BEACON ON THE SHORE

Smelling salts were handed to him by someone in a small crowd which had gathered around them. A whiff of the pungent stimulant was enough to bring the woman back to full consciousness.

Removing his own coat and placing it about her bare shoulders, David was gratified to see the pallid skin take on some colour. What a sweet face it was! From the style of her clothing he had at first thought her to be an older person, but this was a girl, perhaps in her early twenties. A rather severe bonnet had been dislodged during the incident. Bright red-gold curls tumbled down over a milky brow, and a sprinkling of freckles ran riot across the neatest little nose he had ever seen. Her eyes, which were beginning to take in the scene about her, were an amazing green. Realising suddenly that it was she who was at the centre of so much attention, the girl blushed. Desperately she gathered up the edges of her dress where David had unbuttoned it at the throat.

Also by Mary Withall

The Gorse In Bloom

Beacon on the Shore

Mary Withall

CORONET BOOKS
Hodder and Stoughton

First published in Great Britain in 1995
by Hodder & Stoughton

First published in paperback in 1996
by Hodder and Stoughton
A division of Hodder Headline PLC

A Coronet Paperback

British Library Cataloguing in Publication Data

Withall, Mary
Beacon on the Shore
I. Title
823 [F]

ISBN 0 340 64050 2

Printed and bound in Great Britain by
Cox & Wyman Ltd, Reading, Berkshire

Hodder and Stoughton
A division of Hodder Headline PLC
338 Euston Road
London NW1 3BH

To the people of Easdale,
past and present.

THE BEATON FAMILY

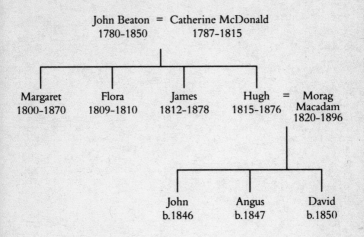

John Beaton = Catherine McDonald
1780–1850   1787–1815

Margaret	Flora	James	Hugh = Morag
1800–1870	1809–1810	1812–1878	1815–1876 Macadam
			1820–1896

John   Angus   David
b.1846   b.1847   b.1850

THE McGILLIVERY FAMILY

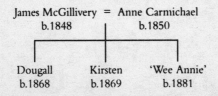

James McGillivery = Anne Carmichael
b.1848   b.1850

Dougall   Kirsten   'Wee Annie'
b.1868   b.1869   b.1881

Beacon on
the Shore

PART I

1

1876

The atmosphere in the crowded hut was becoming unbearable. It was not so much the heat from the round iron stove as the anger – anger and frustration – emanating from the men gathered about it which had raised the temperature to this degree.

'Will you let me speak . . . please!' Malcolm Logie was forced to shout in order to silence the indignant protestations. 'The pump in Number Two requires a whole new piston assembly. There is no way that we can use that exposure until the parts arrived from Glasgow.'

'Three crews will be out of work,' a querulous voice stated the obvious, and the men around the speaker murmured their agreement.

'Where's McPhee?' Sixteen stones of bone and muscle, which had made Alan McLintock weight-lifting and caber-tossing champion for the past five years, now gave him right of passage through the mob. As his mates fell back, the crew captain advanced towards Malcolm Logie. He thrust his face into that of the foreman, his countenance made all the more threatening by the livid scar which stretched from eyebrow to chin.

'The organ grinder has sent his monkey to give us the good tidings again, I see!' He glanced around, seeking support and was rewarded by the nervous laughter of his crewmen.

'Mr McPhee is indisposed.' Hard pressed, the foreman made little effort to suppress his own distaste at the message he had been directed to bring to the quarriers.

'His instructions are that all three of the displaced gangs are to move into Number One and work the south face.'

A tall, muscular figure forced his way to the front. His upright bearing and fiery bush of whiskers gave an air of experience and authority to an otherwise youthful countenance. Standing shoulder to shoulder with Logie, the formidable Jamie McGillivray addressed his fellow quarriers.

'There is no point in arguing like this,' he reasoned. 'The facts are plain. Without the pump, we cannot work Number Two. Until the parts arrive, we will have to operate in more confined areas. Now, we all know what that means. Less control over blasting; more danger from falling rock. Every gang leader will have to be responsible for warning those nearest to him when he begins a major break-out.'

Jamie's words, delivered in the soft Hebridean tones of the outer isles, served to calm the men. One small knot of dissenters, those from Number Two quarry, gathered loyally behind their leader, Alan McClintock, but the remainder of the men appeared to be satisfied.

The crews dispersed one by one, as each boss received his orders for the day. Soon, only McClintock and his men remained. Malcolm Logie pushed back his chair and moved to a large map of the quarries, pinned to the wall. He indicated to McClintock the new locations for the three displaced gangs. When McClintock followed his crew off to the quarry, he was still muttering.

'And what about the loss of earnings? Do you realise how much we were likely to make from that seam in Number Two? Who will compensate us for that, I'd like to know?'

Jamie McGillivray closed the door behind the disgruntled men and turned upon his friend.

'It will not do, man. You know that we cannot go on working in this manner, Malcolm. Look at the accidents there have been in the last few weeks. It is only a matter of time before someone is killed.'

'Do you think I don't know that?' Malcolm Logie sat down dejectedly behind the rough desk. He pushed away a scribbled list of the gangs and their locations. He was taking a risk in reallocating the sections on his own initiative. If anything went wrong he would be to blame, there was no doubt about that. He stood between his inadequate manager and the dissatisfied workforce, the butt and scapegoat for all the criticisms, all the problems.

'The owners sit in their plush offices in Glasgow, while their wives and daughters spend our hard-earned profits on fine houses and silk dresses,' he said, unhappily. 'If only a small part of that profit was ploughed back into new machinery, how much safer and more effective our work would be. Why can they not see it?'

'The men will not put up with matters as they are for long,' warned Jamie. 'McPhee is the Manager. It is for him to demand of the Company lease holders what is to be done.'

'McPhee will do nothing to endanger his own position, you know that. Besides, these days he is aware only of what he sees through the bottom of a brandy glass.'

'Then we must take action ourselves.' Jamie McGillivray rose to his full six feet three inches. 'It is time that someone spoke with His Lordship.'

McGillivray closed the door behind him and paused for a moment to allow his eyes to adjust to the diffuse light which struggled to penetrate a thick sea mist. Drawing about him the canvas cape, which hung loosely over his shoulders, he forced his way forward against the driving rain.

The stone bothy which served as the manager's office stood at the top of the steep zig-zag path, cut out of the vertical face of the quarry. The path had begun, no doubt, as a simple sloping track, allowing the men to make what at the time had been a short drop to the quarry floor. In the course of three centuries and more, there had been many occasions when digging had ceased for lack of means to keep out the water. With each innovation in pumping equipment, further quarrying had taken place. Over the years, the path had changed direction many times. Now a great gaping hole in the ground, fifty yards in diameter and one hundred and twenty feet in depth, it allowed access in several places to rich seams of fine blue slate.

By the time Jamie reached the quarry floor, his own gang of men had assembled their equipment and were already erecting the platform from which he would operate. Balanced precariously, each upon a roughly made wooden ladder, Murdo Campbell and Archie McLean were hammering long iron stakes into cracks in the sheer rock wall. Satisfied at last that the stakes were secure, Willie Campbell called for the first of three sizeable lengths of timber. These, when laid horizontally across the stakes, formed the platform from which Jamie would work.

All about them they could hear the sounds of other crews at work, but the mist was so dense at this level that it was impossible to judge the exact position of any of them.

Jamie, recalling the plan on the office wall, knew that his own position was clear of any other crew.

It was with good reason that Murdo Campbell had earned his nickname of 'Spider'. His lightly-built frame was ideal for scrambling across the sheer rock faces. With great agility he negotiated the fifteen feet between the platform and the ground, and called out to his boss.

'All ready for you, Jamie.'

McGillivray stripped off the canvas cape which would inhibit his activities. He must rely now upon the protection afforded by his thick woollen shirt and a closely woven rough tweed waistcoat which, while keeping out the cold, did little to repel the soaking rain. He gathered up his satchel of gunpowder, checked that the fuses were snug and dry in his waistcoat pocket, and began the climb to the platform. Safely in position, he reached down for a heavy auger with which he would drill holes into the rock, to take the charges of gunpowder. If he did his job properly, a slab of slate rock would be dislodged cleanly, ready for the splitters.

For some minutes the auger appeared to be making no impact at all on the tough slate rock.

He felt the tool turn much too freely and swore, softly. He had struck a band of soft shale and quartz. Now he would be forced to waste precious time removing this rubbish before he could get at the seam of high quality slate below.

The slate quarriers worked in crews of five or six. The two most experienced performed between them the dangerous task of breaking out the slate rock from its natural bed. One or two men would be engaged in hauling away the great slabs of rock as they came free, while two other members of the team first split the rock into thin sheets, and then cut these into suitable sizes for roofing purposes.

The whole team was paid according to the number of slates they could sell. On the effort of each individual depended the prosperity of all. Striking poor rock as he had, McGillivray was only too conscious of the effect upon his workmates' pay packets. With so many stoppages recently, due to faulty equipment and poor organisation, the men had found it difficult to maintain the kind of production which would give them a living wage.

The winter months lay ahead, when production would be slow and sales of slates would certainly flag. With six families dependent upon him, Jamie was anxious to get in a good few days' production before the December gales made it impossible to operate safely in the deepest quarries. There was always the possibility that a high tide with a following gale force wind could create a sea high enough to breach the walls of the quarries and swamp them.

Peering down through the mist, he could barely distinguish the dim outlines of his crew.

'I've struck rubbish,' he called. 'I'll need to move over to the right a little.' He knew this was not in accordance with Malcolm's instructions, but did not recollect another gang working anywhere near. It was worth the risk, to ensure that they would win good slate.

He leapt down from his perch and stood back while the others prepared a new platform.

It was some time before all was ready for him. He selected a suitable position on the sheer face, and began the painstaking task of drilling into the edges of the slab of rock he wished to displace.

He was halfway round, with only six more shot-holes to make, when the rain began in earnest. The wall of rock instantly streamed with rivulets and miniature waterfalls, one of which fell directly on to Jamie's cap, pouring freezing cold water down his neck. He cursed and moved the fuses to an inside pocket.

As a result of the pause in his operations he was able to hear, for the first time, the sound of hammering coming from somewhere above his head.

That's a little close for comfort! he thought, peering upwards to catch a glimpse of whoever was working there. The quarry *was* large enough to accommodate six crews working on different seams at different levels, but it was unlikely that Malcolm Logie, would have set a further crew to work so close to McGillivray's.

Dr Hugh Beaton, medical officer for the Eisdalsa Slate Quarrying Company, heaved himself out of the ferry boat, allowing a forest of willing hands to haul him up the slimy steps to the quay.

He remembered the day when he would have leapt ashore, a bag in either hand, scorning any assistance. Now he was totally dependent upon their help.

Michael Brown, the doctor's young apprentice, watched anxiously to see that his master did not lose his footing. Then, turning to the heap of equipment lying in the boat, he began to hand up stretcher, splints, blankets . . . all items of equipment which recent experience had taught him would be needed.

At fourteen Michael was a tall boy, rather too skinny by his mother's reckoning. He was sufficiently strong to carry the doctor's equipment, however, and fit enough to run his many errands. He took his position very seriously.

'Have a care there,' he cried, remonstrating with some careless person who had grasped the doctor's bag and tossed it on to the quay. His tone of authority was sufficient to make the burly quarryman bend down and examine the Gladstone for signs of damage.

Leaping on to the steps, Michael snatched the bag from his grasp, entrusting no one else with its safe transportation.

A straggling procession was soon making its way along a stony path which passed between rows of low white cottages and around the edge of an extensive harbour, bristling with vessels of every kind. Soon the path turned northwards, towards the great quarry workings.

Eisdalsa was a small island, not much more than a mile in length in either direction. Much of its land surface was only a few feet above high tide mark, but a spine of volcanic rock, rising to a height of one hundred and eighty feet, bisected it from north to south, providing some shelter for the neat rows of white cottages which were grouped about the harbour. The bulk of the houses surrounded a green, perhaps a hundred yards across, while close to the harbour stood the schoolhouse and accommodation for the teacher. Beside this was a large building with a distinctive pyramidal roof, the Volunteers' drill hall. Here the quarrymen could be found on Friday evenings, dressed in their uniform blues, practising the arts of war.

Except for the harbour and the village surrounding it, the whole surface of the island appeared covered with the evidence of the industry which gave it life. Heaps of waste slate provided a certain shallow contouring while discarded machinery lay rusting on every hand. Pulled by tough little highland ponies along a series of narrow-gauge railways, trucks carried the finished roofing slates. One of these rattled past the doctor's procession, approaching out of the mist at speed, spelling danger to the unwary.

'Well, what do we have this time?' Dr Hugh Beaton enquired as Malcolm Logie joined him.

'It is McGillivray, Doctor. His leg is broken and there is a bad wound on his head.'

'There have been too many such accidents lately.' The doctor was forced to pause for a moment, a niggling pain in his side causing him to catch his breath. 'Overcrowding on the face again, I suppose?'

Malcolm Logie nodded. 'It seems that one of the gangs set themselves up in the wrong section. I should have been there to check but . . .'

'. . . you were elsewhere doing your Manager's work, I'll be bound,' Hugh Beaton concluded.

Malcolm made no attempt to reply.

'And where *is* Mr McPhee? Too much to expect him to be at the accident site, I suppose?'

McPhee was, at that moment, seated before a roaring fire, his feet propped against the fender. So deep was his drunken stupor that the smell of scorching leather did no more to waken him than had the tolling of the emergency bell some twenty minutes before.

Dr Beaton was only too aware of the Manager's habits of late. He made a mental note to write a report for His Lordship. This, the latest in a spate of serious accidents, was sufficient reason to bring the matter to the Marquis's attention. It was time that something was done about such a sorry state of affairs.

The bell which had summoned the doctor had drawn to the quarry's edge a small crowd of women and children. They huddled together in a forlorn attempt to escape the driving rain. Each had come there dreading it being her own man who had suffered injury. Now the word was out. Only Annie McGillivray had anything to fear but nevertheless her neighbours remained to give her their support.

Dr Beaton, recognising Annie, left the party to address her.

'Now then, my dear,' he chided gently, 'this is no place for you. Do you get back to your house. Make sure that there is a warm room and a clean bed for your man to come home to. We will have him out of there directly.'

Annie McGillivray looked at the doctor for a moment, as though unable to focus upon him. Regaining her composure, she gave him a fleeting smile and, taking a firm grasp on her little daughter's hand, said, 'We'll away home then, Kirsty.'

Hugh stood for a moment watching them go, the child running to keep up with her mother's purposeful strides. Hugh knew Annie too well to expect her to crumble, no matter how serious the problem. Like so many of her neighbours, she had been born to trouble and had learned to face it head on.

The passage down was difficult for the elderly doctor. But for the steadying hand of the foreman he might well have slipped. Once on the quarry floor he was able to recover his breath before making his way to the scene of the accident.

There was little that Hugh could do for his patient while he remained here in the mud and rain. The old man knelt beside the stricken quarryman, wondering if either of them was going to survive this ordeal.

With Michael's help, he eased the shattered leg into a more natural position. The movement caused the poor man to shriek out in pain.

'Oh, so you felt that, did you?' muttered Dr Hugh. 'There may be hope for you yet, man.'

The apprentice, Michael, laid out the iron splint. It was an instrument in two parts, one half designed to support the back of the leg, the other to be clamped over the shin bone and screwed firmly to the back half. Brought home by Hugh's brother from his service with the army in India, the instrument had proved its worth time and again.

Hugh examined the head wound. It was a gash, perhaps six inches long, across the occipital region of the skull. 'No bone damage there,' he murmured with relief, 'but a great deal of blood lost . . . he is very weak.'

To the men standing around, he said, 'Come along, let's get him on to the stretcher and snugged down before he dies of cold. The sooner we have him away from here, the better.'

For transportation to the top of the cliff, it would be necessary to rope the patient to the stretcher. They used the crane to lift Jamie out of the quarry, on a pallet of timber. Two of his crew squatted either side of the stretcher, to steady it. It was a precarious way to go but quicker, and less likely to cause the patient further pain, than the tortuous climb to the rim.

The flagging doctor found himself being half-dragged, half-carried up the path by two hefty quarriers.

At last, having reached the top, Hugh sent Michael ahead with the stretcher party to prepare McGillivray's house for the operation which would have to be performed. With Malcolm Logie supporting him, he struggled along in their wake.

Annie McGillivray's kitchen had been transformed into an operating theatre. The family table had been covered with a white linen sheet, and the barely conscious master of the house was stretched diagonally across it, to accommodate his height. On the brightly polished cooking range pots of water boiled, while more clean linen covered the clothes chest upon which Michael had displayed the doctor's instruments.

Dr Hugh gently moved aside the wide-eyed Kirsty who clung to the doorpost gaining comfort from a well-sucked thumb. Stooping to avoid the low architrave, he stepped into a dimly lit room, a small, four-paned window providing the only illumination.

'I shall need more light than this,' he declared, shrugging off a soaking

tweed overcoat. 'That oil lamp should suffice. Ah, thank you, Annie
. . . with a good strong dram of whisky, I hope?'

She smiled as she handed him the steaming mug of tea.

'You'll be feeling the cold, doctor.'

Revived by the warming brew, Hugh began to feel stronger. He
examined the gash in Jamie's scalp. Movement had opened up the
wound again and blood had already soaked into the linen table-cover.

He chose his sutures and needles carefully, placing them in one of
the kettles of water. He washed the wound clear of mud and congealed
blood and waited while he allowed the boiling water to do its work.

'Now, Michael, the copious flow of blood should have kept the wound
clean, do you see?' His apprentice was paying close attention, as always,
to his master's teaching. 'But that does not mean that there will be no
suppuration in the wound. No one knows what causes the formation of
pus. Some people even believe it to be essential for healing to occur.
My experience tells me that it does no harm to see that everything
you use for the job is clean as well . . . that is why I use water, as
hot as possible, for cleaning the wound, and boiling for cleaning the
instruments.'

Michael waited for the phrase that would come next. He had heard
it so often he even murmured it in his dreams.

'Always remember, boy, a clean wound is a healthy wound and one
most likely to heal!'

The doctor might be pedantic to the point of boring his apprentice
at times, but Michael was to remember those words in years to come;
years when he would be forced to recognise the wisdom of this old
man who prided himself on his descent from the Beatons of Mull, a line
of physicians whose origins went back to the dawn of history.

The neatly sutured head wound was soon covered in bandages. As
Michael gently lowered the patient's head on to a newly spread towel,
Jamie groaned and his eyelid flickered for an instant.

Inwardly, Hugh swore. He had hoped that unconsciousness would
last until he had been able to deal with the mangled leg. Now, all feeling
would be returning and the poor man was to experience the greatest
of agonies. Hugh stood back from the table and flexed his shoulders.
His back ached and that pain had returned, dull, thudding, constant.
He brushed aside the anxieties which had been torturing him for many
weeks past.

'Michael, will you come here a minute?' Michael bent close to hear
the doctor whisper, 'Mrs McGillivray is in no condition to witness the
next part. Take her to a neighbour and find me two strong men!'

The heavily pregnant Annie was finally led protesting from the scene,
and Michael returned almost at once with Archie McLean and Angus
McTavish from Jamie's crew. Both were looking worn and anxious but

each was eager to render whatever assistance was required, for the sake of his friend.

Taking the two men aside, Hugh gave them very specific instructions before returning to his patient.

'Now then, McGillivray,' he spoke brusquely, 'we have to straighten out this leg of yours. These two fellows are going to give me a hand. It will hurt but, God willing, it won't last too long. Are you ready, Michael?'

At his word, the apprentice placed a pad of leather between Jamie's teeth and said, 'Bite, as hard as you can.'

At a nod from the doctor the two men each grasped the shattered limb as they had been instructed.

'Now, pull!'

As the broken ends of the bones slipped apart, Hugh deftly eased the jagged edges into place.

Jamie's scream of agony stopped abruptly as he sank once more into oblivion. Hugh could proceed with greater speed now that his patient was unconscious. Soon the fractures were secured, the wounds, where the flesh had been pierced, were closed, and Hugh was ready to apply the splint once more.

'Just help me get him into his bed.'

At the doctor's request, the two powerful men lifted their friend and laid him gently in the box bed which Annie had prepared for him.

'Will he walk again, doctor?' asked Archie. 'Being a cripple would come very hard to a man like Jamie.'

'Only time will tell,' Hugh answered, weary now that the task was completed. 'Let us hope that there is no gangrene. That could mean the loss of the leg . . . or worse.' He stopped short for Annie had entered the cottage.

The men left quietly while she ran to her husband's side, scarcely daring to touch him for fear of further hurt.

Hugh came and stood beside her. Placing a reassuring hand on her shoulder, he said quietly, 'I'll be off now, Annie. Keep him warm and see that he eats a little broth when he wakes. Do not touch the leg unless he becomes fevered, or you notice the flesh becoming reddened. I shall be back tomorrow.'

'I think I can manage well enough, Dr Hugh, thank you all the same.' Annie rose to her feet and lifted down an old tobacco jar from the mantleshelf.

'You must tell me what I owe you, doctor.'

She began to count a handful of coins which she had tipped out on to the table.

'You will not concern yourself about the money, girl,' he admonished gently. 'We will talk about it when your man is fit and well again!'

2

Sir Alexander Campbell, Bart.
        of Barcaldine
Eisdalsa Slate Quarrying Co. Ltd
21 Park Lane
London

Eisdalsa Quarry
Office
Eisdalsa
Argyll
3 November 1876

Dear Sir Alexander,

It is with regret that I must inform you of the death, on 30 October, of Dr Hugh Beaton, Medical Officer to the Eisdalsa Quarrying Company.

Two days before his death he had attended an accident in Number One Quarry, The Windmill. The weather conditions being inclement, it appears that the good doctor suffered chill as a result of long exposure and, being weakened in the lungs from previous bouts of bronchitis, he fell into a decline and died in the early hours of Friday morning.

Mrs Beaton summoned her son, Dr Angus Beaton, from his own practice on Mull. Although Dr Angus Beaton has agreed to cover the medical needs of the quarries for a short period it will be necessary to appoint a new medical officer as soon as possible.

The accident, which was the indirect cause of the doctor's demise, was to a crew leader, James McGillivray, who sustained severe injuries to the head and right leg. This man is unlikely to work again at his trade. Perhaps you will give consideration to what compensation, if any, should be due to him.

A full report on the accident accompanies this letter.

I am, dear Sir Alexander, your respectful and obedient servant,

Charles McPhee
Manager, Eisdalsa Quarries

REPORT OF AN ACCIDENT IN THE WINDMILL QUARRY
(NUMBER ONE)
to JAMES McGILLIVRAY, quarryman
Eisdalsa Quarries, Wednesday, 28 October 1876

McGillivray and his crew began work at 7.30 am, the morning being dark and misty.

At approximately 8 am, McGillivray, who was drilling prior to setting charges, discovered a seam of poor rock and ceased work at that site.

Without recourse to my foreman, Logie, McGillivray took it upon himself to move his working site some distance from his allocation. Visibility being poor, he was unaware of a second group working at a higher level and directly in line with his newly chosen site. This crew, having set their fuses, gave the normal warning before blasting.

As a result of the explosion, McGillivray was dislodged from his position and fell fifteen feet. He sustained a large wound to the scalp and two compound fractures of the right leg.

Dr Hugh Beaton was in attendance.

Charles McPhee
Manager, Eisdalsa Quarries
29 October 1876

To The Most Noble   Tigh na Broch
The Marquis of Stirling   Seileach
Aberfeldy Castle   Argyll
Perthshire   31 October 1876

My Lord Marquis,
It is with very great regret that I inform you of the death, on 30 October, of my father, Hugh Beaton.

Having attended an accident at the quarries on Wednesday last, he suffered a severe chill which quickly turned to inflammation of the lung. He passed into a coma from which he never recovered consciousness.

Before his condition deteriorated, my father was at pains to produce the report which I enclose for your perusal. It was clear that he was greatly concerned at the matters it contains, his last words to his grieving widow being: 'Be sure to tell His Lordship.'

I trust therefore that Your Lordship will grant my father's last

wish, and give your urgent attention to the contents of his report.
I am, My Lord, your most humble and obedient servant,

Angus Beaton, MD, BS

To The Most Noble   Tigh na Broch
The Marquis of Stirling   Seileach
Aberfeldy Castle   28 October 1876
Perthshire

My Lord Marquis,
For some time I have been concerned at the escalation in the
number of accidents occurring in the quarries.

Despite my detailed reports to your Manager, McPhee, and via
that gentleman to your lessee, Sir Alexander Campbell, Chairman of
the Eisdalsa Slate Quarrying Company, not once has action been
taken to resolve the problems which are, from my observations and
from discussions with the crews, the main cause of this spate of
accidents.

To be blunt, since Your Lordship's interests in the company were
leased to the Glasgow consortium of which Sir Alexander Campbell
is Chairman, there has been no investment in new plant, and a
number of accidents have occurred due to faulty materials and
equipment. Furthermore, the day-to-day operation of the quarries
has been left in the hands of a Manager who, for whatever reason,
appears to have lost his grip on affairs and seeks solace for all his
ills from spirituous liquor. The foreman, Logie, is an experienced
face worker but is not, and should not be expected to be, capable
of handling the whole enterprise on his own.

Your lessees, not one of whom has visited the area these past
six months, as I am sure that your agent will confirm, have left
everything to McPhee and are content to take their profits with the
least exertion on their own part.

As example of the sorry state to which your business has fallen
I recount the events leading to the most recent, and most serious,
of accidents, one which may indeed still prove to be fatal.

As a result of there being no spare parts to repair a pump in
Number Two quarry, nine crews were set to work in Number One
where there has never been sufficient space to accommodate more
than six.

One of the three additional crew leaders mistook the directions
relayed by foreman Logie, setting his men to work closer to an
existing crew than was safe for blasting.

The day being wet and visibility impaired by the mist, neither crew was aware of the proximity of the other. When the new crew set off a charge, the existing crew was showered with debris and one member, James McGillivray, so severely injured that he is unlikely to work again.

I know that, under the terms of the leasing arrangements, Your Lordship no longer has any control over the operation of the quarries but I am sure that a word from you would bring to their senses those responsible for this sorry state of affairs.

I am, sir, your most humble and obedient servant,

Hugh Beaton, BSc, MD, BS

Sir Alexander Campbell, Bart.   Aberfeldy Castle
        of Barcaldine   Perthshire
Eisdalsa Slate Quarrying Co. Ltd   5 November 1876
21 Park Lane
London

Dear Campbell,

Disturbing reports have reached me as to the management of your operation at Eisdalsa.

Unlike my predecessor, I have little wish to involve myself in the affairs of the quarries on my Lorn estates. I am, however, desirous of having these quarries returned to me, at the conclusion of your tenancy, in good order and capable of making a profit. It is therefore alarming to discover that, through lack of control, and indeed the investment which was part of our agreement, there has been a fall-off in efficiency and an increase in accidents to the men.

Some considerable blame must be attributed to your Manager, McPhee, who by all accounts is an incompetent drunkard. This man will have to go.

If you wish to avoid unpleasantly lengthy and expensive action in the courts regarding your non-compliance with the lease, I would suggest that you accept my nomination of replacement Manager. There is a young man of my acquaintance, presently employed in the Cornish slate industry at Delabole, who should fit the bill admirably. My agent, Mr Lugas, will be pleased to put you in touch with Mr William Whylie who will be more than pleased to accept your offer of an appointment.

I shall expect to hear from you by return.

Stirling

The curved benches of the lecture theatre rose in tiers. Elaborate plasterwork on the ceiling, once white, bore the yellow-brown staining of fifty years' exposure to dense tobacco smoke.

The wooden benches, polished by the elbows of generations of would-be physicians and surgeons, were today crowded not only with the entire student body of Edinburgh University's Medical School, but a fair proportion of its qualified staff as well.

When the Medical Superintendent of The Edinburgh Royal Infirmary was to perform in public, it ill behoved any of his staff to be absent. Equally, any student absenting himself from Professor Hector Munro's classes could certainly forget about passing his examinations!

The hubbub produced by a hundred or more voices was suddenly stilled by three loud bangs made on the operating table which stood on a raised platform before the tiered seating.

The gargantuan figure who currently commanded the attention of the students was built like an all-in wrestler. He wore a grubby singlet and coarse-woven trousers supported by a wide leather belt. The buckle of the latter proved to be of inestimable practical value to its wearer, as wife, whores, fellow drunks and unpunctual students had good reason to remember!

The giant Meek, personal assistant to Professor Munro, was well known to the students as provider of cadavers for the anatomy classes. In this capacity he was a man worth cultivating. From him were obtained the best specimens for dissection. He was besides the source of information about examination topics and likely subjects for interrogation by the fearsome Munro. New students found he was also good for an introduction to the cheaper brothels in the city. Meek enjoyed his work and the many tokens of gratitude which he received from the young gentlemen. From all his sources of income, he probably earned more than many of the qualified medics.

Whether Munro knew or cared about Meek's additional perquisites was debatable. It was on account of his impressive physical strength that he was present in the lecture theatre today.

The Professor was to perform, for the benefit of the student body, the amputation, at the upper thigh, of a man's leg.

For this operation to be performed with all the skill and speed that the surgeon could command, it was necessary that the patient remain immobile throughout. It was Meek's job to see he did not move and cause the scalpel to slip.

Behind the double doors leading on to the platform, the unfortunate subject of the morning's lecture awaited his fate. In charge of the trolley stood a diminutive figure who was, if possible, even less familiar with soap and water than Meek. This was the porter, Longfellow. The contrast in size, and the absurdly inappropriate names they bore, had caused the two porters to be a source of amusement to generations of students.

The patient lay covered by a greyish linen sheet.

Dr David Beaton, MB, dresser to Professor Munro, bent over the sick man and checked his vital signs. He was concerned to find a racing pulse; noted the flushed face and raised temperature.

The amputation to be carried out this morning was long overdue. Professor Munro had kept the case back with a series of excuses which had not convinced David. A day or two before, amputation of the foot would have been sufficient. The delay had meant that the limb must now be severed above the knee with all the problems that this would produce should the patient recover.

'How are you feeling, Mr Adams?'

'Very well, doctor, and thank you for asking.' The man gazed up at him with the beatific smile of inebriation. Several liberal doses of whisky, administered by Longfellow, were taking effect.

David was sure that the florid complexion of his patient was only partly due to the administration of alcohol. He wished Munro would come.

His prayer was answered. The lean figure of Professor Hector Munro could be seen striding along the gloomy, half-tiled corridor towards them.

As he reached the trolley he barked at the patient: 'Your moment has come at last, Mr Adams . . . all over and done with in a few minutes. Not a thing to worry about!'

'Thank you, sir.' Adams attempted to raise his head in deference to his deliverer. Munro acknowledged David with a curt nod and then continued briskly, 'Bit of pain while it's happening, don't you know. You'll soon forget about that! Legs are my speciality. Plenty of practice in the Crimea.'

For the first time, Adams's eyes showed signs of trepidation. Mention of the Crimea brought back memories of terrible carnage which he had witnessed as a young man. He recalled the screams of agony which had emitted from the hospital tent. Suddenly the whisky no longer held sway. Mr Adams was afraid.

David noticed the sudden change in the man's demeanour and gave his shoulder a comforting squeeze. He waited until the Professor had thrown back the doors and entered to a wave of applause. Giving Longfellow a signal to push the trolley forward, David himself stepped out on to the platform and, with Meek and Longfellow to assist, supervised the transfer of the patient to the operating table.

The Professor was a tall, thin figure, sharp-featured and with the most piercing blue eyes. Many a student had quaked before their penetrating gaze, and been turned into a gibbering idiot when asked a question.

For surgery he wore the frock-coat in which he had been presented to the young Queen Victoria upon the occasion of a Royal visit to Holyrood. He considered it an appropriate garment in which to demonstrate his remarkable skills. It appeared at every public operation and was as renowned as the surgeon himself. The blood and pus of many an unfortunate man or woman now contributed to its decoration and provided its unique aroma.

Having assured himself that all was made ready, Munro addressed his audience.

'Gentlemen, our subject today is a forty-five-year-old male who suffered a crushed left foot in a street accident ten days ago.

'The injuries were not in themselves severe. There were deep lacerations dorsally and ventrally; two tarsal bones and three metatarsals were fractured. However, the wounds have become gangrenous and the flesh of the entire lower leg has mortified. It is therefore necessary to remove the limb from above the knee.

'In amputation, the greatest importance must be attributed to speed, gentlemen. The trauma induced in the patient can lead to deep shock and subsequent death. The art is to perform the operation with all speed, but also great dexterity. The only way to achieve success is to practise, practise, practise. Do not expect always to have assistance at your elbow either, gentlemen. Often this procedure is carried out in the open. A person may be pinned by a limb under falling masonry or immovable machinery. In such circumstances you will be called upon to operate in the field. Always be prepared!'

As he spoke the Professor held up one instrument after another, laying them down in the order in which he would use them. This procedure was carefully noted by the students. They would be examined on the list in due course and dared not be found wanting.

'I shall call upon Dr Beaton to assist me. Dr Beaton, if you please . . .'

David stepped forward to join the Professor at the table. He picked up a bunch of ligatures and threaded them through the buttonhole of his lapel. In one hand he took up a pair of fine tapering scissors and in the other a pair of steel forceps.

Professor Munro addressed his three-man team with a theatrical gesture which would have done credit to an Edmund Kean or David Garrick.

'Gentlemen, we will begin!'

Meek held the patient's head and shoulders firmly to the table, wedging a thick leather gag, none too gently, between the poor fellow's teeth. The sheet was drawn back to expose both legs. While Longfellow applied pressure to the free leg, David attached the one to be amputated to an extending arm of the table. This was designed to give maximum freedom of movement to the surgeon as he worked.

The Professor grasped a shining scalpel in his right hand. With another dramatic gesture he tested the blade on the hairs of his own forearm then cast his eye over the sea of faces before him.

'Now then . . .' his eye travelled along the rows, '. . . which of the vessels must have my particular attention . . . Mr McIver?'

This luckless gentleman rose uncertainly to his feet. 'The femoral artery . . . er . . . sir?'

'Just the femoral artery will do, I think. Thank you. Dr Beaton, perhaps you will be kind enough to enlighten these poor benighted half-wits.'

David, not having anticipated that his part in the demonstration would be anything other than passive, looked at his superior in surprise.

'A description of the femoral artery, if you please!'

Desperately searching his memory for the correct form of works, he heard himself speaking, clearly, concisely.

'The femoral artery arises from the external iliac artery at the inguinal ligament. It is situated superficially, running down the front medial aspect of the thigh. Two-thirds of the way down it passes into the back of the thigh, continuing downwards behind the knee, as the popliteal artery.'

'Thank you, Dr Beaton. Perhaps you will also inform our colleagues as to where I must look for the femoral artery.'

'Scarpa's triangle, sir,' said David, 'a triangular depression on the inner side of the thigh, bounded by the sartorius and adductor longus muscles and the inguinal ligament.'

The Professor gave him a long, penetrating stare before commenting with customary sarcasm, 'It appears we have the wrong surgeon performing here today, gentlemen.'

There were a few guffaws from the body of the hall but these were rapidly silenced by another of those fearsome glances.

Professor Munro turned to the figure on the table.

'I have identified Scarpa's triangle and I can feel the pulse of the femoral artery. I shall now ask Dr Beaton to tighten the tourniquet above this point until I can no longer feel the pulse.'

Adams flinched as David approached him. His eyes were wide with terror. The young doctor smiled sympathetically then, signalling to the assistants to strengthen their grip, tightened the strap which encompassed the thigh.

Having satisfied himself that the pulse could no longer be detected, the surgeon proceeded to slice into skin and muscle. Ignoring the writhings and the muffled cries of agony of his patient, Munro isolated each major vessel as it appeared, waiting seconds only as David, with a deft movement, inserted the cat-gut ligatures and tied them off. Cutting, tying and finally sawing, the entire process was completed in little more than three minutes.

A roar of appreciation came from his audience. The great showman

stalked to the front of the platform once more to acknowledge their
cheers. Meanwhile David concentrated on the patient. He it was who
now took up the large flap of skin which Munro had left uncut on the
outer surface of the thigh. This he stretched to cover the raw stump
and then stitched neatly into place. The tourniquet was released in
under four minutes and blood was able to flow freely to the extremity
of what remained of the limb.

Mr Adams, mercifully released from his torment, had subsided into
unconsciousness. In seconds, Meek and Longfellow had the patient
removed to the trolley and Longfellow was rolling him away to the
ward.

Professor Munro wiped his hand vigorously on a piece of linen which
he dragged from his coat pocket. He tossed it to David who followed
suit before handing it on to Meek to wrap up the severed limb.

'Save that for me, Meek, will you?'

The sprightly figure who had leapt on to the stage from the body of
the hall joined Munro and David as the latter began to gather up the
Professor's instruments, placing them carefully in a small basket,

'Good heavens, Lister, what on earth do you do with all this mortified
flesh you collect?' Munro enquired. 'Why, you're a regular scavenger!'

'You will find out soon enough, Professor,' he laughed heartily. 'Of
one thing I can assure you, it does not finish up in Mrs McTavish's
stew!'

'I fear that I owe you an apology, doctor,' Munro addressed David.
'You must not mind my playing to the gallery at your expense. A little
sarcasm does you no harm and amuses the empty-headed. More importantly, the laughter engendered relieved the tension, allowing me to
relax a little.'

It came as a surprise to David to find that this godlike figure was
actually capable of feeling such pressures. The realisation made the
Professor a little more human in David's eyes.

'Ward rounds in thirty minutes, Dr Beaton.' The Professor strode
out through the double doors which opened as though by magic at his
approach. Meek was in attendance.

The scavenger of severed limbs introduced himself.

'Joseph Lister. I don't believe we have met.'

David shook the proffered hand eagerly.

'I cannot tell you what an honour it is to meet you, sir,' he replied.
'It was my misfortune to have been a student here during the years
when you were Professor of Surgery at Glasgow.'

'I trust you were impressed by the skills we have witnessed this
morning?'

'Indeed I was,' replied David. 'Although I wish that Professor Munro
would consider the use of chloroform in cases such as this.'

Lister looked at the young man with interest.

'There are those of us who wonder what would have happened had James Young Simpson chosen to anaesthetise someone other than a woman in labour when he carried out his first operation using chloroform.'

'It seemed certain to take on after the Queen herself gave birth under anaesthetic.'

'That just compounded the notion that chloroform was only for women!' laughed Lister. 'Our dear Professor's reputation rests upon his ability to sever a limb in record time. What merit would there be in having all the time in the world to complete the operation?'

Astonished as he was by Lister's candour, David thought it politic to remain silent.

Lister continued, 'So, you are reading for your Membership of the Royal College of Surgeons, Dr Beaton?'

'That is my ambition, sir.'

'Well then, I wish you every success in your enterprise. Despite my previous comment, you could not wish for a more worthy teacher than Hector Munro.'

'I am conscious of my good fortune, Mr Lister, I only hope that I shall live up to the confidence which he has placed in me by giving me this opportunity.'

'That confidence could be dented seriously if he reaches the wards to find his dresser is not following close behind. You'd better move quickly if you wish to avoid another exhibition of his sarcastic wit! Come and see me in my room when you have time to spare. I would like to become better acquainted with the protégé of Hector Munro!'

The Infirmary had been new when the young Queen ascended the throne. Built as an adjunct to the teaching of medicine and surgery, its beds were filled with the poorest and most direly sick of Edinburgh's teeming population.

People did not submit willingly to hospitalisation. While the skills of the surgeons were never in dispute, the death rate was high. Dirt and overcrowding, the rapidity with which fevers spread through the wards, and the manner in which open wounds became infected, all contributed to the belief that hospital was merely the last step on the road to oblivion.

Twenty and more years before, Florence Nightingale had scandalised the nation by taking a team of women to the Crimea, to nurse the soldiers wounded in battle. Her strict adherence to rules of hygiene which she herself laid down, together with her abhorrence of dirt, had saved the lives of countless men, otherwise doomed to die through ignorance and lack of care. It was to be many decades before her message reached the hospitals of her native land.

Nurses were for the most part drawn from the immediate neighbourhood, which meant that their standards of care and cleanliness reflected the squalor of their own hovels.

Patients were placed upon truckle-beds furnished with thin straw palliasses and it was not uncommon for two people to share a bed.

These were huddled close together in wards littered with unemptied chamber pots, baskets of soiled linen and discarded dressings. Newly admitted patients, none too clean on their arrival, might lie for days amid their own emissions until family or friends provided a change of clothing or bedding.

The foetid smell of humanity, urine and festering flesh was overpowering. The medical staff appeared inured to the stench, and the patients were too sick to care.

Professor Munro entered the lying-in ward with his somewhat breathless acolyte at his heels. He moved from bed to bed, asking the patients solicitously how they progressed. Occasionally he would draw the attention of his assistant to a particular case, or deliver an instruction regarding care.

From time to time he stopped to make a cursory examination of an intimate part of a patient's anatomy. The unwashed hands which had lately severed a limb, now penetrated a recently opened, often lacerated, birth canal.

He stooped to take up a mewling infant. While he conversed with the mother, he held the child gently in the crook of his arm, its head resting against the breast of the famous frock-coat, still damp with the splattered blood and pus of the unfortunate amputee. He handed the child back to its mother and, moving on, reached a corner of the ward where a woman lay in high fever. Tossing feebly and crying out in her delirium, she was still sufficiently conscious to suffer great pain.

'A case of puerperal fever, doctor.' The Professor felt the patient's pulse.' Unfortunately, an inevitable consequence of protracted labour, difficult parturition and a stillbirth. Nothing to be done here but to wait for merciful death.'

David was puzzled at the finality of Munro's statement. He had observed, amongst his father's patients, women who gave birth time and time again without such problems. He recalled only one occasion when a women had died from fever following childbirth, and she was a drover's woman whose child had been born beside the track. By the time Hugh Beaton had reached her, the woman was beyond all help.

David recalled this experience later when, the ward rounds completed, he sat in Lister's consulting room drinking tea.

'You must remember, David, we see here only those cases which require a surgeon's assistance. Most normal pregnancies can be delivered in the mother's own home without intervention. The patients we see here are all suffering complications to begin with. Malnutrition, hard physical work during pregnancy, and the general poverty of life in the city, compound the problems.'

'All that is true,' David persisted, 'but it does not explain why, at Eisdalsa, a quarrier's wife will work quite as hard as any of her sisters in the city, be equally undernourished and poorly housed, yet manage to bear her children without the fear of puerperal fever.'

'I think the time has come,' Joseph Lister set down his cup and rose to his full height, 'to enlighten you. Come on, drink up, there's a good fellow.'

David knew that Lister had some secret project on hand. Rumours as to the nature of his work abounded, especially among the students. In the basement of the hospital a small room had been allocated to him for his research. Lister was interested in more than the day-to-day surgery required of him in the hospital. He was a man of vision, never satisfied with the complacent explanations of such as Munro but always seeking after new knowledge. Such was the climate of medical opinion, however, that it was a foolish man who voiced unconventional ideas without having strong evidence to back them up. Lister worked quietly and alone. For him to invite a young colleague to share his findings was as much a demonstration of his need to share his ideas as it was a sign of his confidence in David's ability to understand them.

The laboratory was no more than fifteen feet square, poorly lit by a single window which looked out on to the brick wall of an area below street level. A large plain table occupied the centre of the floor. This was heaped with papers, all manner of bottles and other paraphernalia. At one end was laid the severed limb from this morning's operation.

Before the window stood a much smaller bench upon which stood a magnificent binocular microscope of a quality and design completely new to David.

Recognising his young colleague's interest in this instrument, Lister observed, 'It is my good fortune to have a father whose hobby is microscopy. He actually makes instruments, every part with his own hands. Over the years his skills have developed amazingly . . . this is his finest piece yet.'

While he spoke, Lister's hands were never still. From an open box, he took a small glass slide. Using a scalpel, from a remarkably clean pack of white linen, he scraped some of the putrefied material of the severed limb on to this slide and placed it on the stage of the microscope.

Deftly, he adjusted the focus before stepping back for David to look. 'There . . . what can you see?'

What he saw was amazing. Under the powerfully magnifying lenses, the putrid material had become a sea of lifelike organisms; clusters of oval-shaped, transparent cells seemed to pulsate. As he watched David realised that this appearance of pulsation was created as the cells divided, increasing their numbers. They enlarged and again divided. He raised his head, astonished at what he had witnessed.

'What are they?'

'Pasteur calls them germs. He has been working with vegetable material, investigating the putrefaction of foodstuffs. He works for the French brewers, you know.'

'I have heard of him,' David admitted, 'but is he not considered to be something of a crank and a charlatan?'

'Only by fools too blind to see the significance of what he says. Having read his papers on the subject, I decided to investigate putrefied flesh from living beings. Hence the rather melodramatic stories concerning Meek and his activities. I use only discarded material, I do assure you!'

'So you have identified living organisms in putrid flesh. How can this help to prevent sepsis? As I understand it, Pasteur prevented further deterioration by boiling the contaminated material in a flask. One can hardly boil a person's limb when it seems to be turning gangrenous.'

'Watch this.' Lister took a small bottle of colourless fluid and, using a glass pipette, he placed a drop on the slide. David focused on the swarming mass of animalcules. To his astonishment, the activity on the slide ceased almost instantly and the creatures showed every sign of death.

'What happened?' he asked. 'What was that you used?'

'A solution of carbolic acid.'

'Can it be that simple?' David envisaged for a moment a world of medicine in which pus did not signify.

'Far from being simple, it has been the devil's own job to find a concentration of carbolic which is weak enough to cause no burning of the flesh, while at the same time strong enough to destroy the microbes.'

'Accepting that these organisms are present in gangrenous material, where do they come from to infect the wound in the first place?'

'That was the first question I asked myself when I set out upon this investigation.' Lister leaned forward in his chair, his face alight with enthusiasm.

'The animalcules, or germs, are all around us. Look here, and here . . .' He thrust one after another of the thin glass slides on to the microscope stage. They were permanent mountings, stained to reveal detail of the microrganisms.

'These samples come from clean and dirty skin of healthy human beings . . . these from clothing . . . from healthy blood . . . scrapings from a table used for surgery . . . a slide, simply exposed to the air, in one of the wards.'

On each of the slides David observed the images of the microbes. Not all were ovoids of the kind from the gangrenous flesh. Some were rod-shaped, some spiral, some came singly, others in massive clusters.

'Why,' exclaimed the younger man, fascinated, 'this is a whole new world of creatures that no one has seen before!'

'But do you understand what it means? If, as I believe, sepsis is caused by these organisms, then by destroying them we will never have to concern ourselves with the problems of infection again. The surgeon's greatest current problem is not so much the plumbing and carpentry he performs on the human body, but the healing, or lack of it, which follows. How many successfully completed operations lead subsequently to the patient's death?'

'What will your next step be?' David asked.

'I am already putting into practice various schemes to test my theory. I have taken over one ward in which everything is done under my personal supervision. Why talk about it? Come and see for yourself!'

The two men set off for the more public area of the hospital. They ascended a flight of steps which brought them into the entrance hall of the Institute. As their footsteps rang out on the black and white chequered floor, a uniformed porter hurried towards them.

'Dr Beaton, sir, there is an urgent letter for you . . . by special messenger.'

David turned over the letter, recognising, instantly his brother's hand. Full of foreboding he tore it open.

Dr David Beaton	Tigh na Broch
Edinburgh Royal Infirmary	Seileach
30 October 1876	Argyll

My Dear Brother,

Sad news, I am afraid. Our dear father died in the early hours of this morning, following an illness of only two days' duration. His lungs became congested following a chill and I am afraid that his weakened heart could not sustain the load.

Mother, as you may imagine, is distraught. It is left to me to carry out the sad duties of arranging the funeral and so forth.

The interment will take place on Wednesday next, to give you time to get here. I fear it will be many weeks before the news reaches John, although I have made contact with a young officer, on leave from South Africa, who has agreed to carry a letter. His boat sails on Monday next from the Clyde.

I sailed across from Bunessan when Father was taken ill and have been looking after things here. I really cannot leave my own practice for long, there being only the two doctors to serve the entire population of Mull.

I suppose that the practice, with the MO job in the quarries, will have to go out of the family now. It seems a pity after such a long association.

In the meantime, they desperately need cover. Since you will be coming for a few days anyway, can you not obtain leave to stay on until something is settled? After all, there is no shortage of men to cover for you at the Infirmary.

Try to let me know, by return, when you will arrive.

Your affectionate brother,
Angus

3

David Beaton made a slow perambulation of the deserted deck. From time to time he stopped to absorb the glorious kaleidoscope of autumnal colours which painted the mountainside on either shore. Brown of dying bracken, yellow and red of oak, ash and sycamore, purple of late-flowering heather, all were reflected in the mirror surface of the loch, enhancing the beauty of the morning.

The November sun, low on the horizon, glowed scarlet through a light mist which shrouded the edges of Loch Fyne. The landscape was suffused with that warm, ruddy glow peculiar to the Highlands at this time of the year.

To David it seemed only a matter of days since he had last made this same journey to Eisdalsa, for his father's funeral.

The morning that they'd laid Hugh Beaton to rest in the old cemetery on the hillside had been wet and dreary. How his father would have delighted in such a sight as today's!

Hugh was now resting amongst his ancestors in St Brendan's churchyard. All of them had been medical men. Each had passed on to his sons the ancient arts of the physician.

David smiled, remembering those long discussions he had enjoyed with his brothers in which the young men had been so full of all the new ideas in medicine, scornful of old tried and tested methods. Hugh would listen indulgently to their conversation, like an old dog watching over his litter of pups. They must learn, as he had, that change comes about gradually, not by heaps and bounds.

David recalled a day in his boyhood when he had sat alone with his father, on the rocks below Tigh na Broch. They had studied the waves breaking upon the shore, some gently, some with greater force.

'Count them,' Hugh had urged him, 'count them and see how they vary.'

The first was a mere trickle which came sliding and sneaking between the stones. The second and third followed on, each a little stronger than the last, reaching a little further, encroaching just a few more inches up the beach. The fourth was much stronger and broke along the shoreline in a tumble of white foam, filling the little pools and wetting the larger boulders before slithering back, leaving a multitude of busy rivulets in its wake. The fifth and sixth waves tumbled forward, probing gently, seeking an inroad between the rocks. And then, far out, they saw the seventh wave approaching. It was a monstrous swell, rolling across the top of its predecessors. As it mounted its attack, the retreating waters scuttled across the shingle to meet it. The wave hit the beach with a mighty roar, foaming spume was flung high up, over the rocks, and the waters broke below the one on which they perched. Hugh had his feet drawn up, to avoid a wetting, and was sucking on his pipe thoughtfully.

'Take a lesson from the sea, Davy,' he had observed. 'Man can change anything with patience and perseverance. One day disease will be conquered, not by miracle cures and wonder drugs but by the obstinate pursuit of better housing and adequate food for all. Ignorance and apathy are the great evils of mankind and only by continuously pushing forward, like the waves, will they be conquered. Remember this,' he had urged his son, 'it is the six gentle waves which do the most work. Oh, the seventh makes more commotion at the time. Sometimes you may feel that all the good work that has gone before has been destroyed by this one wave, but once it has receded the other six will come back to get on with the task.'

During this homily, the next cycle of waves had broken, the final one flying towards them with such force that they had no time to escape it.

Soaking wet, they had scurried up the beach, laughing.

With the arrogance of youth David had smiled to himself, humouring Hugh in his quaint philosophy. Now however, he placed these ideas alongside those of Joseph Lister, and recognised the amazing foresight in his father's thinking.

Angus had been anxious to get back to his own practice after the funeral, but David was obliged to return to Edinburgh for a short time, before taking over at Eisdalsa.

In his mind's eye, he saw again the experimental ward which Joseph Lister had shown him on his return. The beds were set in neat rows, with walking distance between. The bedding was clean, changed several times a week. The floors were polished each day until they shone. The overpowering smell was of carbolic acid, not of suppurating humanity. How David longed to be part of the medical revolution which he knew was coming!

As he had taken his leave of Lister the previous evening, the great man had confided that he had received an invitation to take up a post of Professor of Surgery in London. He was able to appoint his own chief assistant and had offered the position to David.

He was sorely tempted to follow his mentor to London, to seek the prestige that such an appointment would bring. On the other hand, he felt he owed a duty to his father's memory. He knew that his mother expected him to give up his hopes for a career in surgery in order to carry on the work which his father had begun. But surely Hugh Beaton would have wished his son to become a famous surgeon? How proud he had been when David was appointed to serve under Professor Munro at the Royal. He still had the letter Hugh had written, congratulating him. There was no doubt about it, David assured himself, his father would have wanted him to sell the practice, buy a suitable property for his mother with the proceeds and follow his own career.

Finding himself shivering in the cold, clear air, he gathered his warm topcoat about him and descended to the stuffy atmosphere of the gentlemen's smoking lounge.

For many city dwellers in the Glasgow of the 1870s, a trip 'Doon the watter' meant a day's holiday sailing abroad one of the paddle steamers which plied between ports along the river Clyde. To those who lived in the Western Isles and along the shores of the Western Highlands of Scotland, however, the steamers were their lifeline to the cities of the Lowlands.

General Wade had used his army to open up roads through the harsh mountainous regions north of the Highland Line, a hundred years before, but these were now poorly maintained, rutted tracks which only the most hardy, or penniless traveller, would dare to negotiate.

Water was the safest and most reliable means of transport. To reach Inverness, the capital city of the Highlands, a passenger must take the steamer from Glasgow's Broomielaw Quay at the foot of Argyle Street, and sail to Ardrishaig on the Argyll Peninsula. From here he would embark upon a narrow boat, *The Linnet*, for the short journey along the canal to Crinan on the Atlantic coast.

A daily service carried passengers between Crinan and Fort William aboard one of the famous ocean-going paddle steamers of the day. From there, they sailed along the Caledonian Canal, and across the mysterious waters of Loch Ness to Inverness on the North East coast.

What might appear at first sight to be a cumbersome method of travelling proved highly efficient. By careful co-ordination of sea and rail services it was possible for mails posted in Inverness to be delivered twenty-four hours later in London. Letters posted to London from the quarrying villages of Eisdalsa and Seileach could expect a reply within three days.

David decided that he would give himself a fortnight in which to make up his mind about Lister's offer. There was still time for him to find someone to replace him in the Eisdalsa practice, should he wish to do so. He knew that it would be difficult to persuade his mother to accept a stranger into her home, but that was a matter which could be sorted out later. The new doctor would require the use of Tigh na Broch in the first instant, but another house might be sought for him, or Morag might be induced to take some alternative accommodation.

*   *   *

A familiar change in the tempo of the paddle-wheels alerted the more experienced travellers to the approaching landfall. David rose to retrieve his carpet-bag from beneath the polished mahogany table. He gathered up his medical case and made for the stairs to the upper deck.

The pier at Ardrishaig was in sight and passengers were gathering, ready to disembark.

David made his way down the gang plank and on to the crowded pier. Here passengers picked their way between heaps of fish-boxes, bags and trunks, pens of livestock and nets of vegetable crops; cargo assembled for transport to the towns and the city on the banks of the River Clyde. As he hurried towards the barrier, among passengers for Glasgow lined up ready for the return trip, David noticed an old friend, Kenny MacPherson.

'Good day to you, Kenny. Off to the market in Glasgow?'

'Aye, Davy, the last of the potato crop. And what brings you back so soon after your poor father's funeral?'

'Just a short spell, Kenny . . . to sort out the practice and find my mother a place to stay. We hope to find someone new to take over, very soon.'

'Och! the poor woman . . . to lose her husband and her home. Can you not come back and work here in his stead?'

Again, that same question! Why would people not leave him to make his own decision? He attempted to explain the problem to his friend.

'The hospital has given me leave for a few weeks, but I shall have to go back in the New Year if I want to keep my post. I am hoping to become a surgeon, you see.'

The mysteries of medical training meant nothing to the crofter. So far as he was concerned, David was a doctor like his father and brothers before him. There was no distinction between surgeon and physician in a situation in which one medical man served all requirements!

'I must away, Kenny, or the *Linnet* will sail without me.'

'No doubt I will see you before you go back to the hospital, Davy. Goodbye.'

As he lifted his luggage and made for the lock gate where the canal boat, *Linnet*, was moored, a stranger approached him.

He was a short stocky man with jet black hair. His skin had the light olive tint reminiscent of those Spaniards who thronged the port of Glasgow, and the Italian traders who sold their wares on the city streets. This was no itinerant trader, however. His coat was of heavy English broadcloth with a fashionable short additional cape set about the shoulders. His dark locks were almost hidden by the close-fitting deerstalker hat, much favoured by English gentry who came north for the hunting season.

'I beg your pardon, sir, but I overheard you mention the *Linnet*. Can you direct me to her mooring?' the stranger requested.

The accent was certainly English but of a marked brogue, unfamiliar to David's Scottish ears.

'Of course,' he responded cheerfully, 'we will walk along together. It is no distance.'

The *Linnet* was a long vessel of shallow draught, designed to navigate the narrow waterway which linked Ardrishaig in the East and Crinan in the West. In order to accommodate all those who needed to travel this route, the boat had two decks. Its exceptional height meant that it was clearly visible across the fields and looked particularly strange as it sailed alongside the water meadows which fringed its northern banks. It appeared not unlike one of the new horse-drawn trams which were to be seen, in increasing numbers, on the city streets.

David led his companion on board and made for his favourite spot, on the upper deck, in front of the Captain's bridge. His companion followed. When both were comfortably settled the stranger introduced himself.

'My name is Whylie, William Whylie, bound for Eisdalsa quarries.'

'David Beaton.' The two shook hands. 'I am going home to Eisdalsa myself.'

'This is a most fortuitous meeting,' declared William. 'Perhaps you will be kind enough to prepare me for my encounter with the people and the locality? Until I received my appointment, I had never heard of Eisdalsa.'

'Do I understand you to say that your appointment is in the quarries?' asked David. 'May I enquire in what capacity?'

'I have been asked by the Chairman, Sir Alexander Campbell, to take over the management. I believe there have been some problems of late. I am expected to put everything right, and turn a loss into a resounding profit, overnight!'

'I think it might take a little longer than that,' laughed David. 'According to my brother, things have been going downhill for a long time. The Company seems to have been the most at fault, by not investing in new plant, but also there was some difficulty with the Manager . . . McPhee. Have you met him?'

'No, nor am I likely to,' replied William. 'I understand that upon his dismissal he took off, threatening dire consequences. He also declared his intention to sail for Australia on the next boat.'

'Despite the difficulties, I believe you will enjoy life on Eisdalsa,' said David, 'although I think you will find things very different from London.'

'I grew up in Cornwall and have worked there for the past five years.' William smiled ruefully. 'I imagine I know most of the problems of working in a close-knit community!'

'Do not underestimate your workforce,' advised David. 'You will find the men are not as primitive as you might expect. They are, for the most part, literate, hard working, God-fearing people.'

'They speak in the Gaelic tongue, I am informed.'

'Aye, and write it too, but they speak and write English also.'

Time passed easily for them both in mutually agreeable company. They were surprised to find how quickly this stretch of the journey had been completed, when the *Linnet* arrived at Crinan lock.

The ship for the Western Isles awaited them at the seaward side. The *Lord of Lorn* was a paddle-steamer of proportions suitable for addressing the mountainous seas which, on occasion, confronted her. Two funnels denoted the size of her powerful engines. The two enormous paddle-wheels gave great width and a low centre of gravity to the ship. Experts declared that it would be impossible for her to capsize, whatever the circumstances.

A simple wooden gangplank enabled passengers to reach the deck of the steamer. Close beside it a steam crane was lifting huge bales of cargo, bound for the islands.

As William and David prepared to board the steamer, the crane suddenly swung out of control, hurling its heavily laden net against the side of the vessel. The return swing carried the load in such an arc that it crossed over the gangplank, and would have swept away a young woman who was boarding had she not made a grab at the netting. The load swung on until, suspended high above the water between the boat and the quay, it almost made contact with the hull of the vessel. Desperately, the woman tried to fend herself off, screaming and clinging to the netting. On this first swing she was not badly injured, but the pendulum was gaining impetus and it was clear that a second swing and harder impact would prove fatal.

Without hesitation David dropped his luggage and sprang on to the gangway. He made a grab for the woman as she swung towards him, and caught her around the waist. David clung desperately to the woman's body, fearful that he too would be carried away by the wildly swinging load. Undoubtedly this would have happened had not William leapt to control the mechanism on the dock. He thrust aside the operator, who seemed paralysed with fright. Disengaging the gears, William cut off the steam. The mechanism ground to a halt although the load continued to swing, threatening to take David and the woman, over the side.

Fortunately, by this time one of the ship's officers and several of the crew had run forward to assist. Swiftly the monstrous load was brought under control.

So tangled had the woman's garments become in the netting that it was necessary to cut free clothing before she could be carried on board. The fainting passenger was set down on one of the slatted benches. David, quickly recovering from his own ordeal, set about loosening the fastenings of her torn dress to help her breathing. This naturally contributed further to her near-naked condition.

'I say,' exclaimed the officer, 'do you think that really necessary?'

'Of course,' he replied impatiently. Then, perceiving the young man's embarrassment, he added more kindly, 'I am a doctor.'

Smelling salts were handed to him by someone in the small crowd which had gathered around them. A whiff of the pungent stimulant was enough to bring the woman back to full consciousness.

Removing his own coat and placing it about her bare shoulders, David was gratified to see the pallid skin take on some colour. What a sweet face it was! From the style of her clothing he had at first thought her to be an older person, but this was a girl, perhaps in her early twenties. A rather severe bonnet had been dislodged during the incident. Bright red-gold curls tumbled down over a milky brow, and a sprinkling of freckles ran riot across the neatest little nose he had ever seen. Her eyes, which were beginning to take in the scene about her, were an amazing green. Realising suddenly that it was she who was the centre of so much attention, the girl blushed. Desperately she gathered up the edges of her dress where David had unbuttoned it at the throat.

'Do you feel able to stand?' he enquired solicitously. She nodded, starting at a sudden stab of pain. Turning to the officer who had been hovering in the background, David asked, 'Is there a cabin where I can examine this lady properly? It is possible that she has sustained more injury than is immediately apparent.'

A white-coated steward materialised and whispered to the officer who nodded his approval and said, 'If you will follow me, doctor . . . arrangements have already been made.'

David looked about him for his medical bag, mislaid in the excitement. To his relief he found William at his side, with all their baggage.

'What can I do to help?' he asked.

'Just bring my medical case, if you will, and follow us,' said David gratefully.

He helped the girl gently to her feet. She winced as he caught hold of her arm to steady her.

'I am sorry, my dear,' he murmured, taking her other arm instead. 'Do you think you can walk a few steps to the cabin?'

She gave him a wan smile, her large green eyes brimming with tears of shock and pain.

Together they followed the First Officer, passengers stepping aside to let them pass. William trailed behind, carrying David's medical bag.

Having deposited the doctor and his patient in the Captain's personal cabin, the officer led William to a position by the rail. It was obvious he had been warned by his Captain to watch his words.

'I believe, sir, that the Company owes you a debt of gratitude,' he began. 'Without your speedy intervention the outcome might have been disastrous. I can assure you that details of your part in the incident will appear in my report to the owners.' The ship's First Officer took out his notebook. 'May I have your name, sir, for the record, and an address at which we may contact you should there be a formal inquiry?'

'William Whylie. My address will be Eisdalsa Quarries, for some time to come anyway!'

The smartly uniformed figure wrote rapidly for a few minutes, then held out his hand in friendly fashion. 'First Officer Gordon MacIntyre, sir. At your service!'

The two men cordially shook hands.

The steamer, *Lord of Lorn*, made her way sedately through moderate seas, passing between the islands of Islay and Jura on the port side and mainland Argyll to starboard. William and Gordon McIntyre stayed companionably exchanging views and admiring the scenery while they waited for David's verdict on the young woman's condition.

Still in a state of shock, the lady did not resist when David unfastened her jacket and, very gently, slid her arms free. It was immediately clear from the condition of her camisole that she had sustained considerable injury. He undid the garment and removed it to reveal a mass of bruises and extensive grazing. Congealed blood caused the material to cling to a wound on her right side. As this was eased away from the battered flesh, the girl cried out in pain.

'Just one more little tug and I shall have it free.' David's gentle tones soothed her.

'I shall apply a little salve to the grazes,' he continued. 'There is a deeper gash, here on your side, that will need binding tightly if it is to heal.'

'Is anything broken, doctor?' Her voice was strained, but nevertheless he was struck by its softness and pleasant intonation.

She did not move as David slid fingers across her rib-cage, searching for fractures.

'I think not,' he replied reassuringly. 'The bruising is extensive and will be painful for a time, but there is no lasting damage.'

'I don't even know what happened,' she said. 'All I can remember is seeing the sea heaving beneath me as I swung towards the ship's side.'

'I think you should try to rest now,' he advised.

He poured a small amount of a syrupy brown liquid into a small glass and supported her head so that she might swallow the draught of laudanum.

'Drink this, it will help you to sleep.'

'I must not take any drug,' she protested. 'My new employer is meeting me when I get off the steamer at Eisdalsa.'

'If you will give me your name,' David suggested, 'a message can be given to whoever is waiting for you.'

Unable to resist further, the girl swallowed the potion.

Still cradling her in his arms, he waited for the drug to take effect and continued, 'There is no suitable inn at Eisdalsa for the accommodation of a young lady. I must however insist that you rest for a day or two in the Village where I can keep a close watch on your recovery. My mother's house on Seileach seems most suitable. I am sure she will make you very welcome. Should there be any further complications, I would prefer to be on hand to deal with them.'

Her initial unease at his suggestion was quickly dispelled when she recognised its professional intention.

'Then I am much obliged to you, doctor, and accept your invitation. My name is Elizabeth Duncan. I am to be the assistant schoolmistress on Eisdalsa Island.' Her voice was beginning to trail off into an almost inaudible whisper. 'Mr Ogilvie, the dominie, is to meet me when the ship . . .'

Her head lolled in David's arms. With some reluctance, he laid her back against the pillows, in the narrow bunk.

He covered her gently with a blanket, checked her pulse and gathered up his equipment. Before leaving he made one further check on his patient. Without the severe bonnet, with her hair scattered wantonly over the pillow, she looked more child than woman. David was surprised by the strength of emotion which the sight of her aroused in him. Assuring himself that she was indeed asleep, he went to the door and closed it silently behind him.

As he left the cabin, he was immediately confronted by the anxious men who awaited him.

'I have given her a sedative,' David replied to Gordon's solicitous inquiry. 'You may tell your Captain that the young lady's injuries are mainly superficial. She should be fully recovered in a few days. However, that does not exonerate the Steamship Company from liability. It is a matter of gross negligence that such an accident should have occurred at all!'

'Thank you, doctor,' Gordon MacIntyre interrupted sharply. 'The Company will undoubtedly accept responsibility for the accident. The lady was the innocent victim of an unfortunate series of events.' Realising that he was sounding too defensive, Gordon continued in a milder tone: 'I would be obliged if you will make out a written report of the passenger's injuries. Facilities are available for you to do this before you leave the ship. But first the Captain is anxious to speak to you both, gentlemen. Will you follow me, please?'

'Miss Duncan is not to be disturbed,' warned David. 'She should sleep until the boat docks at Eisdalsa.'

'I will order a steward to stand guard outside the cabin.' The First Officer signalled a steward.

'Robarts, see that no one enters the Captain's cabin.'

'If I may,' interrupted David, 'perhaps Mr Robarts might look in on

the young lady from time to time.' To Robarts he added, 'If there is
any sign of distress, fetch me immediately.'

The steward saluted smartly, acknowledging the doctor's request,
and took up his post beside the cabin door.

The laudanum induced a restless sleep in which Elizabeth experienced
a jumble of memories and emotions, items from her past being inexplic-
ably linked with her apprehensions about what was to come in the
future.

She seemed to be travelling at speed along a dark tunnel with no
turnings. As she progressed, the walls closed in around her until she
was sure she could not get through. Suddenly she was out in the open
but enveloped in a white mist. She was swinging, swinging on a rope,
upwards towards a solid wall of iron. At the last moment before impact
she screamed and threw up her hands to protect her face.

'Miss Duncan, Miss Duncan!'

Gordon MacIntyre had thrown his arms around her to prevent her
from hitting herself on the wooden sides of the bunk. He spoke gentle
comforting phrases as he rocked her within his warm embrace. Gradually her frenzied movements ceased and she gazed at him in bewilderment.

'All right now?'

She was looking up into warm grey smiling eyes. The broad intelligent
brow was framed by neatly clipped brown hair, squashed flat by the
uniform cap which had been flung carelessly aside.

'You were calling out. A nightmare no doubt.'

Suddenly self-conscious, he released his hold and laid her head back
against the pillows. Backing out of the cabin, he hurriedly retrieved his
cap, muttering, 'The steward sent for me when he heard you calling
out. The doctor will be here directly.'

Gordon's confusion was not lost upon certain members of the crew
working nearby. He thrust his fingers through his dishevelled hair and
replaced his cap firmly, giving the men a withering look as he did so.
They knew better than to make any comment. Dropping their gaze,
the sailors applied themselves to their work.

Robarts discovered David and William Whylie in the passengers'
lounge.

'Mr McIntyre's compliments, doctor. The young lady is stirring and
the ship will be docking at Eisdalsa in fifteen minutes!'

David and William both rose from the comfortable seats where they
had been resting, sipping large glasses of whisky and enjoying their
discussion.

'You take care of Miss Duncan,' said William. 'I will see that all our
baggage gets ashore.'

David found his patient awake and attempting, with little success, to pull on her clothes. When she tried to sit up a pain shot through her right side and she all but cried out. She was stiff, so very stiff.

'If you will allow me, I will take the liberty of opening your baggage to find a more suitable garment,' he offered. 'Your camisole was soiled rather badly.'

She smiled up at him gratefully as, with considerable expertise, the young doctor helped her to dress. She winced as she tried to stand.

'Thank you so much doctor,' she whispered. 'I believe I owe my life to your prompt action at Crinan.'

David smiled. 'It was nothing, madam, I do assure you.'

If she only knew how much this encounter had affected him. He thanked Providence for bringing her into his life, yet wished fervently that a less painful method might have been devised. Every step she took was obviously agony for her, and he felt the pain as though it were his own.

As they emerged from the cabin, Gordon McIntyre stepped forward to support Elizabeth on her free arm.

Thus they proceeded to the companionway, each young man believing himself to be a prizewinner. William was obliged to demonstrate his devotion to the young lady by taking care of her luggage.

Sighting a lone figure impatiently pacing the jetty, David relinquished his charge to Gordon.

'I must have a word with that gentleman down there, before we disembark,' he explained.

He strode down the gangplank and confronted the Dominie.

'Mr Ogilvie, if I am not much mistaken!'

'That is correct.' The schoolmaster took a closer look at the young man who had spoken. 'You will be Dr David Beaton, the doctor's youngest son?'

Ogilvie was not particularly pleased at this encounter. It was cold, getting quite dark, and he had to see his new assistant into her quarters before he could get home to his supper.

'It seems that I am here on a false errand.' The dominie allowed his gaze to sweep across the deck, searching for a single female person and spotting only a small group of people hovering near the top of the gangplank.

'I believe that you are expecting to meet a Miss Duncan?' David enquired.

'Indeed I am. Do you have news of her?'

'The young lady had an unfortunate accident whilst boarding the steamer at Crinan. I regret to say she has sustained injuries which will require treatment and rest for several days. I intend to take her to my mother's house where she may recuperate.'

'Surely I may have a word with her, at the very least? Having waited here for so long, I would prefer to meet my new assistant.'

'I fear you will have to contain your curiosity for a day or two longer,' David insisted. 'My patient is overwrought after her traumatic experience. She is in no condition to meet her future employer at this moment. Perhaps you will call at Tigh na Broch later in the week?'

Without waiting for a response from the schoolmaster, David turned on his heel and hurried back up the gangplank to oversee the disembarkation of his patient.

4

M orag Beaton stood in the window, watching the *Lord of Lorn* steaming up the Sound from the south. She called out to Michael who was working in the dispensary.

'Dr David should be on this boat, Michael. Will you take the trap down to the pier to meet him?'

'Yes, ma'am.'

The boy scurried away to do her bidding while Morag rubbed purposefully at the already glowing mahogany. It was Hugh's desk which she herself had cared for over so many years. He had never allowed the servants to clean in this, his holy of holies. Only Morag had been allowed to tidy his books and papers.

She felt slightly guilty at the reasons for the great effort she and the servants had been making to have the house spotless for David's homecoming. In her heart, she knew that David's ambition was aimed in quite a different direction, but that did not stop her from dreaming. If only he could be persuaded to take over his father's practice! If only he would appreciate what his father had already achieved, and what his hopes had been for the future!

Already, by rigid application of the law concerning vaccination, smallpox had been eradicated in the parish. Hugh, by his insistence on good supplies of fresh water to all the villages, and by his relentless battle with the factor to improve the housing of the workers, had ensured that the district was free from both cholera and typhoid. These two scourges were the cause of widespread deaths not only in the cities, but also in the rural villages of nearby parishes.

Unlike most other men of his age, Hugh had confided all his hopes and ambitions in the wife whom he regarded as his partner. Together they had planned strategies by which the simple villagers might be persuaded to change their ways for their own good. There were times when it had been Morag's tact and understanding which had won through after Hugh's explanations and reasoning had fallen on deaf ears. She missed this aspect of their relationship almost as much as the comfortable, deep affection in which her husband had held her throughout the years of their marriage.

Once more she ran her duster over the lines of books, leatherbound and heavily embossed with gold leaf. Her eye fell on one particularly ancient and well-used tome. She lifted it reverently from its place and laid it on the desk. At her touch leaves fell open at those pages most often referred to by her husband, and many others doctors before him.

The book was handwritten in an ancient script, difficult to decipher. An ancestor of the Beatons' had long ago written about the plants which grew on his home island. He told of their form, their whereabouts, and the uses to which they might be put for medicinal purposes. The book also included many cures for common ailments which some might laugh off as old wives' tales. Hugh, however, had studied them all, and to many had attributed a degree of efficacy which would have astonished some of his disbelieving contemporaries. Morag smiled to herself as she came across one after another of the more favoured remedies which he had unashamedly applied when all else failed.

So deeply immersed had she become that, although she had been awaiting it, her son's arrival took her by surprise. She heard his familiar call as he leapt from the carriage and ran the last remaining yards to the front door.

She left the book lying open on the desk and hurried to greet him.

Elizabeth sat patiently in the carriage, still trying to throw off the effects of the drug which David had administered. He had asked her to wait while he explained her presence to his mother. She was only too pleased to take advantage of the opportunity to straighten her dress, pat at her unruly curls and retie her bonnet strings. What a place this was for wind, she thought. No wonder the village women wore shawls tied tightly about their heads. She was not unaccustomed to country roads, but this seemed inordinately rutted and muddy. She made a mental note to lift her skirts a few inches higher . . . as she had seen them worn in the village.

Tigh na Broch, 'the house of the badger' according to David's translation, was an imposing residence of two storeys, standing well back from the shore road about a mile outside the village.

The steeply sloping roof of local slates was interrupted by a row of dormer windows which suggested accommodation for servants or perhaps children. It was a fine family house with a welcoming aspect.

Windows facing to the north-west commanded a fine view across the Sound to Eisdalsa Island and the craggy cliffs and mountains of Mull in the far distance.

Windows facing to the south-west overlooked the wide expanse of the Atlantic Ocean with, here and there, scattered islands of the Inner Hebrides. To the immediate south lay the island of Lunga, a little smaller than Seileach but considerably larger than its sister slate island of Eisdalsa.

Built originally for one of the numerous progeny of the Campbells of Argyll, Tigh na Broch was part of the estate of the Marquis of Stirling. The tenancy had been offered to David's grandfather when he was appointed by the Quarrying Company to be their medical officer. Two generations of Beaton children had occupied those attic rooms, and shouted and tumbled across the hillside which towered behind the tall chimneys and grey slate roof.

David was returning, with those quick purposeful strides to which Elizabeth was becoming accustomed. In the doorway behind him she saw a short, rather stocky, woman. Her hair was drawn back tightly into a neat bun. Her mourning dress was cut in a fashionable style. Her erect posture with shoulders held back reminded Elizabeth of Miss Murdoch, her last employer, and as had been the case with the headmistress of the Solway Academy for Young Gentlewomen, a severe exterior had a warm heart. This was immediately made clear when Morag stepped forward to greet her guest.

Having followed her son to the carriage, she came forward to embrace Elizabeth.

'My dear child,' she crooned, 'you have had a terrible experience. David has told me all about it. Now come along inside. We will do what we can to make your stay comfortable. You must understand that in these parts we live very simply.'

The effusive welcome was beginning to make Elizabeth uneasy. Morag, who had never travelled further than from Tobermory to Seileach following her marriage to the young Dr Hugh, was anxious to observe the proprieties. She had read all the journals of the day and understood the kind of hospitality which a town-bred lady would expect. She would not wish David's young lady to think her lacking in social niceties. A fellow passenger, David had said, but Morag had already linked the couple romantically, believing that her son's interest in the girl revealed more than mere professional solicitude.

Having helped Elizabeth off with her outer garments, she led her guest towards the parlour.

David intervened. 'I am sure Miss Duncan will be comfortable in the kitchen, Mother,' he said, gently. 'She needs to get warm and the parlour fire is only just lit. A little food and a long sleep is my prescription.'

Smiling, he raised his eyebrows enquiringly at Elizabeth over his mother's head. She nodded her approval, and smiled back.

Sheilagh, the cook, was stirring a huge pan of broth and singing softly to herself. When David entered the kitchen, she dropped her spoon and ran forward to hug him.

'Why, Sheilagh, just as beautiful as ever I see . . . and what a smell. Delicious!'

'I know you, Master Davy. It's not my looks but my broth that you are after!'

They laughed. David led Elizabeth into the cosy room with its gleaming range and white-scrubbed table.

'Miss Duncan, let me introduce Sheilagh, as much a part of the Beaton household as the walls around you!'

The elderly servant curtsied warily to the younger woman. Elizabeth held out her hand in a friendly gesture. Sheilagh grasped it with enthusiasm, her round red face wreathed in smiles.

'Welcome to Eisdalsa, miss.' She pulled out a chair. 'Now just you sit here and I'll serve the broth directly.'

As David and Elizabeth began to eat, Morag and Sheilagh exchanged knowing glances.

Morag could understand why David should be so taken with the lass. She was pretty, and intelligent too . . . had he not said she was a schoolteacher? Well, if Elizabeth was the means by which David could be persuaded to stay, so be it. He could do much worse for a wife!

After the first few mouthfuls Elizabeth realised that she was not, after all, as hungry as she had thought. She found herself picking at the food before her, while her eyelids became too heavy to hold open. As she nodded over her plate, David became aware of his guest's discomfort and was immediately all solicitude.

'Will you take Miss Duncan to her room, Mother, before she falls asleep in her pudding!'

Morag rose and placed a hand on the girl's shoulder. Elizabeth flinched as pain swept over her. She tried to rise to her feet but it was only with David's firm grip on her undamaged arm that she was able to do so.

Morag was surprised. So the visitor was truly injured? She had done her son an injustice, believing the accident to be an excuse for accommodating the girl in this fashion.

Morag assisted Elizabeth to climb the wide staircase to the first-floor landing, and led her into a low-beamed bedroom of ample proportions. A wide four-poster bed dominated the room. Its hangings were of delicate pastel colours, patterned in flowers and birds. The coverlet and the linen were sparkling white.

'Oh,' protested Elizabeth, 'this must be your own room, Mrs Beaton. I cannot put you to so much inconvenience.'

'Nonsense, my dear.' Her hostess brushed aside Elizabeth's protests. 'I hope you will find the bed comfortable.'

Laid out on the coverlet was a gown of white lawn decorated with exquisite lace.

'I thought you might like to borrow a nightgown,' Morag explained. 'It will save you the trouble of unpacking your valise tonight.'

'You are too kind,' Elizabeth murmured, tears welling in her eyes. The strain of the day, the after-effects of the laudanum, and the overwhelming welcome she had received from this kindly stranger, were all too much. The tears fell.

Morag sat on the bed beside the girl and cradled her in her arms like a child. After a while the weeping ceased and she began, gently, to help Elizabeth undress. When the bruised and battered flesh was exposed she let out a cry of concern.

'Oh, my dear, how could you have borne to sit at my table in such discomfort? David should have warned me. He did not say the damage was so serious!'

Elizabeth smiled wanly as the older woman tucked the snowy sheets around her.

'Please, don't distress yourself. The wounds are all superficial, but I must admit they do not hurt any the less for that!'

There was a sharp tap on the door. At his mother's bidding, David entered, wearing his most professional expression and carrying his medical bag. Behind him stood Michael Brown, holding a tray of glassware and various implements. David took the tray and dismissed the apprentice.

'Thank you for your help, Michael. I will talk with you in the morning.'

With some reluctance, Michael took his leave of Morag and smiled encouragingly at Elizabeth before closing the door behind him.

David had difficulty in disguising the emotions which coursed through his veins when his eyes rested on the girl, auburn curls spread loosely over the snowy froth of his mother's lacy pillows. The sight of her swollen eyelids and blushing cheeks made him want to gather her in his arms to comfort her. With a great effort of will, he pulled himself together.

Deftly, he loosened the neck of the nightgown and, with his mother's assistance, stripped his patient to the waist. With his fingertips he traced the areas of most severe bruising and then proceeded to paint each of the bruises with a solution of sugar water. He reached for a shallow dish in which a dozen skinny leeches wriggled and squirmed.

When she saw what David was about to do, Elizabeth gasped and shrank back from the fearsome dish.

He spoke kindly to her.

'Believe me, Miss Duncan, these little fellows will ease your pain far more than any balm which I can provide.'

He placed one of the little creatures in a wineglass and inverted it over a bruise. Attracted by the sugar coating on the skin, the leech dug in its mandibles and was soon swelling before their eyes. David offered up one after another of the leeches to the affected areas. As each became engorged with blood, it let go its hold and David caught it and replaced it in the dish.

By the time that the leeches had completed their work, Elizabeth had fallen into an untroubled sleep.

David covered the bite marks with calamine lotion, and then removed the dressings from the deeper cuts which he had dealt with after the accident. Satisfied that they would heal if left undisturbed, he replaced the dressings and pulled the sheet up around his patient's shoulders.

Morag had settled herself by the fire in a comfortable armchair. She was examining Elizabeth's gown. Every now and again she uttered a little cry of dismay.

'This dress is ripped to shreds,' she said. 'However could it have got into such a state?'

'The sailors were obliged to cut the young lady free from the cargo net,' he replied. 'It was not the time to worry about damage to her clothing.'

'Well, I shall sit here and repair the gown as best I can,' announced his mother. 'You look as though you could do with some sleep yourself. Away to your bed now . . . I will call you if she wakes.'

David was reluctant to leave the bedside of the sleeping girl. 'Please watch her carefully, Mother. If you notice any change to her colour or her breathing, fetch me at once.'

Morag smiled at this son who looked and spoke exactly like her beloved father. She nodded to him and he went out, closing the door so quietly that she was hardly aware he was gone.

From time to time during the night, she was conscious that David was in the room, watching over his patient, listening to her breathing and gently taking her pulse. At one point she realised that he had covered her own legs with a rug and had replenished the fire.

The morning light revealed a tousled Morag sleeping upright in her chair by a rapidly cooling grate. The young woman tossed restlessly in her bed.

Morag woke suddenly. The sharp cry which had disturbed her was repeated, again and again. Elizabeth half-raised herself in the bed then dropped back upon the pillows in a faint. Beads of perspiration glistened on her brow but, when Morag touched her face, it was cold and clammy.

She found David stretched out, fully dressed, on a little truckle-bed in the small attic room he had occupied as a child. One shake from his mother and he was instantly awake.

'It's Miss Duncan!' Morag's anxiety was clear from her sharp tones. 'She seems to be delirious and is uncommon cold to the touch. Her breathing is very laboured.'

David was away down the stairs before his mother had finished speaking. He shouted a demand for hot water to Sheilagh, who was already busy in the kitchen.

It was as his mother had described. Elizabeth was indeed cold. Her skin was clammy and her breathing irregular. He had to search for a pulse. When detected at last, it was rapid and very weak. He pushed up an eyelid and found a dark dilated pupil staring up at him, unseeing. In her semi-conscious condition, Elizabeth was pleading for water.

David raised her head gently and gave her a few sips then called upon his mother for assistance. Together, they were able to raise

Elizabeth's feet on piles of cushions, so that blood would flow back towards her head.

Sheilagh had brought a pail of steaming hot water. David now sent her off to find salt while he bounded down the stairs to his father's surgery.

For more than two hours, David worked unceasingly. He had observed the administration of hot saline douches, as a treatment for shock, while working with Professor Munro. This, however, was the first time that he had had occasion to use the treatment himself.

At last the pulse rate became normal and the clammy skin dry and less pallid.

Elizabeth's throat felt sore and her voice was croaking.

'Have I caused you all a lot of trouble?' she asked. 'I am so sorry.'

'How do you feel now, my dear?' asked Morag, in her crooning tone. 'Very tired.'

David, finally satisfied with the pulse rate he was counting, lowered her hand on to the coverlet, looked into each of her eyes and pronounced that she would do very well.

He ushered the old servant out of the room.

'Sheilagh, we all need a strong cup of tea. Then I want you to prepare a bed for my mother. I have no wish for two invalids on my hands as a result of this night's work! Oh, and if Michael Brown has arrived, ask him to wait for me in the consulting room.'

Sheilagh departed for her kitchen while David went to wash and change the clothes he had been wearing for the past thirty hours.

When he returned to the sickroom, he found his patient and his mother in quiet conversation. Elizabeth smiled when she saw him, and said she felt quite well again.

'You must rest,' said David. He measured a draught of laudanum into a medicine glass and held it out for her to take.

'Oh dear,' she protested, 'must I really take more medicine to make me sleep? I begin to feel quite myself.'

'I fear I must insist,' he said firmly. She looked as though she would make further protest, but recognising a determined adversary, changed her mind and allowed the syrupy liquid to course down her throat. In a few minutes she was sleeping soundly.

Morag gave her son a long hard look.

'I have seen your father perform a number of extraordinary operations,' she declared. 'Never have I seen such a treatment as that!'

'The young lady was suffering from what is called post-traumatic shock. It happens quite frequently after heroic surgery, amputations and so forth. It is a matter of getting the heart and pulse rate right, and the blood circulating normally.'

David was rather pleased with his night's work. He had only observed the method, as practised by Professor Munro, following a rather protracted amputation. In that case both legs were involved. Unfortunately the patient had eventually died from gangrene. Elizabeth, he felt sure, would have no further complications. Nevertheless, while she slept soundly, he did take the opportunity to replace the dressings on her wounded side and was satisfied that there was no evidence of suppuration.

The waiting-room was full. Word had spread around the Village that the new doctor had arrived. Despite having come home solely to tidy up loose ends, ready to hand over to the incoming practitioner, David found himself obliged to take the surgery.

Michael gave him invaluable help in finding his way through his father's somewhat disordered records. Dr Hugh had been excellent in his practical doctoring, but short of method when it came to keeping accounts.

As the day wore on, David became more and more aware that his father's affairs were in a very bad state. Money was owing to the practice from every quarter. By the same token, unpaid bills were stacked in piles in his father's desk drawers.

When he spoke to Michael about the manner of invoicing his patients, the boy seemed puzzled. He had never heard Dr Hugh discuss money with his patients, and had no idea how the doctor had gone about collecting what was owing.

Asked how Michael himself had received his wages, the boy said that the doctor had given him a few shillings when he thought of it, usually straight out of his pocket. Nowhere could David discover any reference to the boy's employment, or his terms of apprenticeship.

'I hope to be able to continue to engage your services and to keep up with your training,' explained David, 'but you must understand that I cannot guarantee that the new doctor will agree to employ you.'

Michael looked very surprised.

'Oh, but I thought . . .' he began.

'What did you think?'

'Nothing really, something Sheilagh said . . .' The boy stammered in his embarrassment and shut his mouth.

David looked at him narrowly. 'Well, we shall just have to see, shall we not?'

By now the heaps of paper had been returned to the desk drawers, in somewhat better order. There remained only the volume which Morag had been studying while she awaited David's arrival the day before.

He turned over a few pages, struggling with the curious language and the unfamiliar handwriting. This book summed up the practice, in his eyes. Some of the old-fashioned remedies seemed more akin to witchcraft than medicine. Many were not far removed from the category of old wives' tales.

David knew that his father had often referred to this book. As a child, David and his brother had been taken for walks across the hills. Painfully slow expeditions they had been. Every few minutes his father would stop to examine some bush or herb. He would pull up a root, inspect a flower or rub a leaf vigorously between his fingers and make his sons take note of the scent. And all the time he would relate tales of the healing skills of their ancestors, those Beatons from the islands whose work was their memorial.

Annoyed at his father's ability to exert his influence even from the grave, David snapped the volume shut and thrust it into a space in the bookcase.

5

W illiam Whylie gazed after the trap as it rounded the corner of the street and disappeared into the fast-gathering dusk.

Across the narrow strait which separated him from his destination on the Island of Eisdalsa, windows were alive with lamplight. The sounds of the quarries were hushed and an eerie stillness had descended. The cold south-easterly wind, which had blown steadily throughout the day, had dropped to a light breeze and veered to its more accustomed south-westerly direction. The air temperature was low enough to cause William to huddle into the ample folds of his heavy overcoat, its large cape flapping gently about his shoulders.

He glanced around him, seeking out someone to transport him across the water. At the foot of the harbour steps, low voices, the occasional slap of water against timber and the clank of metal upon metal alerted him to the presence of a small wooden craft tied up against the pier. Aboard, and clearly making ready to sail, were two men. In the bows lobster pots were stacked alongside a pile of netting. One of the sailors had set the oars in the rowlocks while the other was about to cast off.

'Good evening,' called William. 'Is there any chance that you might give me passage to Eisdalsa Island?'

There was a muttered exchange between the two men. William, not understanding what was said, supposed it to be in the Gaelic tongue. The youth who was in the act of casting off reached up for William's valise and lifted it into the boat as though it were no heavier than a feather pillow. Setting the bag down upon the bottom boards, he turned to help William aboard. Not one word was exchanged.

It was a tricky operation for a landsman to perform. The tide was rising and the heavy swell caused the boat to lift and fall continuously, as the waves pounded against the harbour wall. William hesitated, finding it difficult to choose the right moment to step across the gunwale with one foot, while the other still clung to the slippery stone step. He had no need to fear. Before he realised what was happening, he had been grasped firmly by the arm and swung across into the boat where he was unceremoniously pushed down on to the heap of netting.

The men never addressed him directly but several short exchanges took place in their own tongue.

Outside the confines of the tiny harbour, the sail was raised and the craft tacked up into the wind. Working against the south-westerly, the short crossing, only five hundred yards at the most, took some fifteen minutes. Once in the shelter of the island, the wind dropped and the sail was lowered. Under oars, the small boat slid silently up to the landing stage.

Although no word of English had been spoken between them, William thanked his benefactors and, as he climbed ashore, asked where the Quarry Manager's house stood.

The elder of the two boatmen raised his eyes and nodded towards a house which stood a little distance from the quarriers cottages which clustered around the harbour.

William followed the man's gaze.

'Up there, under the hill?'

'Aye.'

It was the only indication that the men spoke English though clearly they understood the language. William was uncomfortably aware that he had more problems to face than just the regeneration of a depressed industry. If he wished to integrate fully with these people he would have to learn to communicate with them in their own tongue.

In the wintery gloom of early-evening, the white cottages with their slated roofs looked friendly and inviting. Here and there, an oil lamp created a welcoming glow. In other homes a slender tallow candle provided a more meagre illumination. As night fell the island noises were of the soft chatter of breeze in the rigging of the small boats crowded in the harbour; the mewling of infants; the occasional banging of a loosely fastened door; the gentle neighing of horses, stabled on the far side of the village. Only the steady throbbing of the pumping engine in the quarry, somewhere beyond the ridge, reminded William that this was a place of great industry and no peaceful haven.

Skirting the neatly laid out rows of cottages, he followed a well-worn track around the harbour narrowly avoiding a noisome midden at its head. As he came up to the Quarry Master's door it was flung open to reveal an elderly figure who, with lamp held high, gazed short-sightedly into the surrounding gloom.

'Will you be William Whylie?' he demanded. 'I have been expecting you this half hour. Let me take your bag. Come along in . . . and welcome to Eisdalsa!'

The house was warm and inviting. Placing the valise upon the slate floor, the old man ushered William forward into the room, helped him off with his coat and indicated a comfortable chair by the stove.

'Sit you down, man. You will take a dram to ward off the cold?'

William accepted the proffered glass gratefully. The strong liquor coursed through him, restoring his spirits.

'You will be wondering who I am.' The grey-haired man settled himself on a 'creepy' stool, close to the hearth. 'Archie MacLean is my name. Mr Lugas, His Lordship's Factor, told me to expect you today.

My wife Maggie has cleaned the house and made you a fine stew.'

In his early sixties, Archie MacLean was stooped, gnarled and weather-beaten, but William estimated that he must have been a strapping six foot or more of Highland manhood in his earlier days. His face, etched by time, showed him to be a man of good humour whose ready smile had engraved itself permanently upon his countenance.

'You will be weary from your journey, Mr Whylie. How long have you been on the road?'

William had a struggle to recall the number of days which had passed since he left his home town of Redruth.

'I left Cornwall a week ago, but I had to report to Company Office in London before travelling northwards.'

'Aye, aye,' sighed Archie, 'it is a wonderful thing the steam locomotive, transporting folk such long distances in so short a time. I would that I might experience such a trip myself, before I die.'

'Without doubt, the best part of the journey was aboard the *Lord of Lorn* today,' said William politely. 'Yours is a beautiful country, Mr MacLean. I look forward to making the acquaintance of its people.'

'Aye . . . oh, aye,' mused the old man. 'It is fair enough on a day like today. You may feel differently when the winds are upon us. The high tides at the end of the month will most likely be accompanied by gales. Then you will know what it is to be an Islander.'

As he spoke, Archie tended the large iron pot which stood upon the stove and from which issued the most delicious smell. William was suddenly made aware that he had eaten nothing since breakfasting in the buffet at St Enoch station that morning.

'The house is somewhat lacking in comforts.' Archie handed William a large dish of stew. 'Mr McPhee took away all but the basic furniture when he left. You can set yourself up with what you need at the Company Store. Furniture and such we make ourselves or else send to Glasgow. Maggie will have a catalogue you may borrow.'

'Will you not join me in the meal?' asked William. Archie needed no further bidding. He reached down a second plate from the shelf above the range and filled it.

'Your wife is a fine cook, Mr MacLean.'

'You have no wife yourself, Mr Whylie?'

William shook his head. He thought fleetingly of the dark-eyed girl who had spurned his offer of marriage, and whose refusal had been instrumental in his acceptance of his present position.

When his childhood sweetheart had suddenly begun to show an interest in an older and wealthier man, William's jealous response had merely served to make her more determined to take the other suitor. He realised now that his pride had been injured rather than his heart. He was ready to look elsewhere for a bride, and thought he might have met her already, aboard the *Lord of Lorn*.

'No . . . nor any prospect of one,' he replied.

Conversation lapsed until the entire contents of the pot had been devoured and the dishes cleared away. When all was done, they talked of the quarrying; of earlier days when the Old Marquis had himself directed the quarries and taken an active role in their development. Archie had been the foreman, before he retired. Now he was retained by the Factor to supervise the accommodation of the workers on the island, to collect the rents and see to the maintenance of the buildings. As Archie said, with so little capital investment by the Company, there was little enough funding for him to administer. He was, however, able to see that the tenants performed their duties with regard to the upkeep of their own homes, using whatever materials came to hand.

As time went on, William found he could no longer concentrate on his companion's soft, musical speech. His head began to droop and he could not keep his eyes open.

Archie rose to his feet, tapped out his pipe on the stove and reached for his coat.

'Maggie has made up the closet bed for you.' He indicated an alcove in one wall, where a curtain concealed a box bed. 'She thought it would be warmer for tonight. There is a bedroom up the stair, if you would prefer to use it.'

'Please thank Mrs MacLean for her kindness.' William stirred himself sufficiently to give his new friend a courteous farewell.

He retired to his bed and to a deep sleep, which was disturbed only by visions of hills and white water churning beneath monstrous paddle-wheels. From out of the clouds of spray came the vision of a young girl's face, framed in reddish-gold curls. The skin was blotched and bruised. The mouth gaped wide as though calling out in fear . . . pleading with him to save her.

William was awakened by a thunderous hammering on his door. Wrapping a blanket about him, he padded barefoot across the cold slate floor.

On the threshold stood a tall, gangling fellow, dressed in flannel shirt and moleskin trousers. Over his shirt he wore a colourful tweed waistcoat and, on his head, the bowler hat of his rank.

Malcolm Logie touched his hat to his new boss in a manner which ought to have suggested respect but which might as easily be interpreted as contemptuous.

'I thought you would be anxious to meet the crews before they begin work this morning,' he said accusingly.

It was gone eight o'clock. The men were gathered at the quarry road awaiting their instructions and here was the new boss, still in his bed. Nothing, so it seemed, had changed.

If William was sensitive to the implied criticism, he chose to ignore it.

'Good day to you, Mr . . . ?'

'Malcolm Logie, foreman, Mr Whylie, sir.'

'Step inside for a moment, Logie. It is a confoundedly sharp wind this morning.'

'The men are awaiting their orders, sir.' He removed his hat as he stooped to enter the manager's house.

'Sit you down for a minute while I dress.'

William poured cold water from a blue and white earthenware jug into a similarly patterned bowl and splashed some over his face.

'You catch me unawares,' he observed, as he pulled on his garments which he had left neatly folded over the single arm-chair. 'I was travelling for thirty-six hours without proper sleep,' he continued, by way of explanation.

'I have never travelled further than Glasgow myself,' ventured Malcolm. 'Five years ago that was, when my brother married a city lassie. Och! What a terrible noisy, dirty place it is. You would not catch me going there again.'

William drew on his heavy overcoat.

'You'll no be wearing a good coat like that to go into the quarries.' Malcolm was aghast at such an idea.

'It is the only coat I have,' responded William. 'No doubt I will be able to obtain something more suitable in due course.'

'There may be one left by Mr McPhee,' suggested the foreman. 'Try the closet.'

William opened the door which Logie indicated. Sure enough, inside the closet hung a calf-length canvas coat. It was well-worn, but would serve to protect the new manager from the biting wind. William drew it on.

'Mr McPhee will have left some gaiters there too,' suggested Logie. Indeed he had.

At last, fully clothed to the foreman's satisfaction, William emerged from his cottage to view the island by daylight.

As the two men strode along beside the railway track, they were conscious of curious eyes marking their progress. In this community the Quarry Manager was an important figure whose movements were likely to be monitored at all times.

'Mr MacLean and his wife gave me a fine welcome last evening,' ventured William. He could sense a certain hostility in his companion and felt it was up to himself to break the ice.

'Aye, it was Archie told me you had arrived.' The statement sounded like an indictment.

'Do you think Mrs MacLean would agree to continue to keep house for me?' William knew the importance of following protocol in such matters. He was only too well aware of the problems which could arise from any ill-judged approach, made in such a close-knit community.

'She looked after Mr McPhee, difficult as he was. I feel sure she would not be averse to your asking her.'

'Before we meet the men, Mr Logie, I want you to know that I have met and spoken at length with His Lordship's agent in London and I believe that I understand the problems which you have been having with the lessees. I have some ideas about the means by which improvements may be made in that respect. For the rest . . . the day-to-day working of the quarries and the organisation of the men . . . I shall rely heavily upon your knowledge of the area and your experience. I shall not interfere in such matters unless you specifically request it, or I myself see a need to intervene.'

Logie was relieved. For a long time he had carried the full weight of responsibility for the quarries on his own shoulders. While he had no wish to relinquish his position as foreman, he had resented the responsibilities of management which McPhee's inadequacies had forced upon him.

'I shall be pleased to be of service to you, sir,' he answered. 'I cannot, of course, speak for my opposite number in the Seileach quarries across the water, but I believe he will be equally satisfied with such an arrangement.'

'When will I have the pleasure of meeting that gentleman?' enquired William. He realised that it was important to treat the two foremen with equal deference. To keep careful watch over the quarries on the other side of the water would be difficult if he must rely always on someone else to transport him. He filed away this problem in his mind, for further consideration.

'Dougie Brown will be across tomorrow with his weekly report,' Malcolm added, 'but I can send for him to come today, if you wish?'

'Tomorrow will do, thank you.' William was pleased to find that the chill atmosphere between them had warmed a little.

Malcolm Logie led his new master along a stony pathway beside a narrow-guage railway track along which ponies were drawing small trucks laden with finished roofing slates.

The path took them beneath overhanging cliffs of the one piece of high ground on the island, a narrow ridge of volcanic rock some eighty feet high which ran across the island from north-east to south-west. It was clear to William that while this formation might provide a welcome shelter from the Atlantic gales, it was a major problem to those engaged in winning the slate. At the junction between this tertiary intrusion of molten magma and the uniform beds of blue slate rock, the slate had buckled and twisted. Veins of quartz had formed along the divide.

To the experienced eye of the new manager this spelt trouble. Men set to work in the area where the intrusion was uncovered would have poor results for their labours. Their wages, based upon the number of slates made, would suffer in consequence. William made a mental note to go into this problem with Logie as soon as possible.

They approached an embankment carrying one of the railway tracks overhead, from east to west. It skirted the hill and then wormed its way towards the south-westerly shore.

'That track is specifically intended to carry away the waste slate,' observed Logie. 'On such a small island the refuse is a constant problem. We have tried filling the abandoned quarries, only to have to remove the waste at a later date because we need access to newly discovered slate beds. Dumping in the sea seems the best solution.'

They rounded a corner and there before them was the whole expanse of the Sound of Lorn with the mountains of the Island of Mull in the background. Before them lay two enormous quarries; the outermost, at least two hundred feet in depth and one hundred yards across, was skirted on the seaward side by a stout wall of slate stones set vertically, without mortar, and built with masonry skills which left William breathless with admiration.

'That's a fine wall,' he commented. 'With masons of that calibre you should have no trouble keeping out the sea.'

'Aye,' agreed Logie. 'Would that the younger men were as skilled as the old fellows who built it. That wall has stood there for a hundred years and more.'

William smiled to himself. All workmen hankered thus after past glories. From what he had seen so far, he was well satisfied with the standard of workmanship about him.

Between the large outer quarry and the hill another, deeper but of smaller diameter, was separated from it by a narrow causeway. At the start of the causeway stood a low stone building which appeared to be the company office.

There must have been one hundred and eighty to two hundred men gathered outside. They stood about in small groups, smoking their clay pipes and talking mainly in the unmistakable cadences of the Gaelic language. The men parted ranks to allow William and Malcolm to pass through. A few muttered a 'Good day, sir', some doffed their caps deferentially, but for the most part, they simply stared.

Inside the hut was a smaller group. Logie introduced these as the crew leaders, and as he called out their names, each one stepped forward to shake William by the hand.

He followed Logie to the desk and took the seat he was offered.

'If you can find somewhere to sit, gentlemen, please make yourselves comfortable.' He turned to Logie, expecting him to translate what had been said.

There was no need, the men positioned themselves as comfortably as they could in the limited space available.

William continued: 'As you can tell by my speech, gentlemen, I am not a native of your country. I do however come from another great slate area – Cornwall. If you find my brogue difficult to follow, I hope you will tell me and I shall speak more slowly.' He paused. Not a sound was to be heard. No one moved. No one spoke out.

'I understand that there have been some difficulties here of late,' he resumed. 'What these are, I have yet to determine. Mr Logie will be able to enlighten me. I assure you that I am not unfamiliar with the kind of problems arising from absentee management. With your assistance, I shall endeavour to put matters right when I can, and seek help from above when I cannot.'

There was a murmur of approval from all round.

'Until such time as I am ready to make a move, I would ask you to carry on as you have been doing, under the direction of Mr Logie. I hope to meet you all in more congenial circumstances, and to get to know you and your families very soon.'

He sat back and listened while Logie distributed the work stations amongst the men. Soon they had all gone about their business, leaving Logie and William alone in the hut.

Logie proceeded to explain the method by which allocations were arranged, and the measures he was introducing to make the working practices safer.

Satisfied, for the moment, with what he had been shown, William turned to another subject.

'Do all the men communicate with each other in Gaelic?' he asked.

Malcolm shook his head. 'Only those who were born here, although that is the majority. The men of working age will all have attended the school, where they would have been forbidden to speak anything but English. I suppose that it is a kind of protest that they make, continuing to use the Gaelic amongst themselves.'

'Is it a difficult language to learn?' William queried.

'Perhaps not,' Malcolm replied. 'Although no Englishman about here has ever tried.'

Their conversation was interrupted by a loud rap on the door. Two men entered. Unlike the other quarrymen, these two were dressed in their Sunday best and had been most carefully groomed; their whiskers were trimmed and their hair plastered close to the head with Macassar oil.

'Come in, come in,' Logie invited. Then he explained to William, 'Murdo Campbell and Archie MacLean are leaving us to seek their fortunes in Africa, Mr Whylie.'

'Archie MacLean? Are you related to the Archie MacLean whom I met last night?'

'My grandfather, sir!'

Regarding MacLean more closely, William recognised a remarkable likeness between his bent and frail companion of the previous evening, and this tall, broad-shouldered young man with his fulsome red beard. He was immediately drawn to him.

'I am surprised he did not mention your departure,' commented William.

'I am afraid that he does not approve of my leaving . . . says that I am letting down His Lordship.'

'All the more reason for you to do well in Africa and show the old fellow what you are made of!' Logie said, smiling at young Archie and giving him a friendly handshake.

'Old Archie will forgive you, provided you make a success of things. Be sure to write often to let him know what you are up to.'

'I know you understand how it is, Malcolm. I must see something of the world. I don't wish to spend all of my life working for an invisible master who does not even know that I exist.'

'Good luck to you too, Murdo.' Malcolm shook hands with the other youth who was standing silently, in the background.

Of Archie's companion, William reserved his judgement. A spindly figure, his narrow frame scarcely filled the smartly-tailored tweed suit, obviously worn new for the occasion. His hair, cut short and shaped into the neck, was plastered to his head with oil, making him appear like a wooden soldier with painted-on features.

'Luck, I think, will not enter into it,' Murdo replied, ungraciously. 'Here you see two experienced miners with nothing to lose, and everything to gain from a life of adventure. I can assure you that we shall show the sceptics just what may be achieved by a little fearless enterprise.'

William suspected that this degree of self-confidence might be a veneer of bravado. How would the young man stand up to the inevitable setbacks which the pair must encounter? It was common knowledge amongst the men that, on the occasion of Jamie McGillivray's accident, Campbell had run for the quarry rim while his companions, including Archie, had fought to free their comrade from the rubble. There was a certain shiftiness about the dark countenance, an inability to look one straight in the eye, which gave William some misgivings. He preferred the more modest and thoughtful attitude of Archie's grandson, and trusted that he would not live to rue the day he had chosen Murdo Campbell as a travelling companion. He was, therefore, all the more startled to hear Campbell say:

'Thank you, Mr Logie, sir.' Then, blushing a little, 'I hope you will not object if I write to Miss Katherine from time to time?'

Malcolm laughed. 'My daughter is of age, Murdo. It is up to her to correspond with whom she chooses. We shall all be glad to hear your news.'

Both of the young men also shook William by the hand, and wished him success in his new appointment.

For his part, he was sorry to think that they were leaving now, just when things should be improving in the quarries. It was strong, healthy young men such as these upon whom would depend the recovery he was planning.

'Well, gentlemen,' he said, 'I cannot say I am pleased to see you leaving at this time, but I know what it is to be young and eager for adventure. Let me wish you well and hope that, having found the excitement you are seeking, you will one day return, and give us all the benefit of your experience.'

The two young men thanked him, took their leave of Malcolm Logie, and set off for the harbour. The steamer for Glasgow was just rounding the end of Kerrera Island, and the adventurers would be hard pressed to cross the Sound to the steamer pier in time to board her.

Towards evening, before the late-November sun sank behind the mountains of Mull, William took a climb to the top of the Island's only hill. From there he could look down on the quarries. Those being worked were clustered at the northern end of the island. To the south were two ancient workings, now flooded with seawater. Logie had explained that these two had produced good slate for a while, but when the floor of the quarry sank to fifty feet, there had been no way to keep out the sea. Work had stopped and the quarries had nearly been refilled with waste from the new workings.

To the north-east and stretching southwards towards the harbour, lay the only croft on the Island.

According to Archie, it had been farmed for generations by a family called McDougal.

William could pick out a few cattle in the meadow by the shore, whilst on the sparsely covered hillside, a handful of sheep grazed.

The house and sheiling were tucked in below the sharp dolerite ridge on which he now stood, while high stone walls protected a few small fields of grain and vegetable crops.

William wondered how such a meagre holding could sustain a family, let alone supply the needs of the villagers on the Island.

He watched the men going about their labours.

His eye followed the line of the railway which was used to carry away the slate. For a long time he studied the outcrops of rock and, as he descended the hill, he tapped occasionally with his hammer at a rock, removing a sample here and there. Each of these he labelled carefully, before placing it in a deep pocket of his borrowed overcoat.

Tomorrow he would take a look at those two old quarries at the southern end of the Island. For the moment, he had other plans. Hunching his shoulders against the rising wind, he went in search of Archie MacLean and his wife.

6

The dominie had finished his early-morning preparations. He stepped back from the blackboard upon which, in a perfect copperplate hand, was written the text for the day:

The Son of Man shall send forth his angels and they shall gather out of his kingdom all things that offend and them which do iniquity, and shall cast them into a furnace of fire. There shall be wailing and gnashing of teeth. Then shall the righteous shine forth as the sun in the kingdom of their father. Who hath ears to hear, let him hear.

Elizabeth stood at the open door.

'Good day to you, sir. Mr Ogilvie, is it not? I am Elizabeth Duncan,' she introduced herself.

The schoolmaster turned to face his new assistant. Mr Ogilvie was an unprepossessing person. An oversized belly, which struggled unsuccessfully to escape from his tightly belted trews, suggested a love of good living, an impression which was amplified by a bulbous red nose and the unmistakable odour of whisky which clung to him like a mantle. He peered at her with humourless, piggy eyes, set too close together.

'Yes, indeed, madam, you are addressing Farquhar Ogilvie. I am pleased to see that you have arrived . . . at last!'

His thin lips bisected his face in a sardonic leer.

Inclining her head in acknowledgement, Elizabeth stepped into the classroom and extended her hand.

'I am so sorry that you were inconvenienced last week and must thank you for coming to meet me at the pier. I believe that Dr Beaton explained the nature of my indisposition?'

'He said that you had sustained an injury on the boat from Crinan, certainly. Although to look at you now, one would wonder what kind of trouble it was to keep you from your duties for more than a week! No doubt you will find a way to make up the lost time.'

He turned his back on her abruptly and strode over to the high desk, set to one side of the blackboard and facing several rows of benches on which the pupils would be accommodated. Seating himself upon a stool he withdrew a ledger from beneath the desk lid and took up his pen.

'This is the log which I am obliged to keep for purposes of reporting to the School Board,' he launched into an explanation. 'In view of your late arrival, it will be necessary to deduct one week's wages. You will be paid, during your period of probation, the sum of £30 per annum. From this will be deducted £2 per annum rent, for your accommodation in the schoolhouse. You will be expected to undertake such extramural activities as are required of you, without additional remuneration. Additional payments, for any private tuition which you may be called upon to provide, will be made to myself, a proportion of such monies being made over to you, at my discretion. I hope that these terms are to your satisfaction?'

Elizabeth was not a fool. She could see that the man was avaricious in the extreme. She was alone in the world. Almost everything she owned was packed into the small trunk which the boatman had deposited for her at the school door. She had nowhere else to go. What could she do but accept his terms?

Tentatively she questioned him, 'You mention a period of probation. For what length of time, may I ask?'

'Until the Board considers your work of a standard high enough to promote you to a permanent post.' His cold grey eyes bored into her, challenging any suggestion of further agument.

'I can understand that the Board should wish to ascertain that I am competent,' she replied coolly. 'But you will appreciate that I have been teaching for seven years, three as a pupil teacher and the last four as an assistant mistress. I believe that you will find my work satisfactory.'

'We shall see. Be so kind as to append your signature where I have indicated.' He handed Elizabeth the pen and watched, critically, as she signed her name in the logbook.

'For this morning I wish you to sit here,' he pointed to a chair beside his own, 'where you can observe the manner in which I expect my classes to be conducted. I believe in strict discipline as you will see. I shall require the same from you. My pupils will not be found wanting when the School Inspector arrives!'

As the hour approached for school to begin, the sound of the lively voices of the younger islanders could be heard mounting to a crescendo outside the building.

Ogilvie thrust the ledger into his desk, at the same time extracting his tawes. This implement was not unknown to Elizabeth. Indeed as a very young child she had herself been chastised by the split leather thongs which had been wielded by her own father. While her parent had used the weapon sparingly, however, Elizabeth felt sure that this man would apply it with great gusto. She was unable to suppress a shiver at the thought.

Noticing that she trembled, the dominie snorted, mistaking the reason. 'You will need to wrap up warm to combat the cold. The Board is not generous with its allowance of coal for the schoolroom.'

He rose and stalked to the door, swishing the tawes which he held loosely by its well-polished handle. At the sight of the schoolmaster, the noise from the playground ceased immediately. After a few minutes the children began to file in, taking their places on the long benches in absolute silence.

The youngest children sat on the front row. The little girls wore neat, for the most part, clean, white overalls. The boys, miniature replicas of their fathers, were dressed in shirts and the ubiquitous moleskin trousers. Only one or two had the benefit of a jacket. Most wore guernseys knitted by their mothers, the wool home-spun and dyed in time honoured tradition.

As each child entered the room, he or she placed a lump of coal in the master's basket which stood beside the door. One boy had come without his contribution. Ogilvie grabbed him by the ear, indicated a place on the bench farthest from the small iron stove, and thrust him towards it.

Returning to the front of the class, the master explained, 'Every pupil must contribute to the supply of coal, otherwise we all go cold. Those who do not are seated furthest from the fire. Make sure you maintain this rule, miss.'

He addressed the class.

'Miss Duncan has at last condescended to join us, children. When you rise to make your customary greeting you will include your new teacher.'

With a scuffling, the occasional cough and hastily suppressed giggle, the children rose to their feet.

'Good morning, children,' said Ogilvie.

'Good morning, Mr Ogilvie. Good morning, Miss Duncan,' the class recited.

Uncertain as to what was expected of her, Elizabeth gave a weak smile and inclined her head.

'I am sure Miss Duncan will find her tongue in due course,' Ogilvie observed sarcastically. 'I know she can speak, I have heard her!'

Some of the children sniggered. Ogilvie allowed this acknowledgement of his wit, and after a few seconds, during which Elizabeth continued to remain silent, he shrugged his shoulders in an exaggerated fashion, producing further titters from the children.

'The text for today is written on the blackboard,' he announced. 'Those who can, will write it down and learn it. I shall test you later.'

Addressing Elizabeth he commanded, 'Take aside the smallest children, read the passage to them and have them learn it by heart.'

She had noticed a small space at the far end of the room. Rising to her feet she said, 'Stand up all those children who cannot read.' The entire front row stood, together with a large, gawky boy seated at the back of the room. There was a slight disturbance as his companions gazed at him in disbelief.

'What are you doing on your feet, Mr MacNab?' demanded Ogilvie.

'Please, sir, miss asked all those who canna' read to stand up, and I canna'.'

'I believe what Miss Duncan meant was that Class One should rise. I am sure that she has no time for an illiterate like yourself. Sit down.'

'Now Class One,' Elizabeth intervened, 'please make your way quietly to the back of the room and sit on the floor.'

The little ones did as they were bid. Before moving to join them, Elizabeth turned to Mr Ogilvie. 'If that boy . . . MacNab, was it? . . . cannot read, perhaps he should join my group. I will try to help him.'

'The boy is unteachable. He will be better off working in the quarries. Only the Old Marquis's rules prevent me from dismissing him immediately,' snapped the master. 'As it is, he will leave school when he reached his eleventh birthday in a few weeks.'

'What does he do all day, if he cannot learn?'

'He sits, unless I have some task that he can perform, clearing the ashes, washing the ink pots, that kind of thing.'

'May he not join me, if he is willing to do so?'

'Oh, very well!' Unwilling to prolong the argument, Ogilvie instructed the boy MacNab to carry Elizabeth's chair to the back of the room and to join the children gathered there.

She looked at the passage on the blackboard. It was obvious to her that the words were too difficult for such young children. She was also aware that a further confrontation with the schooolmaster, at this stage, would be most unwise. She began the lesson by reading out the biblical text in muted tones, so as not to disturb the dominie.

As she had anticipated, there were blank looks from most of the children gathered around her.

'Let us take the passage a few words at a time,' Elizabeth proceeded. 'The Son of Man. Who is the Son of Man?' Many hands shot up, all around her.

'Now,' she said, 'as I do not know anyone's name, I shall ask you to tell me who you are before you answer. That way, perhaps I shall get to know some of you by name before the day is over.' She pointed to a little, brown-eyed girl directly in front of her.

'Who are you?' she enquired.

'I am Kirsty McGillivray, and Jesus is the Son of Man.'

'Quite right, Kirsty. Jesus is the Son of Man. Who else was going to say that?' Ten little arms waved in the air.

'Very good. Now, put down your hands and listen to the rest of the sentence. "The Son of Man shall send forth his angels." Who knows what an angel is?'

'Please, miss, my little brother Joe is one!'

The tousle-headed urchin had crept forward and grabbed her skirts in his eagerness to attract her attention.

'Now what did I ask you to do before you answered?' queried Elizabeth.

The infant looked crestfallen.

'Tell me your name and then your answer,' she reminded him, kindly.

'My name is Murdo McEwen, and my brother Joe's an angel.'

There was a titter of amusement from the back row of the senior class, who were finding Elizabeth's lesson vastly more entertaining than their own. A severe glance from their schoolmaster was enough to silence them.

'So your brother died and went to heaven?' she encouraged the boy. 'What do you think he does there?'

'Helps Jesus?' It was a query rather than a statement.

'Yes, I expect so,' Elizabeth agreed. 'Now,' to the rest of the class, 'our passage actually says then . . . Jesus is going to send all his helpers, his angels, to do what . . . "to gather out of his kingdom all things that offend and all them which do iniquity".'

She turned to a rather more silent group on her left side and picked out a fair-haired boy, whose blue eyes were particularly appealing.

'Do you know what iniquity means? Don't forget to tell me your name.'

'My name is Peter McFarlane, miss. I don't know what pinquity means.' His eyes filled with tears.

'All right, Peter, I'll tell you,' she said hastily. 'To do iniquity is to do naughty things, things which the Lord does not like us doing.'

'Like things in the Ten Commandments?' asked another small boy. 'Er . . . Jack Lamont, Miss Duncan.'

'Exactly like that,' agreed Elizabeth. 'Now then, what the piece is saying is that Jesus is going to send out his helpers into the world, to collect all the deeds and objects which offend him, and to gather in the people who do wicked things. What will he do then, do you think?'

'Punish them,' called out several very excited little voices.

'How will he punish them?'

'In the fiery furnace,' the chorus increased in volume.

'And what will all the people say about that?'

The forest of hands shot up again. Elizabeth selected a bright little girl sitting at the back.

'Mary Campbell, miss. The people will wail and gnash their teeth.'

'Can you gnash your teeth?' Elizabeth laughed as they all tried. So absorbed was she that she was startled to find Mr Ogilvie towering over her.

'Such games should be confined to the school yard, Miss Duncan. It is time for the children to work at their numbers. Perhaps you will supervise them at their slates?'

At a signal from Elizabeth, the smaller children filed back on to their front bench. Charlie McNab, who had remained silent throughout her lesson, gazing at her in rapt attention, now asked if he should give out the slates. Soon, all were settled to their numbers, and Elizabeth found herself in constant demand as the brighter children completed an exercise and raised a hand to have her mark it.

It was nearly noon and time, she thought, for a break. For a long while there had been utter silence as children of all ages wrote down multiplication tables on their slates.

The peace was suddenly shattered by the sharp clap of wood upon wood.

'Mr McFadyen, stand up, if you please.'

Ogilvie's voice was loud, rasping, and to a ten year old, terrifying.

'Be so kind as to step forward.' The silence was electric, broken only by the scuffle of a reluctant pair of unshod feet.

'Your right hand, I think.'

There was a thwack . . . then a second . . . and a third.

'Now the left.'

Three more times the awful leather thongs sliced across the child's outstretched palm. The boy, McFadyen, did not cry but his face turned ghastly white, and he winced with the pain as he nursed his hands beneath his armpits.

'What was Mr McFadyen doing, you may ask, ladies and gentlemen? Well, I will tell you. He was speaking, *speaking*, to his neighbour! Now, sir, you will enlighten us with these pearls, so wise they could not be left unsaid until after class. Tell us what you said . . . boy!'

With faltering voice, his head bent low, McFadyen murmured, 'I said that I have cheese for my piece.'

'Have you indeed? Then perhaps you will bring it forward for us all to admire.'

The boy hurried to his place, retrieved a very small packet and returned to the schoolmaster.

'Put it in the waste-basket,' growled Ogilvie.

The child did as he was bid.

'There will be no midday meal for you today. I shall see to it that you are suitably employed. Report to me when class is dismissed.'

McFadyen returned to his seat.

'I will hear the text which you were set to learn last week. Dougal McGillivray, recite what you have learnt.'

A smart boy, in flannel pantaloons and a good tweed jacket over a soft grey shirt, stood up at the back of the room.

'"To him that hath shall be given. To him that hath not shall be taken away even that which he hath."'

'And, Mr McGillivray, can you tell me what those words mean?'

'Please, sir . . . there are two kinds of people, the rich and the poor. If you have plenty of money, you cannot help but make more. If you have very little, even that is taken away from you. At least . . . that's what my da says.'

Elizabeth could have sworn that for a fleeting second a smile swept across the schoolmaster's face. Instantly, it was replaced by the now familiar sneer. 'No, sir. It is not about money, sir. It is about talent, ability, the gifts that God bestows upon us. If you have talents and use them, they grow and flourish. If, on the other hand, you allow what small gifts you have to wither and die, you will end up stupid and without any means of support.'

Elizabeth could not tell if the movement was planned, but as he spoke Ogilvie wandered around the class of seated pupils, until he reached poor Charlie MacNab. His last phrase was accompanied by a sudden thrusting forward of that poor creature's head, so that his forehead was slammed down on to the back of the bench in front. Charlie, accepting his lot as the class dunce, made no sound.

'Very well, children, time for dinner. Those of you who are going home, be sure to be back in thirty minutes.' Pulling Charlie roughly to his feet, he ordered, 'Fill up the ink-wells.'

The luckless McFadyen was sent off to gather wood from along the shore, to feed the stove. Once he was out of the room, Elizabeth noticed Charlie edging towards the waste-basket, and guessed that he was hoping to take the discarded lunch packet. Too slow, he was halted in his advance by the dominie, who snatched the basket from under the boy's nose and thrust the packet in his desk.

Later in the afternoon, Elizabeth was surprised to see Ogilvie taking surreptitious bites of bread and cheese, and wondered at the meanness of the man.

When at last the day came to an end, the dismissed children filed solemnly out into the yard. It was dark and cold, so they did not linger in the school precincts but hurried home, their shrill voices fading on the evening air.

Ogilvie turned his attention to his new assistant.

'You have seen how I run my school, Miss Duncan. I must explain that I am obliged to divide my time between this establishment, on Eisdalsa Island and the school in the village on Seileach where I have a pupil teacher supervising at present. Now you have at last appeared, I shall take charge there, and come across no more than once or twice each week. You will find yourself alone here for much of the time. Do you think you can manage?'

'I feel sure that I can, thank you, Mr Ogilvie.'

In fact, Elizabeth was vastly relieved. She already knew that she could not operate under the regime which Ogilvie employed in the classroom. Left to herself, she believed that she might have a chance with these children, some of whom were inordinately bright.

Although poor and, in some cases, clearly undernourished, there was the spark of intelligence among them. She had never taught boys before and regarded their presence in the classroom as a challenge rather than a threat. In Ogilvie's absence, she believed that she might succeed in widening at least some horizons.

He was obviously anxious to get away. Night was falling and he had to be ferried across to the village, where he lived.

'There is the question of my accommodation,' she reminded him. 'My luggage has been standing on the step all day. Where may I have it taken?'

'Arrangements have been made with the factor for you to use the bothy next-door. If you will wait here, I will call on Mrs McGillivray to show you. For myself, I bid you good night. I will be back at the end of the week, to receive your report.'

'Good night, Mr Ogilvie.'

Elizabeth waited, alone, for what seemed a very long time. Ogilvie had made sure that all the oil lamps, lit during the dark afternoon, were turned out before he left. The fire had been allowed to die down; the room had grown noticeably colder. She wondered who would be responsible for lighting the fire in the morning, and made a mental note to question Mrs McGillivray on such details.

There was a quick step on the path outside and, out of the night, stepped a woman no more than ten years Elizabeth's senior. She allowed her shawl to fall from her head and rest over her broad shoulders, revealing greying hair stretched firmly back behind her ears into a tight bun. Her face was clear of blemishes and the skin around her eyes showed signs of frequent laughter.

'You must be Miss Duncan,' the woman said, in the soft Highland way to which Elizabeth had become attuned during her week in the Beaton household.

'My boy Dougie was just telling me all about you when Mr Ogilvie knocked.' Turning back to the door she called out, 'Dougie, will you pick up Miss Duncan's box and take it to the bothy, there's a good laddie.'

'Thank you for coming out, Mrs McGillivray. It must be an inconvenient time for you. Your husband will be coming home for his meal.'

'That's quite all right, miss,' Annie replied with a sigh. 'My Jamie has not worked this past month . . . nor ever likely to again.'

'I'm so sorry. Has he been ill?'

'Injured, more like. A fall it was . . . in the quarry. But you are not here to listen to my tales of woe. Come along and see your wee house. It is rather small, but cosy enough. I'm sure a young lady like yourself will soon have it comfortable and homely.'

The bothy was a single-roomed house, more precisely a shed. It was built of stone under a slate roof. Outside the door stood a large rainwater butt which served as the only water supply. Judging by the amount of rain she had already witnessed, Elizabeth reflected ruefully, it was unlikely to run dry!

Two small windows, one on either side of the entrance, provided the only source of natural daylight. In one of these, Dougie had lit an oil lamp which gave a welcoming glow.

Stooping to enter by the low doorway, Elizabeth found herself in a sparsely furnished room, some fifteen feet by twenty.

Along one wall stood a truckle-bed, and beside it a small closet, covered by a rough curtain.

Below one of the windows, on a night stand, stood a basin and jug for washing. Beneath the other, a well-scrubbed table and an upright chair completed the furnishings.

At the far end, a small cast iron range burned brightly, giving a comfortable atmosphere to the room, bare though it was.

'When I heard this morning that you were coming, I took the liberty of looking in to light the stove,' Annie explained. 'These old buildings can be very damp. The bedclothes are properly aired. They are my own, as is the lamp. You are welcome to use them until you have found something of your own to replace them.'

Once again Elizabeth was overcome by the kindness of these friendly people. Would that her new superior was out of the same mould.

'Thank you so much for your trouble, Mrs McGillivray. I have a few things in my trunk which will be of use, and in Glasgow there are stored a few pieces of furniture which will fit in here very well. I shall see that you get your lamp back, as soon as possible.'

'I am afraid that you have no supplies of food in the house, Miss Duncan, so I insist that you come and join my family for supper.' Somewhat shyly she added, 'And since we are to be friends, you must call me Annie.'

'Only if you will call me Elizabeth,' responded the young schoolmistress.

Annie and her son departed, after giving Elizabeth instructions on how to find their cottage on the far side of the green.

Elizabeth stood for a moment, alone for the first time since arriving at Eisdalsa. She pulled the single chair before the iron stove and sat down, surveying her new home with a sinking heart. This was a far cry from the comforts of Tigh na Broch, which she had left so cheerfully that morning amid promises of frequent visits from Morag and a host of helpful hints about life on the Island from Sheilagh.

Well, Elizabeth, she told herself. To them that hath . . . we shall just have to see what can be done to make it more like a home. It's either this or the Poor House for you!

She began to unpack her box, in which she had brought a few reminders of her former life.

Her mother, the impoverished widow of a minister in the Church of Scotland, had been forced to relinquish most of her household possessions. She had retained some fine pieces of china however, and these formed part of Elizabeth's meagre inheritance.

She unwrapped a teapot of good Staffordshire pottery, three cups, a few plates – all in the same dainty pattern – and an iron kettle. There was an embroidered linen cloth which Elizabeth had made herself whilst a pupil at the Solway Academy. With this she covered the bare table.

Her small collection of books represented those years when benevolent Miss Murdoch had taken the orphaned Elizabeth under her wing, made her a pupil teacher and provided her with the means of making her own living. She arranged the volumes on the sill of one of the deeply recessed windows.

At the bottom of the box, as protection for its contents, she had folded a colourful rug which her mother had made long ago. She remembered as a very small girl helping to cut up the pieces – here was a sample of the curtains which had hung in her bedroom in the manse, here a piece of her mother's only ballgown, and here – she felt the tears pricking as she remembered – stuff from her own first party dress.

Brushing a hand across her eyes, she arranged the mat before the stove. The colours were set off by the gleaming black ironwork. It was really very kind of Mrs McGillivray to have taken so much trouble.

A charming water-colour of a village on the Solway Firth, where she had spent her schooldays, she hung from a convenient nail above the mantleshelf. She recalled the sunny summer day on which her friend Helena and she had walked across the sands at low tide to that village, and Helena had insisted on stopping for a while to sketch. By the time she had finished the tide was in, and they were obliged to walk back along the road.

Elizabeth had been most touched when Helena had presented her with the framed picture on the day her friend left the Academy.

The last remaining item was a small mirror standing in a frame of German silver. It had been her father's, the only one of his possessions other than his bible which she had been able to retain. She recalled how he would trim his immaculate moustache every morning, twist it and wax it carefully so that the ends turned upward. She could see his twinkling, mischievous eyes peering at her out of the glass as she stood quietly by, holding his collar and studs.

Standing the mirror beside Annie's washing bowl, Elizabeth surveyed her domain.

In the firelight, the room did not look so bare now. Once her mother's few pieces of furniture were delivered from the Glasgow depot in which they had been stored since her death, the bothy would seem just like home.

She took out her few clothes and hung them in the closet, behind the curtain. Pushing the now empty valise beneath the bed, she encountered an old chamber pot. Well, that was another problem solved for the present. An inspection of the school privy during the afternoon had caused her to shudder. She really must speak to someone about that!

She glanced at the fob watch which hung from her jacket. The dainty timepiece had been a parting gift from her dear friend, Miss Murdoch. Elizabeth felt a sudden longing for the school which had been her real home for so long. She wondered what Miss Murdoch would have to say about the manner in which Mr Ogilvie conducted his establishment.

It was time for her to present herself at the McGillivrays' home. Turning the lamp down low, she left it in the window to guide her on her return.

The night was very dark and it was with some difficulty that she found the house for all the buildings looked alike. Once inside, however, all was warmth, bustle and cheerfulness.

Kirsty and Dougie sat at the table with their books. As she stood before the range, no longer muffled in her outer clothing, it was clear to Elizabeth that Annie McGillivray was heavily pregnant. She wondered at the amount of energy the woman seemed able to expend, considering her condition.

A thick, guttural sound, a mixture of cough and throat clearance, issued from the alcove in the wall which divided kitchen from bedroom. Elizabeth peered into the shadows and saw the man of the house, Jamie McGillivray, stretched out on the box bed. His legs were covered by a colourful wool rug and his back supported with cushions made from emptied flour bags which Annie had stuffed with heather.

Jamie made no sign that he had noticed the presence of a visitor.

At the sound from her father, wee Kirsty climbed down from her chair and ran to him. No words were exchanged but the child seemed to know what he required. She reached down a small wooden box from a shelf above the range, and carefully lifted a clay pipe from the rack which stood on the rough wooden dresser.

With practised fingers, she filled the pipe, handed it to her father, and reached for the lighted spill which Annie handed to her.

As Jamie sucked on his pipe, his wife declared, 'Here is Miss Duncan, the new schoolmistress, come to take her supper with us, Jamie.'

He made no acknowledgement.

'Please sit at the table, Miss Duncan,' she prattled on, ignoring her husband's apparent discourtesy. 'Come along, Kirsty, sit down and we will eat.'

The meal was a cheerful enough affair for both the children had plenty to say and were allowed to join in the conversation without restraint. Elizabeth was impressed with Dougie's knowledge of the quarries. It was clear that the boy could not wait for the day when he would leave school and start work.

'Of course,' said Annie, 'before Jamie's accident we had planned to send Dougie away, to learn to be a real engineer. Now it looks as though he will have to start work as soon as he is old enough.'

'I want to work in the quarries, Mother,' declared the boy stoutly. 'My father has no school learning, but he knows everything about the quarries.'

'It is because of all that he knows,' Annie observed, 'that he realises how much more there is for you to learn. He wanted you to become a real engineer, like Mr Whylie.'

'When would you expect to leave school, Dougie?' Elizabeth asked.

'On my eleventh birthday, in just over two years from now.' The boy was determined about his future, all the more so since his father was no longer able to work himself. Someone must bring in a wage to feed the family.

Annie smiled fondly at her son. 'He is a good boy,' she told Elizabeth. 'Until his father broke his leg he was quite content to stay at school but now he feels obliged to go to work. Even now he earns a few pennies by working after school hours.'

Elizabeth hesitated before saying, 'Could he not continue to study, even after he leaves the school? I know that in Glasgow it is quite common for working men to attend night classes.'

'Where would he find night classes in Eisdalsa?' Annie chided kindly. 'We are a hundred miles from the nearest Institute.'

Elizabeth realised that there was no point in persisting with her argument here. She did determine, however, to mention the matter to Mr Ogilvie and perhaps to Dr Beaton, when she saw him again. It must be possible to provide technical education in a community where so many professional and technical experts were at hand. She listed in her mind those she had already met, and was so absorbed that she had to be prompted a second time by wee Kirsty, who demanded to know where Elizabeth had gone to school.

She entertained them for the rest of the evening with stories about the school on the Solway, and the adventures of the girls whom she had known there.

During the entire evening, not one word was uttered by the prone figure in the corner. After her initial discomfiture at her host's behaviour, Elizabeth found it easier to forget his presence in the room.

Apart from an occasional word, directed at him by Annie, one would not have known that he was there at all.

At last Elizabeth rose to leave, and Annie accompanied her to the door. Out of her husband's hearing, she tried to apologise for his behaviour to her guest.

'You would not believe how changed he is, since the accident,' she explained. 'I suppose it is the thought that, even when his leg is healed, he will probably not be able to work at the quarrying again.'

'Surely, with all his experience, they will find something useful for him to do?' Elizabeth responded. 'Has the doctor said that he will not be able to work?'

'It was old Dr Hugh who set his leg,' Annie explained. 'He died soon after the accident. The new doctor has not come to see Jamie, for which I am thankful. I could not afford to pay him, you see.'

Elizabeth felt suddenly guilty that she had eaten food in this house where there was not sufficient money to pay the doctor.

'You have been very kind, making me feel so at home,' she observed. 'There is one last thing I must ask you. It is about the schoolroom fire. Do you know who attends to that, and who does the cleaning?'

'There was an old lady who used to clean but she died in the summer. Since then, Mr Ogilvie himself has done what little he feels necessary. The School Board provides money for it, I know, because Mrs Fraser received a small wage.'

'I will make enquiries,' said Elizabeth, 'but in the meantime, I would be happy to pay a little myself, to have the work done. Do you think Dougie would care to work for me, before school each day?'

Annie's face was suffused with gratitude.

'Oh, I am sure he would be delighted to help,' she exclaimed. 'I will see that he is up in time to light the fire in the morning. Thank you, Miss Duncan.'

'You promised to call me Elizabeth, remember?'

'Good night, Elizabeth!' Annie continued to hold her door open wide while her guest made her way across the square and until she was in sight of her own bothy. Then she closed the door softly and turned to her husband.

He lay against the pillows, staring into space.

'Are you comfortable, Jamie?' she enquired, shaking out the pillows, one by one. 'She seems a nice lass, the new teacher. She has given Dougie a wee job. He will earn a little money helping around the school.'

She chatted on for some time while the children were washed and sent packing up the ladder to their beds under the roof.

Jamie McGillivray made no reply to her conversation. It was as though he was there in body only. His spirit seemed to be far away.

Annie reached for the little china pot in which she kept her scanty supply of money. She counted out the contents, twelve shillings and threepence. She set aside one shilling and replaced the remainder in the pot. Tomorrow she would send word for the doctor. Jamie was not getting any better. She was sure that he had become even more unresponsive during the last few days, and tonight . . . It was so unlike him to be rude to a stranger.

PART II

1

David handed his bag to the ferryman and swung himself up on to the quay. Even in the well-sheltered harbour, the swell of the rising tide, together with the wind-tossed waves, made landing difficult. Reaching down for his medical case, the young doctor thanked his old friend, Iain McInnes, and attempted to pay his dues.

'Since when did the Quarry Doctor pay for a ferry, David?' protested the old man, refusing to take the proffered coins.

'I am not the Quarry Doctor, Iain. Just filling in until a new man can be found.'

'Och, awa' with ye, young David. Ye know full well it is yourself will be the new doctor.' The ferryman refused to listen to argument and David was obliged to accept the concession.

He climbed the steep slope from the ferry steps and paused at the top to look around the place which he had not visited for more than a year.

Into every aspect, the quarries intruded. Seagoing vessels were moored against the harbour wall, taking on board truck-loads of roofing slates. Horse-drawn wagons traversed the Island by way of railway lines, carrying slates to the shore or removing waste from the quarry workings. Everywhere there was noise. The sounds of machinery, winches, pumps, the paraphernalia of industry, mingled with the voices of men at work on the boats, in the harbour. As he neared the village of single-storied cottages, he could distinguish the sounds of children in school, chanting their multiplication tables. When he heard this, David paused, straining to catch that other voice which had lately invaded his dreams. There it was now. The pupils were silent while her clear tones rang out, giving them further instruction. The children began again, and David, smiling, continued on his way.

It was a fine day. The wind had dropped from gale force to a strong blustery breeze. The village women were taking advantage of the change in the weather to dry their washing. David was obliged to dodge beneath lines of white linen and dancing red flannel drawers, coarse-woven shirts and dainty lace-trimmed petticoats.

Shouting out the occasional greeting to old friends, and those he remembered of his father's patients, he came at last to the McGillivrays' door.

His sharp knock was answered almost immediately by Annie. No longer was she the cool and cheerful woman who had entertained Elizabeth so hospitably during her first evening on the island. Annie was deeply disturbed by her husband's deterioration, and was beginning to suspect that she might have left it too long before calling the doctor.

'Good day to you, Mrs McGillivray. Michael Brown tells me that your husband is not so well after his fall,' said David.

'Thank God you have come, Mr David,' cried Annie. 'I am that worried about Jamie.'

'Is it the leg which is bothering him then?'

'Oh, no. At least, I don't think so. I have changed the wrappings carefully, as Dr Hugh said, and kept the splint on, so as not to move it. The wounds are healing and they are not red at all.'

'Then what is worrying you?' he asked.

'It's Jamie himself, doctor. He has changed so since the accident. He won't speak to us. Just sits there, propped in his bed, glowering at anyone who comes in. He's a different person and that's a fact. Only wee Kirsty seems able to understand his wants. She fetches and carries for him . . . but they never speak to each other. Not one word has passed his lips this week past.'

Gently ushering the woman in before him, David entered the little house. The sudden change from bright sun outside to the dim recesses of the ill-lit cottage made it difficult for him at first to get his bearings. A movement from the far corner of the room alerted him.

After the usual throat clearing, Jamie McGillivray lapsed once more into the apparently comatose condition which he had adopted for many days. He stared into space, taking no heed of people or events occurring around him.

Summoning his best bedside manner, David approached him.

'Good morning, Mr McGillivray. I thought I should come and see what kind of a job my father made of your leg. Would you care to let me see it?'

Jamie gave no sign of recognition. As a boy, David had spent a lot of time on the Island amongst the quarriers' children. He had known the young Jamie McGillivray as someone to be looked up to and admired: an energetic youth who was making a name for himself as a proficient quarrier, a fine oarsman and athlete. He had crewed a winning boat in the regatta the summer before David went away to do his medical training. Jamie had also been a hill runner, having won medals at the Oban games. He was unlikely to run like that again, David thought, as he exposed the wounded leg.

Hugh had done his job well. The limb, fractured in several places, was passably straight, and although it would undoubtedly remain stiff, should allow him to walk fairly well. The open wounds had healed beautifully. Not for the first time in the past few days, David silently praised his father for his foresight. Without knowing what Joseph Lister had discovered about sepsis, Hugh, by the application of common sense, had kept open wounds scrupulously clean and avoided all but the most minimal instances of suppuration.

Turning to Annie, who hovered anxiously behind him, he said, 'You have done a fine job of nursing Mrs McGillivray, the leg is good as it could be. We should have your husband up and about in a short while. Just a little gentle exercise at first, to get the muscles working again, then a somewhat longer walk each day, until he gets his strength back.'

'There was a gash on the back of his head as well, doctor, will you take a look at that too?' she asked. The wound had healed, and the hair was already growing back where Hugh had shaved it to clean the cut.

David ran his fingers gently over the scar and then, seeing that his examination did not appear to distress his patient, began to feel more firmly around the base of the skull. His fingers moved to the area of the temporal bone. It was here that he discovered the depression. Hugh must have missed the injury. He had had sufficient damage to deal with at the time, so it was understandable that the slight indentation of the bone should have been overlooked. Although there was no outward sign of trouble, it was possible that fragments of depressed bone were creating pressure upon the brain. In which case, there might well be a change of behaviour in the patient. The situation could not be allowed to continue; any excessive movement, a slight knock, could cause the fractured bone to enter the brain.

David lowered his patient's head gently to the pillow and then examined each eye carefully. He moved a finger from side to side in front of Jamie's face. There was a flicker of movement in the eyes. When a taper was brought close to them, David noticed how slow the pupils were to contract in the more intense light. He did not doubt that the brain was affected and that the slow decline into which Jamie had fallen would continue until he died, unless . . . David stood up. He led Annie out of earshot of the patient.

'Mrs McGillivray,' he said quietly, 'I cannot pretend to you that all will be well with your husband. There has undoubtedly been damage to the bones of the skull, and I believe that this is causing pressure to build up in the brain. Unless this is relieved, your husband will die.'

Naturally, he had noted the woman's condition when he entered the house. As soon as he had spoken, he realised that he should have found some more compassionate way to give her his prognosis. Unfortunately, the harm was already done. As Annie recoiled at his words she was suddenly overcome by a terrible pain. She screamed, then collapsed senseless on the floor.

Alone in the tiny cottage, with a dying man and a fainting woman, David was galvanised into action. Opening the door into the tiny entrance hall he found facing him a similar door which led to the bedroom. The room contained only a double bed and a night stand. Apart from a small closet, corresponding to the alcove of the box bed next door, there was no other furniture. To his relief, he saw that the bed was freshly made up, and the linen clean. He had no doubt that Annie's child was about to be born, and he would need to seek assistance.

Returning to the living room, he gathered Annie's limp form in his arms and carried her to her bed. He removed her clothing and examined her. Labour had certainly begun and, since it was not her first child, was unlikely to be protracted. Covering her with the sheet, he waited for her to recover consciousness, then went out to look for help.

Martha Govan, self-styled midwife of Eisdalsa Island, had conducted a long-running battle with Dr Hugh Beaton. He had done all that he could to stop her from interfering with the accouchements of his patients, but those women who were unable to pay the doctor's bill, and those who still clung to the ancient mythologies of childbirth, could not be prevented from seeking her out. Hugh was not a vindictive man. He did not doubt that the woman, with so many years of experience to rely on, knew a great deal about the mechanics of childbirth. What he could not subscribe to was her complete lack of hygiene, and her adherence to remedies which were more closely associated with a witch's cauldron than a pharmacy.

In the weeks following Hugh's death, babies still insisted on being born in their due time. In the absence of a resident physician, several women had been obliged to seek the aid of the midwife. Martha was beginning to gain confidence and to regain her influence among the village women.

Thus it was that Annie's neighbour, sent by David to find someone able to assist him with the birthing, quite naturally turned to the midwife.

Martha arrived, breathless, and immediately began to bustle about the kitchen, making preparations for the coming event.

She entered the bedroom to find David seated on the bed holding Annie's hand as he quietly talked her through a particularly painful contraction. Martha tried to bustle the young man out of the room.

'Come along, young sir,' she ordered. 'This is women's work. It is no place for a man!'

'This is Dr Beaton, Martha,' Annie explained.

Martha sniffed her disapproval.

'Just out of school and thinks he knows it all, no doubt,' she muttered. 'All book learning and no experience . . . like his father,' she sneered. 'You had better leave this to a proper midwife!'

As she spoke, she turned back the sheet and was about to thrust two filthy fingers into Annie's vagina.

David grasped her hand to prevent her.

'What are you doing, woman?' he cried, aghast.

'We need to know how far she is along. Goodness me, what kind of a doctor are you anyway?'

'Take your filthy hands off my patient and leave this house immediately,' he shouted. 'Call yourself a midwife, when you do not even bother to wash your hands before examining a patient!'

'Do you know how many babies I have delivered in my lifetime?' she screamed at him, as he pushed her out of the bedroom. 'Dozens and dozens!'

'And how many mothers have you killed with your dirty ways and evil potions? My father knew all about your methods of treating patients.'

'And who looked after the poor women who could not pay, may I ask? Who was there to do the work with the doctor dead? Now you come along with your fancy ways and tell me . . . ME . . . that I don't know what I am doing!'

Both the protagonists in this argument were so furious with each other that they did not notice the diminutive figure who stood, thumb in mouth listening to them. As David began again to lash out verbally at the obdurate midwife, little Kirsty McGillivray turned and ran back to the schoolhouse which she had just left. In moments she returned with Elizabeth who, having summed up the situation, sent the child to play elsewhere. David and Martha carried on with their dispute, ignoring Elizabeth's presence. She pushed past them and went into the bedroom to Annie.

'How are you?' she asked. Before she could reply, Annie was again engulfed by a wave of pain such as she had never experienced before. She clasped Elizabeth's hand so tightly that the schoolmistress herself was hard put to it not to cry out.

Gently, Elizabeth released the vice-like grip and stooped to wipe the beads of perspiration from Annie's brow.

'Just you lie quietly now,' she advised calmly. 'I will go and get the doctor.'

In the kitchen the argument continued.

'Whatever you may have to say about your claim to be the official midwife,' David was fuming, 'Mrs McGillivray was my father's patient. That being so, she is now my patient and I demand that you leave this house.'

'You have not heard the last of this,' hissed Martha. She stared at David as though casting some malignant spell, then turned on her heel and marched out of the cottage.

'Oh, dear.' Elizabeth's gentle voice brought David back to normality.

'Why, Miss Duncan, what are you doing here?'

'Kirsty came for me. Is there something I can do to help?'

'I am sure one of the village women will come in, if you would be so kind as to fetch someone?'

'But Annie and I are friends,' protested Elizabeth. 'It is the least that I can do, to help her now.'

'This is not suitable work for a lady,' David insisted.

'What nonsense!' retorted Elizabeth, angrily. 'I can fetch and carry and obey instructions. Just tell me what you require to be done.'

During the next few hours, Elizabeth worked as hard as she had ever done in her life. She boiled instruments, prepared clean linen, attended to the needs of Jamie, as well as Annie, and cooked a meal for all of them, including the children. Dougie ran back and forth on a variety of errands and Kirsty was told to keep out of the way, attending only to her father when necessary. Into the long hours of the night, Annie struggled on in labour. The baby was badly placed, presenting in the breech position.

David had attended a good many births during his obstetrics training. Students were sent out from the hospital, in pairs, to attend to the working-class women of the city. The conditions in which they gave birth were poor and often dirty. It was quite usual to have the rest of the family looking on, there being nowhere else for them to go. At least he had clean conditions here, plenty of boiling water to sterilise his equipment, and a willing pair of hands to help him.

A breech birth had been outside his experience, although he remembered, clearly, the lecture given by the senior obstetrician at the Glasgow Royal. As the hours passed he revised the instructions in his head. When at last the baby was ready to be born, he would be able to turn the tiny body, ease out the shoulders one by one and finally assist the head to pass through the birth canal.

It was now, at the most crucial moment of the labour, that David made his decision to use chloroform. His researches had shown that anaesthesia had its drawbacks as well as its benefits. There had been a number of instances of death by chloroform poisoning, due to inexpert administration of the drug. He had read of side effects, such as burns to the face, damage to the bronchial tissues, even pneumonia, as a direct result of chloroform or ether inhalation. His decision to use anaesthesia in this case was therefore not taken lightly. His patient had been in labour for many hours and was very weak. There was little hope that the child could survive unless released quickly. He would have to assist the journey down the birth canal by making incisions in a controlled manner, to avoid ragged tearing and a wound more likely to become infected than a clean cut.

He called Elizabeth to assist him and instructed her in the use of the face mask and dropping bottle.

With his patient deeply sedated, David cut through the muscle of the cervix neatly in two places, giving the infant's body an easier passage to the outside. This practice had been uncommon before the introduction of aseptic techniques, because of the extreme danger of sepsis and the likely onset of puerperal fever. In the clean conditions in which he was working, David felt that he could take a risk.

The child was born, feet first. When the head finally appeared in the accepted, face down, position, he rapidly severed the umbilical cord and handed the tiny body to Elizabeth to wrap in the clean flannel she had prepared. His attention must, of necessity, be focused on the mother, who would bleed to death if he did not at once attend to the cuts he had made. It was some time therefore before he could take a look at the infant.

Elizabeth, having tucked the child in the cradle, which Dougie had found for her in the loft, had returned to David's side, passing him the instruments he required, and obeying his every grunted instruction.

When at last they could look at the newborn child, Elizabeth let out a cry of despair. The tiny body was no longer pink but suffused with a blueish tinge. She grasped one miniature hand. It was stone cold.

David, who was washing his hands at that moment, turned at her cry.

'Yes, I was afraid of that,' he said, his tone casual. 'It was inevitable that the child would be dead, after such a protracted labour. Asphyxiated in the birth canal. Normally, of course, the head is born first and the child begins to breathe instantly. In this case, as it began to breathe while still in the cervix, it will have inhaled mucus and drowned in its mother's body fluids.'

Elizabeth was crying as though her heart would break. Whether it was for the dead child, the living mother, or for herself, she did not know. David's indifferent attitude to the tragedy was too much for her to bear.

Her wild sobbing struck him to the core. He could not bear to see her so distressed. Would that he might enfold her in his arms and kiss away her tears. With great restraint he took hold of her hand, and gently pushed away a stray lock of hair from her damp cheek.

'How could I have been so cruel and thoughtless?' he said anxiously. 'You are tired and overwrought.'

'If you had had a proper midwife to help you, he might have lived,' she wept. 'I should have seen he was distressed when I laid him in the cradle.'

'There was nothing that anyone could have done,' David assured her. 'If he was not already dead, he could have lived for only a short while. You did all that anyone could to help him, believe me.'

She looked up at him, and saw tears in the calm grey eyes. Elizabeth realised that there was, after all, some compassion behind the veneer of callous professionalism.

She fumbled for her handkerchief, but David forestalled her, quickly producing one of his own. She accepted it gratefully, wiped away the tears, and smiled at his concerned expression.

'At least Annie will be all right.'

'I hope so. Shall we go and take a look?'

He stood back to allow Elizabeth to precede him into the bedroom where Annie lay, exhausted, but now conscious.

She seemed to have aged ten years. Hearing them enter, she opened her eyes and searched each face in turn. Immediately, she learned all that she needed to know.

'Oh, the poor wee bairn,' she moaned. 'Such a hard world he was coming into . . . perhaps it is better this way.'

Elizabeth found it difficult to accept such stoicism. She felt sure that in similar circumstances she would not wish to live herself. Annie struggled to sit up.

'Did Dougie and Kirsty get their teas? Has anyone looked to Jamie, does he want for anything?'

Then it was that Elizabeth understood. For Annie, the world consisted of her home and her loved ones. They were all that she cared for. She would do her grieving for the little lost boy in her own time. For the present, it was the living who mattered. Summoning what little strength remained, she reached out and grabbed David by the hand.

'Jamie . . . will he be all right, doctor? Will you be able to help him?'

David was also startled by Annie's acceptance of the infant's death and taken unawares by her question. His answer was perhaps more abrupt than it need have been.

'He is a very sick man, Mrs McGillivray. I will do my best for him. Now, you must rest and I must take our nurse back to her house, for some sleep, before school starts in the morning.'

He guided Elizabeth out of the room and picked up her cape from the chair.

'Wrap up warm. The air is chill outside.'

'Should not someone look after Annie?'

'I shall come back, when I have seen you to your door, and wait until daybreak. One of the village women will take care of her until she is up and about. You have your own job to do.'

He held her arm firmly as they picked their way across the grassy square around which the houses were built. The moon was still bright enough to light their way, although in a short while it would give place to a watery sun which even now was beginning to lighten the tips of the mountains to the east.

Elizabeth shuddered in the chill breeze and David instinctively tightened his grasp, drawing her body closer to his own. He felt a warm thrill at her closeness. She was grateful for the firmness of his support, for her dainty shoes were no match for the sharp slates over which they had to tread.

She was aware that these events would stay with them both a long while. They had shared with Annie an intimacy given to few and she knew that the experience would cement a lasting friendship between them.

She was troubled, however, that David might be making assumptions about their relationship which she herself did not share, for when they reached the bothy he loosened his grip on her arm only to turn her towards him.

'Thank you for your help tonight. I could not have managed without you,' he murmured.

'It was the least I could do,' she replied, 'after all Annie's kindnesses to me.'

She felt he was about to kiss her. Not yet satisfied in her own mind that this was what she wanted, Elizabeth freed herself from his grasp and went inside.

'Good night, Dr Beaton.'

'Please call me David. After all, we are friends, are we not?'

'Good night, David.' She smiled sweetly at him and closed the door in his face.

'Good night, Elizabeth,' he replied to the door, then turning on his heel strode back to his patients, his step a little lighter and with a song in his heart.

Mairie Campbell had woken earlier, to attend to a feverish wain. The child was sleeping now. Before returning to her bed, she glanced out of the window, in time to see the couple, standing close together, outside the door of the schoolteacher's bothy. She allowed the net curtain to fall back as David approached. Extinguishing her candle, she climbed back into bed. Thrusting her frozen feet into the small of her husband's back, she snuggled down for a few more hours of sleep. His heavy snoring stopped abruptly. She smiled to herself. It worked every time!

Sleep was slow to come. She turned over in her mind the scene which she had just witnessed, her head filled with suspicions. As the minutes passed, the details of what she had observed became more and more elaborately embroidered. By the time that sleep eventually overtook her, it would have been difficult to distinguish fact from fiction.

Dougie knocked sharply for a third time. At last he could hear sounds of movement within. A bleary-eyed Elizabeth pulled her robe more closely about her as she wrenched open the ill-fitting door.

'Good morning, Miss Duncan,' Dougie greeted her brightly. 'Dr David said I should give you a call because he thought you might oversleep!'

The boy was obviously pleased to have been given such an important assignment. He knew that Elizabeth had been up very late helping the doctor and it was he who had suggested to David that there could be trouble with Mr Ogilvie if she was late for school.

'Thank you, Dougie.' Elizabeth stifled a yawn. 'Have you lit the fire in the schoolroom?'

'I am away to do that now,' said the boy. He scampered off round the corner and Elizabeth set about her preparations for the new day.

It was already five minutes past nine when she ushered the children inside and settled them to the first lesson of the morning. Fortunately, the wind had increased since dawn and McInnes had difficulty manoeuvering the heavy ferry-boat across the channel.

Thus it was that when at last Mr Ogilvie arrived to make his weekly inspection, it was after nine-fifteen. He found all the children happily singing a simple hymn which Elizabeth had taught them. The schoolmaster frowned upon such activity in the classroom, but since it was a hymn that was being sung, there was little to which he could object.

Observing his entry, Elizabeth stopped the singing at the end of the verse. There was silence. She motioned with her hands and the children rose, as one, to their feet.

On cue Ogilvie said gruffly, 'Good morning, children.'

In unison they replied, 'Good morning, Mr Ogilvie.'

'Sit down, children,' ordered Elizabeth. Turning to the schoolmaster, she invited him to hear the text the children had learnt for the week.

'This is just a short visit to see that you . . . er . . . have everything you require. I will not hear the lessons today.'

He was clearly embarrassed, and Elizabeth suspected that his visit had been intended to catch her out, with an unruly class perhaps, or teaching something unacceptable?

Ogilvie made a cursory examination of the register, noted without comment the neat marking and careful entry of each day's attendances. Believing that some explanation of his visit was called for, he made out that he was checking to see that members of a certain family were in class, as he suspected that some of the children were truants . . . working in the quarries, when they were supposed to be in school.

Elizabeth saw through his pretence, but she remained dignified, avoiding showing any sign of her contempt for the unsavoury schoolmaster. It was his prerogative to check up on her. She only wished he would be more open about it. After all, she had nothing to hide.

'Since you are here, Mr Ogilvie, there is one thing in particular which is troubling me. It is the condition of the school privvies. I believe it is important to teach the children about cleanliness and good habits, but I can hardly press home the point when the privvies are in such an appalling state.'

'I have spoken to the School Board on many occasions,' lied Ogilvie. 'It is the responsibility of the Quarry Company to put right any defects in the building. I suggest you mention it to the new engineer . . . Whylie, is it?'

Ogilvie was well aware that Elizabeth knew the engineer. Rumours about her accident and the subsequent attention paid to the schoolmistress by both the young doctor and the new engineer aboard the steamer were circulating amongst the gossip-loving members of Eisdalsa society. Elizabeth's sojourn at Tigh na Broch had been elaborated upon; that she had spent the best part of the previous night alone with the doctor, at the McGillivrays' house, would not have gone unnoticed.

'Have I your permission to approach Mr Whylie on the subject?' she asked Ogilvie.

'As you please, madam. No doubt you will have more influence with that gentleman than shall I!'

Elizabeth did her best not to show any reaction to this provocative observation. She was learning quickly that the best treatment for this odious man and his insidious innuendoes was to ignore them. She was determined not to give him the satisfaction of seeing that she was either annoyed or distressed.

His arrows having so obviously missed their mark, Ogilvie was obliged to retreat. He fired one further shot as he opened the schoolroom door.

'The School Inspector will be calling in to see you next month. Be sure that the class is prepared for his visit.' Without any further explanation, he was gone.

Elizabeth looked after him, perplexed. What did an inspection entail? she wondered. How characteristic of him, not to give her any advice. He obviously hoped that by placing her in this predicament he would score off her in some way. We'll see about that! she told herself, and turned her attention to the children.

Addressing the older pupils, she asked, 'Which of you had to speak to the School Inspector when he last visited the school?' Several hands shot up. 'Angus McTavish?'

'Yes, miss.'

'What did you have to do, Angus?'

'Recite, miss.'

'What did you recite?'

'Psalm 21, miss.'

'Who else? Dougie McGillivray, what did you do?'

'I had to work out a mathematical problem, Miss Duncan.' Dougie was obviously very proud of this distinction.

Attracted by the vigorous waving of several hands on the back row, Elizabeth called upon Mary McCulloch. 'Well, Mary, what did you do for the Inspector?'

'Said a poem in French, Miss Duncan, and Jack Buchanan, he spoke to Mr Ford in German, miss, for several minutes!'

'Does Mr Ford always come, or are there several Inspectors?' Elizabeth was delighted at their co-operation.

'We've only ever had Mr Ford.' This from Dougie.

'Tell me, was Mr Ford pleased with your work?'

'Yes, miss,' said a wee girl in Class Two. 'Although Mr Ogilvie said it was a good job he had Charlie locked in the woodshed or he would have spoiled the record.'

Elizabeth glanced at the back corner where Charlie sat waiting to pounce on any little task requiring a volunteer. He could neither read nor write, yet he was the most helpful and willing pupil that Elizabeth had ever encountered. She noted that he sat with a kind of smirk, not a smile, on his face. She could recognise his wounded pride, and her heart went out to him.

'Well now,' she said, 'we shall all have to work very hard so that Mr Ford will see how much progress everyone has made since his last visit.'

For the rest of the morning Elizabeth and her scholars discussed, arranged, searched in the meagre library of books, until everyone in the class had something which he or she would be able to do, if called upon by the Inspector. Only Charlie remained without a task.

At the end of the school day, as the children filed out, leaving Dougie to do his job of tending the lamps and putting out the fire, Elizabeth called to Charlie who was always reluctant to leave her presence.

'Tell me, do you know "The Lord Is My Shepherd"?'

'I think I do, miss,' he said, ever willing to oblige.

'Say it to me.'

'"The Lord is my shepherd . . . the Lord is my . . . The Lord is my shepherd, I . . ."'

'"shall . . .",' Elizabeth prompted.

'"I shall not want,"' chimed in Dougie.

'That is enough, Dougie. Charlie is saying it, not you.'

'That's just the point, miss. He isn't because he doesn't know any more.'

'Do you know it all through?' asked Elizabeth.

'Oh, yes, miss.'

'Then this is what we will do. You, Dougie, will come in and do your cleaning job every day. While you are doing it, you will keep reciting the words of Psalm 23. Charlie, you will come in too, and help Dougie. As he says the words, you will repeat them. In no time at all, we will have a very clean schoolroom and a Charlie who can recite, to Mr Ford, Psalm 23.'

Dougie looked very doubtful, but Charlie was ecstatic.

'Can we start straight away, Dougie? Here, give me that cloth, I'll polish the benches!'

Elizabeth smiled as she closed the door on the two boys, the eight-year-old in charge, with ten-year-old Charlie drinking in his every word. For the first time in his life, he was making a real effort to get a set of words firmly fixed in his memory. The reason for this sudden change in his behaviour was not hard to find. Charlie was in love with his teacher – the first adult to treat him like a human being.

David had sat up until the dawn, watching over his patients. Annie had slept for much of the time. She woke once in considerable pain, but a dose of laudanum had quieted her and she was now sound asleep. Jamie McGillivray gave David greater cause for concern. He had not actually slept at all, just lay, unmoving, his eyes focused somewhere beyond the walls, only the occasional clearing of his throat indicating that the man still lived.

In the early morning David dispatched the children, Dougie to rouse Elizabeth, and Kirsty to seek out a neighbour who, she assured him, would come and look after her mother.

Satisfied that Annie was in good hands, he made his way to the ferry, assuring the neighbour that he would be back as soon as possible.

Archie MacClean was leaning on the harbour wall as David approached the ferry steps.

'Good day to you, Mr David, sir!' he called. 'Taking on your father's work, I see.'

'Only until I can find a replacement,' he replied. 'I understand that the Company will be engaging a new doctor.'

'Dr Hugh will be a hard person to follow.' The retired foreman shook his head sorrowfully. 'He knew every soul on this island . . . saw most of them into this world, and guided as many again on their way to the next. Oh, aye, a sad loss, a sad, sad, loss.' He drew heavily upon his clay pipe and, as he exhaled, a thin blue coil of smoke rose in the still air. Not for a moment did his eyes leave David's face. He knew exactly what the old man was telling him. Hugh Beaton had been an exceptional person. Even his own son would find it difficult to fill his shoes. Why should it worry him? David reflected. He had no intention of burying himself and his talents here. Delightful as the prospect of life in the Highlands might seem to some, it was no place for an energetic, ambitious, young doctor, with the whole of his life before him and the best of career prospects in view.

A sudden thought brought him abruptly to present problems.

'My father used to speak of a retired army surgeon who has come to live on Seileach. Do you know who he meant?'

Without hesitation, Archie replied, 'That will be Major Lovat, late of the Argylls. He lives over the hill, at Ballahuan. He joined our Volunteer Force as Honorary Surgeon some months ago. Mind you, he comes only occasionally to our meetings but he's a grand old fellow, nothing he enjoys more than a ceilidh and a wee dram.'

'Ballahuan, you say? I am much obliged to you, Archie.' He grasped the old man by the hand. 'Thank you for saying what you did about my father. He loved this place and its people. They were his whole life.

Nothing could have pleased him more than to die in harness, the way he did.'

Iain McInnes was anxious to be gone. David jumped down into the boat. As he settled himself in the bows he looked up to wave to Archie and was surprised to see that William Whylie had joined the old quarryman.

'Good day to you, doctor,' called William. 'How is your patient?'

'Which one?' enquired David. 'There seem to be so many.' Then, seeing the look of bewilderment on William's face, he shouted: 'Try the schoolhouse!'

2

William encountered Elizabeth as she was attempting, unsuccessfully, to close the ill-fitting door to her new home. Moving her gently to one side, he was obliged to exert all his force to close it.

'I will send someone to put your door in order,' he declared as he picked up a pile of school books, lying on the step.

'That would be most kind,' she thanked him, smiling. 'Mr Ogilvie tells me that the Quarry Company is responsible for the school buildings. If that is indeed the case, there are a number of much more serious matters to be put right than the door to my house.'

Still carrying her books, William followed Elizabeth to the rear of the schoolhouse where he encountered the obnoxious smell and appalling sight of overflowing privvies. The long, low building was divided into two halves by a flimsy partition whose function was to separate boys from girls. A number of cracked and broken planks, however, provided the very peep-holes which the panel had been intended to avoid.

Each section contained, along one wall, a plank of wood in which had been bored four holes, large enough to accommodate juvenile bottoms. The timber was smooth and polished by years of use, but there was fouling of the seat and floor, and the drainage channel, from beneath the bench, had become blocked. Obviously the building had been unattended for a long time.

William shuddered at the sight, and had difficulty controlling the expletives which came readily to his tongue.

'This is a disgrace,' he exclaimed. 'It will be attended to immediately. In the meantime, I suggest that you send the children home rather than use the place. I feel sure that Dr Beaton would condemn it out of hand!'

'I am so relieved you agree with me,' she replied. 'I can make arrangements to cater for the children's needs until you have completed the work. I have asked Mrs McGillivray to supply me with two buckets which we can set behind screens at the far end of the room.'

'Is there anything further that you consider requires attention?'

'No, nothing, apart from my own accommodation. The bothy roof leaks in one or two places. The schoolroom is sound enough, though inordinately gloomy.'

William glanced up at the tall windows of the schoolhouse. They were glazed, above head-height only, to deter the children from staring out when they should be attending to their lessons. The lower part of each window had been shuttered with stout planking, presumably as an afterthought. The initial design had provided for more light in the schoolroom, and less restriction of the children's vision.

'I will make a complete survey of the school building when classes finish this afternoon,' William decided. Then, snatching at the opportunity of seeing her again that day, he suggested, 'Perhaps we can discuss any changes once I have completed my inspection?'

'I shall be taking tea at four o'clock,' she told him, smiling. 'Would you call in then and join me?'

With this encouragement, his enthusiasm knew no bounds. 'If I may be permitted to enter your own house, in the meantime, I will make an estimate of the work required there also and set it in hand.'

'I will be more than grateful for any improvements. Thank you so much for taking the trouble, when you must have a great many problems to occupy you.' Elizabeth hesitated for an instant, and frowned as she continued, 'I do have one or two suggestions to make about the schoolroom, but I doubt if Mr Ogilvie will agree with them.'

William sympathised with her misgivings. His own single encounter with the schoolmaster had been less than satisfactory. The fellow had not endeared himself to William by his uncharitable complaints about Elizabeth's absence from her duties. The man was an arrogant bully. Only let him make one move against her, and he would find himself looking for employment elsewhere!

'Let me decide what repairs are necessary immediately. Later, we can discuss any strategies needed for obtaining Mr Ogilvie's consent.'

On the schoolhouse step, William handed over the heap of books. He was rewarded with her most dazzling smile and went off, light-heartedly, to instruct his men.

When he arrived at Tigh na Broch, David would gladly have gone to his bed, having slept only fitfully in the upright armchair the night before in the McGillivrays' cottage. After a wash and change of clothing, however, he began to feel more capable of facing a waiting room full of patients.

He was so busy, dealing with the many and varied ailments of a community fallen upon bad times, that the morning passed quickly. Disorders were of the kind associated with poor feeding, inadequate housing, and the apathy engendered by uncertain employment prospects. He was surprised to encounter a number of conditions related to poor hygiene and lack of sanitation. Surprised because, as a boy, David had been made very aware of the importance of both by a father who had spent his life fighting for proper conditions of work and housing for his patients. Neglect of such matters must have occurred since the change of management in the quarries, following the death of the Old Marquis.

It would have broken Hugh's heart to see his work so savagely disregarded. David felt a sudden surge of anger, which was quite out of keeping with his usual attitude to his father's affairs. While David's own sights were set on a lucrative city practice and a prestigious surgical appointment, it did not mean he was content to see his father's accomplishments disregarded, and through the neglect of absentee quarry owners the community slipping back to its former condition of dirt, disease and poverty. He felt a strong urge to do something, to take some action which would put things right again, as Hugh would have wanted them.

The last patient left clutching his bottle of white mixture, which a few decent meals and some permanent employment would have rendered superfluous. Over luncheon, David asked his mother about the retired army surgeon whom Hugh had befriended. Apart from giving his address as a cottage at Ballahuan, Morag could offer little information. Hugh had called on the Major's wife when he had first moved into the parish, and the two men had occasionally encountered each other at gatherings of the Volunteers. Morag had never met him.

Leaving Michael Brown to tidy up the surgery, and replenish the stock of various pharmaceutical mixtures, David set out on horseback to visit Major Lovat.

His mount Bess enjoyed the change from shafts and heavy trappings. With a firm step, she carried her young master over the hill and down the steep path into the next village. David inhaled the good, clean air, delighting in the salty tang which persisted even as they climbed higher above sea level.

From the top of Ben Mor the highest point on the island of Seileach there was an unimpeded view far out into the Atlantic. To the north, the cliffs at the southern end of Mull fell, like the folds of a gown, into a frill of white surf at their base. Westwards, the Garvelochs stretched towards the low-lying sun, while to the south-west the sharp triangular shape of Scarba almost obscured the long flat silhouette of Colonsay, the most distant island, which lay on the far horizon. It was a view that had accompanied his childhood, like a favourite toy. He could feel himself being drawn back into the clutches of this place. Each time he thought about his position, it took a greater effort to shake off the feeling that he was destined to remain there.

Maybe he would be able to persuade Major Lovat to take over, until a new man was appointed. Had not Archie MacLean said that he attended the meetings of the Volunteer Company? That surely meant that he had not completely set aside medical practice.

Digging his heels lightly into the mare's flanks, David set off down the steep path to the village of Ballahuan, taking note of any changes to the road wrought by the passage of time. The sun would be setting very soon, and he would have to return by the same route, in the dark.

As he approached the village David recognised the house that had belonged to his boyhood friends, Stephen and Martin Bellamy. It was a mansion of modest proportions, set in some two hundred acres.

The 'big house' was supported by a number of small cottages, similar to those of Eisdalsa, but having an upper storey, with dormer windows. These were considered to be of superior quality, having originally accommodated the estate workers.

Since the English tenant now restricted his visits to a few weeks in the summer, his only farming involvement was to run a few sheep over the open moorland. What had once been an army of retainers had diminished to a shepherd, a groom and a ghillie. The married couple who took care of the master's household had their quarters in the main house. The remaining cottages had, over the years, been let to incomers like the surgeon Major Lovat, people who desired a remote and peaceful place in which to end their days.

The mare picked her way delicately along the stony track as it approached the village. Soon horse and rider encountered a wider lane which wound its way between the cottages.

David hailed a small urchin who was perched precariously upon an outcrop of rock, towering above the road.

'Can you tell me which is Major Lovat's house?'

The child's only reply was to point towards a well-kept cottage, lying back from the road, with a piece of garden-ground running down to the shore.

'Is that the one, there?'

'Aye.' Shyly, the child slid down the rock face and scuttled off into the cottage behind. At the same moment a woman, doubtless the boy's mother, appeared at the door.

David lifted his hat in greeting. The woman curtsied politely before pushing the child into the cottage ahead of her.

Dismounting before the Major's house, David left his horse to crop the swathe of rich green grass between the wall and the road, knowing she would not wander far.

The Major was a shrunken figure with a florid countenance. He might have been any age beyond sixty. It was likely that he had already passed his allotted span of threescore and ten. David sighed inwardly. No replacement for his father was to be found here.

The old doctor sat on a wooden bench, puffing solemnly on his pipe and gazing out towards the Western Islands. The wintry sun, slipping below a lightly clouded horizon, cast a rosy glow upon the neatly whitened walls of the cottage. Despite the lateness of the season, with the strong afternoon breeze now fallen to a slight whisper, the air was remarkably mild. The only sounds were of waves slapping the shore, and sea-birds crying to their comrades as they flew off to some mysterious rendezvous with the waters of the wide Atlantic.

David trod a little noisily, to give warning to his approach.

'Good afternoon, sir, do I have the pleasure of addressing Major Lovat?'

The older man removed his pipe and gave him a careful scrutiny.

David continued, 'May I introduce myself? I am Dr David Beaton. My father was, I believe, an acquaintance of yours.'

'Aye, you will be Hugh's laddie right enough. There is the look of your father about you.'

'I have come upon a professional matter.'

'It's gie cold out here.' As though suddenly becoming aware of the time and the season, the Major drew his coat about him as he said, 'Come away in.' He rose from his bench and David could have sworn he heard bones creaking.

'You will be thirsty from your ride.' The Major noted the mare, grazing quietly by the roadside. He left his guest standing, somewhat perplexed, while he went over to the well and drew a bucket of water. He carried the bucket to the mare and watched her drink, all the time muttering small endearments which the beast clearly appreciated.

Returning with the empty receptacle, the old soldier smiled wryly at his companion's expression.

'Old habits die hard,' he explained. 'An officer attends first to his horses, then to his men!' Observing David's embarrassment at the implied criticism, he changed the subject. 'Will you take ale or a dram? I have a fine malt somewhere about, if that housekeeper of mine hasna' had it awa'!'

The low doorway led into a narrow hall which, in turn, opened directly into the living-room.

Although the room was small, everything had been chosen in correct proportion, so that the mahogany pieces were dainty enough not to overcrowd the space. Fabrics and carpet were equally tasteful; perhaps rather more faded than one might wish, but of a colour and pattern to set off perfectly the low, beamed ceiling, the deeply recessed windows, and the plain white walls.

Around the room, in glass-fronted cabinets upon the walls, and standing on a number of small occasional tables, were the accumulated souvenirs of a life spent in the far-flung outposts of the Empire. From India, China, Africa and the South Seas, each object carried its own memories, and together they formed a fitting background for their elderly owner.

The house gleamed with polish, responding handsomely to the care which was lavished upon it. David wondered if there was a Mrs Lovat. His unspoken question was soon answered.

'My wife and I dreamed of retiring here,' the Major explained. 'During our wanderings around the globe, Emmy's thoughts were always here, in Argyll. She dreamed of it all the time. At long last we came to live at Ballahuan. She worked so hard to make the house into the home she had always imagined. It took two years to get everything to her liking. Then, when the work was finished, she suffered a massive brain haemorrhage and died, in minutes.'

For a moment there was silence. David was sure that he felt a presence in the room with them, the overwhelming strength of the union of these two people whose lives must have witnessed the whole gamut of human experience and whose love had survived throughout.

Emerging from his reverie, Major Lovat continued.

'I try to keep it as she would have wanted. It gives me pleasure to potter among the treasures we gathered together from around the world. So many memories.'

The old man straightened his shoulders, blew noisily into his pocket handkerchief and put aside his grief.

'Come now, a dram for you?'

Soon, both men were seated comfortably before the fire of peats, which was augmented by a few pieces of driftwood. The coloured flames were reflected in the polished wood and gleaming brasses, giving the men sufficient light to talk by.

David felt weary after the rigours of the past twenty-four hours. The strong spirit and the warmth of the fire conspired to make him drowsy. While his host was busying himself, pouring more drams in the next-door kitchen, David dozed.

'Your father and I were good pals.' The Major's voice broke into his visitor's slumbers. David sat more upright, fighting to keep awake.

'Many were the long evenings he sat, where you are now,' continued the Major, 'while we talked of all manner of things.

'He was very proud of his sons. He spoke often of you . . . what high hopes he had for your career. I believe he would have liked to think of you carrying on his work here, but he knew that your sights were set on higher things. But here I am blethering while you, no doubt, have something important to discuss. A professional matter, I think you said?'

'It is your military experience that I would like to call upon,' he explained. 'You must have a great knowledge of head wounds?'

'Aye . . . oh, aye. But surely there has been no shooting accident?'

'Not a shooting, but a fall in the quarries. My father treated a multiple fracture of the femur, but overlooked a depression of the temporal region also sustained in the fall. The patient's wife noticed that he had become increasingly withdrawn during the past few days. When I examined him yesterday he made no response to my questions and his reflexes were slow. His wife fears that he is losing his mind. I suspect that damage to the skull is the cause of his condition.'

The Major was sitting upright in his chair, his attention held by David's description.

'How severe is the damage to the bone?'

'The depression is so slight as to have been overlooked by my father. He was not a man to miss much, under normal circumstances.'

'Nevertheless, fragments of bone pressing on certain areas of the brain may cause defects of speech, movement and so on. If this is the case, and the increase in pressure remains unrelieved, death is inevitable.'

'I have never witnessed surgery involving the brain,' David admitted. 'Would you be prepared to operate? I am sure there is insufficient time to bring a surgeon from the city.'

'Even if one could be found who was willing to come so far,' agreed the old man.

'Will you do it?' David pleaded.

'My hands are too stiff for such an intricate exercise,' his host protested. 'The arthritis has attacked every joint. No, my boy, I could not undertake such delicate work.'

David's expression showed his disappointment.

'However,' Lovat continued, 'if you are half the surgeon that your father was, you will do it yourself . . . with a little guidance from me. What do you say?'

Still doubtful, David hesitated before replying. He had taken a liking to his father's friend. If Hugh could trust him, then surely he himself could rely upon the man? The operation was a dangerous undertaking for a young doctor with a reputation to build. He made up his mind, however, to take the risk.

'Without your help I could not attempt such an operation. With you to guide me . . . I am willing to try.'

'Well spoken, laddie! Now, there is a great deal of preparation to be done. That you may leave to me. I have a set of instruments here that your father would dearly have liked to get his hands upon.' He chuckled as he remembered how Hugh had coveted the trephine which had been made, to the Major's own specification, by a craftsman in Birmingham.

'You look as though you could do with a good night's sleep. Awa' with you now. I will call upon you at nine o'clock tomorrow, and we will visit your patient together.'

'I do not know how to thank you, sir.' David shook the old man by the hand. 'I only hope that I may justify your faith in my ability.'

'Hugh Beaton's son will do his best. Even the good Lord Himself can expect no more. Away home the now . . . we will meet again in the morning.'

It was quite dark by the time David and Bess reached the highest point of the cliffs below Ben Mor. He had dismounted a short distance from the summit to allow the mare to regain her wind. She stood beside him, quietly shuffling, as David drank in the scene below.

The tiny Island of Eisdalsa seemed to reflect the heavens, with candles and oil-lamps twinkling in every window. It was a haven from life's tumult, and yet it had a powerfully throbbing heart. Lives were lived out here, with all the fervour, the joys, sorrows, loves and hates of any community of souls. Feuds were carried on, battles of conscience fought, folk were born, grew to adulthood, married, gave birth and died, without the need to go further afield than the next village.

David's own parents had put down their roots here, and loved the community in which they had worked together. Perhaps, with the right partner, he reflected, he might do the same.

Could he settle for such an existence? Would he find the opportunity he needed to carry through the work which he felt he had been placed on this earth to do? David was no fatalist; he believed firmly that he was master of his own destiny. A month ago he had known what that destiny was to be. He had been able to see a clear pathway ahead, with great achievements, and their accompanying prestige, just over the horizon.

There was a decision to be made. David could almost believe that Hugh stood at his side at that moment, urging him to take it. As he stared down at the Island, a bright light illuminated the little cottage beside the larger, dark shape of the schoolhouse. The schoolroom door had been flung open, and for a moment David glimpsed two figures standing in the lamplight. It was extinguished, to be replaced a few moments later by a softer glow from behind the curtains of Elizabeth's bothy.

With her, David felt that he might settle down in Eisdalsa. She, like his mother, would not be afraid to take up the reins of a busy doctor's household. Why, she might even be of help to him.

As though she had been reading his thoughts, Bess nudged her master firmly between the shoulders, as if to say, 'All right then, if you have made up your mind, you had better get on and do something about it!'

He climbed back into the saddle, and pulling gently on the rein urged Bess into a steady trot. She pricked up her ears and started off across the heather, gathering speed as the flat plateau gave way to a steady downward slope. At the top of the cliff path she halted for a moment, lifting her head to the night breezes. 'Come on, old girl,' he urged. 'Time we both were home and abed.'

With sure feet and a jaunty spring in her gait, Bess carried on down the narrow path and into the yard of Tigh na Broch. Morag, who had been listening for the sound of hooves, came forward to hold the horse's head as David dismounted.

'What a time you have been!' she exclaimed. 'Supper has been on the table an hour or more. There is a letter from Edinburgh and I have arranged a supper party for Sunday. Miss Duncan and that nice Mr Whylie have both agreed to come!'

When David led the Major into the McGillivrays' house the following morning, they found Jamie McGillivray lying staring into space, seeing nothing. His breathing, laboured and stertorous, gave the only indication that he still lived. For two days he had said nothing, eaten nothing and drunk only small sips of the water which Annie had painstakingly held to his lips from time to time. Thankfully, neighbours had removed the children so that she might concentrate upon her husband's needs. Callous though it might seem, she was glad that the infant had died at birth, leaving one less problem for her.

David introduced the Major. Annie had heard of him, of course. Jamie had mentioned with pride the acquisition of a medical officer for the Battery. Theirs was the only Volunteer Company with its own surgeon in the whole of Argyll!

The Major examined Jamie's skull with great care. His delicate fingers, twisted and painful as they were, gently traced the bones of the cranium while the patient moaned softly, his eyes wide open and fixed upon nothing.

After a few moments the old doctor rose to his feet and, signalling to David to follow, he stepped outside the cottage.

'There is no doubt in my mind that it is the depressed bone which is the cause of the problem. I must warn you that even if you are successful in removing the fragments, after this length of time there is no guarantee that the patient will make a full recovery. Worse, he may live, but only as a vegetable, his mind destroyed.'

'What is the prognosis if we do not perform the operation?'

'As you yourself have observed, the patient is declining. He will be dead in a matter of days.'

'I must talk to Mrs McGillivray. After all, it is she who will bear the burden if her husband lives, but without a mind.'

'I will take myself down to the harbour and have a word with the men. Come and fetch me if you are prepared to proceed. If it is to be done at all, there must be no further delay.'

David found Annie seated before the range, half dozing. As he approached, she was startled into wakefulness. When she read his expression, her eyes filled with tears.

'Mrs McGillivray . . . Annie, Major Lovat, as you know, has been a surgeon in the army for many years. He has considerable experience of men in Jamie's condition. I respect his judgement fully.'

Annie wiped her eyes with the back of her hand and smiled up at him. 'You can tell me, Dr David, bad news or good. I know I can trust what you have to say.'

'Major Lovat believes that Jamie can be saved by an operation to remove the broken bones of the skull.'

At her startled cry of relief, David was forced to calm her, pressing her gently back into the chair before pulling up the fireside stool for himself, and taking both her hands in his.

'Due to arthritis in his hands, Dr Lovat is no longer able to operate. I have never performed surgery on the brain. However we believe that between us, the Major and I may be able to save your husband's life.'

Her eyes were no longer shining, she sensed that there was a proviso. 'Tell me what you must,' she whispered.

'If I can remove the broken fragments of bone which are pressing into the brain, without penetrating the tissues, Jamie might make a complete recovery. Any greater damage, whether it is already done or occurs during the operation, could impair his functions. In short, he might be left alive, but mindless.'

Annie bit hard into her knuckles and for a long while she gazed into the fire. She could cope with a man crippled so that he could not walk, but how would she manage a household with a helpless lunatic to care for? It would have been better if her husband had died outright on the day of his fall. The doctors had agreed that without the operation Jamie would die. Should they just leave it at that? Would she ever forgive herself if she did not allow them to try? Would she wonder for the rest of her life what might have happened?

David had risen from the stool and was standing by the window, looking out on to the everyday scenes of village life. Everything continued as usual, oblivious of the troubles which beset this stricken household.

At Annie's murmur, he turned his head. 'I beg your pardon, Mrs McGillivray. Did you speak?'

'I said, you must try to save him,' she replied.

David was immediately at her side. 'You understand, fully, the implications?'

Again he searched her face anxiously, finding in it a courage and stoicism such as he had never encountered in any woman. He squeezed her hands encouragingly.

'We will do everything we can.'

As he made for the door to go and summon Major Lovat, she called after him.

'I trust you, as I would have trusted Dr Hugh. If you should fail, I will understand that you have done all that anybody could. Please believe me.'

'Thank you.' David slipped away, and Annie knelt beside her husband, stroking his hair and humming a Highland lullaby.

*   *   *

Annie began the preparations she now knew would be required. Clean sheets, clean bowls and a scrubbed table were soon ready and two large pots of water were set to boil on the stove. By the time that the two doctors arrived, everything was ready. Major Lovat was very impressed.

'My word, Mrs McGillivray, one might have thought you had been nursing all your life,' he declared. 'What I would have given for your assistance in years past!'

Annie knew he was humouring her, but smiled her appreciation and stood quietly by, awaiting further instructions.

'Now, Annie,' David was kind but firm, 'Major Lovat and I can manage on our own. I think you should be with your children during this difficult time. I will send for you just as soon as we have finished.'

'Oh, but I thought I might stay to help . . .'

The older doctor took her gently by the arm and steered her towards the door. 'I shall come personally and tell you when it is all over.'

Unable to find any further words of protest, Annie allowed herself to be propelled through the door, where she came face to face with two of Jamie's workmates who had come to assist in lifting the patient on to the table.

The Major laid out the contents of his medical bag on one of Annie's clean sheets. An assortment of instruments soon lay gleaming upon the white linen. For many hours the previous evening, the surgeon had honed and polished drills, scalpels and bone saws until each cutting edge was as sharp as human endeavour could make it. Last of all, he extracted a number of stout leather straps and began to anchor the patient to the table.

'Since the operation is so delicate,' David ventured, 'I wondered at the advisability of using chloroform. I used it very effectively on Mrs McGillivray herself recently.'

'Dangerous,' his companion answered abruptly. 'The level of consciousness is already reduced to a minimum. Anaesthesia could be enough to kill him outright. No, lad, you will have to be quick, and accurate. I will anchor his head as tightly as possible. You must hope that he does not move unduly.'

Under instruction from the Major, David worked steadily, cutting away a neat flap of scalp tissues to expose the shattered temporal bone. The wound bled profusely, suggesting to David that there would be little chance of infection. Nevertheless, he prepared a very mild solution of potassium permanganate and used a Lister spray to permeate the atmosphere with carbolic acid, using this to irrigate the wound, making it possible to see what he was doing, and ensuring that any germs would be eliminated.

Major Lovat watched these manoeuvres with interest, but said nothing. When David had exposed all the broken area of the scalp, the old surgeon took a good long look for himself.

'We may be in luck, laddie,' he said. 'The subdural membranes appear to be intact. We may yet find that the brain tissue is undisturbed.'

With extreme care, David lifted one jagged sliver of bone clear of the open scalp. The membrane beneath, although deeply dented, showed no sign of a tear. With growing confidence, he cleared another three or four pieces, and finally a few tiny splinters. At last the area seemed clear of stray fragments of bone. David stood back for the Major to inspect the wound.

'Aye, it looks clear enough . . . try another irrigation with yon fluid of yours . . . there, I thought so . . . d'you see?'

Davie peered into the opening, clear now of blood. The brain itself could be observed pulsating beneath the final thin layer of protecting membrane. In the corner, resting beneath the edge of the flap he had cut, a tiny white fragment was clearly visible. With a fine pair of forceps he removed the offending splinter.

'That would have defeated the whole operation,' declared the Major. 'Sharp enough to work its way through in time, it could have caused all manner of trouble!'

As he spoke, the Major brought from his vest pocket a clean white handkerchief which he unwrapped carefully, laying its contents on the sheet beside Jamie's head. It was a thin plate of silver, like a small saucer, just large enough to cover the area where the bone had been removed. Around the edge had been drilled a number of small holes, through which a fine surgical needle might pass without difficulty.

'Better do your boiling-up bit on that, too,' the old man chuckled. He had watched David's scrupulous attention to sterility with great interest throughout the operation. Never had he witnessed such a display of clean surgery.

The silver plate was placed in position, over the hole in the bone and lying above the fringe of the scalp, so that it could be sewn to this tough covering, without harm to the delicate tissues beneath.

Even at this stage, David was holding his breath as he worked, for fear of puncturing the brain tissue. The needle he had been handed for the task was curiously curved, to ensure that only the tissues required should be caught up in the sewing. David had no doubt that this was another of the old surgeon's own inventions.

At last the plate was secure along three-quarters of its edge. The flap of scalp was eased over the unattached part of the rim. When the membrane had been stretched and sewn down, nothing could be seen but a row of silk stitches, each precisely positioned, and as neat as would do justice to a lady's sempstress.

So intense had been David's concentration, that it was only now that he paid any regard to the patient's physical response to the operation.

He need not have worried. The Major had, all the time, been monitoring pulse and breathing. It was apparent that McGillivray, having remained unconscious throughout, had felt no pain.

David was pleased to note that Jamie's breathing had changed to the quiet rhythms of a sleeping babe. His pulse seemed strong, and an inspection of the pupil reflexes showed these to be normal. So far it seemed that the operation had been a success.

'The sooner we get our patient back in his bed, the better.' Major Lovat went to the door and, on his signal, the two quarrymen appeared, as if by magic.

'How is Jamie, doctor?' enquired Willie Campbell. It was Jamie's own crew, who had forsaken their work in the quarry to be on hand to help their friend.

'We have high hopes of a good recovery,' replied David. 'Now, if you will lift him into his bed, Major Lovat and I will try to make him comfortable.'

The Major left David to wash and tidy up the mess, while he went in search of Annie.

He was soon back with an anxious little party. Annie went straight in to her husband. Elizabeth remained outside, her arms around the two children, waiting patiently for an invitation to enter.

Annie crept quietly to her husband's side. Instantly, she realised that his breathing was improved, and his colour too was more healthy.

She glanced round enquiringly.

David smiled at her. 'Major Lovat believes that there is a good chance of recovery.'

She got to her feet, and without restraint kissed first David and then the Major.

'How can I ever thank you?' she cried.

'By taking care to see that your husband is left to rest, given wholesome food, a light broth and perhaps some carrageen. He must be made to stay in his bed until I say he may leave it!'

Smiling, Annie indicated her acceptance of David's instructions.

The two doctors finished packing their instruments and prepared to leave. At the door, David nearly ran full tilt into Elizabeth. She released her hold upon the two children so that they could creep past him and into the house.

'Major Lovat, I think perhaps you have not been introduced to our new schoolmistress, Miss Duncan.' David turned to Elizabeth. 'May I present Major Lovat late of the Argylls.'

Smiling, Elizabeth extended her daintily gloved hand.

'Major Lovat, has been successful in saving Jamie McGillivray. At least, as far as we can see for the moment.'

The Major beamed appreciatively at the young woman before him.

'Schoolmistress, eh? Would I were young enough to be your pupil, ma'am!'

Elizabeth laughed, her eyes sparkling.

'Take no heed of this young man of yours,' Lovat went on. 'It was he who saved the patient. What a surgeon, and what stitching! Get him to sew you a gown sometime.'

Turning to David he said, 'I have a mind to stop for a jaw with a few old friends. If you wish to get away home, I will look in on our patient, later this evening. Just to see that all is well.'

'That is uncommon civil of you, Major,' David thanked him. 'Perhaps I may call on you again, soon?'

'Please do. It seems you have a few lessons to teach an old man. I was much intrigued by all the boiling water, and what else was it?'

'Carbolic acid, sir. I will be very pleased to acquaint you with Mr Lister's theories of asepsis.'

'I shall look forward to seeing you then. Good night, Dr Beaton.'

The two men shook hands and the Major departed.

Elizabeth took the arm proffered by David, and together they walked across the green to her cottage.

'I fear that your friend has made a mistake about our relationship. I do hope you will enlighten him,' Elizabeth remarked. She waited for David to push open the door. William's joiner had performed wonders. It now slid open readily, at a touch.

'Oh, you mean when he assumed that you were my young lady?' David blushed slightly as he said the words.

'Exactly.'

'I wish that it was so,' he ventured, somewhat surprised at his own audacity.

'You flatter me, sir.' Elizabeth laughed as she made an exaggerated curtsy.

'My mother tells me you will be dining with us on Sunday.'

'It was very kind of her to invite me.'

'May I offer you a ride to church in the morning?'

'Thank you, but Mr Whylie has already arranged for us to travel in the Company's gig.'

It was a crushing blow. David tried unsuccessfully to disguise his disappointment.

'Perhaps we shall meet after the service then?'

'No doubt. Good day to you, David.'

'Until Sunday then, Miss Elizabeth.'

Disconsolately, he watched her step inside the bothy, and close the door.

3

Dr David Beaton
Tigh na Broch
Seileach
Argyll

Edinburgh Royal
Infirmary
15 December 1876

My dear friend,
Good news! All arrangements are in hand for our removal to
London.

My agent has acquired premises in Harley Street where we may
both have consulting rooms and also reside, at least for the time
being.

I am in constant correspondence with King's College and feel
sure that we will be made welcome when we take post there. Sir
Charles seems eager to get something started on the aseptic
method and has already begun advising his surgeons of what will be
expected of them.

Well, my dear fellow, have you found a replacement for your
poor father? I do hope so. Let me know by return how your search
is progressing. I am loath to travel to London ahead of you, but if
needs be . . .

I must set out myself before New Year, to be well installed by
1 January.

My very good wishes to your mother.

Your affectionate friend,
Joseph Lister

David laid down the letter and gazed through the study window. Waves
were lashing mercilessly at the grey rocks along the shore. Sea-birds
wheeled and cried into the wind. Dark clouds towered upwards from
the horizon, vaulting the heavens.

So, the moment had come at last. He re-read Joseph's letter. It was
so full of anticipation and excitement – excitement in which he too might
have shared. What other young doctor would have turned down such
an opportunity? Was he being foolish?

On the corner of the desk lay his father's ancient book of herbal
medicine. He took it up now, absentmindedly turning the pages. His

eyes glanced over the neatly written notes in the margins. There were
many different hands, for the book had passed through several generations of Beaton medical men.

A note in his father's hand took his attention.

'Mrs O McCaffer, tincture of Hyssop, relieved case of cardiac oed-
ema, July '73. 5 drops in water, tincture made from leaves and flowers.'

Hugh Beaton really believed in this stuff. Well, maybe, given time,
David would follow in his footsteps . . . there would certainly be plenty
of that if he remained here.

He thought again about his deliberations on the cliff the previous
evening. It had been the sight of that slender figure, silhouetted in the
schoolhouse doorway, which had convinced him. If any woman was
worth the sacrifice of his career, it was Elizabeth Duncan! She had
seemed a little reticent on the night of Annie's confinement, but he put
that down to feminine perversity. He felt certain she would consent to
be his wife.

For a moment only, the clouds parted and a shaft of bright sunlight
sprang across the sea, making a shimmering pathway out towards the
distant islands.

David sighed, took up his pen and wrote.

Mr Joseph Lister MB, FRCS   Tigh na Broch
Edinburgh Royal Infirmary   Seileach
                                     21 December 1976

Dear Joseph,

I am in receipt of your letter, for which I thank you.

Appreciating the haste with which the day for your departure
approaches, I write to tell you that as yet I have had no success in
finding a replacement for my father.

There is plenty of work here of an engaging nature and I have
been required to perform two considerable surgical operations within
the past weeks. I have had occasion to enlist the assistance of one
Major Philip Lovat, lately of the Argylls, a surgeon of considerable
experience. Together we performed a repair to a skull fracture with
which I think even you would have been satisfied. Were it not for
his advanced years and severe arthritis, the Major would have been
an ideal stand-in for the practice. As it is, I feel I must remain here
for the time being. There are two thousand souls in the parish,
without a medical practitioner. Even in the short time since the death
of my father, conditions of health and hygiene have noticeably
deteriorated. I feel that I owe it to his memory, if nothing else, to
remain until I can place the care of these people into responsible
hands.

So it seems you must proceed to King's College without me. I am already applying your aseptic methods in my work here, to good effect. I shall keep a journal of all exercises undertaken in this respect which may be added to your own research papers if you so wish.

Conscious as I am of your need to make definite plans for your supporting staff at King's College, I feel that I must absolve you of any obligation which you may feel to retain a place for me. Thank you for the honour which you bestowed upon me in offering me the post of your assistant. You must be aware that it is my dearest wish to see your methods in universal use. You may rest assured that there will be at least one small parish in Scotland which observes your rules!

I trust that you will continue to find time to correspond and that we shall always remain friends.

I am, sir, your obedient friend and servant,

David Alexander Beaton

David sealed the letter and addressed it. Calling out to Michael, he ordered the boy to go with all speed to the pier, to catch the afternoon steamer.

'See that you put the letter into the hands of the deck officer himself, mind. It is most important that it is sent on immediately from Glasgow.'

He gave his apprentice a shilling piece to pay for the delivery. Michael was through the door and halfway down the hall when David suddenly remembered the other decision he had to make.

'Michael,' he called the boy back, 'you should know that I have decided to remain here at least for the present. That being the case, I am happy to continue your apprenticeship and will be calling upon my solicitor, with your father, to sign the proper papers.'

'Oh! Thank you, doctor. Thank you very much.'

Disregarding all previous requests for quiet and decorum, Michael Brown slammed the outer door to the surgery and ran, shouting his good news to the wind.

'I'm going to be a doctor . . . I'm going to be a doctor!'

Morag, disturbed by the noise, came to see what was happening.

'Whatever has got into Michael? What have you been doing to him?'

'I told him that, since I was going to remain here in my father's place, I would continue with his apprenticeship.'

Morag ran and threw her arms about him.

'I am so pleased, my darling, so very pleased!' Then, hesitating, knowing that in her heart she had no wish to deter him, 'Are you quite sure that you would not rather go to London?'

Evading the question deliberately, because he certainly was not at all sure that he had made the right decision, he replied, 'It is too late now to change my mind. The letter has already been despatched.'

'*Feasgar math,*' William greeted Morag.

Delighted to be so addressed by the Englishman, she replied, '*Ciamar a tha thu?*'

'*Tha gu math, tapadh leibh.*'

'*Tha mi toilicht' d'fhaicinn.*'

William had exhausted his repertoire, and David was exploding with merriment at William's anguished expression on hearing Morag's further words.

'She says, she is pleased to see you.'

'Thank you for your invitation, madam.' He took the proffered hand. 'I regret to say that so far my Gaelic is limited to "Good-day" and "How are you"!'

'At least you are making a try at learning the language. Very few Englishmen take the trouble.'

'Archie MacLean is tutoring me, and as Maggie goes about the housework she quizzes me on the previous day's lessons! Between the two, I hope to be able to converse passably well in due course. It is a language with some similarities to the ancient Cornish tongue. I have no difficulty in forming the consonant sounds, as I believe do most English students of Gaelic.'

Elizabeth handed her bonnet to Sheilagh.

'I must compliment Mr Whylie,' she said, smiling. 'Try as I might I cannot get my tongue around the strange words, and the grammatical form appears to bear little or no relationship to Latin or Greek. Perhaps I, too, should acquire a tutor.'

The Sunday evening supper party was a happy affair. The young people shared many experiences from their first days at Eisdalsa, while Morag was delighted to have their bright young faces around her table. She was reminded of earlier times, when her sons and husband had engaged in deep discussions on how to set the world to rights.

The sweet had been consumed with relish. It was a dish strange to Elizabeth, who enquired of Sheilagh how it was made.

'It is only carrageen,' replied the old servant. 'With the mistress's preserved myrtle berries for a sauce.' She gathered up the remaining dishes and left the room.

'What is carrageen?' asked Elizabeth.

'It is a purple seaweed, which we find at low tide in these parts,' David explained. 'It is often used as the basis of puddings for infants and the sick. For my part, it is associated with nursery teas and not much to my liking.'

'Hush,' warned Morag, 'Sheilagh will be offended if she hears you say so. She believes it to be your favourite pudding.'

'I know. Would that some kind messenger would tell her otherwise!'

They all laughed and Sheilagh, who reappeared soon after, was pleased to hear such merriment. The house had been so gloomy since Dr Hugh had died.

A platter of fresh bread and an English cheese, brought in from Glasgow, completed the meal. David placed a decanter of port on the table. Elizabeth looked to Morag for a signal that the ladies should leave. Morag, however, remained seated and accepted the glass which her son passed to her.

Observing the younger woman's perplexed expression, David explained, 'My father always included Mama in discussions at the dinner table. Indeed, he considered her wisdom an essential addition to any discourse. I am sure, Miss Elizabeth, that he would have felt the same about you.'

'For my part,' added William, 'I believe that there are certain conventions which are quite ridiculous and deserve to be ignored. That gentlemen should hold the important conversation of the evening without their fair companions is one such.'

The ladies remained, and the talk moved on to more weighty matters, concerning the village and its inhabitants.

'I have observed,' said Elizabeth, 'that many of the more senior workmen are educated beyond the resources of the village school. Where did they obtain their superior knowledge?'

'It was the policy of the old Marquis,' David explained, 'to seek out the brighter pupils in the school and pay for their further education in one of the academic centres. There are several with engineering qualifications from either Glasgow or London. The accountant is a local man, trained in Aberdeen, and the present Factor, Mr Lugas, studied philosophy at Edinburgh University at the Marquis's expense.'

'What about the this Marquis . . . is he prepared to fund the pupils in a similar manner?' Elizabeth was clearly very anxious to make her point.

'The new Marquis,' observed Morag, 'seems very remote from Eisdalsa. Apart from the few weeks he spends here, during the summer, he leaves the Parish to itself and his affairs entirely in the hands of Mr Lugas.'

'If I have some exceptional pupils, as indeed I have,' persisted Elizabeth, 'to whom should I apply for their support, in the pursuit of further training?'

Again it was Morag who had the answer.

'When Hugh was a member of the School Board, the schoolmaster would provide a list of deserving pupils. The Board determined which of these should be supported and the names were submitted to the Marquis through Mr Lugas. Often the old Marquis would interview the children himself. It was an excellent idea for, as Hugh always said, it was an investment in the future of the quarries.'

'There are two very deserving cases at present,' said Elizabeth.

'Dougal McGillivray is a very clever boy. Because of his father's troubles, it seems that he is bound to begin work in the quarries on his eleventh birthday. That would be a serious loss to the Company, as I believe he would make an excellent engineer.'

'From what I hear of his father's abilities, that may well be the case,' agreed William.

'Mary McCulloch, the minister's daughter, is also a very bright little girl. I believe that there may be bursaries for which she can compete, but nothing likely to cover all the costs of teacher training, which is what she has in mind.'

David had been deep in thought up to this minute.

'Michael Brown, our apprentice, will also require financial assistance, if he is to continue with his medical training,' he remarked. 'The practice can help a little, but from what I have seen so far, there is no way in which it can cover all of the costs.'

'I believe,' Morag observed, 'that there is an obvious solution.'

They all turned to her.

'The elections for the School Board take place at the Parish Council meeting early in January. We have a new doctor and a new Quarry Manager, both of whom should have a say in the running of the school. You must get yourselves elected to the Board.'

William was looking quizzically at David.

'Does this mean that you have decided to stay on after all?' he asked.

When David affirmed that this was indeed the case, Elizabeth seemed pleased.

'That is good news,' she said. 'I am sure that Mrs Beaton must be absolutely delighted.' David might have wished for a more positive expression of her own pleasure at his news. It was, after all, because of her that he had decided to stay, although she of course was not aware of this. So far as David could see, he was without rivals. There was no doubt that Elizabeth showed a certain warmth towards Whylie, while that sailor fellow, McIntyre, had made little secret of his admiration for her at the time of the accident. Whylie was pleasant enough, if a trifle stodgy, but surely Elizabeth was too intelligent to have her head turned by a smart uniform?

If there was a fleeting shadow of doubt, he dismissed it utterly. Seeing her here, so at ease in this homely setting, who could doubt that Elizabeth Duncan was destined to be the next mistress of Tigh na Broch?

Gordon McIntyre listened, with growing alertness, to the tale of woe from the Engineering Officer.

'There's nothing else for it, Mr Mate. We shall have to stop over at Eisdalsa and effect some temporary repairs.'

'Very well, Mr Kelso. I will give your recommendation to the Captain,' he observed, finding it difficult to suppress the elation he felt at this timely news. 'Meanwhile,' he continued, 'you had better muster your skilled men and have them make ready to dismantle the bearing in question.'

'Very good, sir!'

Gordon found himself whistling as he ran up the companion ladder to the bridge. The Captain, however, was not pleased to be faced with a delay. In no circumstances could either Seileach or the Island be considered a suitable place for an unexpected holiday.

'As soon as we dock, Mr McIntyre, you will discover some suitable craft to carry onward-going passengers to Oban or Fort William,' he ordered.

'Very good, sir.'

'While you are ashore, perhaps you will deliver this letter from the owners to that unfortunate young woman who had the accident a while back? The village schoolmistress, I believe.'

'Yes, sir!' he answered smartly. 'Oh, yes, indeed, sir. Thank you, sir.'

Astonished at this outburst, the Captain might have queried his subordinate's strange reaction to his order, but Gordon was already gone about his duties. There was, he remembered a container of furniture from Carter Paterson's store, addressed to Miss Duncan. Now he would have an opportunity to make both deliveries to her, in person!

It took longer than Gordon would have wished to seek out a suitable vessel whose skipper was willing to make the round trip to Fort William with the dozen or so passengers who were making the full journey. When, at last, he had seen his charges aboard, with assurances of a fast passage from the boat's owner, it was already late in the afternoon and dusk was closing in.

Elizabeth's cargo had been lowered from the deck of the *Lord of Lorn*, into a flat-bottomed barge. The crew awaited his order to shove off for the Island.

'Wait a moment,' cried Gordon, 'I'm coming with you!'

On the far side of the channel, he left the crew of the barge to manhandle the crate of furniture and found his way to the schoolhouse, arriving as the last of the children were leaving. He was not unaware of the interest which his appearance had aroused amongst her pupils. Clearly excited by the presence of this tall, handsomely bronzed figure in his smart uniform of blue serge, liberally decorated with brass buttons and gold braid, the girls curtsied and giggled in embarrassment while the boys made no effort to disguise their admiration. Would that their teacher might be equally impressed. Enquiring the whereabouts of Miss Duncan, he was directed inside the schoolroom where he found Elizabeth giving instruction to two young boys.

'Charlie, when you have finished cleaning the ink-wells, you are to help Dougie with the sweeping. How much have you learnt of Psalm 23?'

'Up to the "valley of the shadow", miss,' volunteered Dougie. 'Do you want him to say it?'

Elizabeth had noted the presence of her visitor.

'No, not now, Charlie. Just go on about your work, both of you, while I speak to this gentleman.'

Gordon was pleased when she greeted him by name.

'Good afternoon, Mr McIntyre. Is there something I can do for you?' Recalling the circumstances of their previous encounter, she felt a trifle embarrassed. Perhaps her response sounded rather cold, because Gordon answered formally, 'I carry a letter from my employers, madam. I was asked to deliver it in person.'

He handed over the correspondence: an imposing-looking package, addressed in a fine copperplate hand.

Thanking him, Elizabeth accepted the letter, without glancing at it further. In truth she felt flustered in the presence of this very personable figure. Like her pupils, she found him more than a little alluring. She bade the two boys good night and led her visitor towards her own house.

'Will you take some tea?' she invited. 'Do you have the time to spare?'

'Fortunately, I do,' he replied, unable to believe how well everything was falling into place. He explained about the engineering failure.

'I come on another errand also,' he continued, holding open the bothy door that she might enter. 'A consignment of furniture has been delivered for you. The men are even now carrying it up from the harbour.'

'Oh, how wonderful!' Elizabeth exclaimed, her eyes shining with delight. 'You cannot imagine how I have longed to have my own things about me! As you can see, the Quarry Company provides only the barest necessities when it comes to furnishings.'

By now, a party of quarriers and seamen was at the door. In no time at all, a warm wool carpet from her mother's drawing room was stretched across the slate-stone floor. Two comfortable armchairs were placed on either side of the range and a fine gateleg table with four mahogany balloon-back chairs had replaced the crude scrubbed table and single straight-backed chair which had been her only furniture since her arrival on the island.

Elizabeth's own mahogany bedstead could not be erected in the confined space. She begged the men to leave it propped against the wall at the far end of the room. Her discussions with William had included the proposal that an extension might be made to the building, providing her with a separate scullery and a bedroom. Until that time, she would be obliged to manage with the box-bed which was set into the wall alongside the fireplace. With her parents' fine mahogany tallboy placed in front of it, the bedstead hardly imposed upon the room at all.

Elizabeth ran hither and thither delighting in the transformation of her tiny home. At her command, Gordon obligingly moved a chair a trifle in this direction; the table a little to the side; the tallboy an inch or two forward from the stacked bedstead . . . At last she was satisfied, and, childlike, threw her arms about him in her excitement.

'Oh, Mr McIntyre,' she cried, 'how can I ever thank you enough?'

Startled at first by her innocent embrace, the young man held her gently and gazed into her dancing eyes.

Suddenly overcome by the enormity of her indiscretion, Elizabeth felt the hot flush of blood to her face, and removed her hands from about his neck as though scalded. In the silence that followed a noticeable tension grew between them. It was Gordon who broke the spell.

'While I am on the Island, I have a mind to visit Mr Whylie the engineer,' he said. 'It seems he may be able to give my men some assistance. Would you be so kind as to direct me to his house?'

Elizabeth quickly recovered her composure.

'At this time he could still be in the quarry office,' she said. 'If you follow the path around the harbour, you will probably meet him as he makes his way home.'

Elizabeth accompanied Gordon to the door and indicated the position of William's house which stood out, being the only two-storey dwelling on the far side of the harbour.

Unwilling to let him go without the prospect of another meeting, Elizabeth made a rapid decision.

'There is a great party in preparation for Hogmanay,' she said tentatively. 'I do not suppose that your schedule will include a visit to Eisdalsa on the festive day?' She held her breath as she awaited his reply. Her hopes were quickly dashed.

'Unfortunately I am obliged to join my people in Edinburgh for the festivities.' His regret was manifest. Much as he would have rejoiced to accept her invitation, he knew that his mother would never forgive him if he absented himself from the family gathering.

As he strolled off into the dusk, he turned and called to her, 'Don't forget your letter.'

It was fortunate that he had reminded her, for she had indeed overlooked it. Settled comfortably before the fire in her upholstered armchair, she tore open the paper.

To Miss E Duncan   Clyde River and Western Isles
C/o Eisdalsa Slate Quarrying   Steamship Company, Ltd
          Co. Ltd   Glasgow
Eisdalsa Island   20 December 1876
Argyll

Madam,
Having considered the circumstances of the accident at Crinan, on
26 November last, my Company has decided to accept all
responsibility for the occurrence.

The medical report supplied by your practitioner indicated that
you received some superficial wounds and experienced delayed
shock. The Directors have asked me to convey their sincere
apologies for any discomfort suffered as a result of the accident.
They trust that you are now fully recovered.

Our insurers have agreed to pay compensation of £50 (fifty
pounds) in an out-of-court settlement. A banker's draft to that amount
accompanies this letter.

I would be grateful if you will acknowledge receipt of the money
at your earliest opportunity.

I am, madam, your most obedient servant,

Elgin J. Potts
Secretary to the Clyde River and Western Islands Steamship
Company

She laid down the letter, and began dreaming of the things she might
do with the money . . . new clothes perhaps, books, new china for her
home. She would borrow Annie's catalogue in the morning.

She took out pen and paper and composed her reply to Mr Elgin J.
Potts, thanking him for his attentions and acknowledging receipt of the
draft for £50. If she hurried, she might have the letter carried by the
Lord of Lorn when the steamer made her return trip the next day.

William and Gordon met on the path from the quarry office.

'Why, if it is not First Officer McIntyre!' exclaimed the engineer.
'My word, sir, but it has taken you a long time to make your promised
call.'

'Circumstances were against my visit I fear,' replied Gordon. 'In any
case, your schoolmistress seemed to have forgotten my promise to
visit you all.'

'At the time of our last meeting, she was hardly in a condition for
making new acquaintances.' William leapt to Elizabeth's defence as
though he had some prior right to protect her reputation.

'Anyway,' Gordon tried to mollify him, 'she made me more than welcome when I explained that I was delivering her furniture.'

'I am sure she will be pleased.' William hastily regained his composure. 'Her house was very sparsely furnished, as I remember.'

It was unlikely that he could forget it, having been drinking tea there only two days before!

'I forget my manners.' William led Gordon into his home and bade him be seated. Over a brimming glass of Eisdalsa-brewed ale, the two men renewed their acquaintance.

'With a fractured bearing, the Chief decided it was unwise to risk a major breakdown at sea.' Gordon was explaining the reason for the steamer's overnight stay at Eisdalsa. 'The Skipper has gone on to Oban in the hired barque, on the pretext of ensuring that his passengers reach their destination. Truth is, he has little faith in the ability of the Eisdalsa Inn to provide for his entertainment!'

'So you are left to oversee the repair?'

'That I am, and it is proving to be a problem. The bearing in question must be replaced, and we carry no spares. It seems that a new part has to be manufactured. I wondered if you had the facilities for such work?'

'I am sure that we can do something to help you. Let me come with you to inspect the problem and we will see what can be done.'

William had had a great deal of experience of steam engines in the Cornish mines. Also, in the past weeks, he had been obliged to oversee a quantity of making-do with inferior quarry equipment. The task of putting the *Lord of Lorn* to rights was relatively simple. Once he had been shown the required part, William returned to the smithy with Gordon at his heels. The blacksmith stood by to assist where necessary, while William manufactured the new bearing.

When the task was completed, he sent one of the boys to the steamer with the replacement part so that it could be fitted in time for the morning departure.

'Must you go back aboard the steamer directly?' he enquired of his guest.

'I shall certainly be expected to spend the night on board,' replied Gordon, 'but there is no reason to return immediately.'

'Good, that is as I had hoped. I have asked Mrs MacLean to prepare supper for us. I hope you will join me?'

Delighted at his good fortune, Gordon readily agreed.

The supper was a venison stew and William's guest could not resist a joke about poaching.

'Would that I had time for such capers!' William laughed. 'The meat was a welcoming present from His Lordship's Factor.'

The meal ended, they sat before a roaring fire, sipping a fine old malt whisky.

'I don't know how to thank you for your help, William. The Company will of course reimburse you for your time,' Gordon observed.

'There is something you could do for me, in fact, although I would not wish you to feel under any obligation.' William responded as he refilled his guest's glass.

Gordon waved a dismissive hand. 'My dear fellow, anything at all . . .'

'The Quarry Company's stock of pumping equipment is sadly depleted and what remains is in need of major repairs. I have a mind to acquire some more machines . . . not new, you understand, more likely something discarded from old vessels in the breaker's yard. Should you hear of anything suitable, I would be obliged if you could let me know? I can then come down to Glasgow to inspect what is on offer.'

'Delighted to help in any way I can.' Gordon rose from his chair. 'I had best be off before my crew think they have the steamer to themselves for the night. Thank you again for your hospitality, and for providing the new bearing.'

'I will see you to the harbour,' offered William. 'At this hour it will be necessary to find someone to row you across to the *Lord of Lorn*.'

'Please do not trouble yourself,' protested Gordon, 'I can hail the steamer, for a boat.'

'What time will you sail tomorrow?'

'Probably on the scheduled hour . . . if my Captain returns in time.'

'If you have a half hour to spare in the morning, I would be pleased to show you the quarries at work. It will give you a better idea of the type of equipment I am looking for.'

'Tomorrow then. Good night.'

With a wave of his hand, Gordon disappeared into the darkness.

William considered the clear night sky and felt it was a good moment to address Elizabeth on a matter which had been exercising him for some days.

Having seen the ship's officer depart, he followed some distance behind, skirting the harbour until he came to the green. Cutting diagonally across the square patch of grass, he reached Elizabeth's house just as she was thinking of preparing for bed.

Seeing movement within, he lifted his hand and knocked on the door. She arrived in moments, holding high the lighted oil lamp in order to see who was calling at this late hour.

When she saw who her visitor was, she held the door open, inviting him in.

Having a care for wagging tongues, William ignored the gesture.

'I just called to give you an invitation to the Hogmanay Ball,' he explained. 'I would be so pleased if you will consent to be my partner.'

Elizabeth thought of her invitation to Gordon, earlier that day. She would have preferred it to have been him partnering her, but if not Gordon, who better than William? 'Thank you,' she replied. 'I shall be delighted.'

4

Two days before Christmas, Mr Ford arrived. The schoolmaster, Mr Ogilvie, had been most secretive about the exact date of the Inspector's visit, but Elizabeth had her informants and was not taken completely by surprise when the day arrived for the ordeal.

Mr Ford had visited Eisdalsa on many occasions and knew Ogilvie to be a strict teacher whose discipline could not be faulted. The children were always well drilled in their bible pieces and he had no quarrel with the standard of reading and writing. Indeed, over the years, he had come to expect a high level of achievement from the public schools in the area.

He had spent the previous night lodging with the Ogilvies and was disturbed to hear from the schoolmaster that, because of the insistence of the School Board that the village children should have their own schoolroom on Seileach, he had been obliged to appoint a probationer teacher to take care of the Eisdalsa Island school. According to Mr Ogilvie's wife, Ellen, the girl was rather flighty, and not a lot of learning was taking place. She hinted that there had been complaints from some of the parents, although Ogilvie himself was reluctant to discuss this point. He had, however, intimated that perhaps Miss Duncan's work was unconventional and consequently not up to the required standard. If that were indeed the case, then it would be for Mr Ford to report the matter and have her dismissed.

The Inspector clambered carefully out of the ferry boat, exchanging a cheerful greeting with a group of stevedores who were loading slate from the pier.

He was a well-known figure on the Island, and instantly recognisable in this setting. His clothes, in complete contrast to the apparel of the quarrymen, were what was considered proper for a government servant.

The dark suit was of fine broadcloth, while the linen was spotless and freshly starched. His boots, appropriate for the rural areas in which he worked, were of the finest leather and so highly polished that no speck of mud dared linger long upon them.

A high forehead and aquiline nose, upon which perched a pair of rimless, pince-nez spectacles, left the observer in no doubt about the man's intellectual status. Mr Ford tried hard to maintain the aloof attitude which, he felt, was expected of a government official, but he was quite unable to disguise the fact that he was a kindly human being. If he wished to appear serious, his wide-set grey eyes and the upward curving creases at the sides of his mouth betrayed his natural good humour. Indeed, there were times when he was hard put to it to refrain from bursting into gales of helpless laughter, particularly when in the company of children.

The School Inspector accepted the deference paid to his position by the teachers whom he visited, but did not encourage it. He was pleasantly surprised therefore by his initial encounter with Elizabeth Duncan.

At first glance it seemed that the class was without a teacher at all. There were several small groups of children standing out front. On the left, a single boy stood alone. To his right there were two girls and beyond them three boys. A group of two boys and two girls made up a fourth set and finally three girls and two boys were gathered on the far right.

Elizabeth was conducting a game of numbers, from the body of the room. The groups out front were added, subtracted, multiplied and divided, by the simple expedient of moving the children about and counting the results. Even the infants, at the front of the class, could make their calculations by this method.

So absorbed were the participants in this exercise that it was a while before anyone noticed that Mr Ford had arrived. Having stood for some moments inside the door, which he had been obliged to close for himself, he had been able to assess the activity in the classroom unobserved. He found Elizabeth's method simple but effective. Most interesting was the fact that, although there was much movement and some discourse between the pupils, in no way could the class be said to be disorderly.

At last, Elizabeth's attention was drawn to the presence of the School Inspector. She moved towards him in a friendly manner, her hand outstretched in greeting.

'Mr Ford? How good of you to call upon us.' She turned to the children, motioning them to return to their places. When everyone was still, she commanded, 'Children, let us welcome Mr Ford.'

In unison the class chanted, 'Good morning, Mr Ford. Welcome to Eisdalsa.'

'Good morning, children,' he replied and beamed upon them.

'I am afraid that I have had no experience of a school inspection, sir,' said Elizabeth. 'Perhaps you will tell me what you wish to see of the children's work?'

'If you will set your pupils some quiet individual work, I will examine your log and glance at the older children's exercise books.'

Each child had already been given a suitable task to cover this eventuality. Soon absolute silence reigned as the Inspector studied the attendance register.

'There seem to be an inordinate number of absentees, particularly in certain families,' he commented. 'What is the explanation for so much truancy?'

'I fear that some families are so poor that the older children are sent to work in the quarries, to help to feed their younger brothers and sisters.'

'The fathers are out of work, so the children are taken from school and made to labour in their place? Pray what is the logic of that?'

'There is none,' replied Elizabeth, 'except that a ten-year-old child works for less money than his father!'

'It is against the law for a child to be kept from school under the age of eleven. Parents of these children should be summoned.'

'They could not pay the fine. By committing the father to gaol, you would condemn the whole family to starvation.'

He gave her a long, penetrating stare over the top of his pince-nez, but ended the discussion by saying, 'Let us see what progress has been made by those who do attend.'

Mr Ford looked first at the books of the older children, already laid out for his inspection. Then, suspecting that he was seeing only the best, he began to walk around the room. He glanced here and there, at a slate of one of the younger children or the exercise book of an older pupil to check on the work that was actually going on at the moment. From time to time, he stopped to speak to a particular child. In Dougie McGillivray's book he found an intricate drawing of what appeared to be a piece of machinery.

'What is this, boy?' he asked. 'Where in the curriculum are you required to undertake work such as this?'

Dougie was quick to reply. 'It is an extension of a geometry lesson, sir. See, here is constructed a right-angled triangle, and there a perpendicular; an isosceles triangle here, and a circle whose arcs form the edges of a hexagon.'

Mr Ford was impressed, not only at the knowledge that the boy had of what he had been doing, but by the neatness and accuracy which the exercise displayed.

Mary McCulloch was reading a small book of Latin poetry. He asked her to read aloud, which she did in a sweet voice with inflections which showed clearly that she understood the meaning of the text. Nevertheless he asked her to translate, and was rewarded for his pains with a rendering which was poetic in itself.

Not all the children performed so well. Peter Lugas, the Factor's son, relied upon his father's position and his own strong fist to gain ascendancy in the schoolroom. His work was often copied from his more timid classmates, so that the contents of his exercise book belied his limited amount of learning. Under the direct scrutiny of the Inspector, however, he was made to look foolish.

'I see from your writing that you are describing the crops which are grown in the West Indies. On which of the islands would you expect to find sugar cane?'

It was a reasonable question for one who had apparently investigated the subject. Peter turned bright pink, then white, and in a strangled voice ventured, 'Madagascar?'

There was a titter from those around him, his immediate contemporaries. Even Charlie joined in, although he did not understand the joke. Peter Lugas scowled at the most vulnerable of his classmates. He would soon wipe the smile off Charlie's face, just let him wait!

Beginning with the very young children, Mr Ford now picked on one pupil after another to recite a passage from the bible. As each stood and said his or her piece, it was clear they had been well drilled, not only in the words, but in their rendition. Whether or not Mr Ford was favourably impressed it was impossible to tell. He listened attentively to the children and occasionally made a note against a name, but his comments were few and unrevealing.

Charlie and Dougie had worked so very hard on Psalm 23 that it would have been an anticlimax had Mr Ford failed to call upon Charlie. The great gangling body stood out so from the other children's that it was impossible for the Inspector to overlook him.

'Now, young man, what have you to recite to me?'

Charlie rose to his feet, all his confidence fading away under the steely eye of the School Inspector.

'Well then, come along, boy, what are you going to recite?'

Charlie glanced around, his gaze resting at last upon Dougie. His friend mouthed the first line. Charlie immediately responded.

'"The Lord is my shepherd
I shall not want.
He maketh me to lie down in . . ."'

'Cow dung,' whispered Peter Lugas.

'"He maketh me to lie down in cow dung,"' Charlie repeated. The children sniggered, and Mr Ford looked very surprised.

Desperate now, Charlie turned again to Dougie.

'"Still waters,"' prompted his friend.

'"He leadeth me beside the still waters.

'He restoreth my soul.

'Yea, though I walk through the valley of the shadow of death . . ."'

He liked that part.

'". . . Though I walk through the valley of death . . ."'

'I will catch no bed-bugs,' prompted Peter, helpfully.

'That's not right, miss,' cried out Charlie! 'That's not what I learnt!'

As the large boy, tears streaming down his face, fled from the room, Peter Lugas was the only person smiling. The rest of the children were aghast.

Elizabeth intervened. 'I am afraid that Charlie is overcome by the situation,' she explained. 'He has been working very hard on his piece. I do hope you will forgive him?'

Mr Ford had already summed up the situation. The boy was so noticeable, it was curious that he had been absent from the class on previous occasions. He walked to the front of the room and picked up the register. Turning back to a date when he had previously visited the school, he searched for Charlie's name. He checked over several weeks and then turned to Elizabeth.

'That young man may not have a retentive memory, but at least his attendance is one hundred per cent.' To himself he added, So why have I never seen him before?

Elizabeth hesitated to tell him what the children had made clear to her. Charlie had been kept out of the way on Mr Ford's previous visits. She was concerned that the Inspector should understand about Charlie.

'He has difficulty with his lessons, but a more helpful and willing boy it would be difficult to find. It is doubtful if he will ever learn to read and write, except with personal tuition. This I am willing to provide, but I am afraid that his mother could not afford the cost.'

Mr Ford was surprised; Miss Duncan did not appear to be a mercenary woman.

'Would you be obliged to charge so much?' he asked.

'I would not charge him at all,' she responded. 'The terms of my contract demand that all additional fees are paid to Mr Ogilvie. It is he who insists upon ten shillings for a term.'

'How much of that would be your portion?' Mr Ford was very interested now. He had long suspected that Ogilvie was less than honest in his dealings with the School Board, and could recall no reference to additional fees in all the years that he had visited Eisdalsa.

'I am to receive what Mr Ogilvie deems to be appropriate.' Elizabeth was feeling more than a little nervous. She spoke only the truth, but had no wish to antagonise the dominie. He would be a dangerous foe.

'At present there are only four pupils having private tuition. Mary is taking Latin and German, the McNeil boys are doing extra study in order to catch up in mathematics, and I have one older pupil, the doctor's apprentice, who is to begin Latin and Greek after the New Year.'

Mr Ford wrote for some moments in his notebook. At last he looked up at her. His thin face broke suddenly into a beaming smile.

'I think that I have seen enough, Miss Duncan. Thank you for your help.'

He walked towards the door, pausing to turn to the class when he reached the threshold.

'Good day to you, children.'

There was a scuffling and scraping of benches as the children rose to their feet.

'Good day, Mr Ford.'

To Elizabeth, who had accompanied him to the schoolroom door, the Inspector said, 'My report will be made to the School Board which meets in January. Why Mr Ogilvie has you down as a probationer I cannot understand. I see by your letter of application that you have taught for several years.'

'I think that, quite rightly, Mr Ogilvie wished to ascertain the quality of my work before making my appointment permanent.'

'I shall certainly make my own views plain to the Board,' declared Mr Ford. 'Au revoir, Miss Duncan, I believe we shall meet again, very soon.'

As the following day would be Christmas Eve, Elizabeth dismissed the class at lunchtime.

'Now, children, tomorrow is Saturday but it is also Christmas Eve. Christmas is a very special birthday. Who can tell me whose birthday it is?'

'Please, miss,' piped up a little voice from the front. 'Please, miss, mine, miss!'

'Is it indeed, Angus?' Elizabeth laughed and the older children joined in too. 'Then we must all wish Angus a very happy birthday! Who else has a birthday tomorrow?'

Kirsty McGillivray answered. 'Jesus, Miss.'

'And how are we to wish Jesus a happy birthday?' Elizabeth enquired.

There was silence. Every shining pair of eyes showed an interest in finding the answer.

'Why, by going to church and singing carols,' Elizabeth declared. 'And, before we leave school today, we will sing the special carol that we have been learning this week. The one which begins: "Hark the herald angels sing".'

The sound of childish voices rang out joyfully across the Island, gladdening the hearts of the men at work in the harbour, and the women hanging out their washing in the square. Jamie McGillivray hobbled to his door to listen, his face lighting up with pleasure when at last, the singing over, he saw his small daughter come tumbling out of the schoolroom with a dozen other children at her heels. William heard the carol from his office desk, and David, who had just landed from the ferry, was in time to hear the last verses and to witness the headlong flight of that mass of small humanity which had been set free for the holiday.

He reached the schoolroom just as Elizabeth emerged, her arms full as usual. His offer of help with her burden was gratefully accepted. He accompanied her to the door of the bothy, and stepped inside to lay down the pile of books and papers.

It was the first time he had seen the room since its transformation. It was as neat and cosy as anyone could wish. The combination of wood smoke, beeswax and lavender was familiar, and yet unique to Elizabeth. The scent would always remind him of this moment.

'Your house is very comfortable,' he said, taking in the pictures, fine china, ornaments and the handsome pieces of furniture.

'It will be better still when William's men build me my new bedroom and a separate larder closet. He has promised to begin the work after Hogmanay, when the quarries will not be busy.'

'When did your furniture arrive?'

'It was delivered last week, the day that the steamer developed a fault and was obliged to stay tied up overnight. Mr McIntyre himself saw to the delivery. He also brought me a letter from the Steamship Company with the compensation for my accident.'

'I trust that they were generous? It was, after all, a serious accident caused by gross negligence. You might have been killed.'

'I think fifty pounds was very generous.' Elizabeth reached down the banker's draft to show him. 'Perhaps you can tell me, is there a branch of the Royal Bank in Oban?'

'Fifty, is that all?' exclaimed David. 'Why, that is a miserable sum from so wealthy a company. I trust you have not sent an acknowledgement?'

'By return.' Elizabeth looked worried. What was David implying? Had she made some terrible error?

'Oh, dear, that could damage your case,' he rejoined. 'However, a good lawyer could plead ignorance of the law on your part. You really should have spoken to William or myself before taking such a precipitate step.'

'But I don't understand, what I have done wrong.' The girl was quite mystified. 'I have received compensation and I have written to thank them for it. What else should I have done?'

'But it is not enough, don't you see? You should have demanded more, even threatened to take the matter to court.'

'Fifty pounds seemed more than adequate to me,' she insisted. 'After all, I was scarcely hurt at all.'

'Sufficiently so that I was obliged to attend you through the night and lodge you in my mother's house for a week!'

'If it is your own compensation you are concerned about,' she retorted, 'I am sure that my money will cover your bill, whatever it is.'

'Oh, dear,' David fumed, exasperated, 'I do not intend to send you a bill. I was pleased to be of service. But I do not wish for others to take advantage of your innocence.'

'I do not agree that any advantage has been taken.' His persistence only made her the more determined. 'I am perfectly satisfied with fifty pounds.'

'Oh, well, you will just have to leave the matter in my hands. I will speak to my solicitor. I have to see him upon other business next week.'

'Dr Beaton,' Elizabeth said icily, 'I have no wish to pursue the affair further, and I should be obliged if you would not mention it again.'

Her words stung him into silence for a moment, but quickly recovering his composure he replied, 'As you wish.'

It was obvious that he was humouring her.

'But I think you will see it differently when you have had time to reflect upon the matter.'

He was filled with admiration for her mettlesome nature, and despite his irritation at her refusal of his advice, found himself even more enamoured of her.

There was an awkward silence. David fumbled uncomfortably with his hat, which he had laid down beside the books on entering.

'I was on my way to see Mr McGillivray.'

'Annie tells me he is making excellent progress.' Elizabeth's tone was still frosty. 'I believe I saw him actually standing at his door this afternoon.'

'The operation on his head seems to have been a success. His leg will always prevent him from taking active work in the quarries, I fear, but at least his mind is unimpaired. For that he must be thankful.'

'Yes, indeed. Poor Annie has more than enough troubles to contend with.'

'Will you be attending the Hogmanay Ball in the Drill Hall?'

'I believe so, is not everyone invited?'

'Oh, yes indeed, but I had hoped to be permitted to escort you myself.'

'I think that will not be necessary,' she replied. 'Mr Whylie has already offered his services.'

'Oh, I see.' For a moment, David was at a loss for words. He had assumed that she would be expecting his invitation. 'Well then, I trust you will save a dance for me?'

'That is as maybe,' she retorted, anxious now for him to be gone. His interference in her personal affairs had infuriated her. He treated her as a fool, with no mind of her own. How dare he!

Abruptly, she closed the door on the doctor and for the rest of the evening chastised herself for her behaviour. David was probably acting in her own best interests, she told herself. She would try to make reparation for her rudeness when next they met.

*   *   *

The quarry office was cold. The rain, which all morning had been driving in sheets before a north-westerly gale, was causing smoke to back down the chimney and William had been obliged to douse the fire or suffocate.

There was a tap on the door before it was thrown open and two figures, wrapped up tightly against the weather, all but fell into the room.

Malcolm Logie unwound his long wool muffler, and would have removed his overcoat had not William warned him, 'You had best keep your coat on, man, it is very cold in here. I have had to put out the fire because of the smoke.'

'Oh, aye,' laughed Logie's companion, Douglas Brown. 'I mind the times I had to do the same, when I worked here with Mr McPhee.'

'There must be some way of improving matters,' protested William. 'A cowl perhaps?'

'I believe everything that can be, has been tried,' said Logie. 'The fact is, when the wind is in the north-west, nothing will keep it out. Most of the cottages have the same problem.'

'I feel sure there must be a solution,' insisted William. 'However, it was not to talk of smoky chimneys that I have brought you here today.'

He motioned to the two foremen to make themselves comfortable. Producing a thick pile of documents, he proceeded to summarise the position of the quarries, as shown from his investigations.

'As I suggested, when I first arrived in November, I have spent most of my time going over the transactions of the last few years and also examining the working methods which have been applied. While it is true that the lessees have been at fault in refusing to invest capital, it is also the case that the quarries themselves have been working at less than their full potential output. There is no coherent plan, and as a result one set of workings tends to interfere with others, instead of all the faces working to their mutual benefit.'

The two quarrymen looked defensive.

'We have only operated under orders,' Logie protested, angered that his integrity was in question.

'Now then,' William tried to smooth ruffled feathers, 'this is no time for recriminations. I am simply pointing out the reasons why there must be changes in the way we work.'

Douglas Brown was keen to understand what William was driving at. He had realised for a long time that the operation could be better handled. He too gave Logie a restraining word.

'Let us hear what Mr Whylie has to say first, Malcolm, you can make your protests later.'

William looked with gratitude at the man from Seileach. He had had little opportunity to get to know his foremen well, but had seen enough of Brown's work to realise that the man was a valuable asset to the

Company. It was understandable that Hugh Beaton had sought out Douglas Brown's son, Michael, to be his apprentice. The lad must surely have inherited his father's intelligence.

'Let us look at the faces which have been most recently opened,' William resumed. 'What was the first operation which had to be carried out?'

'Well, before we could expose the new seams, we had to clear out the rubbish from previous workings,' said Logie.

'And if I were to suggest that pumps were available to empty the two southern quarries, how soon would we be winning slate there?'

'It would take weeks to remove the waste slate that has been used as infill,' Logie muttered sullenly.

'Precisely,' said William. 'In other words, we have no proper means of disposing of our waste rock. We fill in behind us as we go, which is all well and good until the day comes when we wish to go deeper into one of the old workings. Supposing we were to have a sudden demand for roofing slate – an order, say, for a million slates?'

The other two men exchanged glances. The Englishman must be out of his head. Where would they be getting an order for a million slates?

'We could only recover the old quarries at the south end if we had the pumps,' Logie argued, 'so it's not worth worrying about.'

'At the moment orders for slate are on the low side,' William agreed, 'but that is because we are relying entirely on the home market. Around the world, great cities are growing up in places where roofing materials in the European tradition are unavailable. There is no slate in the West Indies. In Australia and New Zealand, the mineral resources remain untouched because of the remoteness of the sites and the lack of transport. While those countries are trying to solve their local problems, the people who have been transported out there to do the work need housing – and of a kind that they are used to. We should be supplying the roofs for those buildings.'

Brown nodded solemnly. 'When I was a lad, the old Marquis had connections in Canada and America . . . mostly friends who had acquired land and were building new industries, housing the thousands of emigrants who were going out there seeking a new life. The quarries could not supply enough slates at that time.'

'What happened to that market?'

'As our production declined, because of the lack of interest of the new Marquis and the poor management, contracts were not fulfilled. I suppose that the orders went to our competitors.' Brown thought for a few minutes and then added, 'I am told that the Ballachulish quarries have been sending large shipments to Philadelphia in recent months.'

'In other words,' suggested William, 'there is a market for our slate, and at any time we could find ourselves under pressure to fulfil an increased demand.'

'It would take a month or more to open up any new workings,' Logie pointed out.

'As far as I can see,' declared William, 'the most important problem we have is how to dispose of the waste slate, without filling in potential future sites as we have been doing.'

'In the past,' volunteered Douglas Brown, 'the waste was used to build the causeway linking two small islands to Seileach . . . the Village on the other side is actually built on rubble. In the end such dumping was stopped because there was a possibility of the harbour becoming blocked.'

The harbour was a most important feature of the Island. Deep enough for the craft which carried cargo back and forth between the islands and the Clyde, it provided shelter from even the most severe gales. The heavy slate-stone could not be moved by any method other than the sea, and to load such a cargo a safe haven was essential.

'If we cannot refill the quarries, and we can no longer dump in the channel, what can we do with the waste?' Logie's question was rhetorical, but William's answer was to give a practical solution.

'We extend the railway, by a series of causeways, to carry the waste away to the western shore. We'll build a ramp out into the sea, and run the trucks far out, before dumping at low tide. Any movement by the tide will carry the rubble away to the south. Thus there will be no fear of clogging up the shipping channel.'

William went to a freshly drawn map of the Island which he had spread out on the drawing table. He showed the two quarrymen where his new, high-level railway track would go. He pointed out how the track would cross the Island by a series of bridges, so as to avoid interfering with the present system of rails which already carried the finished slates down to the harbour.

'We can use what we move out of the southern quarries to begin building the causeways,' Brown suggested enthusiastically. 'We will have to put in a new track to those quarries anyway.'

'We still have to solve the problem of pumping the quarries,' Logie protested. 'Where is the money to come from for the new pumps?'

The past years, working on a miserably low budget, having to go cap in hand to McPhee for every chisel, every bolt and hammer, had made him cynical. Why should Mr Whylie have any greater resources than his predecessor?

'Already I have someone scouting for pumps at the Glasgow docks,' William informed them. 'I have a promise from Sir Alexander's agent that funds will be made available to invest in better equipment. Provided we are not greedy in our demands and can justify any expenditure that we make, I believe there will be no problem.'

Logie was three paces ahead in thought by now. 'If we use the waste slate piled in One and Two workings, we can begin immediately on constructing your ramp. Then, when we have pumped the old quarries dry, we will be ready to build the causeway. At least we shall be able to keep more men in work over the slack season.'

William still had to persuade the agent to invest the initial funding, in order to get the men back to work. He was not sure whether Campbell would agree to this. He would have to understand that, until the clearance was completed, no further slate would be produced. At least William now had two enthusiastic foremen, ready to do their best to make the scheme succeed.

'Well, gentlemen, with your agreement I think I can proceed,' he decided. 'I have to take a trip to Glasgow to see some pumping equipment. I shall use the opportunity to visit our masters, and put to them what we have been discussing.' Seeing the doubt beginning to creep back into Logie's eyes, he hastened to add, 'I shall, of course, keep Mr Lugas informed of what we are proposing, and will be making a report to His Lordship in the same vein.'

'Shall we see you at the Hogmanay ceilidh?' asked Douglas Brown. 'It has always been the custom for the Quarry Manager to chair the meeting.'

'So I am informed by Archie MacLean,' laughed William. 'I believe that I am to make the speech of welcome to the New Year?'

'Aye, and you'll be required to give us a song too, no doubt!' joined in Malcolm Logie.

'So long as it does not have to be in the Gaelic!' William had been struggling with the language he had set himself to learn, but his competence did not as yet stretch to singing the traditional songs. He would leave that to his fellow workers!

5

O n New Year's Eve, it was customary for the islanders to gather in the building which the old Marquis had provided as a Drill Hall for the Volunteers. This was the citizens' army which Queen Victoria had been obliged to raise in order to protect her more remote boundaries from yet another threat of invasion by the French. In recent years, so many of the regular regiments had been distributed among Her Majesty's territories overseas that there were insufficient troops to quell any onslaught upon mainland Britain. To a man, the quarriers had offered their services, and the activities of the Volunteers had become an integral part of the life of Eisdalsa.

As compensation for time given freely by the Volunteers, the Drill Hall had been made available to the islanders as a general meeting place. It now served a number of functions which were in no way connected with the defence of the realm!

Hogmanay was one of the few occasions when islanders and those from Eisdalsa Village across the Sound joined forces to celebrate.

For an hour or more, a series of small boats had been carrying folk across from Seileach. The Island women had been cooking all day, while the men were told off to carry in the ale and the whisky, and to hang garlands of leaves and coloured paper flowers which the children had been busy making all the week. Elizabeth had shown a few of the older pupils how to construct Chinese lanterns in which could be fixed real candles. When the festivities began, these would be lit and carefully strung up on high.

She had put on her one evening gown for the occasion. The richly glowing emerald velvet set off her auburn ringlets to perfection. Applying a little powder for the first time since her arrival, she considered for a moment what the reaction of some of the members of the Ladies' Guild might be. Quickly she brushed the thought aside. Everyone dressed up and wore powder for a party. It was only polite to make the best of oneself.

The vision of loveliness displayed before him gave William Whylie the kind of jolt which most men experience only once in a lifetime. Against the brightly glowing coals in the open stove, her auburn hair shone like a flaming torch. Her green eyes sparkled in the soft lamplight and the rich colour of her gown set off the swan-like delicacy of her neck and shoulders. He was entranced.

Elizabeth, in return, was not disappointed with her escort. William had pondered over the question of formal evening attire, but had at last decided upon a simple dark suit, made festive by a fine lawn shirt with ruff, and an elaborately embroidered waistcoat. The rich colours of the latter, a combination of red, purple and silver, although only glimpsed beneath the folds of the sombre jacket, were sufficient to set off his dark curly hair and rugged manly features. She had never before thought of him as handsome.

'How fortunate that you are wearing green.' William smiled as he brought his hand from behind his back and revealed a corsage of pink and white gardenias. 'I hoped that the colours would be suitable.'

Elizabeth took the flowers, unable to conceal her amazement.

'But where on earth . . . ?'

'As luck would have it, I was paying my respects to Mr Lugas this morning and was able to beg a posy from His Lordship's conservatory.'

'Why, I believe these are the first flowers I have set eyes upon since I came here,' she cried. 'What a delightful surprise!'

She ran to the night stand and fumbled in the mirror drawer for a moment. 'Will you help me to fasten it, please?'

Handing him a small gold pin, with an artless gesture she indicated a spot above her left breast where she wished the flowers to be fixed. As he stepped forward to carry out his commission, William was made aware of her heady perfume, a mixture of attar of roses and a faint whiff of the lavender which had been packed away with her gown. It seemed quite natural for them to stand together there while he performed his simple task.

Resisting the temptation to kiss her, and make her his own right then, William led her to the door, where she paused for a moment to hand him her stole.

Solicitously he wrapped the finely woven garment around her bare shoulders, allowing his hands to rest upon them for a moment longer than was absolutely necessary.

Together, they stepped out into the cold night.

They made their way towards the Hall where already the music had struck up. The room was full when they arrived, William having been warned to wait to make his entrance. As Chairman for the evening he was to receive the honours. He had decided not to warn Elizabeth, lest she refuse to accompany him.

The small orchestra, consisting of two fiddles and an accordion, struck up a chord as William and Elizabeth entered, and then began to play a popular waltz tune. William led his partner on to the floor and they moved gracefully together to the music. After the pair had made one round of the room, other couples joined in and soon the hall was full of whirling dancers.

William danced well and Elizabeth, having overcome her momentary dismay at being the centre of attention, was soon enjoying herself. When the band struck up a reel, he excused himself, but Elizabeth would have none of it.

'You cannot live in the Highlands and not learn to dance the Highland way!' she assured him. Soon the sets were formed, and the dancers spinning away to the distinctive rhythms, augmented now by the pipes of Archie MacLean.

As she was whirled in and out of the mêlée by her partners, Elizabeth caught sight of David, standing stiffly behind his mother's chair. She waved in passing, catching his eye, and he responded with a tight smile.

In a corner near the door, his crutches thrust out of sight beneath the table, Jamie McGillivray sat surrounded by his workmates who were doing their best to include their crippled friend in the festivities. He could participate only in the drinking, but was making a very good effort in that direction. Annie, who sat beside him, watched anxiously as, time after time, his tankard was emptied and refilled. The children had made up their own set and were happily dancing to one side of the room, Kirsty and Dougie among them. Annie smiled when she saw their happy faces. The troubles of the past weeks seemed to fall away as she watched the colourful scene.

The women had dressed up their grey or black Sunday gowns with ribbons and bright scarves. The men had forsaken the moleskin trousers of the quarry for the kilt, in a multitude of colourful tartans. Predominant among them was the dark green and black of the Campbells of Argyll, but McKenzies and Stewarts, MacLeans and McDougals all added their own particular hues. Setting off their kilts, the men wore frilled shirts and tartan stockings in whose tops glinted the jewelled and silver handles of the *sgian dubh*. Some even sported sporrans and velvet jackets with silver buttons. As the evening wore on, the jackets were abandoned and the shirt sleeves rolled up. At the same time, the women discarded their scarves and shawls, and were to be seen openly mopping perspiration from their glowing brows, ignoring all those rules of etiquette so carefully studied for this very special occasion. Painstakingly curled ringlets fell straight, and delicately perched chignons became dislodged. Kilts and sporrans flew as couples gyrated in time with the music, which became more and more frantic as the hour of midnight approached.

Elizabeth had danced every dance, so it seemed. She had been handed on from William to David, to Malcolm Logie, and back again to David, who always managed to be hovering nearby when each dance ended.

William, having lost his partner, found his way to the McGillivray court where he had noticed that Annie sat on the edge of the group, looking on. He invited her to dance and soon the two of them were swinging around the room to an energetic waltz tune.

'Are you enjoying the dance, Mrs McGillivray?' he asked.

For the first time that evening Annie really felt that she was.

'It is a rare sight to see so many of our friends and neighbours in carefree mood,' she remarked. 'There has been little enough to rejoice about in the year that is past. Let us hope that there will be something better to look forward to in 1877.'

'Surely hope is what Hogmanay is all about?' suggested William.

'Yes, I suppose it is,' she replied, smiling.

As they swung together in the dance, he tightened his grip on her waist and lowered his head to hers, that she might hear him above the noise.

'I believe that I may have some good news for your husband,' he had to shout, 'will you ask him to come to the company office, as soon as he is able to walk so far?'

'He has already managed to reach Number One quarry where his crew are working,' Annie said. 'I will tell him to come in the morning.'

'Not this morning!' exclaimed William, as the quarry bell sounded out the New Year. 'But tomorrow, by all means.'

The dancing had stopped. There was much milling about and toing and froing as partners, families and friends gathered together, for the joining of hands and the singing of 'Auld Lang Syne'.

Elizabeth found herself standing with William on one side and David on the other. It was David who was the first to demand a kiss, but William was quick to follow suit. With the singing and the cheering ended, it was time for him to step on to the platform to propose the toast to the New Year. As he began to speak, David, complaining of the need for a breath of air, steered Elizabeth away from the throng to the rear of the hall.

'My good friends,' William began, 'although my time here has been short, it is as a friend that you have welcomed me to your Island of Eisdalsa. My friends, the past year has brought great burdens to some of you. You have endured sickness, injury, despair at the lack of work. There is nothing worse than the fear of poverty. At the turn of the year, we all look forward to better things. A spirit of hopefulness is in the air.

'I believe that this New Year holds many surprises for us all. When I tell you that I dare to hope for better things, it is in the certain knowledge that I have an able, experienced and dedicated workforce behind me. Men who, with God's help, will come out of this terrible depression with their heads held high. I believe that on this same occasion next year, we will have much greater reaason to give thanks for our good fortune, and wish each other: *bliadhna mhath ur, slainte mhath!*'

'*Slainte mhath*, good health!' came the cry from every side. The toast was drunk and the music began once more. While the older folk began to move to the sides of the hall to rest their weary feet, the youngsters set themselves to dance until first light.

William, his speech over, looked for his partner in vain. Neither Elizabeth nor David was to be seen. He moved to a group of grey heads, amongst which he had recognised those of Archie MacLean and his wife.

'Archie, *de ghabhas tusa?*' William asked if he would take a drink.

'*Uisge beatha ma 'se do thoil e.*'

'Mairead?'

The jolly woman who kept house for William laughed at his use of her Gaelic name.

'Och, Maggie will do fine, Mr Whylie,' she said, 'and I will have a small whisky too, thank you.'

'I do not recall asking for a "small" whisky,' protested Archie.

'And I certainly did not interpret your reply so!' William was still laughing when he reached the bar to order the drinks.

David had persuaded Elizabeth to walk a little, to cool down after the dancing. The night was clear. Silver stars pierced the deep blue canopy above them. The moon, low and bright in the south-west, gave the whitened cottages an eerie glow and cast long shadows across the frost-crisp grass.

Beside one of the sea-filled quarries they stopped, and leaned against the barrier which prevented the unwary from slipping down the steep bank. All the starkness and untidiness of the workings was covered by the water, and the reflections from the surface produced their own sparkling fairyland of light.

Elizabeth sighed. 'It is so beautiful and peaceful tonight. No one would believe how different the Island is on a working day.'

'One often hears the islanders talk of the magic of Eisdalsa,' observed David. 'It is only on a night like this that one can appreciate their meaning.'

'I begin to understand what a hold this place has upon the people who are born here,' Elizabeth confided. 'I suppose that is why, in the end, you have decided to stay?'

'It may have played its part in my decision,' his voice was modulated and deep, 'but there was an even stronger attraction.'

Elizabeth shifted uneasily. She sensed his mood and hastened to change the subject.

'I met Michael Brown when I was over in the Village last week,' she said. 'He tells me that his apprenticeship papers are now all in order. It seems he cannot wait to begin working for his scholarship in the New Year. Perhaps we can consult William, and between us draw up a plan of study for him? When do you think he should apply to the University?'

'They will not consider his application until he is sixteen,' David replied, somewhat impatiently. 'In any case, in the Classics he is far behind most privately educated boys. I suppose that in Mathematics and Science he may be further advanced.'

'I have suggested that Mr Ogilvie, or even the minister, might be better tutors than I,' Elizabeth continued, 'but he seems determined that I shall be his teacher.'

'Any young man with red blood in his veins would say the same. How do you suppose Ogilvie or McCulloch compare with you in Michael's eyes?'

David could not see her blush in the moonlight as he turned her towards him. The look in her eyes warned him he was being too hasty. He dropped his hands and grasped the rail fiercely in an effort to control his passion.

'I meant to tell you. When I visited my solicitor to have the apprenticeship papers drawn up, I discussed the matter of your compensation.'

David was quite unprepared for the vehemence of her response. 'I wish you had not,' Elizabeth said harshly. 'I told you that I had no intention of discussing the matter further.'

'You must forgive me for being anxious on your behalf.' He put his hand over hers. 'I hope that soon you will allow me to take all your problems upon myself.'

'Why, I . . .' She did not know how to fend off that which was to follow.

'Don't you understand? Do you not know why I decided to remain here for good? It was so that I might be near you, share my life with you. Elizabeth, I am asking you to be my wife.'

She was dismayed. She had come to look upon David, in matters concerning the school, as a champion in her battle with Ogilvie. She saw now that what she had imagined were the attentions of a good friend had held a much deeper meaning.

'Dr Beaton . . . David . . .' She drew back, deliberately putting distance between them. 'You do me too much honour in asking me to become your wife. We have known one another for such a very short time.' Allowing him no opportunity to interrupt, she continued, 'I cannot agree that I am in any way responsible for your decision to remain at Eisdalsa. Please tell me it is not so!'

By his silence, the doctor confirmed her fears.

Elizabeth continued, 'David, please do not ask me to make such an important decision in haste.'

'I have loved you, from the moment I set eyes upon you,' he declared. 'Surely you must have guessed what was in my thoughts?'

She had found him attractive certainly, but never once had she considered that he regarded her as other than a patient and a friend. His declaration filled her with consternation.

'I have seen you at work, and greatly admire your skill as a physician. It may be that you have interpreted wrongly the esteem in which I hold you.' How was she to tell him that she did not love him? 'I do not yet know you well enough to consent to share the rest of my life with you.'

David was not about to accept rejection out of hand.

'I fear that I have been a little too precipitate. You naturally think that I am carried away by the atmosphere, and the fact that we are alone together at last. I feel sure that on reflection you will come to appreciate the sincerity of my feelings toward you, and look more favourably upon my proposal.'

How was she to convince him that his proposal was unacceptable without hurting his pride?

'Please let us continue to be friends, as we have been. I too have a career, about which I care a great deal. I would like to give my full attention to the school for the present.'

Wisely, David refrained from uttering the disparaging remark which leapt into his thoughts. No woman with any sense would turn down a proposal of marriage in order to follow her profession! Elizabeth was simply using those feminine wiles of which he had often heard. She would soon tire of the schoolroom and the obnoxious Ogilvie. Then she would be only too pleased to accept his offer.

'Come,' he said, as though their conversation had never taken place, 'the night is cold. We had best be getting back into the warm.'

He gave her his arm to lean upon. Together, in silence, they returned to the hall.

Through the open doorway came the sound of singing. A mellow female voice soared in warm, vibrant melody. Soon, the singer was joined by a chorus of voices, singing and humming, like the sound of the waves on the shore. When the music ended there was silence for a few seconds and then the whole hall erupted in wild acclaim. Abruptly the music changed to a lilting working ditty, such as the fishermen would sing as they hauled in the nets. Everyone joined in the chorus and cheered as the music came to an end.

Now it was the turn of Archie MacLean with his pipes. He played a well-loved lament. Many an eye was filled to overflowing at the sound. Even William, who had no love for the pipe music, was moved to blow his nose loudly as the piper finished his piece.

Suddenly Malcolm Logie leapt on to the platform beside the players and called for silence.

'It is time for our new Manager and Chairman for the evening to do his piece!' he cried. 'Mr Whylie, to the platform, if you please.'

William was hardly taken by surprise, he had been warned that this would happen. When the moment came, however, he was overcome with embarrassment. It was the gentle squeeze Elizabeth gave his arm which encouraged him to step forward. On re-entering the hall, she had found her way to his side, apologising for her absence with the excuse that she had been in need of some fresh air.

William had a quiet word with Spider Campbell, but the fiddler shook his head apologetically and laid down his instrument. Turning to the audience, William explained: 'Your musicians are unable to help me, I am afraid, so you will have to put up with my unaccompanied singing.'

There was a roar of approval. At this stage of the night, the melody and harmony of what was sung had become less and less discernible. A good noise was the main thing!

William began to sing in a fine baritone voice. The tune was a powerful one, and the singer held it well, very well.

'As I walked out on a summer night
All the stars were shining bright . . .'

The words of the 'Cornish Floral Dance' were soon coming to an end. Elizabeth was entranced. She'd had no idea that William was so gifted. She had heard him in church, of course, but this was different. It was a remarkably fine rendering of the song. Even the most parochial of the Scots could not but applaud their Quarry Master.

The fiddle now struck up a well-known Scottish air, and it was Annie McGillivray's voice which rose above the rest.

'Oh where and oh where
Has my Highland laddie gone . . .'

The melody was taken up all around the hall. Even those small children, who had managed to stay awake until this late hour, could join in.

The last notes died and, as if in response to an unspoken order, the islanders began to depart. The musicians packed up their instruments, and the ferrymen gathered together their passengers for the trip across to Seileach.

William, Elizabeth standing close beside him, wished everyone goodbye and exchanged New Year greetings. David, with Morag on his arm, hung back until the crowd had dispersed.

'It has been a great evening,' declared William. 'I must congratulate you on your Scottish hospitality.'

Morag laughed. 'It is surprising how mellow the most cantankerous of us become, with a whisky or two inside us! But you are right, of course. This is the one night of the year when we Scots, whatever our leanings, live and let live. On Sunday there will be those of us needing to repent our excesses, no doubt.'

'Earlier even than that,' agreed David, who anticipated a full surgery on the morrow.

'Good night, Elizabeth.' David held her hand a fraction of a second longer than was necessary. Otherwise there was no indication that anything had passed between them that evening.

'Goodbye, David,' she replied, 'and a Happy New Year.'

Morag and Elizabeth exchanged friendly kisses, and the Beatons, mother and son, passed on into the night.

Jamie and Annie McGillivray had remained until the last. Jamie was having a little difficulty getting to his feet. It had been a long night and he had had several weeks of drinking to catch up with.

'Good night, Mr Whylie.' His speech was slurred, but only slightly. 'It was a fine ceilidh.'

'Good night, McGillivray, did Annie give you my message?'

'Indeed she did, sir. I shall be in your office first thing tomorrow.'

Annie exchanged kisses with Elizabeth. 'Good night, my dear.' She looked intently at the young schoolmistress, sensing her unease. 'Is everything all right?'

'Yes, thank you, Annie dear. A Happy New Year to you both.'

William and Elizabeth were at last alone.

'Did you enjoy your evening?' he asked, as he led her down the steps and on to the path to the bothy.

'Oh, yes indeed,' she replied, for although her conversation with David had disturbed her, the rest of the evening had been most enjoyable. She had been surprised at the quality of the entertainment which the community had been able to muster and the degree of goodwill engendered.

'I have never enjoyed a Hogmanay more,' she declared.

They had reached her house. William opened the door and stepped back that she might enter.

'Thank you so much for escorting me.'

'It was a pleasure, ma'am.' He made an exaggerated bow, took hold of her hand and kissed it.

Elizabeth was charmed by this gallantry. William was such a warm personality. While always ready to take charge of a situation, he nevertheless deferred to her, taking all her proposals very seriously. He could make a woman feel significant in a man's world. He was a man to whom any woman would feel proud to be attached.

Her earlier confrontation with David, which had threatened to mar the evening, had faded from her thoughts.

If William had proposed at that moment she might well have accepted him. She half-expected him to take her in his arms and kiss her. Making no such move, he stood smiling down at her.

'Good night, William,' she said softly.

'Good night, Elizabeth,' he replied, and walked away into the night.

The slaty path was picked out clearly in the moonlight. William took a deep breath, and smiled happily to himself. It had been altogether a most successful evening. He sauntered along, imagining those auburn tresses stroking his cheek and his arms about those delicious shoulders. Then he began humming softly, his feet skipping to the rhythm of the tune. At last, unable to contain his elation for a moment longer, his clear baritone voice turned up to full volume, he burst into the words of the final verse of the 'Floral Dance'.

6

Morag and David arrived at Tigh na Broch at four in the morning. Morag went straight to her bed and remained there for much of the following day.

David found himself unable to sleep. In his mind the events of the previous evening were churning over and over. At one moment he was elated that at last he had made his intentions known to Elizabeth. At the next, he was angry because she had seen fit to refuse him.

He was accustomed to the near-adoration bestowed on him by the women in his household. As the youngest child in the family, affection had been lavished on him throughout his childhood, and Morag, realising there would be no more babies to cherish, had been more reluctant to loosen her apron strings in David's case than she had been with her two elder sons. When John and Angus were sent away to school, David became the centre of attention. Morag and Sheilagh were his devoted slaves. It was therefore hardly surprising that he was nonplussed by Elizabeth's refusal to marry him.

Assailed by doubts about his decision to stay in Eisdalsa, he searched for Joseph Lister's last letter and allowed himself a moment of self-pity, blaming Elizabeth for diverting him from a career in the shadow of his famous colleague. Finally there came to him a ray of hope that Elizabeth had merely followed normal female convention in refusing his offer on the first occasion. He persuaded himself that, given time, she would be happy to marry him. On that positive thought, he fell asleep, but his sleep was chaotic with dreams.

By eight o'clock he was fully awake again, and far too restless to remain in his bed. The house was silent as the grave; even Sheilagh was not yet going about her accustomed duties in the kitchen. He breakfasted upon bread and cheese and a flagon of porter, then went into the study.

The first day of a new year seemed appropriate for putting the practice's finances in order. He set about the matter with a will. From the jumble of notes, written on scraps of paper, and from his father's appointment book, David began to piece together a record of the work carried out during the past year.

A much neater journal, kept by his mother, told him how infrequent had been the payments in return for these services. The amounts of money outstanding were greater than those which had been collected.

Careful to assign treatment given to the appropriate part of his father's scale of charges, David compiled a list of debtors. From this he extracted those who worked for the quarry company. As Medical Officer attached to the Company, Hugh Beaton had an arrangement to collect sums owing at the time when the men were paid. This occurred, so David understood, on each Quarter Day. He set this list aside to be sent to William Whylie.

There remained a number of patients, other than the quarry workers and their families. Again, David extracted from the pile those poor crofting families which might be supported by the Parish. He would need to discuss these with the minister, Mr McCulloch.

The remaining group of patients were from the middle and upper classes. David began, in a meticulous copperplate hand, to address invoices to each of these.

To Mr Lugas, Factor to His Lordship, on account of attendance upon Master Peter Lugas and Mrs Lugas, on 14 April 1876 . . . 10/-

To Mr McCulloch, The Manse, Seileach, on account of attendance upon himself (8 June 1876), Mrs McCulloch (4 August 1876), and Miss Mary McCulloch (10 September 1876) . . . 15/-

To Mr Stephen Bellamy, Ballachuan House, Seileach, on account of attendance upon Walter Leven, gamekeeper, 19 September 1876 . . . 10/-

He worked on, steadily, until Morag disturbed him, late in the afternoon. Surprised to find him so engaged, she peered over his shoulder and read the addresses on the outside of his growing pile of letters.

'There will be some sour faces at the kirk on Sunday, I am thinking,' she observed. 'Your father always hated to ask for his money. I had to force him sometimes to carry out that task!'

'The finances of this practice are in a sorry state, Mama. I must gather in some funds in order to keep things going as they are. On the present reckoning it will not be possible to improve the equipment as I would wish, nor to retain young Michael Brown.'

'Well,' she replied doubtfully, 'you can but try. Do not be surprised if you meet some resistance. There are those who might expect that their debts died with your father. Those who can afford to pay are the most likely to avoid doing so.'

'What of the quarry people?' David queried. 'As I understand it, they are paid each quarter, and medical bills are extracted before payment.'

'That was the case, certainly,' his mother agreed. 'Since sales of slates have been falling off, really since Mr McPhee took over as Manager, the men have been paid only for slates sold, and then only twice a year. It is unlikely that they will receive enough at the next pay-out to keep themselves for the rest of the winter, let alone pay your father's bills.'

'There must be some better method of dealing with the men than this. When my father attended accidents in the quarries, the Company should have been billed.'

'Indeed they were. I saw to that myself. We are still waiting for a response from the Glasgow Office on account of James McGillivray's accident.'

'I must see Whylie, and have the whole matter sorted out.' David snapped the ledger shut in a determined manner, stretched his cramped writing arm and leaned back in the tall-backed leather chair.

'I must tell you, Mother, that yesterday evening I asked Miss Duncan to be my wife,' he confided.

Morag put her hands together in a gesture of delight. 'Oh, my dear, I am so happy for you, what a perfect match! I could not have chosen you a better partner.'

'She refused me.' He spoke quietly, staring out on the grey sea which stretched to the horizon. There it met a mountainous bank of black cloud as gloomy as his thoughts.

'She refused you?' Morag echoed in surprise. 'What reason did she give? Is there someone else that she cares for?'

'She says that she wishes to continue with her career.' David still found it difficult to accept this idea. To Morag, however, it seemed understandable. She laid a consoling hand upon her son's shoulder.

'It is natural, having spent time acquiring the skills of her profession, that an intelligent girl should wish to practise them for a while. The day will come when she will see that there is more to life than the schoolroom. Give her time. Show her that you are willing to wait, no matter how long it takes. After all, you have known each other a very short time. I am sure she will come to love you eventually.'

'She did not say that she did not love me,' he replied. 'But then, neither did she profess to like me either.'

'Come now,' said Morag, as though his hurt was nothing more than a scraped knee, 'Sheilagh has a meal waiting. You know how distressed she becomes if she sees good food going cold!'

William was surprised when informed that Dr Beaton was waiting to see him in the office. He had had to leave Logie to supervise the installation of the new pump in the southern quarry. The first part of his scheme to reopen the old working was well underway. Gordon McIntyre had been as good as his word. Two pumps had been acquired from the breaker's yard in Greenock. The first of these was already beginning to lower the water level in the long-abandoned quarry. With a wave to Logie, William made quickly for the far end of the island.

David was pacing up and down in the office, attempting to keep warm. William greeted him, pleased at the unexpected diversion.

'I am sorry to take you from your work.' David seated himself on the chair offered to him. 'There is a pressing matter of some unpaid bills, I am afraid.'

'Now there is a coincidence! Why, only this morning I was going over some records with Malcolm Logie and came across a series of payments made to Dr Hugh Beaton, nearly a year ago.'

David leaned across the desk to place a sheet of paper before William. 'I have made a list of attendances on behalf of the Company, mainly accidents in the quarries. In addition, this is the list of private attendance on the men and their families. I believe that these sums are deducted from the pay packets at each quarterly pay-out?' David delivered the second paper and sat back expectantly.

William scrutinised both lists without comment, then he too relaxed in his chair.

'This could be difficult,' he began. 'Money owing to you from the Company I can pay by a bank draft, if you will accept it. I am authorised to make such expenditure without reference to Head Office. As for the money owing from the men . . . it seems that there has been very little slate sold this past half year. It is doubtful if they will receive any more than half the usual wage.'

'Despite what some people in the district may have come to believe, this medical practice is not a charitable institution,' David complained.

'I have been toying with some thoughts on the matter of the medical expenses of the men.' William's tone was sympathetic. 'Logie and I were discussing it only this morning. What I have in mind is a pre-payment scheme. The men pay a sum of money at the beginning of each year; for that they receive whatever medical treatment is necessary for themselves and their families.'

'Supposing one family receives an inordinate amount of treatment?' David enquired doubtfully.

'For every family with more sickness than usual, there should be others with none. This way, those in greatest need will receive whatever help is required, irrespective of their ability to pay.'

'The idea has its merits,' David assented, 'although I wonder how those families who do not fall sick will view the scheme. For my own part, there would be some certainty as to income, something which concerns me greatly. How could such a scheme be got underway? The men have no money to pay even what is owing from last year.'

'Those men with whom I have discussed the idea seem to feel that the people will appreciate the logic of the scheme. There is not a family in the district which does not dread the possibility of sickness and the additional expenses involved,' William assured him.

'If I am able to persuade the Directors,' he continued, 'and I believe

I have a strong enough argument to put to them – that it is in their interests to have a healthy, untroubled workforce – then I shall ask for the Company to foot last year's bills and to subsidise the first payments under the new scheme.'

'Why on earth should they consent to such an arrangement?' David was incredulous. The Quarry Company's Directors were not known for their philanthropy.

'I have plans to re-open two of the old quarries, which have particularly rich seams of slate,' William explained. 'Logie and Brown have been talking to the captains of the slate boats, and we believe that there is a market in New Zealand waiting to be exploited. I have suggested to Sir Alexander Campbell that he might use his influence with the powers-that-be.'

'If the old quarries have so much potential, how is it that they were abandoned in the first place?' David asked.

'They were abandoned because it was impossible to keep the sea out.'

'What has changed then, to make it possible now?' David was sceptical.

'I am here!' William was not given to self-commendation. Indeed, David had found him to be the most modest of men. He stared at the engineer in astonishment.

In his turn, William could not resist the chuckle which turned quickly into a hearty laugh.

'The fact is that in Cornwall we have been fighting this battle with the sea for generations. I propose to wall off the quarries with substantial masonry. The men have a particular skill in drystone walling. I shall then employ additional pumps which I have acquired from a breaker's yard at the dockyard in Greenock.'

'So that is the explanation for all the new activity at the Camas quarry,' observed David. 'There has been much speculation at Tigh na Broch, I can assure you.'

'We shall be able to go down another hundred feet at least,' William asserted. 'There will be a need for expenditure on winding gear, but I think the Directors will accept the necessity for that. I happen to know that the Marquis has them under close scrutiny. It seems that they have failed to make the amount of investment agreed in their contract with the Estate.'

'So you are striking while the iron is hot?' concluded David.

'What else would you expect from an engineer?' William enquired innocently.

The Annual General Meeting of the Parish Council was held in the Seileach schoolroom, on a very cold night in January. A large number of the male residents of the Parish attended, including a contingent from Eisdalsa Island. Both William and David were present, hoping to be elected.

The meeting progressed in a desultory fashion, the Secretary mumbling through the year-old Minutes in a dreary monotone. Mention of new water supplies to the village caused David to prick up his ears. He had noted with some distaste the corroded condition of the iron pipes carrying water from the cistern above the village.

The Chairman, in a manner more suitable for an address to Parliament than to his fellow villagers, thanked the Secretary effusively and would have moved on had not David interrupted him.

'Mr Chairman, I believe we have an item: Matters Arising from the Minutes?'

The Chairman, a stout gentleman of florid complexion, blustered, ''Er . . . of course . . . not usually necessary, y'know.' Then, addressing the meeting as a whole, 'Is there any business arising from the Minutes?'

'Yes, Mr Chairman.' David was on his feet again. 'The question of the water supply. What has been done?'

'Done?'

'Yes, sir. What has the Committee done about replacing the old water supply, which was clearly inadequate a year ago and appears to have remained so?'

There was a murmuring around the hall. Several words of agreement floated on the air.

'Mr Secretary?' The Chairman was deftly passing the buck.

The Secretary leafed through his various documents, searching for a satisfactory reply.

'I have no reference to any action having been taken, Mr Chairman,' he said at last. 'But I feel sure that there has been verbal discussion with the District Council.'

There was an audible sigh of relief from several members of the Committee. The truth was that the matter, which had been put forward by a quarryman during the previous Annual General Meeting, had been ignored. The Committee members had not seen fit to discuss it at any of their subsequent meetings where their own particular hobby horses held priority.

'This is a matter of great importance to the health of the whole community,' David persisted. 'I would like it to go on record that this meeting, appalled at the inactivity of the Parish Council with regard to the matter of the water supply to Eisdalsa, insists that the matter be taken in hand without further delay, and that application be made to the appropriate authorities to have a new water supply installed.'

Edward Murray, the Chairman of the Parish Council, was one of the wealthier tenant farmers whose lands were scattered the length of Seileach, away from the quarry villages. He had arrived in the district only five years ago. By sheer weight of his personality, and with the help of a very substantial bank balance, he had amassed a surprising amount of influence in a very short time. While associating freely with the farming community, from whom he could extract local knowledge and a transient workforce, he held himself aloof from the quarries and the quarry workers and made sure that his family had nothing to do with the working classes.

He looked at the speaker with undisguised distaste. Who was this little whippersnapper to talk about the Parish Council in such terms?

'May I ask by what authority you suggest that the water supply is inadequate?' he demanded.

'By virtue of my medical qualification, sir!' David declared.

The Secretary whispered to the Chairman who looked hard at David, nodded to the Secretary and then continued.

'I understand, gentlemen, that we have to welcome in our midst Dr David Beaton, son of our much loved and late lamented Dr Hugh Beaton.'

There was a little laughter at the Chairman's confusion and some ironic clapping from somewhere in the rear of the hall.

'Well, Dr Beaton,' the Chairman went on, 'if as you say there is a need to consider the installation of an improved water supply, I have no doubt that your newly elected Committee will take it in hand.'

'Mr Chairman, there is a motion on the floor.' It was William who was on his feet now. 'I wish to second that motion.'

Again, there was general acclamation from the body of the hall.

This time, the Secretary did not wait for the Chairman to make another faux pas. 'The motion on the floor, proposed by Dr Beaton and seconded by Mr Whylie, the Quarry Manager' (this for the benefit of the Chairman), 'is that . . .' He then repeated David's motion.

The vote, which was in fact a motion of censure upon the Committee, was carried by a large majority. Neither David nor William felt any elation at this victory. They had made some powerful enemies tonight.

The meeting continued with a round of reports from the various Sub-Committees of the Parish Council. Both the School Board and the Committee dealing with the poor of the Parish interested David, but he said no more until the time came for the election of the new committees.

For the elections, the Chairman, with a great show of self-effacement, surrendered his chair to the Vice-chairman, who was Lugas, the Marquis's Factor.

Lugas studied a list on the paper before him.

'Gentlemen, there is only one nomination for Chairman on my list.' He beamed at the incumbent. 'Mr Murray has kindly agreed to be nominated for a further term.'

Malcolm Logie, from the back of the hall, called out, 'I would like to nominate Mr Whylie, if he will agree to stand?'

'And I will second that!' The voice was that of Dougal Brown, Michael's father.

There was a hurried exchange between Lugas and the Secretary, before Lugas responded to the new nomination.

'Mr Secretary issued a written notice of the Annual General Meeting in the prescribed manner requesting nominations, in writing, to be received five days before the meeting. This is in accordance with the constitution. I cannot therefore accept a further nomination at this stage.'

Members of the retiring Committee nodded their heads sagely. They had all seen to it that their names had been submitted for re-election, and were confident of the outcome of the ballot. From the body of the hall, however, there were some angry mutterings.

Suddenly a hush descended on the proceedings as the white-haired Archie MacLean, stiff with the rheumatism which was the mark of the older quarrymen, rose painfully to his feet. He spoke in the soft Highland brogue but his words were heard clearly. The village elder was treated with the greatest veneration by the younger quarriers, while the farming community knew better than to show disrespect to the old man.

'Mr Secretary, sir, I mind well the day that this constitution of ours was agreed upon. There was a considerable discussion, at that time, about the system of nomination to the Council. It must be remembered that, in those days, many isolated farmers had some difficulty communicating with the rest of the Parish. For them, attendance at the meeting was a major event in their lives. To receive notice of the meeting, and to return a written nomination, was nigh impossible in the time allowed. There was also provision to be made for those who had not the benefit of literacy but ought not be denied their right to a say in Parish matters.'

Murray and several of his supporters shifted impatiently. When would the old man come to the point? What was appropriate for a bunch of ignorant stone gatherers hardly applied in these enlightened times.

Pre-empting any comment along these lines, Archie concluded his intervention. 'If, Mr Secretary, you will refer to item 6 of the constitution, Nominations for Election, you will find that there is a rider to the rule concerning notice of a nomination. "A proposal for a nomination for election to any seat on the Parish Council may be accepted, at the meeting, without prior written notification, if it is the will of members present that the nomination be so accepted".'

There was a general buzz of conversation which ceased only after the Secretary had rummaged through his notes once again and discovered the rather tattered copy of the council's constitution. He read quickly, while an expectant silence descended upon the meeting. Finally he raised his head and acknowledged that Archie MacLean was quite correct. The old man had good cause to be so sure of his ground. He had been the inaugural Secretary of the Eisdalsa Parish Council, established, under the reforms of 1834, to administer Poor Relief to the district.

The existing Committee members were all visibly shaken by what was happening. Logie and Brown between them commanded the respect of all the quarriers on Eisdalsa Island, and in the Village.

Some of the Committee searched the faces in the hall, seeking out their supporters; others merely shifted uneasily in their seats.

'Do you accept the proposal that Mr Whylie be nominated for the position of Chairman of the Parish Council?' the Vice-chairman enquired of the meeting.

There was an overwhelming shout of: 'YES!'

Nevertheless, Lugas called for a show of hands. It was quite clear from this that there was a majority in favour of including William's name on the ballot paper.

'Are you willing to stand in this election, Mr Whylie?'

'Yes,' he agreed.

David had exposed the retiring Committee as being in dereliction of its duties. Many people, who had come to the meeting quite prepared to support the farmer's re-election, were inclined to switch their allegiance to the new Quarry Master. William's own workforce stood by their boss. Murray's support came solely from the members of the retiring Committee.

'The votes for Chairman of the Parish Council of Eisdalsa and Seileach, having been counted,' Lugas announced pompously, 'are: eight votes in favour of Mr Murray . . .' there was a breathless hush as he continued '. . . and fifty-five in favour of Mr William Whylie.'

A tremendous roar of approval went up and William found himself overwhelmed by those villagers, some complete strangers, who were anxious to shake the hand of the new Chairman of the Parish Council.

There was a shuffling of places at the top table to allow him to take the Chair.

He referred to the Secretary's list of nominations for other positions on the Committee. The proceedings now took their normal course, Lugas, the Secretary and the Treasurer being re-elected.

'We come to the election of three Ordinary Committee members,' William announced.

He consulted the Secretary, nodded in understanding, and then addressed the meeting. 'Gentlemen, I understand that it is the responsibility of the Parish Council to decide the composition of those Boards which deal with the School and the Poor of the Parish.' He looked towards Lugas for confirmation, which was given by a quick nod of the head. 'It is my belief that the minister, Mr McCulloch, should have the right to vote on these two Sub-committees, and I therefore propose that Mr McCulloch should be a full member of the Parish Council, not merely attending meetings in an advisory capacity.'

There was some muttering around the hall but, when the matter was formally proposed and seconded, there were no dissensions.

William now proceeded with greater confidence.

'The meeting will be pleased to know that Dr David Beaton has consented to take over the practice of his late father. It will be the duty of the Parish Council to appoint him officially as MOH.' There was general concurrence. 'As in the case of the minister, may I suggest that the presence of the local doctor, as a voting member of the Committee, would be of inestimable benefit when dealing with matters concerning Public Health and the Poor.'

The suggestion was immediately taken up, and David was duly elected.

When the meeting was finally brought to a close, David invited William to walk back to Tigh na Broch with him.

'My mother will be pleased to entertain you. I happen to know that there is venison stew for supper.'

'I would be delighted to join you,' William replied, 'but I fear that I shall not be able to get back to the island tonight if I stay too late.'

'It is time that you had a boat of your own,' suggested David. 'It will not do for the Manager of the Quarries to have to depend upon the public ferry.'

'Nevertheless,' William protested, 'on such a night, who will be willing to turn out for me?' He regarded the driving rain ruefully.

'Young Michael shall be engaged to row you back tonight,' announced David, disregarding William's protests. 'I will see that he is alerted, when we get to the house.'

Morag greeted the two men as they entered, shaking the rain from their heavy coats.

'How did the meeting go,' she asked.

'Better than we could have hoped,' said David. 'William is the Chairman!'

'But that is splendid news,' cried Morag. 'It is time they were all shaken out of their complacency. That Murray has been in the Chair for so long one might believe he was rooted to it!'

'Our new Chairman did not let the grass grow, believe me, Mother.' David was laughing and clapping William on the back, so hard that the engineer could scarce catch his breath.

'You know how Father always complained that whatever suggestions he made could be ignored by the Committee, because he was only an ex-officio member and did not command a vote?' he reminded her. 'Well, William persuaded the meeting that Mr McCulloch should be a full member with voting rights.'

Mystified, Morag felt she was expected to be pleased at this announcement and smiled politely.

David enlightened her.' And when it came to filling Father's place,

William put forward the same argument for me. Well, they could hardly refuse me voting rights when they had already agreed them for the minister, could they?'

'Whylie by name and the same by nature,' laughed Morag.

'I would have looked to see a little more weight given to the quarry workers on the Council,' said William reflectively. 'It seems that it is the professional men and property owners who have all the say in running the Parish.'

'At least we can begin to change a few things with regard to the schools,' David observed. 'Elizabeth's plea for bursaries for the poorer children, for instance.'

'Yes,' agreed William, 'and we shall certainly pursue the matter of the water supply.'

'And what about the drains, while we are on the topic of public health!' David landed heavily in Sheilagh's favourite chair beside the kitchen stove.

William chose to stand with his back to the fire, steam rising from his wet trousers.

'This is just a beginning,' William responded, his face alight with enthusiasm. 'Drains; public privies; ash-pits. With a proper scavenging service the whole area could be tidied up.'

'The people will be much the healthier for it,' David added. 'Let us hope that your influence with the Quarry Company is sufficient to fund these improvements.'

'Surely, as Medical Officer for Health, you will have some sway with the District Council?' suggested William.

'That is a matter yet to be arranged,' replied David. 'It is for the Parish Council to nominate its Medical Officer for Health.'

'Well,' joined in Morag, 'that would not seem to be an insuperable problem!'

Laughing, they sat down to their meal.

While the men attended the Annual General Meeting of the Parish Council, the ladies of the parish had gathered, at Mrs Lugas's invitation, at the Castle.

The fortified house known as Creag Castle stood on a rocky promontory overlooking the Sound. At one time it had been the permanent seat of the Marquis's family. Now, His Lordship chose to spend most of the year at his mansion near Edinburgh, visiting Creag only in the late summer, for the shooting. For much of the year, the Castle was occupied solely by Alexander Lugas and his wife Alicia. Their son Peter attended the school on Eisdalsa Island, and boarded with a kinsman during termtime. Soon he would be sent away to Edinburgh, to the Academy, always assuming that he managed to pass the entrance examination. In his capacity as representative of the Marquis's interests in the district, Alexander was obliged to entertain distinguished visitors and to keep contact with the gentlemen of the parish. The child would have been an embarrassment in the circumstances and was, as his mother frequently found herself explaining, better off living the simple life of the villagers.

Peter Lugas did not share her contentment at the situation in which he found himself. He considered the village houses and the island school to be beneath him, and resented his exclusion from the activities at the Castle. At the school he had gathered a sycophantic following and, using his father's position, lorded it over the other children on the Island, bullying the more defenceless among them, such as Charlie MacNab. Elizabeth had been quick to realise the unfortunate influence that Peter Lugas had upon his classmates, but whenever she attempted to bring the matter to the attention of Mr Ogilvie, her comments were disregarded. In Ogilvie's eyes, the Factor's son could do no wrong.

Elizabeth found herself constantly obliged to criticise both the boy's work and his behaviour. She realised that she was on dangerous ground. Her period of probation had still not been concluded, and she was dependent upon the members of the School Board for her permanent appointment. Mr Lugas was an influential member of the Board, and Mrs Lugas had already indicated her disapproval of the new schoolmistress; her notes to Mr Ogilvie, on the subject of her son's progress in English Language, leaving no room for doubt about Elizabeth's inability to teach him anything!

Had she been able to overhear the conversation at the Castle that evening, her hopes of a permanent post would have been completely dashed. It was not her teaching abilities which were exercising the ladies' tongues.

'I am surprised that you have not invited the new schoolmistress to join us this evening,' observed Myra McCulloch, the minister's wife. 'I was rather hoping to meet her in a social capacity. Whenever I have attempted to call upon her she has been otherwise engaged.'

'Alicia was wise not to include her in her invitation,' Ellen Ogilvie observed. 'From what my husband tells me she is hardly fit company for the ladies of this parish.'

'The young hussy!' Alicia Lugas sniffed in indignation. 'Do you tell me, Myra, that she actually spent the entire night alone with Dr Beaton in the McGillivrays' house?'

'Well, not exactly alone, dear,' the minister's wife twittered like a robin. 'The McGillivrays were both there too, of course.'

'Confined to their beds, and sleeping.' Ellen Ogilvie pursed her lips and nodded significantly at her companions. 'Anything could have happened.' She continued with her condemnation of the new schoolmistress.

'What kind of a woman arrives at the Ball on the arm of one gentleman, and then disappears for fully half an hour with another?'

'This really happened at the Hogmanay Ball?' Alicia sought confirmation from Myra McCulloch.

'With my own eyes I saw her step outside with Dr Beaton, just after Mr Whylie gave his speech.'

'It is only a short distance to the bothy from the Drill Hall,' observed Myra. 'Who knows what they got up to in half an hour?'

'And there is all the work that Mr Whylie is undertaking at the bothy. Her own privy indeed . . . and a separate bedroom! It is quite indecent for a gentleman to discuss such matters with a young, unmarried woman.'

'Particularly,' added Alicia, 'a person engaged to impart not only knowledge but moral standards to our children!'

'Well, I for one have seen quite sufficient of the woman's antics,' declared Ellen Ogilvie. 'I have told the dominie. I have said to him: "mark my words," I have said. "If that woman stays, it will be the worse for the village."'

'Surely, once she has been appointed, only the School Board can dismiss her?' Myra McCulloch had no intention of stealing her companion's thunder, but to Ellen this appeared to be a direct attack on the importance of her husband's position.

'School Board,' she snorted. 'They do what they are told. If the dominie says she must go, then go she will!'

Myra and Alicia exchanged glances. They were both aware of certain controversies in the Ogilvie household, the question of who wore the trousers being one of them.

Alicia summoned the butler, and ordered the carriage to be brought to the door.

'Mark my words,' declared Ellen, as she rose to go, 'the Duncan woman will be gone before Easter. Come along, Mrs McCulloch, our menfolk will be on their way home from their meeting and we have two miles to drive.'

PART III

1

William Whylie Esq.,   21 Park Lane
Eisdalsa Quarries   London
Eisdalsa   27 January 1877
Argyll

My Dear Whylie,
Delighted to hear that you have settled in to your new post, and
that things are moving at last in the matter of breaking out some
new seams.

Congratulations on your initiative in purchasing pumping gear.
The financial transaction has been dealt with by my office and all is
in order.

With regard to your request for a gratuity to be paid to Mr
Gordon McIntyre, who acted as go-between on your behalf, I think
this must come out of your own budget. The usual would be about
2%, in this case, £6.

The Directors have given careful consideration to your proposal
to introduce a medical insurance scheme. While agreeing in principle
with the scheme, the Directors consider that for them to shoulder
the whole burden of back-payments might be to encourage the men
to think money is easily come by. Your forceful recommendation
had some bearing on their decision, however. They are prepared to
foot the bill for all accrued debt to the doctor, for the last half year.
For the coming year, they will pay the first six months' contributions,
but consider that by June 1877 the men should be earning enough
to pay their own contributions for the remainder of the year and
thereafter.

As to the amount to be paid by each man, annually, once the
scheme is underway, it would seem that the doctor's proposal of
12/6 is somewhat excessive. We would propose 10/6 and that he
charge the families 10/- per confinement in addition. This seems to
be the arrangement in the collieries where a similar scheme is in
operation. If nothing else, such a curb will make the people think
twice before adding to their already overpopulated households.

Finally, in the matter of compensation for the accident to James
McGillivray of Eisdalsa Island, the Board is reluctant to admit liability.
From the report submitted by your predecessor, Mr McPhee, the

man was clearly in the wrong in moving his worksite, contrary to instruction from the foreman, Logie. It is considered that McGillivray was fortunate in that he, alone, received injury. He might be facing charges of manslaughter had one of his colleagues been killed in the rock-fall.

Again, your own argument was taken into consideration. It is noted that you consider that there were too many crews working on the one face. If this were so, then clearly Logie was at fault. Should you consider this to have been the position, your foreman should be dismissed forthwith.

If you feel that McGillivray's case is the stronger, then compensation will be paid. The sum of £75 has been suggested.

Now to more important matters. I enclose a copy of a letter received from a friend in Auckland, New Zealand, concerning a contract to supply slate to the newly developing town of Dunedin. Should you consider following his suggestion, the Board will endorse any action you may wish to take. Clearly, it is imperative that there should be as little delay as possible, if you intend to act at all.

We shall await your decision in these various matters, with interest.

Alexander Campbell, Bart. of Barcaldine

William read the letter a second time to assure himself that there was no ambiguity. No, it was clear that he had been left with the decision. Either James McGillivray went without his compensation for the severe injuries which had left him crippled for life, or Malcolm Logie, a most excellent foreman, was to be made a scapegoat. He glanced up at his companion who was seated at the second desk, crammed into the darkest corner of the miserable little office.

Jamie McGillivray was enjoying his new position as clerk to the Quarry Manager. As the title implied, it was a desk job involving a great deal of writing and figuring. He could not hope to equal the wages that a crew chief would command, but it was a steady income. No man could hope for more in these troublesome times.

McGillivray had never been entirely happy with the pen, and when William had originally suggested the post to him, he had been inclined to refuse.

It was not Jamie's writing skills that interested William, however, but his long experience working as a quarrier himself, and, more importantly, as the leader of the most productive gang in the workings.

It was now Jamie's responsibility to keep a record of the position in which every crew was working each day. He noted the quality of the seam being worked and the output of the crew. By applying his own knowledge of the seams, he apportioned the payment for slate produced. Because of the immense diversity in quality of slates from different seams, and the varying degree of difficulty experienced in cutting out the slate-stone, there had always been endless bickering between crews as to who would work any particular seam. Jamie devised a rotation of the crews which ensured that each worked in both poor and good seams. Provided the men applied themselves equally, crews could be equally productive and, most importantly, earn similar wages.

By making certain that the conditions under which the men worked were as equal as he could contrive, William had provided a climate in which competition might flourish. There was a new excitement in the daily routine, engendered by the introduction of a bonus to the crew producing most slates over a monthly period.

With Brown and Logie taking charge of the day-to-day organisation of the crews, and Jamie recording the work done and calculating the wages due, William could afford the time to pursue his other commitments.

The matter of the medical insurance scheme had been put to the Directors. As anticipated, they were not entirely in agreement. Any suggestion which might cost them money was treated with great suspicion. When William had begun to send in monthly production figures, justifying his decision to re-open two of the old quarries, they became somewhat more amenable to his other proposals.

He had made the case that, if the men were untroubled by the prospect of starvation should they be injured or become sick, and if they had no worries concerning the health of their families, they would perform their work better.

Clearly, the owners had recognised the wisdom of this. He was pleased with the outcome of his negotiations, although doubted that David would be so easily satisfied.

William read once again the letter from the Chairman of the Board. It was grossly unfair to dismiss Logie, the one man who had kept the quarries operating despite the deficiencies of a drunken Quarry Master. He glanced across at Jamie, laboriously entering the previous day's production figures in the ledger.

The clerk's stiffened right leg stretched awkwardly before him, obliging him to sit sideways-on to the table. Hair had grown back patchily over the scalp wound. Except when he was alone, Jamie had taken to wearing a flat cap to cover the spot. He was never seen without it. The men joked about it, taking bets on whether he took the cap off when he went to bed at night.

Jamie's thoroughly deserved compensation, or Malcolm Logie's job – what was William to do? His eye fell upon the other letter which Campbell had sent him.

To Alexander Campbell, Bart.   Auckland
                    of Barcaldine   New Zealand
21 Park Lane   1 December 1876
London

My Dear Campbell,
I write in haste, in hope of catching the clipper *Arestes* before she
sails on the morning tide.

You asked me to look out for opportunities to sell slate in the
newly developing towns here. Strangely, soon after receiving your
last letter, I attended a soiree at the Governor's Mansion, where
I encountered a gentleman who is a member of the Town Council of
Dunedin in the South Island.

It seems that Scots, in great number, are flocking to that area,
the sheep farming being exceedingly promising. Along with the farms,
there is a need for other industry and commerce. The outcome is
obvious. A great town is developing on the shores of Otago Bay,
built by Scots who cling to their traditional forms of housing. The
one material which they lack is suitable slate for roofing.

My source tells me that the people will give anything to get their
hands on a large and regular supply of roofing slates. To this end,
they are preparing letters, inviting the major quarry companies in
Scotland and Wales to tender for the contract.

I know that they are not yet ready to despatch these letters and
hasten therefore to send you advance warning. Should you be able
to get a man out here by the next packet, you would be in an
excellent position to secure the contract before your competitors are
on the scene.

Your agent should arrange to go directly to Dunedin, for
cross-country travel is slow here. Most vessels now continue on to
Dunedin, after calling at the major ports further north.

I am, sir,
Your obedient servant,
Silas Robbins

William knew that this was the opportunity for which he had been
waiting. If he did not act immediately, the New Zealand market could
be lost to their competitors.

Out in the sheltered bay, two or three ocean-going barques were
loading slates from their tiny slave boats. Under sail or rowed, these
vessels plied back and forth continuously, transporting their weighty
cargoes. In a few months, those few could become fifty . . . a hundred
even. He could almost hear the heightening of activity in the quarries,

the multiplication of pump noises, the rumbling of wagons and the screech of winding engines.

Why should he not send an emissary immediately? And who better than Malcolm Logie, who knew not only the quarries on Eisdalsa, but also the potential output of those on the other islands? What was more, Logie had the capacity to talk to all manner of men and would not feel out of place among the business fraternity of Dunedin.

By sending Malcolm, William could honestly say that the foreman no longer worked in Eisdalsa. He could report having sent an envoy without giving him a name. The Directors would be satisfied, and Jamie would receive his compensation.

William went to the door of the office and shouted for one of the boys who could be found at any time of day supplementing the work of the ponies by hauling the heavy slate trucks along their railway lines.

'Boy! Do you know where Mr Logie is at this minute?'

'Yes, sir. Camas Quarry, sir.'

'Go and fetch him for me . . . tell him it is a matter of some urgency.'

To Jamie he said, 'McGillivray, will you be good enough to take these time sheets across to Mr Brown? It is late enough for you to stop off for your dinner on the way back.'

Jamie gave William a knowing look. It was obvious that the Manager wanted a private word with Logie. Whyever did he not say so?

'Very well, Mr Whylie.' He pushed back his chair and hobbled to the door. 'Will I have Annie make you up a can of broth for yourself?'

'That would be very kind, thank you, Jamie.' William had a weakness for Annie McGillivray's cooking which outclassed that of every other woman on the Island, including, he had to admit, his housekeeper Maggie MacLean.

William set about collecting all the information he could lay hands on which he thought might be useful to Malcolm. By the time the foreman entered the office, a small pile of documents lay on the desk. On top of the pile was the letter from Dunedin.

'Come in, Logie,' William greeted him cheerfully. 'Come sit you down. We have weighty matters to discuss.'

He handed the letter to Malcolm and watched the foreman's face as he read the contents.

'Well, we knew that New Zealand was a good prospect,' he commented when he had finished reading. 'What an opportunity! If only there was someone who could go and speak for us.'

'Precisely why I have called you in here.' William smiled broadly at him. 'Tell me, Malcolm, you are a widower, is that not so?'

'Yes, that is true.'

'You have a daughter. I believe she is already working? Could she manage without you for, say, a year?'

'There are no prospects of her marrying for many years yet,' Malcolm answered. 'But she is old enough to fend for herself, and well on the way to becoming a fully fledged teacher in the school on Seileach.'

'It may be that I can put you in the way of making sufficient money to see her set up for life, and yourself also. You could be a man of means when you return!'

'Return . . . from where?'

'New Zealand.'

'You want me to go to New Zealand, to sell slate?'

'Yes, exactly that. This letter gives us an advantage over our competitors who will not receive their official invitation to quote for some weeks. Our agent will receive the Eisdalsa Company's invitation at the same time, but you will already be on your way to meet the Dunedin Council with our offer.'

'How competitive can we be in our prices?'

'I have sufficient information here for you to work on. In the six weeks which the voyage will take you will have time to plan a variety of strategies and pricing methods. We need the market. We will have to make a profit, of course, but above all, you must secure the business.'

William continued, in more practical vein, 'There is a vessel sailing from Tilbury on the tenth of February which gives you just the week to prepare for your departure. Come, man, what do you say? Will you go?'

Malcolm did not hesitate.

'Of course I'll go. What fool would refuse such an offer of adventure?'

'What of your daughter?'

'She is well settled as pupil teacher to Mr Ogilvie. Her fiance is in Africa. You met him, Murdo Campbell. She is a good girl, is my Katherine. She can take care of herself.'

'I will make out a banker's draft to cover your expenses. Payment for any sales that you arrange, will be . . . let us say, five per cent of the profit. How does that sound?'

Malcolm was making some rapid calculations in his head. Suppose he could sell five million slates, why, he would earn more than £200 for himself!

'I think it is a very fair offer, Mr Whylie, I shall be happy to shake hands on that.'

'I will have a proper contract drawn up which both of us shall sign. You will receive your portion of the profit when you return from New Zealand. Your maintenance during your stay abroad will be provided by the Royal Bank of Scotland of which there is certainly a branch in Auckland, possibly also in Dunedin itself. These details I will arrange with the lawyers before you leave.'

'I am truly grateful for this opportunity, Mr Whylie. My only regret will be that I cannot be on hand to help you in setting the quarries here to rights.'

'You will be doing your share.' William shook his colleague warmly by the hand. 'Indeed, if you do not secure the contract, we will be hard pressed to sell the slate we produce elsewhere. We both have a difficult task ahead of us.'

Unconsciously, he allowed his hand to stray towards his breast pocket where lay the letter from his employers. He hoped he would never be obliged to reveal its contents to either of the men whose fate it had determined.

2

The School Board was a Sub-committee of the Parish Council, the local representatives being elected from amongst that august body. Among its members were the Chairman of the Parish Council, His Lordship's representative Lugas, the doctor, the minister, the schoolmaster, and as representative of the Argyll Council, Mr Ford.

Lugas, as Convenor, had arranged for the Board to meet at the Castle on a chilly wet day in early March. The drawing room on the first floor of the ancient fortified house had been set out for the meeting. The dining table, extended to its full length, occupied the centre of the room. Six high-backed, heavily carved oak chairs were arranged to seat the members.

A fire of peats and driftwood filled the great stone fireplace, but made little impact upon the chill atmosphere of the lofty apartment. Huge tapestries, which hung from floor to ceiling, swayed in the draught from the ill-fitting windows in their crumbling stone mullions.

William, as Chairman of the Parish Council, also took the chair at these meetings. David, who was seated opposite him, could feel the cold air oozing between the floorboards under his feet. The thin, ancient carpet did little to address the problem.

William glanced across at Lugas, who had taken one of the chairs at the foot of the table.

'Perhaps, Mr Lugas, I may ask you to make notes of our discussion . . . act as Secretary, as it were?'

Lugas looked a trifle uncomfortable and glanced sheepishly at the schoolmaster, Ogilvie, hoping for guidance.

'Mr Ogilvie usually makes the notes on these occasions,' the Factor explained, 'and produces the Minutes for the Parish Council.'

'I am aware of that,' said William. 'I have been studying the Minute Book rather carefully these past few days.'

He did not add that he had experienced considerable difficulty, initially, in extracting the book from the hands of the schoolmaster. Nor did he make any observations on the contents and nature of the notes kept by Ogilvie. He had found the record full of platitudes, lacking in any real detail, and without reference to expenditure or income. These matters could, however, wait until their present business had been completed.

William chose to ignore the implication arising from Lugas's explanation.

'I think it fitting that it should be His Lordship's agent who keeps the Minutes, Mr Lugas. If you will be so kind.'

He silently accepted the rebuke and acknowledged, with a sharp nod, David's offer of a sheaf of paper upon which to write.

Mr Ford, Inspector of Schools for Argyll County Council, took his place at the opposite end of the table from Lugas. He had arrived carrying a heavy portmanteau whose contents he was now assembling in neat piles in front of him.

William opened the meeting formally, then introduced himself and Dr Beaton to the County Inspector.

'The other gentlemen will be well known to you, Mr Ford. Mr Lugas, the Factor for the Estate of the Marquis of Stirling; Mr McCulloch, Minister of the Church of Scotland; Mr Ogilvie the schoolmaster.'

Mr Ford paused for a moment in the arrangement of his various documents, glanced over his spectacles, and nodded briefly in the direction of his fellow Committee members.

'Since I have some matters to discuss at a later stage, relating to the Minutes of previous meetings,' William began, 'I propose to proceed without the usual reading of the Minutes of the last meeting. Instead, I think it appropriate to begin with a report from Mr Ford, who carried out his inspection last December. Mr Ford . . .'

'My written report is before you, gentlemen,' he began, in a manner which showed that he was an old hand at making presentations of this nature.

'I visited both schoolrooms in December last. The Seileach school was conducted satisfactorily, with a high standard of performance in every grade. The children are well versed in the scriptures,' McCulloch was observed to nod his head approvingly, 'and number. The reading skills of the older children are good, but I would take issue over the paucity of reading matter available to the very young children. Some of the passages seemed to be outwith their understanding.'

William interrupted at this point. 'Mr Ogilvie, do you have any comment to make at this juncture?'

He was quick to cover himself.

'With two schoolhouses under my care, it has been necessary to delegate responsibility for the choice of reading material to my pupil teacher, Miss Logie. I fear this may be the reason for Mr Ford's unease. I shall certainly look into the matter.'

William gave the schoolmaster a penetrating stare before turning back to Mr Ford.

'Pray continue, sir.'

Mr Ford reached for a second document.

'My visit to the Eisdalsa Island schoolhouse was a very different experience. Here I found the children undertaking work entirely suitable to their ages and abilities. Among the older children are a number who have made remarkable progress, and easily match their counterparts in the town. I was, however, particularly impressed with the way in which the new schoolmistress has worked with the less able children. Her method of using older, more capable pupils to assist the younger ones appears to be of benefit to both.

'The atmosphere in the schoolroom I found to be happy and productive. The children actually seem to enjoy being there!'

There was an undisguised snort of disapproval from the other end of the table. Ignoring this signal from Ogilvie, William invited Lugas to make the comment which he was clearly eager to voice.

'Mr Lugas?'

'I am informed that this practice of using older pupils to teach the younger ones is very disruptive, and leads to some of the older pupils having to abandon their own important studies. My own son, Peter, seems to have failed badly this last term. Since he was doing so well under Mr Ogilvie, I can only assume that this set-back is a result of the new regime.'

William was down upon him immediately.

'Mr Lugas, we are all here as members of the School Board. If you have any complaint to make as a parent, I suggest that you do this through the schoolteachers themselves. It is not for us to discuss the merits of individual pupils, unless it is for some particular purpose over which we do have jurisdiction.'

Mr Ford nodded his approval. Too often he was subjected to such outbursts when these meetings were not so tightly managed.

'This brings me to the question of the status of Miss Duncan, the Eisdalsa schoolmistress.'

David had been dozing, despite his cold feet. The mention of Elizabeth brought him instantly on the alert.

'I find it difficult to understand,' Mr Ford continued, 'why it is that a woman of seven years' experience was appointed in a probationary capacity. Miss Duncan is a person of very considerable skill. Any educationalist should have observed her potential at the first demonstration of her abilities. To have maintained her in this capacity for several months seems to me to portray a deficiency in those appointing her.'

In truth, the previous Chairman of the Board, the farmer Murray, had delegated all responsibility for the school to Ogilvie. Such meetings as had been held since the demise of the old Marquis had been jolly affairs, with the sharing of a glass or two. The last had culminated in a shoot over the Estate lands. Lugas seemed to recall that when Mr Ford had attended last spring there had been discussion about appointing an additional teacher. At subsequent meetings, the choice of teacher and her conditions of appointment were left in the hands of the school-master.

All eyes were now upon Ogilvie.

That gentleman, bristling with self-righteousness, began to defend his position.

'Miss Duncan had served her apprenticeship in an academy for young ladies. She herself admitted that she had no experience at all of teaching the male sex. I considered it only right to proceed with caution, appointing her for a probationary period of undetermined length. In view of subsequent events, there is no doubt that this was a wise decision.'

William did not pursue this remark. Instead he invited Mr Ford to give his opinion of the matter.

'I believe that Miss Duncan is an excellent teacher,' the Inspector offered. 'I can see no reason at all why she should not be appointed on a permanent basis. This Committee will do well to snap her up. I can think of a number of schools in my district which would welcome such a person with open arms.'

'Has anyone anything to add to Mr Ford's comments?' William asked.

The minister and Ogilvie exchanged glances. McCulloch turned a little pink, and offered his first words to the meeting.

'We . . . er . . . we should, I think, be a little concerned about the moral position.'

William was genuinely astounded.

'What on earth are you saying, Mr McCulloch? Are you calling Miss Duncan's morals into question?'

Like a timorous snail, who stretches his neck to test the weather and finds it not to his liking, McCulloch shrank back into his seat and nervously shuffled the papers in front of him.

David, leaping perhaps too readily to his chosen one's defence, was on his feet in a second.

'What's this?' he exclaimed. 'Sir, you insult the lady!'

Ogilvie supported the minister. Now that he had everyone's full attention, he smiled slyly.

'There have been a number of incidents,' he announced, with assumed regret, 'observed by the ladies of the village, which suggest that Miss Duncan pays less attention to her pupils than she does to her admirers.'

It was too much for either of them. David, positioned on the far side of the table, was disadvantaged. William was already on his feet. The stockily built Cornishman had been the wrestling champion of the Tresgarth Mine when he was only eighteen. His short stature and gentle nature belied his real strength. In an instant he had Ogilvie by the necktie and was dragging him to his feet.

The schoolmaster, his breathing constricted, turned red then purple.

'How dare you besmirch the reputation of a fine young woman in such a way?' shouted William. 'The tittle-tattle of village gossips is no subject for discussion amongst gentlemen. I will have no more of it. You will apologise to the meeting, sir, or leave the room immediately.'

He shook the schoolmaster so that his teeth rattled. So tightly was his throat constricted by William's grasp that he could not have replied had he wished to.

Mr Ford, acting with great agility, placed himself between the struggling opponents and managed to apply his own considerable strength in order to force William to relax his grip.

Once Ogilvie found himself able to breathe freely, he wasted no time in retaliating.

'I shall have you for assault, sir, you may be sure of that. See, I have all these witnesses!'

The other gentlemen were standing uneasily about the room now. William, breathing heavily, was still being restrained by the Inspector. McCulloch was mopping his brow with an enormous silk handkerchief and muttering incoherently.

David, boiling with the pent up rage which he had been unable to release, paced the room. He strode, head down, hands clasped tightly behind his back as though to prevent them from taking any further action.

Mr Ford, having assured himself that William had regained his composure, was the first to resume his seat. Very deliberately he straightened the skirts of his frock-coat and sank into his chair.

William followed suit, deciding that he was unlikely to receive any apology now!

David, his moment of frenzy past, also sat down.

Ogilvie, however, had no intention of letting the matter rest.

'I shall have you arrested for assault,' he cried again. 'Alexander, send for the Sheriff at once!'

Alexander Lugas had moved over to the window and was, even now, gazing out at the rain which fell in sheets, driving against the panes of ancient glass. It was clear to him that William Whylie was more than a match for Ogilvie. He was also painfully aware of the shortcomings in his own administration of His Lordship's affairs. Who knew what can of worms might be opened by a judicial investigation of the cause of this fracas? Best let the matter lie. At Ogilvie's request, he turned slowly and gave the schoolmaster a long, hard stare.

'Why should you require the Sheriff, my dear Farquhar?' he enquired, as though he had not been present in the room all this time.

'I have been assaulted by this . . . this buffoon of an Englishman. That is why!'

'Assaulted, my dear fellow? Rather strong words, wouldn't you say?'

Ogilvie now turned his attention to his other witnesses. 'Mr Ford, you saw what happened, you will be my witness.'

Ford, who was examining some papers with more deliberation than was quite necessary, replied, 'I fear that I was not attending to the conversation at the time. I saw nothing.'

'But you intervened in the attack!'

'You appeared to be somewhat distressed. Your collar a trifle too tight perhaps? I feel sure that any one of these gentlemen would have done the same.'

Ogilvie stepped back as though stung by the Inspector's reply. When the schoolmaster approached McCulloch, that gentleman sheepishly shrugged his shoulders and returned to his seat without a word.

'Perhaps we can make some progress now, gentlemen?' William seemed to have forgotten the entire event and was once again playing the role of the perfect Chairman.

'We have a suggestion from Mr Ford that Miss Elizabeth Duncan be appointed a permanent teacher at the Eisdalsa Island school. Is everyone in agreement?'

He cast his eyes around the group, his gaze resting only momentarily upon Ogilvie.

'Good, all in agreement. What would be the usual salary for such a post, Mr Ford?'

'Since the young lady receives free accommodation from the Quarry Company, I believe that £75 per annum would be appropriate. This may, of course, be supplemented by any private tuition which Miss Duncan may choose to provide. I believe that, at present, only Mr Ogilvie receives payment for extramural activities.'

William gave him an enquiring glance. The schoolmaster, straining a little from the soreness in his throat, agreed that any monies accruing from such sources came first to himself. 'I pay the pupil staff what I consider is an appropriate share.'

'Is such an arrangement usual?' William enquired of Mr Ford.

'Certainly it would be expected in the case of a pupil teacher. One who might have to call upon a mentor for assistance in devising a programme of tuition for a student. It would not, however, be appropriate in Miss Duncan's case, since she is unlikely to require Mr Ogilvie's assistance in her private teaching.'

'Then we will have it written into Miss Duncan's appointment,' William addressed the Secretary, Lugas, 'that any fees for private tuition shall be retained in their entirety by Miss Duncan.'

'I think it is fair to say,' intervened Mr Ford, 'that the pupil engaged in the Seileach schoolhouse, Miss Logie, should receive eighty per cent of any fees, the remainder to go to Mr Ogilvie for his supervision and assistance.'

David tried hard to hide his smile. He sensed that Ford was as keen as he himself to see Ogilvie put in his place. It was very clear that the old skinflint had been milking his pupil teachers for all he could get over the past years.

Hearing no word of dissent, and ignoring the glowering countenance of the defeated schoolmaster, William moved on to the next business.

'This should not take more than a moment, gentlemen. It appears that the Marquis's predecessor was a philanthropic gentleman who contributed handsomely to the further education of deserving pupils from the village schools. I gather that there has been no attempt made to ascertain the feelings of the present incumbent concerning the matter of educational bursaries?' He glanced enquiringly in Lugas's direction.

'There has been no proposal to support any pupil since the old Marquis died,' Lugas confirmed.

'So we have no idea whether the present Marquis will support such activity?'

'None,' Lugas agreed.

'Gentlemen, I have received a list of pupils who would be eligible for further education should the funds be made available. Will you allow me to read out the names?'

From where did this list originate?' enquired Ogilvie. He was trying desperately to reassert himself. William had no desire to prolong their disagreement, and was willing to allow him the dignity of his position.

'The list is one drawn up by Mr Ford, with the help of Miss Duncan,' he explained. 'Perhaps there are others from the Seileach school?'

'There may be,' grunted Ogilvie. 'I would need to give the matter some consideration.'

'Perhaps Mr Ogilvie will provide his list for our next meeting?' ventured McCulloch, who felt he really must have something to say, to justify his presence there.

William had taken the precaution of showing Mr Ford Elizabeth's list to avoid any accusation that the schoolmistress was receiving special favours from the Chairman. How thankful he was now that it was Ford who could be called upon to justify the choice.

'Mr Ford, if you please?'

Ford lifted yet another of his carefully arranged sheets of paper and read out the name of Mary McCulloch.

'Mary is ten years old. She is proficient in all the subjects of the normal curriculum, but in addition she has mastered the essentials of Greek and Latin grammar and is remarkably able in translation from these languages into English. I understand that she wishes to become a teacher.'

All this while, the minister had remained silent. He remembered William's warning to Ogilvie and was anxious not to appear in any way partisan, when his daughter's future was under discussion. But his heart swelled with pride at the thought of his little girl being considered for teacher training, and he had great difficulty restraining himself.

William turned to him. 'Mr McCulloch, would you support your daughter's application? Are you prepared to allow her name to go forward?'

'Of course!' he said enthusiastically.

Ford continued.

'Dougie McGillivray has a remarkable aptitude for science and mathematics. He would certainly benefit from a training in engineering. Since this is an area in which the Quarry Company would be interested, I would propose that he is put forward for consideration.'

Lugas was quick to comment on this proposal. 'It is true that the old Marquis supported training for work in the quarries. This particular pupil might be the one to promote when making the case to His Lordship.'

'There is one further case that I would bring to your attention,' interrupted David. 'This is perhaps a more immediate need. My apprentice, Michael Brown, left school two years ago and is now approaching the age at which he must prepare himself for University entrance if he is to become a doctor of medicine. While the practice can support his small wage at present, it will not be possible to pay for his tuition as well as employing another apprentice in his place. There is a need for continuity in this respect. The Parish needs medical staff, particularly in the quarries. It would seem to be a good investment to send Michael away to train.'

William looked around for any other suggested names. Hearing none he said to Lugas, 'May we leave the presentation of this proposal, and the list of names, in your hands, Mr Lugas? Perhaps you will report the Marquis's reaction at our next meeting?'

William glanced at his agenda.

'I see that we have one further item, the report from the doctor. Dr Beaton?'

'I will make my report very short, Mr Chairman. Its brevity in no way trivialises the problems of health in our schools, but the details of what is to be done are so extensive and specific that I feel they are best left to the experts. Suffice it to say that I have found the two schoolhouses to be poorly heated, badly lit, dirty, and inappropriate for the education of children. I have presented to Mr Whylie my list of requirements to bring them up to standard. He assures me that the Company will provide materials if the men will give of their time to improve the buildings. A meeting of the workers has taken place, and agreement has been reached to this effect. Work will start on the Eisdalsa latrines immediately. Other renovations will follow. The Seil-each buildings, being newer, are in better condition, although their cleanliness leaves much to be desired. A sum of money is set aside for the cleaning of both schoolhouses. It is difficult to understand why they have been allowed to deteriorate in this fashion.'

There was an exchange of glances between the longer standing members of the Board. There was clearly implied criticism in the doctor's report. Should one of them protest or let the matter ride? It seemed that the Quarry Master had matters in hand. It was Lugas who spoke for them all.

'It seems to me that this is a case of two new brooms literally sweeping clean!'

There was general laughter which eased the tension brought on by David's exposition.

'Well, gentlemen, are we agreed that these improvements shall go ahead?' William looked at each member in turn. There was no dissent.

'Finally, I think that I have made clear to you my intention of keeping a tight rein on the conduct and the recording of these meetings. I have good reason to believe that matters have been allowed to become a trifle slack in recent years. I am sure you will all agree that our time is too valuable to be wasted on matters which are not followed up, or have little bearing on the task we have been set.' It was a statement, not a question. William paused only to allow his words to penetrate the thicker skulls.

'Is there any other business?'

There was no reply.

'Then I thank you for your attendance, and have the pleasure to pass on to you Mrs Lugas's invitation to partake of luncheon before you leave.'

William stood up. Lugas went to the bell-pull which hung beside the fire, and summoned the servants.

Soon the table was cleared of papers and a sumptuous repast of cold meats, vegetables and a choice of sweetmeats was laid out. All the gentlemen reseated themselves, Ogilvie choosing to take the chair next to his one remaining ally. Poor McCulloch looked a little crestfallen that he had been so singled out, but smiled politely and offered the schoolmaster a dish of potatoes.

To William Whylie Esq.   Clyde River and Western
Eisdalsa Quarries   Isles Steamship Co.
Argyll   Greenock

My Dear Friend,

I have received your generous commission of £6.0.0. for services in connection with the purchase of steam pumps for the quarries.

You must know that I would have helped you without recompense in view of your own timely assistance when we were in trouble. Nevertheless, the money will be useful. Many thanks to you and your company.

The *Lord of Lorn* goes into dry dock for repairs next month, giving me the opportunity for a welcome period of leave. May I prevail upon your open offer of hospitality to come and stay on Eisdalsa from 4 April for a few days?

I send this note by a Mr Ford who, I understand, will be attending a meeting with you shortly. As he will be boarding the steamer again, after the meeting, perhaps you will let me have your reply by this gentleman?

I remain,
Your obedient servant and friend,
Gordon MacIntyre

William glanced up from the letter which the Inspector had handed to him at the close of the meeting.

'You will be seeing Mr MacIntyre again this evening, I understand?'

'Most certainly,' Mr Ford replied. 'Gordon and I are kinsmen. We always spend a little time together when I am on one of my coastal circuits. I sail up to Fort William and then take the coast road back to Oban, calling at all the schools on the way.'

'Would you be so kind as to carry my reply verbally?'

'Naturally.'

'Tell Mr MacIntyre that he will be more than welcome to stay as long as he wishes. I shall look forward eagerly to his visit.'

'I shall be happy to do so.' The Inspector's smile turned to a frown as he noticed the schoolmaster approaching.

Ogilvie had had a bad morning and was determined to take his revenge on this wiseacre of an Englishman, this upstart who had seen fit to interfere with long-standing arrangements which had been of benefit to all concerned.

Alexander Lugas had been more than generous with His Lordship's cellar during their luncheon. The dominie, filled with Dutch courage, now cast discretion to the winds.

'Do not think that you have heard the last of this morning's episode!' he snarled, his venom inflamed by excess of alcohol.

'What, pray, do you intend to do about it?' William enquired, not in the least intimidated by the sorry figure the schoolmaster cut.

'I shall take you to court, sir! I shall see my solicitor and have you summoned for assault. That is what I intend, sir!' These last words were uttered in a passable imitation of William's own Cornish accent. So good was the attempt, in fact, as to attract David's attention.

He had been deep in conversation with Mr Ford when Ogilvie's temper exploded. The two men exchanged knowing looks. Ford placed an encouraging hand on David's shoulder as if to push him forward into the fray.

'A word with you, if you please, Mr Ogilvie.' David took a firm grasp of the schoolmaster's arm and led him, stumbling slightly, into the tiny pantry which served the dining room. He forced Ogilvie to take the only seat, a low stool, before reaching behind him to close the door.

Uncomfortable in his position on the stool, which left him at a disadvantage, with David towering above him, Ogilvie tried to rise to his feet but his swimming head made it impossible. He sank down again and surrendered to the doctor's powerful presence.

'I believe that you will wish to withdraw your accusations against the Chairman when you hear what I have to say.' David had to place both hands on the teacher's shoulders to prevent him from swaying.

'Nothing will stop me from taking action against that unspeakable monster!'

'Mr Ogilvie, during my survey of the condition of the school buildings, I prevailed upon the Treasurer of the Parish Council to allow me a sight of the financial transactions which have taken place recently in connection with the maintenance of the school. An examination of statements presented to the Board by yourself over the past two years has revealed a number of discrepancies.'

'I kept those records for the benefit of the Treasurer. They are a matter for Mr Murray and myself. He has never found cause to criticise any of my actions.' There was a shifty expression in the schoolmaster's eyes. What was more, he was rapidly becoming sober. David noticed the change and proceeded with greater confidence.

'On the contrary, Mr Ogilvie, those financial records are the property of the Parish Council and should be made available to all who are eligible to elect the Council.'

Ogilvie made no comment and David continued.

'There are a number of discrepancies and omissions which require explanation. No mention is made, for example, of fees collected from private pupils. This morning you agreed that private coaching does take place.'

Still blustering indignantly, Ogilvie retorted, 'What is it to do with the Board if I choose to use my free time thus?'

'You are employed by the Board, sir. All teaching activities and monies accrued thereby are the property of the Board! In any case, it was not you yourself who carried out these duties, I believe.'

'What do you know of the matter, sir?' Ogilvie was now so red in the face that David began to fear the man would suffer a stroke. He softened his tone a little in an attempt to take the heat out of the discussion.

'Mr Ogilvie, you cannot disguise the fact that both Miss Logie and Miss Duncan have been taking extramural classes for which you have received payment. The pupils themselves, and their parents, have confirmed this. Your two assistants, although reluctant to admit the defect, have agreed that there has, as yet, been no mention of recompense from yourself for this work. Now,' he raised a hand to prevent Ogilvie's intervention in his own defence, 'that is not to say that you do not intend to make such payments. After this morning's motion on this matter, there can be no misunderstanding as to the amounts owing to the two ladies. I am sure that you are as anxious as I am to see that they receive their just desserts.'

His thunder stolen, the schoolmaster could only nod his head in acknowledgement.

'The provision of coal for the two schoolhouses is another matter, of course.'

Ogilvie was startled. The sudden switch in subject caught him off balance. He was immediately on the defensive.

'Coal? What about the coal?'

'I find,' David continued smoothly, 'that the Quarry Company makes a generous allocation of coals for the purpose of heating the school-houses. How is it, then, that the teachers are obliged to insist that the children themselves supply fuel? One piece of coal per child per day is, I believe, the required amount.'

'The rooms are large, the supply from the Company is inadequate.' The schoolmaster's protests were becoming more feeble. Every word he spoke signalled acceptance of his defeat.

'There is no coal in the bunkers of either schoolhouse, Mr Ogilvie. I suggest that this is because, under your instructions, the deliveries are made to your own house, on the far side of the village.'

'I am conscious of the risk of pilfering from the schoolyard,' Ogilvie protested. 'That is why I have it delivered directly to my house. From there it can be carried daily to the two classrooms.'

'Certainly it could be,' agreed David with a surprising degree of affability. 'But is it?'

Knowing full well that the schoolmaster had no answer to this last query, he continued, 'There is also the matter of the cleaning of the schoolrooms. I understand that the woman who undertook this work died in June of last year and has not been replaced?'

Ogilvie nodded. 'It has not been possible to find a suitable person as yet. Mrs Ogilvie has been asking around.'

Ignoring the stupidity of this reply, since David and Ogilvie were both aware of the countless number of women who would welcome such an opportunity, the doctor went on.

'Can you explain, therefore, how it is that the sum of sixpence per day for cleaning is entered in these accounts and claimed by you for payments to such a person? By my reckoning, there has been no clean-ing woman for thirty-nine weeks. It would therefore appear that you have claimed, fraudulently, the sum of five pounds seventeen shillings to date. I would suggest, sir, that this money has been stolen from the Board!'

His fish was thoroughly hooked now. The game was played out, and David was beginning to feel bored with the whole affair.

Ogilvie, white as a sheet, had risen to his feet. He stood trembling before his tormentor, the high walls of the narrow room closing in upon him. He was trapped, vanquished. He wanted only to be allowed to go, away from the whole sorry mess.

'What action do you propose to take, Dr Beaton?' he asked, struggling to regain some modicum of composure.

'Mr Ford believes that you are a very able teacher. He tells me that, for many years, he has admired the results which you are able to achieve with the more gifted of the children. He also assures me that, with your two very able assistants, Miss Logie and Miss Duncan, to take care of the smaller pupils, he can see no reason why you should not continue in charge of the two schools. We are agreed, however, that it would be wisest if matters of finance, provision of teaching materials, and additional coaching fees etcetera, should all be handled directly by the Treasurer of the School Board.'

'I was not aware that the Board had elected a Treasurer.' Ogilvie was anxious to know to whom he would be accountable.

'Mr Lugas has agreed to combine the duties of Secretary and Treasurer.'

Ogilvie was relieved. Lugas was at least an old friend, and could be trusted to view his demands sympathetically.

'Of course Mr Whylie, as the Company's representative, controls the purse-strings. Should you find it in your heart to apologise for the unfortunate remarks which led to this morning's unhappy events, I am sure that he will be more than happy to let drop the matter of the anomalies in your records.'

As he finished speaking, David reached for the door handle. He concluded, 'Providing, of course, that from now on you obey the ruling of the Board in these matters.'

Ogilvie acknowledged his agreement with a dispirited nod of the head.

'There will be no more talk of a summons for assault?' David pressed.

Again, Ogilvie concurred. The two men slipped back into the room where their fellows were engaged in a heated discussion of the efficacy of a peer in the role of Prime Minister. The Earl of Beaconsfield, who only a year ago had been plain Benjamin Disraeli, had been invited to form a government.

Lugas, a staunch Tory, was declaring the merits of the situation. Argyll was, however, a Whig stronghold. That a member of the English aristocracy should hold the principal position in the Commons was quite unacceptable to the Scottish members present. William, although careful not to make a display of his political loyalties, naturally supported any attempt to improve the lot of the working man, and leaned towards the philosophy of the new Liberal Party and Mr Gladstone. At this moment he was describing the medical insurance plan which he had at last persuaded his employers to support.

'It appears to me,' Lugas was saying, 'that the one person to benefit from the scheme will be the doctor! He will have his money, whether or no the men become sick.'

'He will not benefit when there is an epidemic. There will be no extra pay because a whole family falls ill,' David responded.

'All the more reason to pursue, with vigour, the improvement in the water supplies and drainage to the villages!' laughed William.

A look from David alerted him to the need to detach himself and pay attention to Ogilvie. The dominie stood, somewhat dejectedly, outside the cheerful group.

As he approached the chastened schoolmaster, William stretched out his hand.

'Well, Mr Ogilvie, what do you say? Shall we let bygones be bygones?'

'I believe that I was a little precipitate in the estimation of Miss Duncan's abilities as a teacher,' confessed Ogilvie. 'I apologise for anything which I have said to imply that her approach to her work is in any way other than impeccable.'

William shook the man more warmly by the hand than he deserved.

'I believe,' he announced to the company in general, 'that we all understand one another now. Mr Ogilvie, you have the full support of this Committee. We look forward to great progress in the year ahead and will anxiously await your report at our next meeting.'

Ogilvie sensed that it was time for him to go. He thanked his host for the luncheon before lifting his hat and stick from the stand and making his way to the front door.

Lugas accompanied him.

As they shook hands, the schoolmaster indicated his pleasure that it was the Factor with whom he would have most dealings.

Lugas viewed his friend with pursed lips and narrowed eyes.

'Times are changing, Farquhar. We must all watch our step with our new Chairman around. There is nothing so dangerous as a truly honest man!'

3

David had been quite right in suggesting that the Quarry Manager should own a boat of his own. William was not content, however, to go for one of the small rowing boats, favoured by most of the islanders.

As a boy, he had grown up amongst the fisherfolk along the North Cornish coastline. At the age of ten he had managed to steer home his uncle's fishing smack when the old man had been suddenly seized by a stroke. Silas Whylie had lived, a helpless cripple, for some years after that event. William continued to sail the vessel, catching fish on occasion and even, when the weather was calm and the day warm, taking his uncle out to the deep waters of the Bristol Channel.

Old Silas had died eventually, leaving his only earthly possession, *The Saucy Nancy*, to his nephew.

William had been at Eisdalsa for only a few weeks when he wrote to a boyhood friend asking him to find a crew and to sail *The Saucy Nancy* north.

The journey was a long one for a small sailing craft. The waters of the Irish Sea and the Sound of Jura were notoriously dangerous in bad weather. It was late March, therefore, when William received a note that his friends had left Newquay and were making their way to Scotland.

He hoped that his boat would arrive before 4 April when Gordon MacIntyre was due to visit him. A good sailor himself, he was only too aware of the dangers of these unpredictable Hebridean waters and welcomed the opportunity to make his first voyages in company with someone familiar with the charts and the nature of the tides.

From the top of the hill, William gazed out over the sea to that line of triangular, rocky islets known locally as the Isles of the Sea. That was where they would sail on the first fine day of Gordon's holiday.

He scanned the horizon, identifying many of the vessels, small and large, lying at anchor in the bay or loading their cargoes of slate. He hoped to see the familiar outline of his own craft. Constructed by Cornishmen, for Cornish waters, it would be instantly recognisable here.

Each day, when the office was closed, he had taken to coming up the hill in the hope of catching sight of *The Saucy Nancy*. Any day now her brown sails must appear over the horizon, flying up between the islands of the Sound, blown by the strong south-westerly gales of March.

Not for the first time, the Quarry Master reflected upon the day when he had received Gordon's request to visit him, the day of his confrontation with Ogilvie.

Only Ford's timely intervention had prevented him from choking the man to death. How grateful he was to the School Inspector!

He had thought often since then of the real reason for his violent reaction. His temper was normally well under control. It had amazed him that he could become enraged over the spiteful tittle-tattle of a few village gossips as related by the sanctimonious Ogilvie.

He thought very highly of Elizabeth. He was stirred by her beauty and admired her intelligence, a quality so often lacking in the girls of his acquaintance. He found her a most agreeable companion, and delighted to escort her to the various village functions.

Was it possible that his feelings for her were warmer than simple friendship?

He had been in love once and understood how strong emotion could distort a man's behaviour. A vision of the dark-eyed, pixie-like face of his little Cornish cousin returned to haunt him.

Millie had been taken from his reach by her avaricious father who planned to marry her off to a wealthy older farmer. She had claimed undying love for William, declaring that she would never forget him and protesting that she could not love another.

She did not look unduly distressed, however, when, attired in her bridal gown, she tripped down the aisle of the village church. She was now the mistress of a fine house, and probably raising a bevy of little Cornish farmers for all William knew.

The experience had taught him to keep a tight rein upon his feelings; to harden his heart against the wiles of the females he encountered; to guard himself against any future hurt.

Until now he had been successful. Elizabeth Duncan, however, was different from other girls he had met. Elizabeth would not knowingly hurt any man. She was pure gold, sweet and kind. It had been the sheer injustice of Ogilvie's insinuations which had enraged him. Of all the women William had known, Elizabeth was the least deserving of such slander.

From the top of the hill, he could see far to the south where the narrow strait between the islands poured its waters into the wide bay of the Sound of Lorn. He raised the old spyglass which had belonged to Uncle Silas, and scanned the horizon.

He swept the glass from east to west, catching sight of the landing at the mouth of the strait, to which the villagers sailed to church each Sunday, providing the tides were favourable. He scanned the narrow gap between Seileach and Lunga and on towards the tall triangular outline of Scarba. So clear was his view and so intense the magnification, that he could see red deer, grazing on the lower slopes, just above the treeline.

Now he took a sweep from west to east. There . . . was that a flash of brown? He concentrated so hard upon the view in his spyglass that he did not hear the ladies approaching.

Hot and tired from their exertions, Elizabeth, followed closely by Katherine Logie, who had been transferred to the Island to become her assistant, flopped down upon the close-cropped turf at the cliff's edge. Both were too out of breath to speak. It was some seconds before William turned. Then, full of apologies, he came and sat beside them.

'Forgive me, ladies! So intent was I on making out the vessel which has just come into view, that I did not realise you were here.'

'It was such a beautiful evening we could not resist the temptation to come and look at the sunset,' Elizabeth explained. 'I fear that I, for one, am out of condition for such strenuous exercise.'

'I come up here every evening in fine weather.' William indicated the broad sweep of the Atlantic. 'I love to watch the activity of the boats in the bay. The more vessels there are, the better business for the quarries!'

'You were so engrossed that we had climbed right up before you realised we were here.' Suddenly Katherine's attention was taken by a patch of colour in the longer grass. She jumped up, greatly excited. 'A wild orchid . . . and another. See, here is another!' The girl darted hither and thither through the heather, discovering more of the elusive blooms. Soon she was out of sight.

William again trained his spyglass on the brown sails. The ship should be identifiable by now.

Yes, there she was, *The Saucy Nancy*, beating proudly up the Sound against the flow of the tide. The vessel, with her deep keel and long, narrow hull, dipped into the ocean swell and cut a swathe through the glistening foam. In William's eyes she was a joy to behold, so different was she from the dumpy, shallow-drafted vessels of the Hebrides.

For a moment he was overcome by a surge of homesickness, greater than he could have believed possible.

'What is it?' Elizabeth was sensitive to this moment. 'Do let me look!'

William held out the spyglass and she placed it to her eye, as she had seen him do. There was a blurred image of what she took to be her own eyelashes.

'Oh, dear,' she cried in frustration. 'I see nothing, nothing at all!'

William came and stood behind her. He held her hands beneath his own, grasping the telescope, his arms encircling her shoulders.

He twisted the focussing ring until she gasped, 'I see it now . . . and so close! What a marvellous instrument. It is as if I could reach out and touch the sails with my hand.'

Her hair smelt of heather and lavender. It felt like silk against his cheek. He could feel the soft roundness of her breast against his arm, through the thin material of his shirtsleeve.

Abruptly, he released his hold, and for an instant the spyglass wavered as she adjusted to the greater weight. For a long time the girl stood before him, the glass trained on the distant brown sails. Her voluminous black skirts blew in the wind, revealing a tantalising glimpse of snowy white petticoats. Engrossed in the scene, brought so clearly into view by the instrument, Elizabeth moved forward, precariously close to the cliff edge. William feared for her safety. He lunged forward to grasp her around the waist and drew her towards him. She turned, holding the spyglass out sideways to avoid hitting him with it. Her look was one of surprise rather than fear.

William was suddenly covered in confusion. He released his hold on her and explained, somewhat lamely, 'You were getting too close to the edge. I had to pull you back.'

Anchoring her unruly skirts with her free hand, Elizabeth handed back the spyglass. There was nothing in her demeanour to suggest that she disbelieved his explanation.

'Is there something special about that particular vessel?' she enquired.

'Indeed there is,' he replied, his equilibrium restored. 'She happens to be mine!'

Astounded, Elizabeth looked out again at the little craft with the brown sails. She was close enough now to be seen clearly with the naked eye. 'I don't understand,' she said, 'where has she come from?'

'From Cornwall,' he told her proudly. 'She is *The Saucy Nancy*, out of Newquay. A proper Cornish fishing smack. I sent for her some weeks back, but the voyage was delayed by bad weather.'

'You will be taking her out in these waters yourself?'

'Of course. I have been sailing her since I was a boy.' William smiled at her. 'Don't look so surprised, even engineers may learn how to sail and fish!'

Her eyes were shining with anticipation.

'I have wanted so much to visit the Islands of the Sea. Annie tells me that there is an ancient chapel on Eileach an Naoimh.'

Katherine had returned in time to hear what Elizabeth said.

'I have been to the islands,' she declared. 'They are truly beautiful. Wild . . . unaffected by man, except for the old ruins of course.'

'When Gordon MacIntyre comes to stay, at the weekend, I intend to take a few days away from my work to try the *Nancy* out. I would prefer not to venture out alone until I have had guidance from someone familiar with the waters. Gordon's visit seems an ideal opportunity.'

So wrapped up was William in thoughts of the blissful days of sailing which lay ahead that he hardly noticed the increased excitement of his two companions.

'Oh, then you must take us along with you!' Katherine cried. 'You will take us, Mr Whylie, will you not?'

He laughed at her girlish excitement.

'If the weather stays calm, we will go on Sunday.' He raised his eyes questioningly at Elizabeth who smiled her approval.

As they clambered down the steep path, William indulged himself in a vision of streaming red hair and billowing skirts against a background of brown sails, the ship running westwards towards a glowing sunset.

Elizabeth's dream was different. She stood in the bows of *The Saucy Nancy* enfolded in strong arms, clad in a harsh dark blue woollen material whose gold braid trimmings brushed her cheeks. She could almost smell the salty tang of the uniform and the sharp scent of tobacco on Gordon's breath.

Gordon MacIntyre, in holiday mood, sprang ashore from the *Maid of Argyll*, taken into service to replace the *Lord of Lorn* while she was refitting. He gave a cheery wave to his friends aboard the steamer and sauntered along the pier to take a ferry to the island.

It was Saturday. At midday the quarries had closed down. Industrial noise was reduced to the soft putter-putter of the pumps, which never slept.

Sea-birds wheeled and cried above the boats of those quarrymen who were spending their afternoon at the fishing in the hope of replenishing their larders.

Children played by the shore, skimming stones across the mirror-like waters of the Sound.

It crossed Gordon's mind that Elizabeth too must have a free afternoon. He wondered what the pretty schoolmistress did with her spare time.

As he crossed the wide green, surrounded on three sides by neat white cottages, his question was answered.

Annie and Elizabeth sat outside the McGillivray house. Elizabeth was struggling to learn the art of spinning wool, while Annie was convulsed with laughter at the teacher's unsuccessful attempts to obtain a single, unbroken length of yarn.

Attracted by their merriment, Gordon approached the two women and took off his hat.

'Good day to you, Miss Elizabeth,' he said. 'I trust I find you well?'

'Why, Mr McIntyre!' Elizabeth rose to her feet, blushing and scattering her tools.

There was a mad scramble to retrieve the objects. Two heads, one black, one red-gold, came close. As both stretched out a hand to retrieve the spindle, their fingers touched and dark brown eyes looked deep into green. The moment was past in an instant and the two young people stood up, laughing to overcome their embarrassment.

Annie had observed the encounter with interest. She too had risen to her feet and waited patiently for Elizabeth to introduce her to her handsome friend.

'Annie, I think you do not know First Officer McIntyre of the *Lord of Lorn*. He was very kind to me when I had that fearful accident last November. Mr McIntyre, this is Mrs McGillivray.'

Annie shook the young man by the hand and made a slight curtsey. 'Mr McIntyre.'

'A pleasure, ma'am.' His face broke into smiles as he turned once more to Elizabeth.

'I am here for a week at least, Miss Duncan. I do hope that there will be some occasion for us to meet during my stay. I must have a word with William.'

'There are already plans afoot.' She smiled, eyes dancing. 'I will leave it to Mr Whylie to inform you of his intentions.'

'Now you have me really intrigued!' He did not exaggerate. 'I will hurry away to find William, and learn of my fate.'

Doffing his hat politely to the two women, he strode off around the head of the harbour towards the house of the Quarry Manager.

'Well,' said Annie, 'I wondered what was holding you back from accepting one of your two attentive suitors. Now I know!'

'Whatever are you talking about?' Elizabeth protested, 'Mr McIntyre is merely an acquaintance who has been very kind to me on more than one occasion.' She tried to make light of Annie's remark but her bright eyes and glowing cheeks belied the protest.

Annie said no more. She was too wise to make fun of her friend's feelings for the young seaman. It was clear to her, if not to Elizabeth herself, that the die was already cast for the two lovers.

Gordon was delighted at William's suggestion that they take *The Saucy Nancy* for a sail on the following day. There had been a fine spell of weather for a week or more. Those elders of the Island community who studied the vagaries of the climate had assured William that the clear skies and firm breezes would last for another twenty-four hours at least. Good weather, combined with a holiday from work, presented the ideal opportunity to try out his precious boat.

With Elizabeth in the party, William had thought it only natural to include David also. Since their arrival at Eisdalsa, last November, the three had tended to take their entertainments together. It was fortunate that Katherine Logie would also be present, to stop the gossips' tongues from wagging.

When she heard what he had planned, Elizabeth agreed readily. There was safety in numbers. What could the gossips have to say about a day trip on which she would be accompanied by at least two chaperons? Surely they could find nothing wrong in a party of friends going off together for a few hours?

Elizabeth lay on a bed of coiled rope on the well deck. The spring sunshine beat down upon her, the chill breeze deceiving her into thinking it was too cold for sunburn. She was beginning to realise, however, that David's warnings had been well founded. She could feel her skin beginning to smart. She pulled the silk scarf which was tied around her hair forward over her face, and resumed her dreaming.

The three men, all accustomed to the sea, were enjoying their freedom from the daily round. They had quickly merged into an efficient crew. David instructed Katherine in controlling the tiller, while William directed Gordon in handling the sheets.

Malcolm Logie's daughter was no stranger to sailing ships; she had been handling her father's craft for almost as long as she could remember, but she had no intention of enlightening David as to her experience of seamanship. She was enjoying the pretence of being an anxious beginner. If he found her to be a surprisingly able pupil, he made no comment.

Elizabeth, observing the glint in Katherine's eye when David gave yet another pedantic instruction, was the only one on board to realise that the girl was taking a rise out of him.

The rigging was a mystery to the two Scotsmen, but William quickly satisfied them that the system was simple and effective. Within the hour, both Gordon and David had mastered it.

William was absorbing the running commentary which Gordon provided on the nature of the currents, the distribution of rocks, and the relative depths of the ocean bed. All these details he needed to know for those occasions when his companions might not be available to accompany him.

Towards noon they anchored in a well-sheltered bay beneath a sheer cliff which towered some three hundred feet above the masthead.

In the cool shade, Elizabeth shivered and went below, to collect a shawl. As she came up the steps from the cabin she saw a movement, high on the cliff.

There was a flash of gold and white across the face of the rock. A dark shadow passed overhead and then, suddenly, the great eagle folded its wings and dived into the clear still waters. In an instant, it broke surface. There was a flurry as it struggled with the weight of the huge salmon which it gripped in its fearsome talons. The giant bird shed seawater in a shower of droplets, and with powerful wings beating strongly, returned to its eyrie near the top of the cliff.

'I wish I had my shotgun with me,' sighed David.

'You don't mean to say that you would kill a beautiful creature like that!' Elizabeth was aghast.

Gordon, who a moment before might have agreed with David, wisely disassociated himself from the argument and moved towards the stern where he had left a line trailing in the hope of catching something.

William, on the other hand, sprang to David's defence.

'Eagles catch the salmon and deprive the fisherfolk of a livelihood.'

'I cannot believe that a single pair of eagles and their brood have any effect at all upon the fish harvest,' Elizabeth protested. 'Why is it that men are never content unless they are going about killing something?'

'If the good Lord had not intended us to kill other living things, he would never have inspired us with technical ability to do so,' was David's pompous rejoinder. 'The reason that we are the superior species is because we have the ability to control, not only our own lives, but those of other creatures also.'

'I do not think it appropriate to lay the blame at God's door,' declared Elizabeth. 'That is to suggest that Man does not have free will. No, the fault is in yourselves and your destructive instincts, which are evil and have nothing to do with the Almighty!'

'Seals, otters, sea-birds, all take their toll of the fish harvest,' William remonstrated. 'There would be insufficient if these predators were not hunted.'

'I feel quite sure that there has been ample provision made for all.' Katherine tried to take the heat out of the discussion.

Elizabeth was not to be silenced. 'The fact remains that men are not satisfied with taking enough for their needs, but kill for pleasure. I am sure that David did not give a hoot for Archie MacLean's larder when he said he wanted to shoot the eagle. He thought only about the sport he was missing.'

By now her face was burning hot and her head was aching.

David, not to be outdone, pursued another avenue.

'No doubt you own a black bonnet with feathers adorning it?' He knew very well that she did, for she wore such a hat to church every Sunday.

'What of it?' Elizabeth demanded.

'Where do you think those feathers come from?'

As though on cue, a pair of blue-black birds flew down from above and skimmed the surface of the waves, their red legs protruding from beneath shimmering tail feathers like a rudder. They performed some acrobatic manoeuvres and then, as abruptly as they had appeared, returned to their perch on the cliff face.

'A pair of choughs will fetch as much as five shillings in Oban market, for their skins alone,' David pointed out. 'Would you deny the quarrymen their bonus? It is their only means of making that little extra money to buy something special for their families.'

Elizabeth shuddered, and vowed that she would never wear a feathered hat again.

William now joined in with equal gusto.

'Where do you suppose the plumes come from to decorate the hearse at funerals?'

'I had never really considered,' she admitted. 'I suppose I assumed that the feathers had been shed by the birds and were gathered up.'

'Thousands of birds are shot every year, just to adorn ladies and to provide funereal trappings,' proclaimed David. 'So why make a fuss about a single eagle?'

'But if that is the case, soon there will be no choughs left alive!' Elizabeth's eyes were wet with frustration or headache, she was not sure which.

'And if the eagles are allowed to raid the fishing grounds, soon there will be no more salmon.'

David was teasing her now, but she was beyond appreciating that the remark was meant to be humorous.

'It matters little what I say,' she replied. 'But I tell you this, one day women will have an equal voice with the men. Then we shall see if you are allowed to continue the wanton destruction of God's creatures.'

'Without a vote in Parliament, you will never be able to change the laws,' he taunted.

'And who says that women shall not have the vote one day!' Elizabeth knew that they were deliberately trying to provoke her but was now on to a topic which she relished. She knew that women's enfranchisement was a subject which shocked not only her male companions, but also many of her female acquaintances.

'You begin to sound like my mother!' he exploded. 'Women with the vote, indeed! A sorry state the country would be in, if women were to control its affairs.'

'I had not noticed anyone criticising the rule of our dear Sovereign,' Elizabeth retorted. 'Is she not a woman?'

'The Monarch does not make the laws, as well you know, madam!'

It was now David's turn to lose his temper. Katherine felt it was time to intervene. With the kind of movement that only a skilled hand could achieve, she luffed, causing the crew to grab sheets and duck as the heavy boom swung over.

By the time everyone had regained their positions and David had issued a stream of superfluous instructions to his pupil, the heat had gone out of the argument.

'I have a mind to explore these cliffs, to see if I can find the eagle's nest,' William announced.

'I had hoped to see the ruins of Brendan's chapel. I am told it is on the southern side of this island.' Elizabeth looked wistfully at William, hoping to remind him of her initial request to visit Eileach an Naoimh.

Her host, recalling his promise, would have changed his plans had not Gordon come forward at once and offered to accompany her.

'I enjoy exploring old ruins,' he declared, adding for William's benefit, 'Let me escort the ladies, then you may pursue your ornithological interests.'

'That is very kind of you.' Elizabeth rose to her feet. She turned to David, meaning to invite him to accompany them in an attempt at reconciliation.

'I shall stay aboard the boat,' he declared, forestalling her. Their exchange had become more bitter than he had intended. Why did they seem always to be on opposite sides in any argument? Perhaps it would be as well for him to avoid further conflict while she was in this mood. Once they were married and she had a house and babies to keep her occupied, no doubt she would put all this political nonsense behind her.

'Someone must stay with the boat and hold her off the rocks while the tide falls,' the doctor declared. 'Anyway, I think I had better do a little fishing, before the eagles take away the entire piscine population of the North Atlantic!'

Elizabeth was in no mood to enjoy the jibe. William and Gordon exchanged meaningful glances, but neither commented. Gordon felt it wisest not to declare for either side in this battle.

Katherine, amused at the exchange, had kept out of the argument.

Glancing from Gordon to Elizabeth, she sensed the bond which was forming between them. Elizabeth's steady gaze when their eyes met gave an unmistakable message. Realising instinctively what was required of her, Katherine turned to William.

'I have visited the ruins many times, Mr Whylie,' she said, 'but I have never seen an eagle's nest.'

Dismayed that his search might be inhibited by her presence, William was about to protest that the climb was too difficult and dangerous for a lady. Nevertheless, he relented when he saw her appealing look. Gallantly he agreed to take her.

'Very well, Miss Katherine,' he answered. 'I trust you are wearing suitable shoes.'

David, suddenly aware that Gordon McIntyre now had Elizabeth to himself, felt a tinge of unease, and a moment of regret for his precipitate announcement of his own plans.

At the present state of the tide, it was possible to draw *The Saucy Nancy* in close enough to a shelf of rock which the explorers could gain by leaping from the deck. Once all four were safely on dry land, David used a long oar to push her off. Still using the oar, he manoeuvred her out into the deepest water and dropped anchor.

He spent a little time tidying the deck, seeing that the sails were properly furled and ready for use as soon as the wanderers returned. From a locker he withdrew fishing tackle, and from his pocket a notebook. While the fish sought out his bait, in the dark waters, he drew sketches of the rocks and the wild birds. As he drew, he studied the shape and the antics of the marvellous creatures about him and thought of Elizabeth's tirade against wanton killing. In his heart he was obliged to concede that the destruction of a whole species was a possibility. To suggest, however, that the one or two creatures which he killed were of any significance was ridiculous. Anyway, he enjoyed shooting. Was not a man entitled to a little sport now and again?

The sun was warm and the air still. Soon his eyelids drooped, the pencil slid from his hand and the pages of his book flapped lazily in the light breeze. When his fishing line suddenly became taut, David was quite unaware of it. Whatever took the bait managed to eat its snack without snagging the hook.

Not for the first time, Elizabeth resented the fact that she could not dress like a man. The terrain was a rock-strewn slope, covered with last year's dead heather, newly sprouting bracken, and in the gullies between the boulders, the strap-like leaves of the wild yellow iris. At least these gave warning of a boggy patch. Otherwise her skirts would have been as wet and muddy as her lightweight boots.

Gordon was as gallant as circumstance allowed. He helped her over the widest chasms and up on to the higher boulders. For the rest, however, it was each one for himself.

After half an hour, they reached the first of the monuments which they had come to see.

A tall beehive-shaped structure, fashioned cunningly of dressed stone, rose out of the heather. To form the roof, the blocks had been placed slightly off centre at each level, so that the circular walls closed in towards the middle as the building reached its full height. At the top, one single, carefully carved block filled the gap and at the same time gave strength to the entire building.

Gordon and Elizabeth examined every inch of the monument, which was some twelve feet in diameter and fifteen or more high at the centre.

'What was it, do you suppose?' Gordon asked.

'Annie told me that this is the chapel belonging to a small monastery built by St Brendan eight hundred years ago,' Elizabeth replied. 'A hundred yards from here, just over that mound, we should find the remains of the monastery buildings.'

The path to the monastery, although overgrown by brambles and nettles, was well defined. A closely cropped, fine turf indicated that it had been maintained by the sheep who, no doubt, sought shelter amongst the ancient ruins.

Most of the walls had long since fallen down. Much of the stonework had been carried away by sheep herders, who visited these uninhabited islands to tend their flocks in the summertime. The two explorers had noticed a number of small stone huts and rough shelters for the sheep as they made their way across the island.

The foundations of most of the ruins were obscured by trailing plants. Had Gordon not lost his balance, and fallen into the opening, they might never have found the hermit's cell.

At one moment he was striding across the heather; the next he had disappeared completely.

Elizabeth clambered more cautiously towards the place from which issued a flow of naval profanity which might have brought a blush to the face of even the most hardened quarryman. At least he is still alive, she thought, and not much hurt if he is making such a noise.

At last she came to the spot. She was hard put to it not to laugh aloud. Gordon had stumbled into an area which was usually approached by a short flight of steps. It was obviously the entrance to an underground room. He had caught his foot at the top of the steps, and fallen backwards into the opening of the cell. The momentum with which he had been propelled had forced him into the narrow opening where he was now firmly stuck. The quality of his protest assured Elizabeth that he had suffered no injury, other than to his dignity.

She descended the steps herself, climbing over his prostrate body in her attempt to reach the opening and help to free him. She found that it was his boot which was the cause of the trouble. Tightly laced, and protected by heavy steel caps to toe and heel, it had lodged itself firmly between two blocks of unyielding stonework. The more he struggled, the deeper into the fissure between the stones the boot was forced.

'Stop struggling,' she commanded in her best schoolroom tone. 'And less noise would be helpful.'

Having at last remembered that he was not in the engine room of the *Lord of Lorn*, Gordon apologised sheepishly for his bad language.

'Try to ease yourself from the doorway.' As he began again to protest, she cajoled him with soothing sounds. 'Just a little . . . try.'

Red in the face from his exertions, Gordon attempted to pull his shoulders back from the opening to the ancient cell. With his foot held fast, he had no purchase against which he could push himself free.

Despairing of ever moving him, Elizabeth changed tactics by putting all her effort into freeing his foot. She pushed and pulled, but no amount of straining would dislodge the boot. Finally she declared, 'There is no other way. I shall have to cut the lace. Do you have anything that I can use?'

Here they were fortunate. No seaman ever travels without his knife. Gordon's, however, was in his trouser pocket, on the side on which he was lying. He indicated its position and Elizabeth, after a momentary hesitation, began to reach around, feeling for it.

As she struggled to get her fingers into the pocket and grasp the knife, she had a fleeting vision of Ellen Ogilvie and Myra McCulloch. At the thought of their expressions, had they been present at this moment, she began to giggle. Once having given way to her feelings, she laughed aloud and then, because Gordon obviously thought she was laughing at his predicament, she had to explain.

He joined in her merriment and as the tension eased, she found that she had managed to grasp the knife. In an instant, she had it free.

Relieved, yet strangely sorry that she had retreated from the position of intimacy he had so much enjoyed, Gordon allowed his aching hip to relax again against the ground.

It took some minutes for Elizabeth to saw her way through the strong leather thongs, but at last she accomplished it. There was a twang as the two ends flew apart and Gordon found he was able to ease his foot out, leaving the boot still firmly wedged.

Once free to move his leg, Gordon could take sufficient purchase on the rock to extricate himself from the narrow doorway. He sat up, tenderly examining his knees and ankle which had been badly scraped in the fall. Elizabeth retrieved the empty boot with minimal effort and helped him to struggle to his feet.

They clung together for a fraction longer than was absolutely necessary. Gordon would have thrown all caution to the winds at this point. His lips were about to meet hers when Elizabeth, realising his intention, brushed aside his restraining hand and turned back to the entrance.

'Do you suppose some ancient hermit dwelt here?' she enquired brightly.

'Who can tell? It seems likely.' His response was automatic; he was still imagining the feel of her soft lips against his own. His senses were filled with her perfume and his ears were ringing, as though he had been struck by a prizefighter.

'Now the way is clear,' Elizabeth continued provokingly, 'perhaps I may see inside this hermit's cell?'

She passed into the underground place which was hardly large enough to accommodate one average-sized man. The wall to one side had been hewn so as to leave a narrow ledge which served as a seat.

Elizabeth sat down, still holding Gordon's boot, and attempted to tie the cut lace. It was more difficult than she had imagined. The leather was tough and unyielding. When he came and sat beside her, to relieve her of the task, she gave up gratefully.

There was barely room for both to sit side by side. His footwear restored, it seemed necessary for Gordon to slide his arm around Elizabeth's waist to prevent her falling off the end of the ledge.

She was still laughing when he placed his other hand under her chin and turned her face towards him. They gazed for a long time into each other's eyes. Then, slowly, his mouth came down to cover her own.

The kiss was long, lingering; neither of them willing to break the spell. Elizabeth had never experienced such a feeling of complete unity with another being.

His hands fondled her swelling breasts. She gave a gasp as his fingers touched one erect nipple, and then the other.

One large warm hand now held her firmly behind the head. He bent her along the hard seat as his knees slid on to the floor. Rocking her in his arms, he kissed her again and again.

She could feel herself sinking, sinking, into sweet oblivion.

She felt him shift his position. Gently, he grasped her hand and guided her fingers towards his swelling manhood. She forced him away from her, not roughly but with a gentle pressure to reassure him that she was not alarmed, only cautious. Her body cried out to belong to him, but her head told her that this was not the way.

Gordon, too, was amazed at the power of the attraction between them. There had been other women, many others, but none like this. This was something far too important to be marred by a stupid indiscretion.

There was no need for words. They stood up and left the cell, he leading her by the hand, up the stairs, and out on to the open hillside.

William held out his hand to Katherine as they climbed cautiously down the cliff. With his free arm he steadied his knapsack, keeping it away from the sharp rocks. He could see Elizabeth and Gordon waiting patiently while David brought *The Saucy Nancy* close inshore. The climbers hailed their friends from their perch on the cliff face, but Elizabeth and Gordon appeared to be too absorbed in conversation to pay them any attention. It was not until they reached the rocky beach and declared their treasure that Elizabeth acknowledged their arrival.

William opened his bag carefully, so as not to disturb the contents. Lying comfortably cocooned inside his woollen muffler were two enormous eggs, at least three inches in length, white, with reddish spots.

Gordon was impressed.

'So you reached the eyrie! That was quite a climb.'

'Not without its exciting moments, I can assure you,' Katherine agreed as she rubbed ruefully at a bruise on her shin.

William, still elated with his find, lifted one of the eggs up for Elizabetha to see it more clearly.

'I cannot believe that you have robbed the bird of its young,' she said coldly. 'After all that was said earlier, about Man's destruction of God's creatures.'

'Oh, come now,' William exclaimed. 'No harm has been done here. The nest had three eggs. The largest was already cracking. Once the first chick is hatched the parents will turn out the others, they cannot feed a large family.'

Elizabeth was still not satisfied. She turned to Gordon for support.

'Surely you do not condone the removal of wild birds' eggs from the nest, Gordon?'

The seaman, who in his youth had made a fine collection of eggs himself, was hard put to it to find a diplomatic turn of phrase.

'I think William is correct in what he says, my dear,' he ventured, after a moment's hesitation. 'The adults will not raise more than one chick. Although,' turning to William, 'they usually allow all the chicks to hatch and choose the strongest to rear, after a few days.'

'What if something happens to the remaining chick?' Elizabeth was not convinced. 'Then the parent birds will have no offspring.'

'They will lay another clutch of eggs,' Gordon assured her.

If William had given this explanation, she would not have accepted it. As it was, she bowed to Gordon's wisdom, smiling sweetly at him as she surrendered to his superior knowledge.

William was too elated with his find to make any close observation of the demeanour of his two friends. Katherine, however, perceived a subtle change in the manner in which they regarded one another. The schoolteacher was flushed with an excitement attributable to something more than the ruins which they had just visited.

Katherine felt her own grinding agony of separation. Her thoughts were of her own darling Murdo as she gazed upon these two young lovers.

By the time that David had manouvered the boat against the rock shelf, and helped the adventurers to jump aboard, Elizabeth and Gordon had somewhat regained their composure.

While the crew took up their former occupations, Elizabeth set about providing for the inner man, finding provisions for a picnic supper in the generous hamper which had been supplied by Maggie MacLean. Gordon took the tiller to steer the little craft away from the dangerous coastline. As he did so, he pointed out to William the unmistakable fin of a basking shark.

David, who was busy with the sheets, also noticed the great fish, but refrained from voicing his disappointment that he was without his gun.

4

The summer of 1877 was unusually dry on the West Coast. The small patches of garden, so carefully tended by the islanders, quickly began to show signs of drought. The potato crop proved small and riddled with diseases of every kind, while cabbage, kale and other green plants, essential to the well-being of the community, withered and died for want of moisture.

Worse was the effect upon the supply of well water on the island. There had been two wells at one time. Now, one of these had been encroached upon by quarrying, and the water was definitely tainted with sea water. The brackish fluid was finally discarded when it was noticed that surrounding plant life was being killed off by the spillage.

To add to the problem, the mountain streams dwindled to nothing and the Seileach loch, which supplied piped water to both the Village and the Island, shrank, causing graceful rushes and yellow irises on its banks to die.

David went about the Parish warning people to boil all their water, but he knew that there would be resistance to using up precious stores of fuel which were being put by for the coming winter. He had little hope that the poorest families would obey his instruction.

In one cottage he found six members of the family lying sick in one tiny room. Three children lay tossing in their fever in one box bed. Three-year-old twins, too weak to move, occupied a part of what was clearly their parents' bed, while on a pallet in the corner lay an elderly grandmother. Within the same confined space, the mother attempted to cook for her patients and boil water for the endless round of washing of soiled linen. Within the week David had signed death certificates for the babies and their grandmother. Of the remainder, only the father managed to follow the hearse on its two-mile route to the cemetery. David was still fearful that others of the family would not survive.

The disposal of human waste was also a matter of great concern to the doctor. From the Village houses, soil was normally thrown into a narrow open drain which ran down the centre of the main street.

In normal climatic conditions, rain could be relied upon to wash the noxious contents of this ditch into the sea. During the months of June and July no rain fell, and the ditch became clogged.

On the Island, lacking even the benefit of a street drain, the people dumped their waste at the head of the harbour, in the knowledge that at each period of high tide, all would be washed clean. The abnormal lack of rain had no effect upon the tides, so the nuisance was no more than usual on Eisdalsa.

As the number of cases of enteric fever mounted, David became more and more alarmed. Families of six or more, crammed into tiny two-roomed cottages, stood no chance of avoiding disease once one of their number succumbed.

At the end of each long, tiring day, the doctor spent more of his time writing to the Chief Medical Officer, to Lugas, and eventually to His Lordship himself, entreating them to make improvements in the water supply. He enlisted William's support in his pleading. The engineer prepared plans for a new water supply, although promise of future improvements could be of no help in the present situation.

'At least we will not have to go through this particular torment again,' David declared when they had completed their proposals for a huge water reservoir to be constructed above the village.

'Always supposing that our request will be considered.' William was only too well aware that there had been a number of suggestions for improvement in living conditions which had been shelved for lack of interest on the part of His Lordship's agent.

It was perhaps fortuitous that the Marquis of Stirling had chosen this period to visit the district. His young wife was pregnant, and he had a particular wish that his heir should be born in Lorn, the home of his ancestors.

Lugas and his family had moved out into one of the estate cottages to give their noble employer the freedom of the Castle. Alexander accepted this situation without complaint. He recognised that his own family's occupation of the main house, in His Lordship's absence, was a privilege. He was quite indifferent to his wife Alicia's angry response to his instruction to remove the household to less prestigious accommodation for a short while. She went about all summer with a disgruntled air, resenting her perceived loss of status in the community. She longed for the child to be born, and His Lordship, together with his slip of a girl-bride, gone from their midst.

His Lordship spent much of his time visiting his tenant farmers. It was on these occasions that he began to hear rumours of the problems being experienced in the quarry communities. Concern for the health of his own household prevented him from going himself to view the situation. Instead, he sent for his Quarry Manager and the young Dr Beaton.

'Whylie, my dear fellow, Alexander Campbell has nothing but praise for your work. He tells me that sales have increased a hundred per cent and that you have opened up two new workings!'

His Lordship motioned the two young men towards seats before taking up his favourite stance beside the rather cumbersome marble fireplace in the great hall of the castle. The Marquis had enjoyed an eventful career with The Argyles, before inheriting his title. His tall, straight figure, assured bearing, and penetrating gaze were the unmistakable marks of a military man. There was however a tendency towards a thickening of those tightly muscled limbs. Without the regular exercise of an active working life he had tended to run to fat and although no one could accuse the Marquis of Stirling of living the dissipated existence embraced by so many of his class, he enjoyed the fruits of his inherited wealth to the full. His florid countenance confirmed it.

'And you, doctor.' His Lordship addressed David. 'Are you content to take over your father's work? There was some talk of a London appointment, I believe?'

David should not have been surprised at His Lordship's knowledge of his affairs. The previous Marquis had been something of a philanthropist. He had endowed the University Hospitals of both Edinburgh and St Andrews, and kept a close watch upon the progress of those young men who were sponsored by his vast estates. His successor had access to the old man's records and seemed to be taking an active interest in them.

'It was appropriate that I should come back to Eisdalsa, under the circumstances,' David murmured, unwilling to be drawn into a discussion of his decision.

'Well, gentlemen, let us not waste time on idle considerations,' continued His Lordship. 'I have brought you both here to discuss the unfortunate conditions in the villages hereabouts, due I believe to this unprecedented drought?'

'While it is true that the drought has exacerbated the situation,' said William, 'there is no doubt in my mind that the water supply is inadequate. With the opening of the two quarries you have mentioned, I have been obliged to bring even more families into the area. This has not only caused congestion in the houses but has placed a further demand on the water supplies. Were it to rain tomorrow, we should still have a problem.'

David was quick to follow up with his own argument.

'Whether or not the quantity of water is increased,' he declared, 'it is the quality of the supply which gives most concern. The drainage system, particularly here on Seileach, is abysmal, there are no official scavengers, and the villagers themselves appear unmoved by my entreaties that they clear the nuisance for themselves. If waste is not washed into the sea, but backs up into the habited areas, then it is almost inevitable that the water supply will become contaminated.'

'I had not realised that this was more than a temporary problem caused by the drought. That was how it was put to me by Mr Lugas.'

'With all due respect, My Lord,' David asserted, making little effort to disguise his indignation, 'your agent has not seen fit to visit the villages at all during this crisis. I do not consider him in a position to express an opinion on the matter.'

David had sent several notes to Lugas during the past weeks, begging him to come and see for himself the condition of the villagers. On every occasion, the Factor had found more pressing matters requiring his attention.

'The immediate problem of water supplies,' William intervened, sensing that David's bluntness could injure their case, 'may be solved by carting in supplies on a daily basis. There is a good well at Clachan, sufficiently deep to have been unaffected by the dry weather. If Your Lordship will agree to the use of Estate horses and drays, I will be happy to organise a team of quarrymen to transport supplies, until the weather breaks.'

The Marquis nodded his head. 'I will notify Lugas that I approve of the arrangement,' he declared. 'Meanwhile you may proceed without further delay.'

'There is still the matter of the long-term solution.' William drew out a sheaf of drawings. 'These are diagrams of a system for storing water in a large reservoir, and piping it to the villages. It will require the water to be pumped up from Loch Craim, which is large enough to maintain a good supply.'

'Will that not require a steam pump to be installed, and a man to operate it?' His Lordship cast an experienced eye over the plans, making a rapid calculation. The result left him somewhat less than enthusiastic.

'I have recently acquired a number of excellent pumps from the breaker's in Greenock,' William hastened to reassure him. 'Among them is one which would be more than adequate for the task. As to maintenance, the quarry engineer can easily take the new installation under his supervision. Only a stoker would be required, paid at a labourer's rate. It is a job for an older man, no longer useful in the quarries.'

'You come armed with sufficient ammunition to overwhelm my every objection,' laughed the Marquis. 'How much do you believe it will cost to build the reservoir and lay the pipes?'

'As for the reservoir, the quarry masons may be engaged to carry out the work, using local materials. The cost will be restricted to their normal wages. Only the pipes will need to be brought in, and a man employed who is proficient in their laying.'

'You have certainly thought of every angle.' The Marquis found the self-assurance and general bearing of this young engineer to be all that his London agent had suggested. He was well satisfied with the appointment. 'Do you have an estimate of the total finance required?'

'I believe that the whole matter of water supply may be resolved for approximately three hundred pounds,' replied William.

Noting with some relief that the Marquis was not unduly perturbed by this quotation, David ventured to press home his own proposition.

'There remains the vexatious problem of the refuse dump at Eisdalsa and the open drain in Seileach village.'

'What are your proposals in that respect?' The Marquis directed his question at William.

'I would suggest that the drain be closed in, and that proper ash pits are constructed to replace the midden. A scavenger would need to be appointed to keep these cleared regularly. As for the midden on the island, the people should be instructed not to use it. Again ash pits, emptied regularly, should be installed.'

'Is not the scavenging a matter for the Local Authority?' asked the Marquis. 'It seems to me to be pointless to have local Medical Officers of Health and not back them up by providing proper sanitation.'

William found difficulty in restraining his anger and frustration. This was precisely the argument put by both the Company and the Local Authority. Neither was prepared to shoulder responsibility for this distasteful task. It was David who now took up the cudgels.

'I have already approached the Sanitary Engineer in Oban,' he protested. 'He appears to think that the Company has full responsibility for refuse in the quarry villages.'

'Then, maybe you should go to the Board of Directors on the matter?' The Marquis clearly considered the topic closed, for he now went on to discuss with William the proposals made by the School Board for bursaries for promising pupils. This was a matter of far greater appeal to him than drains, middens and cesspits.

The question of Michael Brown's training was soon dealt with. The Marquis liked the idea that the professional people on his estates should be his own men. Michael's future was assured. A promise that further consideration would be given to others on the list of applicants ended the discussions. As David and William rose and prepared to leave, the Marquis drew David aside for a private word.

'Dr Beaton, my wife will be confined towards the end of August. I have of course arranged for a consultant to be in attendance for the birth, but in the meantime I would like you to look in on her occasionally, to make sure all is well. It is our first child. I should not want there to be any mishaps.'

'I shall be happy to oblige, My Lord. Perhaps you would convey my respects to Her Ladyship and tell her that I will call upon her on Wednesday next at twelve o'clock?' David tried hard to disguise his elation at this invitation. His mother would be delighted to know that her son's skills were sought in such exalted circles!

'Splendid,' cried His Lordship, rubbing his hands in genial fashion. 'I will tell her to expect you . . . perhaps you will join us for luncheon after your consultation?'

William considered the offer of a free meal poor compensation for disregarding David's concern for the health of the villagers. A feeling which he was quick to express during their ride back to Tigh na Broch.

'It is something to have made contact with the man,' David replied with uncharacteristic complacency. 'When I get to know him better, I will try again. At least the matter of the water supply is settled. Let us be thankful for that.'

'He was certainly more amenable when it came to the children's schooling. Michael Brown will be overjoyed. I will tell his father before I cross over to the island.' William climbed down from the trap as David drew up before the house.

'You cannot go just yet,' he said. 'My mother has been pestering me for weeks past, to ask you to take a meal with us.'

Always reluctant to turn down the offer of Sheilagh's cooking, William readily assented to stay for dinner. David handed the reins to the stable lad, who had emerged from the stable while they were talking. Smiling and relaxed, the two friends strode into the house.

William had left at four o'clock, protesting that he must inspect work at the Seileach quarry, as well as the two new workings on Eisdalsa before the men finished for the day.

David went into the study to examine a mysterious parcel which Morag had mentioned more than once during their meal. One might think the package had been addressed to her, so keen was she to discover its contents.

Even as he cut the string, and began to peel off the many layers of thick brown paper, David found his mother at his elbow.

'Really, Mama, it is not Christmas Eve. This is only a parcel from Joseph . . . books perhaps. It is certainly heavy enough.'

'It is not books,' she exclaimed, unable to restrain her excitement. 'The man who brought it had strict instructions to carry it one way only. If it were books, it would not matter which way up the parcel was carried!'

As she protested further about his slow progress with the wrappings, David removed the last sheet to reveal a polished wooden box. Fitted with best quality brass handles and hinges, it was clearly a container for something of special value.

He fiddled with the lock for a moment, adding to Morag's impatience. Then the door of the small cabinet flew open to reveal a microscope such as David had seen only once before.

The binocular instrument was made of brass, burnished so that it gleamed in the bright July sunshine. Every moving part slid smoothly into position when the knurled edged wheels were turned. Mirror and lenses, each expertly fashioned, were mounted in finely wrought metal.

The monogram JL, the letters beautifully entwined, formed an intricate pattern on the front of the barrel.

Joseph Lister's parent had clearly put as much love and care into the construction of this magnificent instrument as he had into that which he had built for his own son.

Morag was awestruck by the quality of the gift. Nothing would satisfy her but that David should mount something on one of the set of glass slides, which accompanied the microscope, that she might see how it worked. He swatted a bluebottle and pulled off one wing. With a drop of glycerine, he mounted the delicate material and focussed on it. The intricate pattern of veins jumped into view. When he was satisfied that she could see clearly, he left Morag to admire the fly's wing while he read Lister's letter.

The London
Hospital,
9 July 1877

My Dear David,

It seems a long time since I heard from you. I believe that in your last letter you mentioned a sailing trip at Easter . . . that shows how long ago it was!

You have kindly agreed to record your successes, and otherwise, with the Lister aseptic system. I trust that this instrument will assist you in your researches. It is one of my father's finest pieces, to date. There are refinements which even my own microscope lacks.

Word is that there is a serious outbreak of cholera in Glasgow, owing to the humid weather. I trust that you are not yourself plagued with anything so terrible.

I attended a meeting at the Royal Society last month at which a paper was given by one Robert Koch. He has devised a method of staining bacteria so that they may be seen under a microscope. I attach my notes on his method and a list of the chemicals used. You will probably need to experiment to get just the right density of stain but I feel sure that this instrument will be powerful enough for your purposes.

You mentioned in your last letter that you were advising villagers to keep windows closed to avoid noxious night airs. Are you aware that it is now thought that there is no reason to suppose it dangerous to open windows at night? Typhoid and cholera germs are carried in water, not air, according to the latest thinking. Indeed, there are those who would advocate sleeping with the windows open, in cramped conditions, to avoid tuberculosis.

Well, old friend, no need to tell you how much I miss your company, and your support. It is hard going here, amongst so many sceptics. I have three wards which are aseptic now. Results have been remarkable, particularly in the maternity ward. Nevertheless there are still surgeons on the staff of this hospital operating in their frock-coats and not washing their hands between patients!

Congratulations on your appointment to the School Board. I agree entirely with your surmise that a healthy childhood is more likely to lead to a healthy, and long, adult life. I thought I had seen the worst poverty possible in the Glasgow streets, but the conditions in which people live in the East End of London are quite as appalling. There is a local philanthropist, a Mr Peabody, who has designed and begun building model housing for the poorest people. I shall await the medical statistics related to this improvement with interest.

All good wishes to your mother. Are any other congratulations in order yet? I seem to recall mention of a beautiful schoolmistress in distress?

I am, my dear fellow, your respectful and devoted friend,

Joseph Lister

David caressed the microscope with loving fingers and thought with longing of that world in which his friend moved. Not for the first time did he wonder if he had been foolish to abandon all thought of the prestige and wealth which might have been his had he followed Joseph to London. Was the fiery little schoolmistress worth such a sacrifice?

Many times, in the last few weeks, he had wanted to take hold of her and shake her to her senses. His mother had advised patience. He had tried to understand Elizabeth's desire to show that she was capable of doing her work at the school. Indeed, she had more than succeeded. Even the most venomous of the Eisdalsa women had been forced to concede that the girl knew what she was doing. As for the children, they loved and respected her in a manner which was very strange to one who had been forced to suffer the terrors and indignities imposed by a boarding school education. Even David's early years in the Village school had been an experience dominated by fear of the tawes and the stern-faced, unrelenting dominie who wielded it. Oh, yes, there was no doubt that Elizabeth was an excellent teacher, but how could she suppose that a profession, however appropriate, could be a satisfactory substitute for marriage and motherhood?

Removing the slide from the stage, he replaced his new microscope carefully in its box.

Then, casting aside his gloom, he led his mother out through the garden door, to the little terrace where they took their afternoon tea.

'I have such news for you, Mother. I am to take luncheon with the Marquis and his lady on Wednesday next.'

5

Alexander Lugas collected together the piles of paper which had become strewn across his desk. He was not sorry to see the back of the lawyer, Martin Scott. It had been a tough struggle to get him to agree to the arrangements, but it seemed that he would be prepared to go along with them, for a consideration.

As he slid the vital documents into a stout canvas folder, his gaze fell on a note he had received that morning from the Marquis.

Whylie had been whining to him, no doubt, about the water supply. Had he and that fool doctor nothing better to do than fuss about drains, ditches and water? Now they had His Lordship running around for them. Well, let them get on with it. If Whylie was going to arrange transportation of water supplies from the Clachan well, he himself need not take any part in it!

He reached for his hat and called to his wife.

'Alicia, I am riding down to the pier. I have a package which must reach Glasgow tonight.'

'Surely one of the servants can go?' she protested. 'Really, it is most undignified for the Estate Factor to be seen scurrying to catch the steamer!'

'I would rather take it myself,' he insisted. 'There are special instructions for its delivery.'

Without waiting for further argument, he picked up his riding crop and hurried to the stable.

When old man Bellamy had been declared bankrupt, nearly a year ago, he had been forced to give up the Ballahuan estate. For some months Alexander had been at pains to find a suitable tenant to replace him.

Eventually it was Edward Murray, already a tenant of one of the smaller farms on the Stirling Estate, who declared an interest in both the house and farm. Murray had come relatively recently to the district. A manufacturer of woollen textiles, he had made his fortune during a succession of military conflicts, around the world, supplying uniforms to Her Majesty's Armed Forces. Having relinquished responsibility for the running of his factories to his two sons, Edward had decided to retire to a life of ease in the Highlands. He quickly discovered that it was no easy matter to become accepted within the community he had chosen. While there was a great gulf between the circumstances of the landowners and the working classes, there was an understanding and a great comradeship between all native parishioners, no matter what their status. No outsider could hope to force himself upon them. Strangers must earn their respect and their friendship.

Edward soon found that money held very little sway with these people. In the Lowlands, where his factories employed the bulk of the workforce in the town, he had been used to a form of deference. His was an elevated status, consequent upon his influential position as the major employer. On the island of Seileach, and amongst the quarry workers of Eisdalsa, Edward Murray's presence was tolerated with nothing more than indifference.

Believing that in order to be able to associate with the nobility and the dignitaries of the area he should push himself forward as a benefactor of the poor, Edward had become acquainted with Alexander Lugas. Flattered by the attentions of his wealthy neighbour, the Marquis' Factor had used all his influence to have Edward Murray accepted in those circles where decisions concerning the social life of the district were made. In due course, he had been elected to the Poor Law Committee, and it was then only a matter of time before he had become Chairman of the Parish Council. The generous donations to worthy charities were, he considered, a price worth paying for acceptance by his fellow parishioners.

To become a member of that society which orbited around the Marquis and his noble family, however, would take more than a little money scattered amongst the poor. He required a country seat of some importance, and a sizeable area of land, well stocked with game.

The fact that Ballahuan had very little rough shooting within its feu had not deterred Lugas from clinching a deal with the former manufacturer. There were, after all, a number of farms and crofts which were sublet, constituting some seven hundred acres in all. The ploughed land was fertile and yielded good cereal crops, supplying the quarry villages with all their requirements of oats and barley, at a reasonable price. The grazing land supported cattle and sheep sufficient to provide milk and meat for the whole area.

At first, Edward Murray had been reluctant to take on the responsibility of the working farms, since he planned to spend only a few months each year on Seileach. It was only when Lugas pointed out to him that all the tenancy agreements would be coming up for review at the end of the year that he at last agreed to take the lease.

In his dealings with Lugas, Murray had stressed his intention of disbanding the farms and converting all the land to rough shooting. He had made it clear to Alexander that he would be more than generous in the matter of compensation if the Factor was able to clear the farms without fuss or too much publicity.

Lugas had chosen not to enlighten His Lordship on the terms laid down by Mr Murray. Indeed, until today the business had been a closely guarded secret between himself and Edward.

It had been difficult to persuade Martin Scott, the solicitor, to draw up the new rent demands. He was clearly uncomfortable about the terms to be issued to the tenant farmers, and convinced that the rents proposed were too high for the men to pay.

'Some of these farms have been in the same family for generations,' he had protested. 'If they cannot meet Mr Murray's demands, they will be turned out of their homes, their living destroyed.'

Lugas had shrugged his shoulders. 'What am I to do?' he had asked. 'My instructions come directly from the new tenant of the Ballahuan Estate. I am simply carrying out his wishes.'

'Does this Edward Murray not appreciate the high regard in which the tenants are held on this Estate? The loyalty and good husbandry of generations of one family cannot be disregarded on the whim of a newcomer, ignorant of local custom. What has His Lordship to say upon the matter?'

Lugas had sighed convincingly. 'These newly rich landlords have no respect for our customs, as well you know,' he had declared. 'As for His Lordship's opinion, Mr Murray is an acquaintance of his, and he presumably was aware of the man's intentions when he purchased the lease.'

In the end Lugas had been forced to suggest to the lawyer that if he were not willing to draw up the new agreements, then he might be obliged to persuade His Lordship to engage another legal adviser. Mr Scott was finally persuaded by the promise of a handsome commission on each tenancy he retrieved.

When the legal documents were at last complete, and ready for Murray's signature, Alexander Lugas was anxious that they should reach the new tenant without delay.

He cantered past a field where the men were building the first hay-stooks of the season. By next year, or perhaps the year after, all these fields would be laid to waste. Bracken and heather would soon take over, providing cover for partridge and pheasant.

Not for one moment did Alexander Lugas consider the effect of his activities upon the population of Seileach and Eisdalsa. It was not his responsibility to provide supplies of food for quarrymen. They would have to import their meal by sea, as indeed they got most other things. That the cost of transport would be too high for most of the poorer people, was no concern of his.

Down by the quay, the *Lord of Lorn*, her fresh paintwork gleaming, and her newly cleaned boilers emitting only the whitest of smoke, was bustling with the activity of imminent departure.

Lugas kicked his heels into his mare's flanks and galloped along the back street, to the pier.

*　　　*　　　*

David presented himself at the Castle precisely at twelve o'clock on the following Wednesday.

The housekeeper was a stately, almost handsome, figure of a woman. Her neat grey head was held proudly above a stiffly boned collar. At her waist hung the reticule which was the symbol of her status.

Acknowledging the youthful doctor with a dignified, although not unkindly, smile, she led him up the great staircase to Her Ladyship's withdrawing room. Leaving David standing outside on the landing, she entered the chamber and closed the door.

David, feeling as though he was back at school and awaiting a summons to an interview with the headmaster, absent-mindedly rubbed the palm of his hand across one buttock. Then, recalling the actual purpose of his visit, he pulled back his shoulders, brushed a hand over his spotless lapels and prepared to meet the Marchioness of Stirling.

She was standing at the wide bay window, her flimsy gown concealing nothing of the slight, almost elfin, figure beneath. Only as she turned to meet him was David able to observe the advanced state of her pregnancy.

'That will do, Mrs Meecham, thank you.'

As the housekeeper was about to leave, David placed a restraining hand on her arm.

Hesitantly, he addressed Her Ladyship. 'Forgive me, madam, but I think it best if you are attended by a female companion for this examination.'

The girl shook her golden curls pettishly. He thought she might have stamped her foot in indignation had not the decorum of womanhood, so recently acquired, dictated her actions.

'You heard the doctor, Mrs Meecham,' she said sharply. 'Ask the nurse to come down at once!'

Mrs Meecham retreated, leaving David alone with his spirited little patient.

'While we are waiting,' he ventured, 'perhaps you will tell me a little about yourself?'

At her silent invitation, he sat down beside a small rosewood writing desk and took out his notebook.

'Your age, madam?'

'I shall be seventeen years old next month.'

David looked up, quickly. She had moved away from the window and come to sit close by him on an elaborately carved chaise longue. The rich, rose-coloured silk brocade seemed to emphasise her ivory-white complexion. Now that he could study her more closely, what he saw alarmed him.

With the exception of her ripening abdomen, the girl was painfully thin. Purple shadows ringed her pale blue eyes and the area around her mouth. Her lips, lacking any artificial enhancement, were also tinged with blue.

Her initial reaction to his presence, which he had taken to be the petulance of a spoiled brat, he now recognised as abject fear.

He continued to question her gently, watching her carefully as she made her hesitant replies.

Both her parents were dead. The Marquis, being a close relative, had made her his ward while she was a young child. Waiting only until she reached an age acceptable to the society in which they moved, they had been married two months after her sixteenth birthday.

'Was there an older woman in the household, to whom you could turn as a mother-figure?' David's question had a purpose. He believed that he understood the nature of her fears, but she must tell him herself.

'I had a governess, a spinster cousin of my guardian. She was my sole companion for many years.'

'Was there no married woman? Someone with whom you could discuss the intimacies of married life? Someone to answer the questions which all young girls must ask, before their wedding day?'

'There was no such person, sir.'

The colour which now suffused her cheeks was due to embarrassment, he realised. He was much troubled by the waxy nature of her skin beneath.

She flinched away from him as he leaned towards her, to take hold of her wrist. He smiled reassuringly and she relaxed a little. Her pulse was racing.

The door opened and closed softly, and David looked round at the short, heavily-built woman in her early forties who had entered the room.

'Ah, nurse,' David greeted her, as one professional to another. 'Perhaps you will assist Her Ladyship to uncover her chest so that I may listen to her heart.'

'Is that really necessary, doctor?' The haughty tone suggested that the nurse considered him to be little more than an incompetent student. 'Mr Gillespie always manages without disturbing his patients.' So far as the nurse was concerned, the matter was closed.

She took up position behind the chaise longue, folding her hands in an attitude of defiance.

'I cannot make a proper assessment of the lady's condition through several layers of material. Please do as I ask, nurse.' David asserted his authority.

The woman would have continued to resist him, had not the Marchioness herself begun to unlace the bodice of her gown.

'Oh, come along, Pearson, do as the doctor asks,' she commanded.

He warmed his stethoscope in his hands for a few moments, but even so, she flinched when he placed the instrument on her skin. Her heartbeat was strong enough, but she still showed signs of undue stress.

Once having gained access through the protective layers of clothing, David did not hesitate to move down to the lady's abdomen, seeking out the tiny foetal heartbeat. Yes, it was there, steady and strong.

'That sounds like a healthy little heir for His Lordship.' David stood back, while the nurse made an unnecessary show of covering her mistress.

'Oh, can you hear him? Can you really hear my baby?'

Mention of the child seemed to dispel the girl's anxieties for the moment.

'No doubt you feel him kicking, from time to time?'

'Oh, yes,' she cried, obviously relieved to be able to mention something which had troubled her for weeks. 'Is it right that I should feel such movement?'

For weeks past, whenever she had said anything to the nurse about discomfort or any other phenomena of her pregnancy, Pearson had pursed her lips and told her not to be a foolish girl. Such things were part of the suffering she could expect in retribution for the carnality which had brought about her condition.

'Now, madam, I shall need to examine the birth canal to ensure that the baby may be born without difficulty.'

The Marchioness gaped at him, not comprehending his meaning. The nurse drew herself up to her full five feet in readiness for the battle.

'Indeed, you shall do no such thing! Doctor or no, there are limits to the extent to which I will allow you to molest Her Ladyship!'

'Good heavens, woman, are you a nurse or are you not?' thundered David. 'Had I wished only to take my patient's hand and make soothing noises, I would not have asked for a chaperone. Either do your duty by remaining, or fetch the housekeeper.'

'Mr Gillespie never considers it necessary to make such an examination, not when the patient is of so high a rank,' Miss Pearson reiterated.

'Oh, I see, a person's rank determines their ability to give birth satisfactorily, is that it?' David was so angry, he forgot for a moment that the argument was taking place in the presence of his patient. It was only when he heard a sound from Her Ladyship that he remembered his manners, and apologised.

'Forgive me, madam, I fear that I have overstepped the bounds of decorum. I must insist, however, that I continue my examination. You have a very small frame. I must satisfy myself that you will be able to deliver the child without assistance.'

Her Ladyship was torn between her satisfaction at the manner in which the doctor was getting the better of the odious Pearson, and anxiety as to what the proposed examination might entail.

The determination of the doctor inspired her own assault upon the nurse. 'Pearson, you will do whatever the doctor requires . . . NOW!' she added, raising her voice as the woman hesitated.

David carried out his examination, to the increasing embarrassment of the Marchioness. At last, he straightened up and smiled reassuringly at her.

'All is well,' he said, trying to avoid the expression of terrified disbelief in her eyes.

Although he gave his patient every assurance that all was well, he was very perturbed by what he had found. The Marchioness was, as he had suspected, extremely small-boned. Her pelvis was unlikely, even with the natural flexibility developed during the process of parturition, to expand sufficiently to allow for a normal delivery. The Marquis was a tall, heavily-built man; there was every likelihood that the infant would be large.

'When is Mr Gillespie expected to call upon you again, madam?' David enquired.

'Not until the child is due to be born,' the nurse took it upon herself to reply. 'Why do you ask?'

'I presume that he will arrive some days before, in case of an early delivery?'

'That is his usual practice with his more important patients, yes.'

'Very well. Thank you, nurse. I shall not require you further.' He was relieved when Miss Pearson did not protest but walked from the room, tight-lipped, her face suffused with suppressed rage.

'I note that you have an unusually pale complexion, madam,' David observed when the nurse had gone. 'Is this attributable to some concoction you have been persuaded to take?'

'My fairness of skin has always been admired,' she agreed. 'Because of my condition, I find that I am often ugly and red. I have been taking a powder recommended by the pharmacist.'

'May I see the packet?'

The lady went into her bedroom and returned shortly, carrying a small twist of paper.

David spread out the package and dipped the tip of his finger into the white powder. He touched it to his lips. Immediately, his worst fears were confirmed.

'This is a compound containing arsenic. You are poisoning yourself, and the child, with this stuff!'

'But my husband prefers me to look pale and slender. I have had to concede to the swelling of my abdomen. Surely I must not deny him my complexion also?'

'The bloom of motherhood is a delight in itself, My Lady. I am quite sure His Lordship will agree with me. I must insist that you take no more of this substance. In fact, I shall take it away with me!'

He would brook no protest. With surprising equanimity, his patient conceded defeat.

David continued, 'My Lady, I am much concerned that you have no female friend with whom to discourse freely. During pregnancy most ladies gain great comfort from the company of others in the same condition. I wonder if I may be so bold as to suggest that you should make the acquaintance of some of the local ladies? I know that my mother would be pleased to entertain you, and introduce you to her friends.'

The Marchioness smiled politely, thanking him for his concern for her welfare.

'I believe that if my husband felt it was in my best interests to meet the local ladies, he would already have arranged it for me. However, should your mother be so kind as to issue an invitation, I am sure he will give it his earnest consideration.'

David bowed himself out of her presence and went in search of the Marquis.

'Her Ladyship begs to be excused, My Lord,' Mrs Meecham announced, as she heralded the arrival of a team of servants bearing luncheon.

'Her Ladyship has had . . . er . . . a somewhat tiring morning,' the woman continued, casting an apologetic glance in David's direction. 'She has decided to take some light refreshment in her room.'

'Oh, very well, Mrs Meecham, thank you. Tell her I shall be up to see her when she has had her rest.'

Waving David towards the table, the Marquis seated himself and fell upon the sumptuous food with the appetite of a hungry cur.

David found it difficult to consume even that which courtesy demanded. He was very troubled about his patient, and uncertain as to His Lordship's likely response to what he must tell him.

'Come along, my dear fellow!' The jovial host swallowed his second glass of wine, crammed a further loaded forkful into his mouth and belched freely.

'Take another glass, even if you have lost your appetite. Can't understand you young fellows – no stamina, no head for liquor. All this book-learning . . . bad for the digestion, what?'

David smiled politely as the servant replenished his glass. The heavy wine, taken with so little food, was, he knew, a mistake. It did however give him sufficient courage to speak his mind.

At last the servants were dismissed and he felt free to unburden himself.

'My Lady's obstetrician . . . Mr Gillespie . . . has he expressed any concern about his patient's condition?'

'He's always saying she's too damned thin!' laughed the Marquis. 'But you know what these women are, fussy about their figures, desperate to force themselves into the latest fashion in gowns.'

'Has he made comment about her bloodless appearance? I believe that she may be anaemic.'

'Oh, her pale skin has always been a feature of her complexion. Never known her to look otherwise. Damned attractive, don't you think!'

'You encourage her to look thus? She has confessed to taking small doses of an arsenical compound, to achieve the appearance you so admire.'

'Arsenic? Poison, do you mean?' His Lordship was, much to David's relief, concerned rather than angry. 'Damn me, what fool of a pharmacist provided her with that?'

David made no attempt to reply to his rhetorical question. Instead he continued, 'If, as I suspect, she is suffering from a deficiency in the blood, the consequences could be very serious during childbirth.'

'Gillespie did not think anything of it.'

That seemed to settle the matter. Like her nurse, the Marchioness's husband clearly set great store by the opinion of her consultant.

'There is another matter which concerns me, My Lord. I find that Her Ladyship has had no contact with other ladies in similar condition. I find that it often helps, during pregnancy, for the mothers to exchange confidences. Unfortunately, we mere males are totally without experience in these matters and can offer little encouragement.'

'Oh, you don't need to worry about little Jane,' the Marquis laughed again. 'She has been surrounded by womenfolk all her life. Made sure she grew up a lady and all that.'

'Her Ladyship told me of her early life, sir. She also confided that the women of her acquaintance were all spinsters. She has had no contact with any married ladies, who have themselves borne children.'

'Well, damnation, ain't they all the same?'

'Her companions have all been without experience of sexual relations, let alone childbirth.'

'As for the first,' the Marquis gave David an eloquent wink, 'I taught her all she needed to know.'

If the Marquis's sexual proclivities were as gross as his appetite for food, thought David with distaste, then his sympathies went out to the poor girl upstairs.

The Marquis took up a long clay pipe from a rack on the side table, indicating that David should follow suit.

When the doctor declined, he continued: 'As for having babies, well, the women on the Estate seem to have them like shelling peas. Up and about same day, working in the fields. Nothing to it, old boy!'

David was shocked at the ignorance and indifference of the man. By all accounts he was a kindly enough person. Had he not already agreed to improve the lot of the villagers, and pay for the schooling of the

brighter young people in the parish? Yet, in the matter of his child-bride
and her welfare, he appeared to be quite unconcerned.

'My Lord, you have requested that I ascertain the state of the Marchioness's health in the absence of her regular physician. I have to
report that your wife is in need of fresh air and exercise. Her diet
should be improved to include substantial quantities of red meat. If you
agree, I will instruct your housekeeper as to a suitable menu. In particular, she should refrain from taking any compound designed to sustain
her pallor, at least until the child is born.'

The Marquis was clearly shaken by David's summary of the situation.

'You really believe that there may be trouble?' he queried, obviously
surprised.

'I have very great doubts about Her Ladyship's ability to sustain the
rigours of childbirth, sir. She is a sick woman, in need of great care. As
important as her physical condition is her mental attitude to her pregnancy. She is very young, and like all young women conscious of her
appearance. In her attempts to retain her attractions for Your Lordship,
I believe that she is in danger of harming her own and the infant's health.'

The blustering, good-natured swagger had gone. The Marquis stared
at David in dismay.

'What would you have me do?' he asked, eager to grasp at any crumb
of comfort.

David had been contemplating the manner in which he would put his
proposal, throughout the meal. It was apprehension of the Marquis's
reaction which had taken away his own appetite.

'I suggested to Her Ladyship, that she might call upon my mother
who would introduce her to some of the ladies of the parish.'

The Marquis hesitated. 'Perhaps she does need some other companionship,' he agreed, somewhat doubtfully. 'Possibly, if my wife made
your mother's acquaintance, it might benefit her.'

'My mother would be delighted, My Lord.' David was suddenly struck
by the temerity of his suggestion and wondered how Her Ladyship
would react to the humble surroundings of Tigh na Broch?

With the young lady's health at stake, however, he nerved himself
to continue.

'Perhaps it could be arranged for the Marchioness to take tea with
my mother one afternoon?'

The Marquis nodded decisively. 'Very well, I am much obliged to
you, doctor. You will appreciate that I must insist on Mr Gillespie being
in attendance at the actual delivery. That is all arranged.'

'Naturally,' David agreed. 'I would, however, be gratified, if you will
arrange for us to consult together, immediately upon his arrival.'

'I shall bear that in mind, doctor. Thank you for coming.'

'Good day, My Lord.'

*   *   *

Two days later, Morag was fussing over the final arrangements for her tea party.

She was looking forward to meeting the Marquis's young bride. Rumour had it that she was quite a little firebrand. The thought of playing hostess to one of her rank was rather daunting.

At three o'clock, Elizabeth came walking up from the village. Morag had asked her to be in good time so that they might seem comfortably at ease when Her Ladyship arrived.

'What a glorious afternoon,' exclaimed Elizabeth, as she seated herself on one of the garden chairs, arranged upon the terrace, facing the sea. 'David tells me that you are expecting a very special guest this afternoon!'

'Both of my guests are special,' responded Morag, with a smile. Whatever David said, she still believed that one day Elizabeth would be her daughter-in-law. She was determined that nothing should mar their relationship.

'David says we are to treat her like any other young lady. She is too much accustomed to servants, bowing and scraping. He feels she should be treated as a friend, rather than a grand visiting dignitary.'

'How typical of a man,' scoffed Elizabeth. 'The lady will behave in whatever way she chooses. There is little that we can do to influence her reaction to ourselves!'

The conversation was brought to an abrupt halt by the approach of Sheilagh, ushering in their distinguished guest.

Morag dropped a deep curtsey.

'Mrs Beaton?' The diminutive figure stretched out a tiny hand which Morag grasped lightly. She was momentarily deprived of the ability to speak, but quickly regaining her composure, said, 'Welcome, madam, it is a great pleasure to have you visit my home. May I present Miss Elizabeth Duncan, a friend of my son David's.'

Elizabeth's curtsey was rather less obsequious than Morag's. She was one who believed that such honours should be earned, not simply acquired by marriage.

The Marchioness smiled stiffly in her direction, then took the proffered chair. Sheilagh hovered nearby and at Morag's signal the tea-tray appeared.

The ladies exchanged pleasantries, the Marchioness keeping the accustomed distance between herself and her companions. It was all very well for George to arrange for her to call upon the local people, but he did not have to converse with them. Had it not been for the promise of a change of atmosphere for an hour or two, from the dreary Castle, she would not have consented to come at all.

'Have you lived long in the district, Mrs Beaton?' she enquired, not really interested in hearing the answer.

'Since I was married,' Morag replied. 'I came here with my husband on our wedding day, thirty years ago.'

'And you, Miss Duncan, have you been here all your life?'

'No, madam. I came only last November, to take a post in the village school.'

'Indeed? A schoolmistress?' she commented haughtily. Whatever could her husband have been thinking of, she wondered, causing her to associate with these people?

'Indeed, madam, that is my privilege.' Elizabeth was only too aware of the condescension being shown to them by this little baggage, a chit who was at least five years her junior! She found it hard to stomach Morag's obvious pleasure at entertaining nobility, despite the visitor's unsubtle incivility.

'Forgive me for mentioning it, madam,' Morag ventured, 'but when do you expect your happy event?'

The heir to the Stirling title chose this moment to awaken, giving the Marchioness a mighty kick, up under her ribs. She started, and Morag was instantly all solicitude.

'Are you uncomfortable, madam? Would you care for another pillow behind your back?'

'It is nothing, I assure you.' The girl softened a little towards her hostess. 'Dr Beaton assures me that it is in order for him to kick out from time to time!'

'He should know,' laughed Morag, 'carrying him was like accommodating a prizefighter!'

'Will it get worse, do you suppose? There are six more weeks of this to be endured, I am not sure that I can stand being so buffeted by him for that length of time.'

'Towards the end, they become quiet, but I am afraid that you will suffer for some time yet.'

'You seem very certain that the baby is a boy,' remarked Elizabeth.

'But of course it is a boy!' Her Ladyship asserted, scandalised that Elizabeth should suggest the alternative possibility. 'This child is the heir to the Stirling inheritance.'

Morag sensed that the girl would have asked further questions, had they been alone. Turning to Elizabeth, she said, 'I think Sheilagh must have forgotten us. Will you go in and ask her for some fresh tea? I know I would like another cup.' She turned to the Marchioness enquiringly.

Her Ladyship nodded her assent and Elizabeth, detecting Morag's desire to be left alone for a few minutes with her guest, went to seek out Sheilagh.

'What a spoilt little brat she is!' she exclaimed as she entered the kitchen.

Sheilagh, who in the style of her peasant ancestors did not approve of eating out of doors, even when the weather was hot, snorted her disgust.

'Such a carry on,' she complained, filling the kettle and taking the teapot from Elizabeth.

'Did you ever know the old Marquis and his lady?' Elizabeth asked. 'According to the men, they were a friendly couple, much given to joining in with the villagers, attending ceilidhs and sporting events.'

'Och, so they were!' Sheilagh agreed. 'But he was a real Marquis, of course. Sadly they died without children. This Marquis of Stirling, George, is only a cousin. He has no feeling for the place. He comes here merely to shoot during the season . . . leaves everything in the hands of that scoundrel Lugas. A sorry state he will make of things, just you wait and see!'

Elizabeth felt sure that Sheilagh exaggerated. Nevertheless, it would explain the Marchioness's unnecessarily stiff behaviour. Maybe she felt as insecure as they did.

'Do you have a fine layette prepared for the baby?' Morag homed in immediately on the point of the conversation she had so expertly engineered.

'I have left all that to nurse,' the girl replied. 'She has ordered everything necessary, from Edinburgh.'

'Oh, have you made nothing yourself?' Morag was genuinely surprised. 'I always enjoyed embroidering the tiny garments . . . part of the pleasure of a confinement.'

'I do not know how you can describe any aspect of it as pleasurable,' Her Ladyship shuddered fastidiously.

'Tell me, my dear,' Morag drew her chair closer, that she might lower her voice, 'do you have any fears about the coming event?'

Seeing her guest hesitate, she continued, 'It is not unnatural for a young mother, awaiting her first child, to be anxious about the outcome.'

'It would not be so difficult if I knew what to expect.' The girl leaned towards her older companion, hauteur forgotten in this moment of confidence. 'No one will tell me what it is like, because no one I talk to has ever experienced it. Shall I know when the baby is coming? How long will it take? Will there be pain?'

The questions had begun to tumble forth. In her eagerness for information, the Marchioness had grasped Morag's hand so fiercely that the older woman was hard put to it not to cry out in pain.

'My dear child, has not your physician told you what to expect?'

'Oh, Mr Gillespie merely holds my wrist . . . listens through his stethoscope . . . asks my nurse vague questions which, apparently, he assumes only she is capable of answering. They never discuss with me what is going on, Mrs Beaton. I have no idea how the baby is formed or how it will come out!'

There, she had said it. At last she had been able to confess her extreme ignorance. She began to weep, sobbing like a lost and frightened child.

Morag cradled her in her arms until the crying ceased. 'There, there, my dear, you are overwrought. Whatever would my son say if he found his patient in this state, and entertained in his own house too?'

As the girl dried her eyes on a foolish wisp of lace handkerchief, Morag said comfortingly, 'You must have an opportunity to talk about these things, but for today it is sufficient that we have broken the ice. We may be friends, may we not?'

'Oh, yes, I should like that very much.' Her Ladyship clung to Morag as if she was indeed her own mother.

'Mrs Beaton, will you do something very special for me . . . will you be a real friend, by calling me Jane? Only my husband uses my name . . . and his friends, who do so in a patronising manner which makes me hate them for it!'

'I shall do so on one condition, Jane, you must call me Morag. Will you do that?'

The girl nodded, managing a wintry little smile.

When Elizabeth returned with the fresh tea, she was surprised to find them both talking easily together, discussing the design of a christening gown for the baby.

'Ah, Elizabeth,' exclaimed Morag, 'Jane has agreed to visit me again very soon. I do hope that you two young ladies are going to be great friends.'

Elizabeth raised her eyebrows at Morag, finding the changed atmosphere difficult to comprehend.

It was left to Jane to convince her that the situation was indeed very much changed.

'Miss Duncan, I would so like us to meet again. I am sure that you have much to tell me about the children in your care, and I am intrigued to know what it is like to live on an island.'

Elizabeth was more than willing to meet the girl halfway. 'Perhaps you would like to come across to Eisdalsa one day, and see the school for yourself?' she suggested.

'Thank you, I would be delighted.' The Marchioness rose to leave.

'Sheilagh, call Her Ladyship's carriage, if you please.' Morag summoned her reluctant servant.

As the carriage drew away, Her Ladyship leaned out of the window, 'Until we meet again, Morag.' Then, like an excited child, she added, 'Oh, how I am looking forward to my next visit!'

His Lordship's carriage, its black lacquer glittering in the bright sunshine, turned at the gate, and began the steady climb up towards the Castle.

'How did you accomplish such a sudden transformation?' Elizabeth enquired, bemused by the events of the afternoon.

'She is just a very frightened, very lonely little girl,' said Morag. 'Once she admitted it, the rest was easy.'

6

Jane had most certainly benefited from her discussion with Morag.
On reflection, however, she wondered if it was wise to become
more intimate with her, kindly though she was. She was particularly
embarrassed when she recalled some of the admissions which she had
made, as all her worries and fears had come flooding out.

Replying to her husband's polite enquiry as to the success of her
expedition, she told him of Morag's suggestion that there should be
further visits to Tigh na Broch. She was confident that her husband
would resist the idea, and advise her to refuse.

On the contrary, to her great surprise George encouraged her to
accept, declaring that, since he would be very much occupied with the
Estate during the next week or two, it would be good for her to have
some diversion.

Her Ladyship therefore, being obliged to put aside her misgivings,
determined to make the most of the experiences offered, and began to
anticipate the next invitation with mounting enthusiasm.

She was not disappointed.

When David next attended Her Ladyship, at the Castle, he carried
with him an invitation from Elizabeth for the Marchioness to visit the
school on Eisdalsa Island. He had been a little reluctant at first, in view
of the amount of fever among the quarrying families. As Elizabeth had
pointed out, however, such cases were restricted to the Village. There
were none on the Island itself.

On the appointed day, Jane was driven to the pier in His Lordship's
carriage. She was greeted by William, who at the Marquis's request,
was present to escort her across to the island.

Even the short boat trip was an adventure for the young Marchioness. Her eyes shone with anticipation, stray hairs escaped from the
carefully arranged coiffure, and she looked, for the first time since he
had met her, like a healthy young girl.

William escorted Jane to the schoolroom door. Here he surrendered
his charge into the capable hands of Kirsty McGillivray who awaited
the honoured guest, crisp starched pinafore crackling as she made her
carefully rehearsed curtsey.

'Will you be so kind as to step this way, Your Ladyship.'

The child stood aside so that Jane could enter.

It was a very different schoolroom from the one which Elizabeth had found, nearly a year ago.

At the schoolmistress's request, the windows had been enlarged to allow light to stream in, allowing the pupils a glimpse of the outside world. Unlike many educationalists of her day, Elizabeth believed that such outside scenes and activities as were visible fed the imagination and were a benefit to learning rather than a distraction.

Two partitions served to divide the huge room into smaller, more intimate, spaces. The oldest children occupied one end of the building, each seated at a desk where he, or she, could study individually.

At the far end, the infants were busily arranging their nature table, with the treasures they had gathered on their morning walk.

The centre of the schoolroom was occupied by the bulk of the pupils. Seated on benches, arranged before the blackboard, they were industriously working out multiplication sums.

While no one could claim that it was a silent classroom, the sound was one of healthy activity, not indiscipline.

As Her Ladyship entered, Elizabeth put down her chalk, and signalled the children to stand. Jane approached the teacher's desk and, as she passed, the girls curtsied and the boys made a stiff, embarrassed bow. Elizabeth had drilled them well.

The schoolmistress invited her guest to take a seat, while she instructed the children to carry on with their work.

'I trust you are feeling well, ma'am?' Elizabeth enquired, a trifle stiffly. She was still not accustomed to the idea of paying deference to a girl so much younger than herself.

'Thank you, yes, Miss Duncan. Do you not see an improvement? Dr Beaton declares that I am fairly blooming with health.'

'Yes, indeed, Your Ladyship's appearance is much improved.'

'Both Dr and Mrs Beaton have been more than kind,' Jane enthused.

Elizabeth found herself bristling again.

'Would you care to see some of the children's work?' She indicated that it was time for a number of pupils to bring forward their slates for the Marchioness's inspection.

When the older scholars had been visited, and had demonstrated the range of their achievements, Elizabeth conducted her visitor to the infant section where the little ones were gathered about their instructor. Katherine Logie was reading them a story.

'Now, children,' Elizabeth interrupted, 'we have a very important visitor today. Can anyone tell me, who is this lady?'

Several little hands waved anxiously, one small boy so determined to give his answer that he was on his feet and edging towards them.

'Well, Murdo?'

'Please, miss, it's Her Ladyship, miss!' he cried, confidently.

'Yes,' Elizabeth steered the child back to his seat, 'this is Lady Jane,

Marchioness of Stirling.' Looking to her guest for confirmation, she continued, 'But I believe she will be pleased to have you address her as Lady Jane.'

'Good morning, children.' Jane took up Elizabeth's cue exceedingly well. 'I am sorry we have interrupted your story. Can anyone tell me what it was about?'

'A princess, miss . . . Lady Jane,' the child caught Elizabeth's frown, and made a hasty correction. 'She is in disguise, and the peasant's wife is going to prove she is a princess, by putting a pea under her mattress.'

Johnny McInnes could contain himself no longer. 'Please, Lady Jane, are you a princess, miss?'

Jane smiled. 'Not exactly.'

'But you do wear a crown sometimes, don't you, Lady Jane?' Jeanie Campbell smirked at her friends. 'My mummy says you do.'

'Not a crown exactly,' she replied. 'When I go to Court to meet the Queen, I shall wear a coronet.'

'There, I told you so,' crowed Jeanie, who had spent the morning trying to persuade her sceptical companions that if you married a Marquis you wore a crown.

'She said a coronet, not a crown,' muttered Billy Watson. 'Ouch!' as Jeanie stamped on his foot to silence him.

'Would you get black and blue if you slept on a mattress with a pea under it?' The question came from a timid little girl, her elfin face almost completely hidden behind her hand.

'I don't think so,' said Jane. 'No more than anyone else.' Then, hastily, because the little girl looked as though she might cry, 'But, you see, I am not a princess. I expect a princess would go black and blue!'

Seeing that matters might be getting out of hand, Elizabeth suggested that the infants should recite and sing for Her Ladyship.

As this entertainment was conducted in Gaelic, Jane was obliged to listen to the words without understanding the meaning. The poems were short, and she had to admit that the sweet little faces bore so much expression that it was not difficult to follow the gist of what was said. The songs were those that the fishermen and the weavers sang while they carried out their more monotonous tasks. There were many verses, and since it was nearly midday and the temperature had increased, Jane found her eyelids growing heavy. She had almost dropped off to sleep when she was startled by Elizabeth's voice instructing the children to stand. She, too, rose unsteadily to her feet.

'Now, children, you will all say goodbye to Lady Jane, and thank her for visiting us.'

At Elizabeth's signal the children repeated their teacher's words. The girls curtsied and the boys bowed as Jane moved to the door, escorted by the teacher.

One disappointed little voice was heard to complain, 'She didn't wear her crimson velvet robe.'

Elizabeth could not help smiling, and Jane laughed aloud.

'They are delightful children,' she cried. 'Why, Miss Duncan, I almost envy you your occupation.'

'It is not always like this, I can assure you,' Elizabeth replied. 'They were excited at your visit, and warned to be on their best behaviour. Sometimes they can be very trying.'

Having arranged with Katherine Logie that she should undertake the supervision of the children, at their midday break, Elizabeth was free to conduct the Marchioness to her own house where Annie McGillivray had laid out a cold luncheon for them.

When she had carried out the introductions, Elizabeth invited the Marchioness to remove her hat and jacket.

Annie came forward to receive them and, laying the velvet garments carefully over a chair, she made to leave.

'Can you not join us, Annie?' Elizabeth begged her. 'Kirsty told me that you have given the children their pieces to eat in school today.'

'Yes, please do stay,' urged Lady Jane. 'I am quite sure that Miss Duncan and I cannot do justice to this fine spread.'

Annie, blushing with pleasure at the unexpected honour, bobbed a curtsey before taking her place at the little table. Elizabeth found it hard not to show her displeasure at this action. Not only did she consider that there should be equality among women, particularly those visiting her home, but it was especially disagreeable to her to see Annie humbling herself before someone whose sole claim to superiority was her rank, and that acquired by means of a propitious marriage.

'Tell me, Mrs McGillivray, how many children do you have?' asked the Marchioness. 'I believe that I have already met your daughter, a delightful child!'

At their last meeting, Jane and Morag had talked endlessly about babies. Now that she had access to an unlimited fund of knowledge on the topic, childbirth was an all-absorbing subject with her.

Glowing with pride at Her Ladyship's reference to Kirsty, Annie proceeded to engage Jane in animated conversation about the traumas and delights of raising a family, from which Elizabeth was quite excluded.

The hostess busied herself, helping her guests to food and drink, and tried hard not to feel affronted.

Annie and Jane found an immediate rapport. Even the details of that last, disastrous pregnancy were gone over. Here at least Elizabeth could supply her experience of the event. The result was that the Marchioness was left fearful of what could happen, but reassured that David would rescue her, should difficulties arise.

It was time for afternoon school to begin. At that precise moment, William appeared, ready to conduct Her Ladyship on a tour of the slate workings.

Her Ladyship was, however, feeling the heat and looking rather tired. Annie suggested that she might care to visit a typical quarryman's cottage and invited her and William to take tea in her own home. Gratefully, the Marchioness accepted the offer and the party set off, absorbed in discussion, leaving Elizabeth with all kinds of conflicting emotions churning inside her.

As she made her way back to the schoolroom, she comforted herself with thoughts of Gordon, and the anticipation that she herself would one day be in a position to have babies. And, she assured herself, she would do it with a great deal less fuss than the Marchioness!

As though on cue, the afternoon steamer announced her approach to the pier on the far side of the Sound. Elizabeth could not resist the temptation to turn her steps towards the shore, in the hope of catching a glimpse of First Officer McIntyre, on the bridge of the vessel.

The deck was seething with people, summer visitors to the Highlands no doubt. It was impossible to distinguish Gordon in that crowd.

With each consignment of materials for the school, Elizabeth could expect a separate, unstamped communication, addressed to herself. Would there be a delivery today?

She retraced her steps towards the schoolhouse. The children were all inside. Katherine had obviously decided it was time to end their extended break. From within, she could hear the girl's ringing tones as she settled the classes to work.

Elizabeth was pleased with Miss Logie's progress. It would be very satisfying to be able to hand over the school, when the time came, to someone who believed, as she did, that corporal punishment and fear had no place in the classroom.

Elizabeth had settled her older children to their afternoon reading task, and was taking over from Katherine in the main room, when the ferryman entered, carrying a large packing case.

'My, and isna' that one the great weight?' he grumbled good-naturedly as he lowered his burden to the floor. The children began to chatter excitedly amongst themselves, until Elizabeth gave them a reproving glance. They fell silent, each trying hard to concentrate on the exercise they had been set.

Elizabeth greeted Ian at the door. There was a short silence, while she examined the box with interest, and Ian hunted through the numerous pockets in his well-worn overcoat. At last, with a shout of triumph, his hand emerged from the voluminous folds of material, clutching a much-thumbed, rather scruffy envelope.

'I knew it was here somewhere,' he declared. 'That young officer aboard the *Lord of Lorn* asked me to deliver this "Into Miss Elizabeth's own hands" was what he said.'

The old ferryman continued to cling on to the note, his eyes dancing with merriment. His occupation placed him in a privileged position with regard to the more personal and intimate aspects of island life. No one came to, or went from the island without his knowledge. No package or other communication evaded his sharp eye. Over the years, the gentle fellow had watched many a drama unfold, without comment. He kept his observations to himself, avoiding the temptation to make capital from the secrets of others.

This did not prevent him, however, from teasing his clients occasionally, when he felt it would do no harm.

He held the paper at arm's length in order to check on the address. He laid it down on top of the packing case, and tried smoothing out the rumpled surface, and then, by this time straining Elizabeth's forbearance to breaking point, he laid his cap on top of it, while he made a further search for the consignment slip. This Elizabeth signed in such haste that her name became an indecipherable squiggle, and she must needs go over it again to satisfy the ferryman.

At last, his business transacted, Ian lifted his cap, gave a cheery wave to the children, whose eyes had been trained on this interesting scene throughout, and left.

Elizabeth made a grab for the letter, and stuffed it hurriedly into her pocket. Then she called upon two of the older boys to come and open up the case.

Mr Ford, true to his word, had sent a large collection of reading books for the school library. On his last visit he had been pleased to find that Miss Duncan had collected together a number of volumes which the children could take home to be read at leisure and he had promised to approach a certain benefactor, a Mr Coats of Paisley, who made gifts of books to educational establishments for the working classes. Obviously his appeal had been successful.

There was a buzz of excitement among the pupils as the two boys held up one volume after another for their inspection.

'Thank you, Martin and Angus,' called Elizabeth. 'Before any of the new books are handed out, I shall have to write in them, and enter the titles in the catalogue. Go back to your work now. Tomorrow you shall all write a letter to Mr Coats, thanking him for his generosity.'

Elizabeth sat at her desk and watched the class resume its normal activity. She must herself write to Mr Ford, to tell him the books had arrived.

Her hand went to the pocket in which her precious communication lay. She withdrew the envelope and, with one eye on the bent heads in front of her, tore it open.

Out fell a flimsy sheet of paper: a steamer ticket for Fort William,

for a Saturday in August. Elizabeth smiled to herself, remembering
Gordon's hesitation before inviting her on this expedition to meet his
kinfolk in the northern town. It was the first acknowledgement between
them that at some time in the future she was to become a part of his
family.

Accompanying the ticket was a single sheet of notepaper on which
was written in the familiar neat handwriting:

> *I take no pleasure from exotic blooms*
> *Those garish flowers with Eastern, cloying scent.*
> *Give me the snow-white Scottish rose*
> *Whose sweetness fills my every sense with longing*
> *And breaks my heart with its simplicity.*

She did not know the verse; could it be that Gordon had written the
words himself? How much she hoped that he was the poet!

She had thought long and hard about the reason for her preference
for Gordon.

David was a good man. His dedication to his work and concern for
his patients had been apparent from their very first encounter. Why
was it then that she had drawn back from the greater intimacy he had
offered? In his presence Elizabeth felt more like a treasured possession
than an individual. She could see herself being completely overwhelmed
by the strength of his personality, a situation from which she was
bound to break out eventually, probably with catastrophic consequences. There was no doubt in her mind that David was in love
with her. Whether she could love him, she did not know. Perhaps
this in itself was an indication that her affections must be directed
elsewhere?

David was a man of ambition and determination and, she suspected,
not unduly concerned how his actions might affect those around him.
She wondered if perhaps his path through life had been just a little too
smooth up to this point – perhaps he needed a few set-backs to make
him a little more understanding of other people's imperfections? She
valued him as a friend but his wife would need to be someone more
pliable than herself.

William she regarded as a kindly older brother; a figure to lean upon
in time of trouble, a willing partner when one required an escort.

He had taken care of her material needs ever since they had arrived
on the island. Her house was now extremely comfortable, with its
separate bedroom, kitchen and outside closet. The roof had been
repaired, so that she no longer needed to scurry round with pots to
catch the drips during the heavier rainstorms.

With his elevated position in the community, he had been able to
smooth her path when things became difficult at the school. She felt

sure that it was due to him that her post had been made permanent, and that she was at last receiving the proper rewards for her efforts.

Mr Ogilvie's attitude towards her had changed, also. He no longer came creeping round, hoping to catch her out in some dereliction of her duties. He had even been known to consult her about certain matters to do with the curriculum. For the most part, Ogilvie remained at the Village school, and left Elizabeth in charge on the Island. Having taken on an additional pupil teacher, he was content to leave Katherine Logie in Elizabeth's charge for the remainder of her training; a situation which suited both of the women admirably.

Her relationship with Gordon having blossomed throughout the last few weeks, Elizabeth could see no cloud upon her horizon. He was strong, reliable, handsome and amusing. And made no secret of his admiration for her.

He had a talent for springing surprises, seeming to know just what would please her. Like this little poem. She re-read the verse and committed it to memory. Folding the sheet of notepaper, she placed it, together with the steamer ticket, in her pocket, and turned her attention back to her pupils.

Towards the end of July, after an unprecedented six weeks without rain, the heavens opened. The accumulated refuse was swept from the midden heaps, and the weight of water, pouring off the mountains, was too much for the festering drains to contain. It swept along the Village streets, carrying all before it. As the lochs and wells were refilled, the villagers sighed with relief that the endless carting of water was at an end.

Fortunately, the time for her confinement fast approaching, the Marchioness had already immured herself in the Castle before the weather broke.

It was a very different young woman who was greeted warmly by her solicitous husband that morning at the breakfast table.

'Upon my word, Jane, but you look bonny today. That young doctor has worked a miracle!' The Earl held his wife at arm's length and admired the bloom in her cheeks, the shining hair hanging gracefully over her shoulders and forming a perfect frame for the sparkling blue eyes. 'So, what do you think of my little army of quarriers now, eh?'

He teased her for she had been reluctant to come to Argyll for the birth of their child.

Depending solely upon the unreliable evidence of her Edinburgh acquaintances, Jane had come to Seileach expecting to meet a collection of ignorant country yokels. Her visits to Tigh na Broch and Eisdalsa had taught her that there was more to life than idle tea party chit-chat, and according to Mrs McGillivray's account, greater fun to be had at a village ceilidh than at the most extravagant city ball.

Most important of all, she had made some real friends, a luxury denied her, throughout her childhood.

'Oh, George, they are wonderful people!' she exclaimed. 'I cannot tell you how grateful I am to Mrs Beaton for her hospitality. How I wish that Dr Beaton was to be attending at my confinement!'

'How can I put off Mr Gillespie, my dear? He has been the family physician since I was born. It would be an affront to the poor man to deny him the privilege of delivering the new heir. Dr Beaton has agreed to attend if Gillespie is delayed, or if there is need of a second opinion.'

For a moment, a cloud seemed to settle over the young Marchioness. She shivered. The Marquis, fearing that she was chilled on this dull day, ordered the housekeeper to make up the fire in Her Ladyship's withdrawing room.

By evening, with the storm at its height, Jane was glad to sit beside the roaring flames, contemplating the child in her womb and trying to ignore the excitement, tinged with fear, engendered by her approaching ordeal.

In the Camas Quarry, the men worked fast to clear away the great slabs of slate rock resulting from the day's blasting. The last pallet was piled high, and the heavy load moved slowly up the incline.

There had been some problem in siting the winching gear for the inclined plane. Surrounding the old quarry was a rim of solid rock, but in places this had been undermined in previous quarrying operations. Although every precaution had been taken to stabilise the great steel framework of the machine, these measures were no match for the deluge of rainfall that afternoon.

As the last heavy load was dragged up from the quarry floor, one hundred and eighty feet below, the steel framework shifted. The loose packing around its base had been washed away. With so tremendous a weight acting upon it, there was no way to prevent the heavy construction from tipping forward, other than to discard the laden pallet.

Jamie McGillivray, making his round of the quarry faces at the end of the day, was the first to notice the danger to the winding gear. He had a momentary vision of the great steel framework, and the mighty engine itself, toppling over the edge and plunging down, carrying with it all their hopes for a better future, and the threat of a return to the poverty which had, until very recently, gripped them in its strangling tentacles. He lifted a heavy club hammer and brought it thundering down on to one of the linchpins which secured the chain. His muscles, out of tone from months spent at an office desk, were no longer able to respond to the demand made upon them. His crippled leg made it difficult for him to wield the hammer and retain his balance.

Understanding Jamie's intention, another of the men took the hammer from him and completed the task. The great chain parted and the heavy pallet tipped over, showering the quarry floor with massive lumps of rock.

Afterwards Jamie blamed himself for not having established that all the men were clear of the quarry before he attempted to release the pallet. Those who were present at the scene, however, knew that it was only McGillivray's prompt action which had saved the valuable machinery, and with it their livelihoods.

The men had, indeed, left the quarry floor and were making their tortuous way up the steep path to the top, when Colin McClintock, fourteen years of age and proud to be working in his father's gang, realised that he had dropped his hammer in his hurry to get out of the storm.

The hammer had been given to him by his grandfather on the day he began work in the quarries. It had been used by the old man himself for thirty years, until he was forced to retire, crippled with rheumatism. The boy could not bear to think of his precious tool left lying in the mud all night. He stopped, called something inaudible to his companions and went back, down into the quarry bottom.

As he reached the spot where the gang had been working, he felt a few exceptionally heavy drops fall on his head. This was not just rainwater, he realised. He looked up the steep incline and received a dollop of mud, smack in his face. He wiped his hand across his eyes and was horrified to see a moving tide of slurry, rocks and mud, bearing towards him down the steep rock wall. He could not move out of the way. He threw himself to the ground and covered his head with his arms.

Now, out of the cacophony of noises from the storm and falling rocks, he heard another sound . . . hammers striking steel. Seconds later, came the rattle of the loosened chains, and an avalanche of the very slate blocks which Colin had been helping to dress during the long sultry afternoon.

In all the confusion at the quarry's rim, no one noticed his absence. It was an hour later when his mother, concerned that her boy was loitering somewhere, still in his wet clothes, came knocking on her sister's door.

'Is my Colin here, Molly? If he is, it's a skelping he'll be getting. Staying out, and him wet through!'

Molly emptied a large tub of dirty water outside her door, and hurried in out of the rain.

'He's no' here,' she assured her sister. 'Kenny, did Colin say where he was going after work?'

Young Kenny McPherson came in from the other room, furiously rubbing his hair on a towel.

'Did he no' come hame?' he asked, then suddenly he remembered. Colin had been behind him, coming up the path. Kenny thought he had said something but couldn't hear what it was, in all that wind and rain. Had he gone back down into the quarry?

The scene returned to him, vividly. The screaming chains . . . the upturned pallet . . . the hail of giant stone blocks, crashing against the quarry wall as they hurtled downwards. He let out a cry of horror.

'What is it, Kenny?' his mother demanded, alarmed at the whiteness of her son's face.

'He went back,' sobbed the boy. 'He must be down there, in the quarry.'

The two women looked at him, uncomprehending. If Colin had gone back down, he would be home as soon as he had fetched what he had forgotten.

Donald McPherson, his face shining from his recent washing, had come into the room.

He grasped his son by the shoulders, shaking him to bring him to his senses.

'What's this you are saying, boy? Are you telling me that Colin was down in the quarry when the pallet fell?'

Kenny nodded unhappily, unable to speak.

McPherson pulled on his heavy overcoat.

'You will all stay here,' he ordered, and when Kenny made to join his father, 'you too, laddie. Look after your mother and your auntie now.'

In minutes McPherson had alerted his workmates. One was dispatched to fetch out Mr Whylie, while another ran to the ferry house to send for the doctor. Unless the boy had suffered some injury, he would have been home by now. As the men started off for the Camas Quarry, McPherson went in search of his brother-in-law, Alan.

The evening was beginning to brighten as the bedraggled band of workers arrived at the southernmost quarry. The rain had eased to a fine drizzle and the evening sun could be glimpsed through the heavy layer of black cumulus, drifting away towards the mountains of Mull.

At the bottom of the quarry they found Colin McClintock. A thin, bare arm indicated the position of the youth's body, pinned under a great mound of rock. To remove the heavy boulders took superhuman strength, but the men, somehow, summoned it.

At last, the fragile body was cleared of rubble. Their flat caps screwed up tightly in their hands, the band of men stood around, heads bent in silent prayer.

The boy had clearly died instantly in the fall. In his right hand was the hammer he had come to retrieve.

*   *   *

David, having had no previous experience of reporting a fatal accident, was not familiar with the correct form of words to apply. He turned to his father's notes of other such cases.

Looking through the pages, all written in that familiar scrawl, he began to appreciate how the old doctor must have felt as he wrote about the death, not of a stranger, but of a fellow worker, perhaps a good friend; someone whose family had been in his care for twenty years or more . . . maybe someone whom he had brought into the world with his own hands.

There had been many deaths in those last years of Hugh's life. Thankfully, since William had taken over the quarries, there had been fewer serious accidents. In the last year, David had attended minor fractures and abrasions, but this was his first accidental death.

W Sproat Esq.	Tigh na Broch
Procurator Fiscal	Seileach
Tobermory	Argyll

On 27 July 1877, I examined the body of Colin Fergus McClintock.

This was a boy, fourteen years of age, and in robust health. I understand that he had been employed by the Eisdalsa Slate Quarrying Company for a period of three months.

The body presented multiple contusions to the head and upper trunk. The chest cavity was crushed. There were compound fractures to both legs.

All the wounds were consistent with the victim having been crushed by a fall of rock.

I hereby certify on soul and conscience that Colin Fergus McClintock died as a result of asphyxiation, due to crushing of the thorax and the trachea.

David Alexander Beaton, MB, CM   29 July 1877

The aftermath of the accident in the quarry had kept David occupied for the past two days. Colin's mother had been distraught. It had been necessary to sedate her for some hours, and he was still concerned that she might injure herself in some way. McClintock, the father, always a morose character, had become even more introspective since the accident. He spoke to no one, but glowered at those who attempted any sympathetic approach.

Annie McGillivray had done her best to comfort the bereaved mother. Death was no stranger to the women of Eisdalsa, but the loss of a child touched them all.

On the morning following the disaster, Annie had visited Mairie McClintock, bringing her broth and offering to make tea. Moving quietly about the tiny kitchen, Annie seemed to discern a slight improvement in the woman's demeanour and ventured a few cheering words.

'Come now, Mairie,' she said encouragingly. 'Take this wee cup o' tea. It will make you feel better.'

Silently, Mairie took the tea and sipped it.

'When you have drunk your tea, you must get out of that bed and take a wash. See, I have the kettle full of hot water. You will feel better when you are dressed.'

Mairie, responding like some automaton, finished her tea and did as she was instructed. Annie busied herself with straightening the bedcovers. She tried to avoid glancing at the small truckle-bed in the corner whose covers would not be disturbed, ever again, by the lad for whom the bright patchwork quilt had been so lovingly stitched.

Nor did she venture into the only other apartment, where lay the poor mutilated body.

The room tidy, all the crocks washed and put away, Annie sat herself on the three-legged stool which stood beside the range, and clasped both of Mairie's hands in her own. Neither woman spoke for a long time, but Mairie, responding to the warmth of her friend's sympathy, seemed to relax and after a while her eyelids drooped and she fell into a deep sleep, unassisted by any drugs.

Gently releasing Mairie's fingers, Annie rose and was about to leave when the door from the bedroom opened, slowly. Annie was startled. She had not realised that Mairie's husband was in the house.

McClintock stood for a moment in the open doorway, then, suddenly aware of Annie's presence, seemed to lose all control.

He grasped her tightly by the upper arms, making her cry out with the pain. He stared into her face, shaking with anger.

'What are you doing wi' my woman, eh?' His voice was low, as though he was unwilling to disturb his sleeping wife. 'Get you back to that murdering husband of yours, and dinna come near ma hoose again. D'yer hear me? Do you understan' what I'm saying?' With each question he tightened his grip, but Annie made no response. The sooner he calmed down and released her, the sooner she would be out of it.

Suddenly, McClintock collapsed. Releasing his hold upon Annie, he sank to his knees and, sobbing, he buried his face in his wife's lap.

Annie left them alone. Rubbing her arms, to restore the circulation, she walked slowly back to her own cottage. Perhaps it was the shock which had made the poor man say what he did? Why should he accuse Jamie of murdering his boy? How could he have been involved in what everyone agreed had been an accident? Concerned though she might be, Annie McGillivray kept the incident to herself. Her husband had quite enough to worry about, without paying heed to the ravings of a poor bereaved father.

*   *   *

The day of Colin McClintock's funeral dawned bright and warm. It seemed that every member of the Parish must be present. Like one huge family, the quarry workers clung together in times of trouble. There was no shortage of volunteers to carry the lightweight coffin, and to row the boat which was to carry it across the bay to the landing at Sgeir na h-Aireig.

From the shore to the little church on the hill was a steep climb of more than a mile. A steady stream of people wound its way, behind the pallbearers, up the narrow, rutted pathway.

During the journey from the church to the burial ground, another mile or so of walking, the number of mourners seemed to swell, as those from outlying farms and from the Seileach quarries joined the throng.

Behind the coffin walked Alan McClintock, his arm tight about Mairie's shoulders. The boy's mother, heavily draped in black, was supported on her other side by her brother-in-law, Donald McPherson. Other members of the two families gathered closely about their kinsmen as the coffin was laid across the grave, dug deep into the green hillside of the ancient kirkyard.

All around the mourners gathered. The minister raised his voice that all might hear the ritual prayers. There was not a dry eye in that multitude of people.

At the roadside, beside the churchyard gate, Annie and Jamie McGillivray stood waiting for the doctor who had kindly offered them a ride back to the village in his gig.

They hardly noticed the steady file of people passing by. All the more startled were they, therefore, to be confronted by an angry Alan McClintock.

'What's this, McGillivray? Come to gloat over your fine deed, are ye?' His unsteady gait betrayed the excessive amount of whisky which he had consumed since daybreak.

Annie caught her breath, Jamie looked startled for a moment, then, good-natured man that he was, he held out his hand.

'Come now, Alan,' he reasoned with the distraught father, 'you don't know what you are saying, man. Whatever you may think, it was an accident. The boy was supposed to have come up with the others. No one knew he was there.'

'And how much check was made before you let go the pallet?' McClintock was raging now. 'None, I tell ye. None at all! You murdering *madadh*! I'll see you swing for this if it is the last thing that I ever do!'

Jamie looked the man straight in the face. He clenched his fists but held his arms close by his sides, struggling to preserve his composure.

William and Elizabeth came upon the unhappy scene in time to hear McClintock's accusation.

As McPherson and another colleague made to restrain Alan, the Quarry Manager stepped in front of McGillivray and, speaking quietly but firmly, said: 'Come now, Mr McClintock, this is no time to be airing your grievances. There will be an official enquiry into the accident. Let us leave it until then to apportion blame, if there be any.'

Reluctantly, McClintock allowed himself to be led away by his kinsmen while McGillivray, still quivering from the shock of the encounter, sat down abruptly upon the stone wall and dropped his head in his hands.

'Get along home now, Jamie,' William tried to rally him. 'There is no blame attached to you over this matter. The lad should not have been in the quarry. You did the only thing you could to avoid an even greater disaster. If the gear had gone, there would have been weeks of work lost while we replaced it.'

Even as he made these comforting remarks, William's attention was distracted by a movement on the opposite hillside. Travelling as swiftly as he could, against the flow of people leaving the cemetery, a horseman was approaching from the direction of the Castle.

At last the rider was close enough to be recognised. It was Lugas the Factor.

Catching sight of a familiar face in all that crowd, Lugas rode up to the little group standing beside the cemetery wall.

'For God's sake, Whylie,' the Factor called across the heads of the departing crowd, 'where is the doctor? Have you seen him?'

PART IV

1

David pulled up Lugas's horse and dismounted before the castle door, thrusting the reins into the hands of the stable boy who had run forward to receive them.

He took the steps two at a time. In the entrance hall he was met by an anxious Mrs Meecham, who directed him into the library.

George, Marquis of Stirling, sprawled in an armchair, clothes in disarray, face unshaven and the whisky bottle at his elbow half-empty.

Before the marble fireplace stood a tall, thin figure, whose sharply pointed chin curved upwards appearing almost to touch a nose which reminded David of a puffin's bill.

The dark city suit, of tailcoat and pin-stripe trousers, seemed strangely out of place against the ancient stonework of the castle walls.

At David's entrance, His Lordship struggled to his feet, swaying dangerously, so that the doctor felt obliged to step forward to lend him a steadying hand.

'Thank God you have come at last, Beaton. She has been calling for you all morning.' His Lordship gasped out the words.

David's eyes met those of the stranger. 'Mr Gillespie?' he enquired.

The tall gentleman stepped forward. With some reluctance, it seemed to David, he extended his hand in greeting. The fingers, long, cold talons, served only to emphasise the impression of some monstrous bird of prey.

'Good day to you, Dr Beaton,' said Gillespie, in a thin, high voice. His black, boot-button eyes peered through the thick lenses of his gold-rimmed spectacles.

'How is Her Ladyship?'

Gillespie gave David a warning glance. With a brief nod in the direction of the Marquis, he indicated that they should withdraw to the other end of the room where they could not be overheard.

'Lady Jane has been in labour for twelve hours,' the physician explained. 'The child is large, perhaps too large for such a small frame.'

It was as David had feared. 'What do you propose to do then, sir? A Caesarean operation perhaps?'

Gillespie's features displayed no emotion as he replied.

'Do, sir? Why, we wait and see what the good Lord has in mind. I do not believe in interfering with His Will.'

'What are you talking about, man?' demanded David. 'Surely there is something we can do to ease her labour? If it is too late for a Caesarean . . . then forceps?'

The older man's expression was stony as he insisted: 'I will not interfere with the natural process. Parturition is, in my opinion, one aspect of our work where the physician's task is to comfort and encourage. Intervention is against the principles laid down in the Good Book.'

'Good God, you will be telling me next that the pains of childbirth are in retribution for the sins of Eve!' David exclaimed. Then, as the family physician stared back at him with a sardonic smile on his lips, realisation dawned. 'Why, that is exactly what you do believe!'

David turned on his heel, and went to shake the Marquis out of his stupor.

'My Lord,' he insisted, as the nobleman complained about the disturbance, 'I must have your permission to attend Her Ladyship. Mr Gillespie seems unwilling, or unable, to help her.'

'. . . Told you before, Beaton,' the Marquis's words were slurred but quite definite, 'Gillespie . . . knows best . . . always attends family . . . tradition . . . understand?'

David understood only too well. Without His Lordship's permission he was powerless to do anything to help the poor girl lying upstairs.

'May I at least see Her Ladyship?' he requested.

George forced open one eye and muttered, 'Of course, that's what you're here for, ain't it? She has been asking for you.'

From above there came one soul-searing scream, followed by another . . . and another.

David did not wait for a sign of consent from his professional colleague. He strode from the room without giving Gillespie a second glance, and bounded up the staircase to the Marchioness's apartments.

He opened the door cautiously to find his way barred by the nurse, Miss Pearson. That stout body attempted to keep him from the patient, but David thrust her aside in his agitation.

The lovely girl seemed to have shrunk away to nothing. Her fevered brow, and the deep dark shadows under her eyes, told their own story. She was exhausted. Any possibility that she could deliver the child by her own efforts was now gone. She had no strength left.

As he took her hand in his, he felt the feeble flutter of her pulse and knew that her agony could not last much longer.

Sensing his comforting presence, Jane opened her eyes and smiled faintly when she saw him.

Her words were whispered so softly that he had to lean over her to hear them.

'It is all over with me, Dr David. Take care of George . . . he will miss me.' Her knees drew up in pain and she gave one final anguished cry of agony. Her fragile hand gripped David's fiercely for an instant, and then fell lifeless to the counterpane.

David sought in vain for even the slightest flutter of a pulse. There was nothing. He drew back the sheet. The child was nearly born. Its head, covered by a mop of gold-brown hair, was clearly visible.

Casting his eyes around the room, David saw Gillespie's medical bag. 'Bring that here,' he demanded of the truculent nurse. Reluctantly she came forward, holding the bag open.

He sorted swiftly through the instruments. Finding the scalpel he sought, he turned his attention to his patient.

Working quickly, for there was no time to lose, David sliced into the muscular tissues of the birth canal to ease the passage of the baby's head. In a matter of moments, the tiny body lay on the sheet, beside that of its mother. Without waiting to sever the cord, David picked up the child, scooped mucus from its mouth and nostrils and began to breathe air into its lungs, gently, rhythmically. Suddenly, the infant let out a wail, coughed up more mucus and gave a lusty cry.

Satisfied that the child could now breathe on its own, David tied off the cord and handed the baby to the nurse. Given a job to do which she understood, the woman set to with a will and soon the new heir to the Stirling fortunes was clean and comfortably swaddled in his new clothes.

His mother, who so recently had sewn the garments with such loving care, lay as though sleeping. All travail past, her colour drained, she was once again the pale young girl whom Dr Beaton had observed at their first encounter.

David became aware of Gillespie's presence in the room. The physician stepped up to the bed, observed the mutilations which David had been forced to make in order to free the child, and pursed his lips. He went to the door and called for the housekeeper, Mrs Meecham. Quietly he instructed her to assist the nurse in tidying the room and making Her Ladyship presentable.

Returning to the bedroom, he signalled to David to pick up the babe, now lying wide-eyed in his crib. With David carrying the child, they descended to the library.

Gillespie opened the door and strode into the room. His Lordship was still stretched out in his chair, although he had stopped drinking and seemed a little more sober. So much so, that David felt it safe to lay his tiny burden in the Marquis's arms.

'Your son, My Lord,' he said, and stood back, unable to disguise his own anguish.

His Lordship looked down at the wrinkled little face and two bright eyes gazed back at him. He held up one finger and a tiny fist closed around it, as though it would never let go.

The Marquis looked enquiringly at each of the medical men in turn. 'Jane . . . how is Jane?'

David glanced across at Gillespie who, after the initial shock of realising that, against all odds, the child was safely delivered, had resumed control of the situation.

'I regret to inform you, My Lord, that Her Ladyship passed away, giving birth to your son.'

David was angered at Gillespie's bluntness, but then, he reminded himself, there was no easy way to tell it. George looked from Gillespie to the child in his arms, in disbelief.

'But how can he be alive, and she dead?' he asked.

Looking straight at Gillespie, defying him to make any comment, David replied, 'The final effort of delivering the child was just too much for Her Ladyship's frail body. Her last action was to give you your son.'

The Marquis rose unsteadily to his feet. Still clasping the tiny infant to him, he said, 'I must go to her. Oh, my poor little Jane . . . what shall we do without you?' Still nursing the child, he made his way slowly towards the door, which David hurried to open for him.

Alone with Gillespie, David turned on that individual.

'No doubt your nurse will tell you what occurred. As the patient breathed her last, the child was nearly born. I released it by cutting into the birth canal. Had you performed a similar operation earlier, the Marchioness would still be alive.'

'I have nothing with which to reproach myself,' declared Gillespie in his bland fashion. 'I did all that was expected of me.'

'The village midwife would have served her better,' David retorted, outraged by the complacency of his colleague.

'Dr Beaton, you are a young man with a long way to go in order to reach the status which I already enjoy. I trust that no indiscretion on your part will force me to reveal that, at the risk of ending Her Ladyship's life, you performed surgery to release the child.'

David could not believe what he was hearing.

'The patient was already dead before I cut the child free,' he cried. 'The nurse was there, she will confirm it.'

'I think you will find that she will support my own opinion,' Gillespie observed, 'which is, that you did not make certain of the patient's demise before you went for the child.'

'But it was obvious . . .' David blustered helplessly. It was true. He had assumed death without testing for all the vital signs. It could have been that she was still alive . . . but only just. But certainly the child would have been dead had he delayed another second.

Satisfied that David had appreciated his warning, Gillespie resumed his former chilly professional manner.

'His Lordship will require my services now, I think. The nurse will attend to the child. Your presence is no longer required, Dr Beaton.'

David picked up his hat, and not even stopping to acknowledge Gillespie's sharp 'Good day!' he strode out of the castle and down the steep flight of steps to the stable yard.

Lugas had thoughtfully instructed the lad to see that the doctor had a mount to carry him home.

As David allowed his horse to amble slowly along the drive, the Factor came out of his house and called to him.

'What news of Her Ladyship, doctor?'

David, startled by the sudden intrusion into his thoughts, looked blankly at Lugas for a few seconds before answering.

'His Lordship has a male heir,' he replied, and then, as Lugas was about to voice his pleasure, 'Her Ladyship is dead.'

He rode on, leaving Lugas standing in the middle of the road, gazing after him.

In the Great Hall of the Castle the Parishioners of Eisdalsa and Seileach were paying their last respects to their young Marchioness.

From early morning, tenants and employees had shuffled through the silent building, its dark interior a fitting contrast to the brightness of the cloudless August skies without.

The room was lit only by the rays of the sun. Entering through the great stone-mullioned windows, they pierced the gloom and focused upon the high catafalque which was the only object in that vast space, all furniture, pictures and ornaments having been removed.

In her ornately carved oak coffin lay Jane, Marchioness of Stirling. Her face, beautiful in repose, was white as the marble bust, already commissioned, which would soon be the only tangible sign that she had ever existed. A single white lily lay under her folded hands, across the froth of Brussels lace which reached to her chin. Two white satin shoes, peeping out below her silk gown, showed those who had not known her in life just how small and dainty she had been.

At either end of the catafalque stood huge vases of exotic blooms, their stark whiteness set off by contrasting green foliage of every shade and variety.

Beside the door, supported by his Factor and Mrs Lugas, the Marquis received the condolences of his people with a solemn handshake and sometimes a murmured response or a smile of recognition for a particularly favoured retainer.

From all over the Parish they had come: lawyers and fishermen; quarriers and clergy; bankers and crofters; to show their respect for their Laird, and their support for him in his hour of greatest sorrow.

William and Elizabeth were accompanied by the McGillivrays. Elizabeth gazed on the girl, lying so still as though asleep, and chastised herself for all those uncharitable thoughts with which she had clouded their infrequent meetings.

Annie recalled the hours that she had sat with the Marchioness as they sewed and exchanged confidences. She seemed to hear, as clearly as though the poor corpse herself was speaking, the words of excited anticipation, and the fears which they had shared. Clinging to her husband, she was led away, weeping.

Late in the morning, when most of the people had departed, David introduced Morag to the Marquis.

'I have to thank you, Mrs Beaton, for the kindness and comfort which you brought to my wife during her last weeks,' His Lordship murmured. 'She spoke often of your friendship and how much it meant to her.'

David's mother made a low curtsey. 'I came to love Her Ladyship as a daughter, sir,' she replied, trusting he would not find her presumptuous. 'Indeed, I had looked forward to many years in which our friendship might grow.' She fought back her tears.

David squeezed her arm gently, to let her know that he understood her grief, and ventured to relieve the tension of the moment.

'How is your son, My Lord?' he enquired. 'Miss Pearson has made satisfactory arrangements for his feeding, I presume?'

For a moment, the Marquis looked blankly at him. Mrs Lugas answered for him.

'I have engaged Martha McDougal as a wet nurse,' she told him. 'Miss Pearson seems quite satisfied with the arrangement.'

David nodded his head. He knew of the girl, a crofter's daughter who had recently borne an illegitimate child. Her family would be more than grateful for her employment.

'I think we are nearly finished here, Beaton,' the Marquis interjected gruffly. 'There is a matter of some importance I wish to discuss with you. Would you be kind enough to wait for me in the library?'

'I would be pleased to, My Lord,' he replied hesitantly, 'but I must attend my mother. As you see, she is very distressed.'

'Morag shall come along with me,' Alicia Lugas determined. 'You will find us at the house when you are ready, Dr David.'

With some reluctance, he allowed Alicia to lead his mother away.

Morag had been acutely disturbed by Jane's death, and he feared greatly for her health. Anxiously he watched their departure before slipping unobtrusively into the library.

It was there that the Marquis joined him some time later.

'Good of you to wait, my dear fellow,' George Stirling declared, making a bee-line for the tray of spirits standing beside his own favourite chair. 'Will you join me in a dram?'

Without waiting for a reply, he poured two generous measures of whisky and handed one of them to his guest.

'*Slainte mhath!*' the Marquis toasted him, with somewhat forced good humour. Grateful as he was for the wholehearted support of his people, the morning had been a long and tiring one.

David raised his glass in reply, but could not bring himself to utter the time-honoured greeting.

'Fact is, doctor, I have a favour to ask of you.'

'My Lord?'

'Seems a bit of a cheek really, considering how I prevented you from attending poor Jane at the last . . . but it's the young 'un, d'you see?'

'Whatever service I can perform for your Lordship, you have only to ask.' David realised that this bluff but warm-hearted character had found it difficult to apologise. He bore the Marquis no ill-will over the events surrounding the birth of his son. The poor man had relied upon his family physician. How was he to know that Gillespie was an incompetent charlatan?

'Edinburgh is no place for a child.' George voiced the thoughts that had been plaguing him ever since his wife's death. 'The women here seem competent, and Mrs Lugas has grown attached to the boy. Much as I would like to have the little beggar with me, I think he will be better off with the ladies. I love Argyll, you know, always regard this as my true home.' The Marquis became misty-eyed as he gazed on the hills and the distant sea. 'It's the best of places for a little sprog to grow up.'

David could find no fault with this reasoning.

'What I want from you, doctor, is to keep an eye on the little fellow, and write me a report from time to time on his progress. Will you do that for me?'

'Nothing would give me greater pleasure, My Lord,' he replied. 'I understand that Mrs Lugas has charge of the child. I shall be happy to liaise with her, if that is your wish.'

''Pon my word, that's good of you, doctor!' cried the Marquis, greatly relieved.

He poured another generous glass for the doctor which David refused, excusing himself on the pretext of having a number of calls to make upon his patients.

The following morning the Marquis escorted the body of his young wife the one hundred and eighty miles to his castle on the banks of the Tay, and laid her to rest beside the remains of his forefathers.

2

On a fine Saturday in late August, the *Lord of Lorn* drew away from Eisdalsa pier to the shouts of the sailors and the last-minute farewells of the passengers and their friends on shore.

Elizabeth, privileged to be welcomed on to the bridge, settled herself quietly in a corner until the steamer was underway.

With a heart full of pride, she watched her lover going about his duties. He was so sure of his every action, so efficient, so handsome in his uniform . . . she wanted to go up to him and throw her arms about him.

Gordon, in the meantime, was carrying out the various tasks associated with leaving harbour in an automatic fashion. While he might give the impression of being in charge, it was the crew, performing their duties as they had done a hundred times before, who made up for his lack of concentration. The First Officer's mind was upon the fiery-headed goddess whom he could not see from this point, but whose presence was all about him.

Perhaps it was not such a good idea, after all, to have her along on a voyage when he was working. Tomorrow, on the return trip, he would be free to attend to her, but today, with the skipper ashore at Fort William, Gordon was in charge.

As the steamer glided through the Sound of Kerrera, under the towering cliffs of Mull, Elizabeth moved to the side of the deck to gain a better view of the birds wheeling about the rocky shore.

After a few moments, Gordon could resist no longer. He came and stood beside her, their hands resting side by side on the wooden rail.

'It is so beautiful,' she cried. 'Look how bright the colours are . . . the sky so blue, the rocks every shade from grey to red. Were an artist to paint this, no one would believe that such a variety of hues could exist together.'

Gordon looked at the scene through her eyes, and agreed with her. He had become so accustomed to this journey that he had ceased to be moved by the sights which so thrilled Elizabeth. In her presence, he rediscovered the delights of viewing the reflections of the light on the water, the changes of mood of the sea and the movement of the clouds.

'Shall your aunt be expecting us?' Elizabeth asked anxiously.

When he first suggested the trip to Fort William, she had been a little apprehensive. There was enough gossip about her activities as it was. What would the old wives have to say about a stay in Fort William with a sailor? It was only when Gordon assured her that they would spend the night at his aunt's house at Corpach that she agreed to the trip. At least she was able to say that she was visiting a lady friend. Only Annie, and perhaps Katherine, appreciated the significance of the journey.

'I have a confession to make.' Gordon turned to look at her.

'Do not tell me now that you have no aunt in Corpach!' She sounded concerned but her eyes were dancing.

'Oh, never fear, my aunt exists as you will soon discover. My confession is that you will also meet my mother today.' As she drew back in dismay, he laid a hand gently upon her arm.

'I assure you that this was not part of my plan. My aunt must have mentioned your visit in a letter, and Mama, who has been fishing around ever since she suspected that I had a more than passing interest in a young lady, was determined to come and meet you. Without telling me, she arrived aboard the ship at Crinan yesterday and travelled to Fort William.'

'I suppose it had to happen sometime,' said Elizabeth far more cheerfully than she felt. From what Gordon said about his mother, she knew that she would have difficulty gaining that lady's approval. Mrs McIntyre clearly thought very highly of her son. No girl he had ever presented in the past had been good enough for him, as Gordon had pointed out, laughingly, on one of their infrequent walks around the island.

'It is just as well that you have left it until now to warn me,' said Elizabeth. 'Were it not such a long walk back from Oban, I would leave the ship now and run home!'

He knew that she was only joking. That was the wonderful thing about their relationship. They could laugh together. Never had Gordon felt so much at ease with a member of the opposite sex. He could feel for her as a friend, as well as a lover. She was an intelligent companion, unlike those simpering, affected females that his mother invited to the house to meet him.

What, he wondered, would Mama think of Elizabeth, and her 'Votes for Women' campaign? He must be careful to steer clear of those shoaly waters!

As the *Lord of Lorn* pulled in to the Ballachulish pier, Elizabeth was startled by the sight of a familiar figure, that of the previous manager of the Eisdalsa Quarries.

She had met Mr McPhee only once, in the McGillivrays' house some months ago. He had called to see Jamie in order, he said, to assure himself that the Company had treated the injured quarrier properly in the matter of compensation. William's predecessor had gone on to explain that he was now engaged as an agent, selling slates for another company. Elizabeth never heard the remainder of the conversation as McPhee had made some excuse to take Jamie outside, away from the ladies' hearing, but Elizabeth had received the impression that McPhee was there for some more sinister purpose than to allay any personal fears about McGillivray's injuries.

To see the man here, at Ballachulish, was very worrying indeed. William had confided in her when he had decided to send Malcolm Logie to New Zealand. She knew how important it was that the reason for his visit should be kept secret. How discreet had Jamie McGillivray been in his conversation with his old boss?

She wished now that she had mentioned that encounter to William at the time. The Ballachulish quarry was a fierce rival to Eisdalsa in the slate markets of the world. This new association of McPhee's could cause inestimable damage to William's enterprise.

Elizabeth thought it unlikely that McPhee would recognise her from this distance. She decided to keep out of sight until he left the boat at Fort William. There was no need to alert him to the possibility that his movements were under surveillance. When she returned to the Island, she would make sure that William was told of the ex-manager's connection with a rival company.

The evening sun was descending behind the Ardnamurchan peninsular as the *Lord of Lorn* slipped into her berth at the journey's end.

Elizabeth's fears of encountering McPhee were quickly dispelled as she watched him hurrying ahead of most of the other passengers along the quay. She herself must wait until Gordon was free to leave the vessel.

Their journey to Corpach was by one-horse chaise, over rutted tracks, beside the still waters of the Caledonian Canal.

As they drew up outside a whitewashed, two-storey building standing beside the canal, a cheerful-looking woman, her grey hair flying in untidy wisps about a round and rosy face, came out to greet them. She wiped her hands upon a less than clean apron before making a slight curtsey and shaking hands with Elizabeth.

'Mary, I am so sorry, we seem to be rather later than I would have hoped.' Gordon enveloped the woman's large, comfortable body in his broad arms, and gave her a bear hug.

'This is Mary, our old nanny,' he explained to Elizabeth. 'Since there are no more children for her to fuss over, she has come to live with my aunt to keep her company.'

'Your mama is waiting in the parlour, Mr Gordon.' The old nursemaid made it sound as though he had committed some crime for which retribution was inevitable.

When she entered the parlour, Elizabeth was immediately transported back to the manse where she had spent her childhood years. Heavy mahogany furniture filled the room. Every leg of each piece of furniture was carefully frilled. Antimacassars hung over chairbacks and chenille cloths, with their tasselled overhangs, covered every shelf and table.

The curtains, which matched the chenille covers, obscured most of the light, so that the red rays of the setting sun were denied the pleasure of playing over the picture-covered walls.

Although it was still late summer, rather than autumn, Elizabeth shivered in the gloom.

Seated on either side of a well-burnished, unlit grate were two ladies who, in the dim light, might have been twins. Each had her hair, greying at the temples, piled high and drawn tightly back into a severe bun. Both ladies wore the black garb of widowhood, but there the resemblance ended.

The hostess rose to her feet as they entered and, flapping and twittering like a small bird, greeted her nephew and then his companion.

'Aunt Elphie, may I introduce Miss Elizabeth Duncan? Elizabeth, this is my aunt, Mrs Wallace.'

Elizabeth managed to catch the thin delicate fingers in mid-flight and shook the lady carefully by the hand.

'It is very kind of you to invite me, Mrs Wallace,' she said politely. 'I do hope we shall not cause you too much trouble.'

'Nonsense, my dear,' chirruped the little woman, 'it is a pleasure to have young people in the house. Gordon does not call in nearly often enough . . . the naughty boy.'

Elizabeth's mind shot momentarily to the deck of the *Lord of Lorn*. She smiled at an inner vision of the faces of the crew hearing him addressed thus.

Gordon, meanwhile, had advanced towards the other lady who remained seated, a stony expression on her white face.

'Mama, may I introduce Miss Elizabeth Duncan?'

Elizabeth found herself, quite contrary to all her principles, curtseying to this formidable personage. Summoning a hesitant smile, she greeted the woman who could become her future mother-in-law.

'It is a great pleasure to meet you, ma'am. Gordon has told me so much about you.'

'I wish that I had been equally well informed about you.' Mrs McIntyre raised her lorgnette and peered rudely at the schoolmistress, as though she were a particularly shabby item in a house-clearance sale.

Elizabeth was rather amused to see that Gordon apparently found his mother as formidable as she did herself.

'Miss Duncan and I hope to be married, Mama,' he volunteered. Then, persuasively, 'I believe that you will soon come to know her, and love her . . . as I do.'

'Since you are of age, and I am dependent upon your support, there is little that I can do to prevent you,' his mother replied repressively.

Turning to Elizabeth, she thawed sufficiently to invite the girl to sit on a chair, so placed that her features were illuminated by the fading light.

'Gordon has always been susceptible to a pretty face,' she mused. Before Elizabeth could take even a crumb of comfort from this reluctant approbation, she barked, 'Well, girl, where do you come from? Who are your people?'

'Before his death, my father was minister in a small parish outside Edinburgh,' Elizabeth replied quietly. 'My mother died two years ago.'

'You have inherited at a very young age. I trust that you have invested your fortune wisely?' Gordon's mother was unmoved by the startled cry of indignation which came from her son. 'No doubt your father's lawyers advised you. Who are they, pray?'

This was too much for Gordon. 'Really, Mama, I do not think it is any concern of yours what Miss Duncan has or has not done with any money she may have. I shall be able to make all necessary provision for her when I am appointed to my own command.' He came to stand protectively at Elizabeth's side and took her hand in his. Only the tightness of his grip told her of the strength of his anger at his mother's impertinence.

Elizabeth responded to the woman's question with a tight smile.

'Alas, Mrs McIntyre, I have no fortune and therefore have no need of advice from lawyers. I am obliged to make a living for myself, by teaching in a public school.'

Mrs Wallace, who all this time had been hard pressed to keep her tongue still, could contain herself no longer.

'Oh, my,' she cried. 'How interesting it must be to be a lady of learning. I have often tried to read deep works of philosophy and such, but a threepenny novel is all that I ever manage to finish. Tell me, do you speak foreign languages as well? I have often wondered what it would be like to travel abroad and to speak to all those people in their strange tongues!'

Elizabeth smiled at the bright little woman, so simple and yet so anxious to please. It was difficult to understand how the two sisters could be so different.

'I am able to speak and write in French and German,' she replied politely, 'but my real love is for the Classics and for English Literature.'

There was a disgusted snort from Gordon's formidable parent. 'Elphie, is it not time that you were preparing the evening meal?' she broke in. 'I can imagine that Mary will need some help to set out the table.'

The younger woman, accustomed to taking orders from her sister, even though she was mistress of the house, rose reluctantly and bustled out. Gordon, who had hurriedly opened the door at his aunt's enforced departure, now took up a commanding position before the fireplace. Encouraged by Elizabeth's affectionate glances and inspired by her forthright reply to Mrs McIntyre's questioning, he informed his mother of their plans to marry and to set up their home on Eisdalsa.

'My new command should be ready for scheduled sailings by March next year,' he explained.

Elizabeth, who had been thinking hard as to how she was to ease the tension between herself and her future mother-in-law, had a sudden inspiration. 'Mrs McIntyre, why do you not join Gordon and myself at Eisdalsa for the New Year festivities?' she suggested. 'It would be a grand opportunity for you and I to become better acquainted.'

There was a sharp intake of breath from Gordon's mother before she replied stiffly, 'Gordon and I will be spending Hogmanay in Edinburgh, as we always do.' She looked sharply towards her son for confirmation. Seeing that his attention was taken up by activity in the street outside, she added, 'I hardly think that Eisdalsa Island can provide accommodation suitable to a lady of my sensitivities.' She rose majestically from the straight-backed armchair.

Elizabeth could not help but admire the woman's spirit. Aware that she had lost all power to control her son's activities, and was forced to concede defeat in the matter of his choice of a bride, a petulant reaction to Elizabeth's invitation was the only weapon left to her.

Elizabeth suspected that her relationship with her future mother-in-law would always be one of thinly disguised hostility on both their parts.

'There are some months to go before we need decide anything,' she offered as a crutch to lean upon. 'I am sure that you would find my own small house acceptable accommodation should you wish, after all, to spend New Year at Eisdalsa.'

Gordon took hold of Elizabeth's hand and kissed it. With his other arm, he encircled his mother's waist, and hugged her tightly. Even she could not resist this show of affection for the two women whom Gordon held most dear. Relaxing within his grasp, she cleared her throat noisily and remarked, 'Whatever can Elphie be thinking of? The supper must be ruined by now!'

The tragedy which had befallen George, Marquis of Stirling, was to be of life-saving benefit to a poor crofting family, the McDougals. Martha McDougal was the eldest of three children. Jack, her brother, had recently finished school and helped his father farm their small croft on Eisdalsa Island. The younger daughter Ellen was still at school. Martha had become pregnant out of wedlock, thereby bringing disgrace upon herself and her kinfolk. She had paid the price of her waywardness by receiving her admonishment in the kirk before the whole congregation.

The girl's mother, hard pressed to feed the family she already had, despaired of being able to provide for yet another mouth.

Martha's child was born, a surprisingly lusty baby, only days before the Marquis's son fought his way into the world. Alicia Lugas, presented

with the responsibility of caring for the motherless infant, arranged for
Martha and her child to be brought to the Castle where she was given
a room to herself, new clothes, and all the food she could eat, in
exchange for the largesse of her overflowing breasts.

The McDougal household benefited immediately by having one less
mouth to feed. As time went by, their larder was supplemented by
small gifts from the Castle kitchen. These Martha was allowed to carry
home to them on the rare occasions when she was given leave to take
her own child to see his grandparents.

The nurse, Miss Pearson, soon tired of the miserable autumnal gales
and rain, and began to long for the diversions of her home in the city.
When she packed her bags and left, at the beginning of November, no
one at the Castle was sorry to see her depart.

Martha was a sensible girl. Despite her lowly upbringing, she was
quick to acquire the manners of the Castle staff. She soon merged with
her new environment and became accepted. The housekeeper, Mrs
Meecham, realising the importance of a stable and loving environment
for little Edward, encouraged the girl. She took her under her wing,
defending her against the unpleasant backbiting and condescension
meted out by other members of the household.

In her dealings with the nurse, too, Martha had been dutiful and
polite, despite the withering remarks which constantly assailed her
every effort to please the fastidious Miss Pearson. The girl was taught
to care for the babies, and was soon considered sufficiently competent
to look after them on her own. On Miss Pearson's departure, Martha
was promoted to nursemaid. When little Edward was fully weaned and
had no further need of a wet-nurse, she continued with her duties in
the nursery, her own son being allowed to grow up as companion to
the heir to the Stirling fortune.

The gales and the consistently wet weather of November kept everyone
in their houses. Only the men continued to work outside, struggling to
fulfil the increasing orders for roofing slates from around the world.

William's venture in New Zealand had paid off. The success of Malcolm's negotiations with the citizens of Dunedin was such as to embar-
rass the Eisdalsa Company. The demand for slate shipments began to
outrun the capacity of the quarries to provide the slate. Several new
workings were opened on Seileach and the neighbouring islands, and a
number of new families was brought into the district to increase the
workforce.

His Lordship, burdened with his grief, left everything in the hands
of Lugas, and William was obliged to negotiate with that gentleman for
quarry sites and new housing for the workers. He found it hard to
understand the Factor's reluctance to release certain areas on the
Ballahuan estate, and was particularly incensed when Lugas insisted

that any houses built should be situated close to the existing villages, despite the fact that this would mean some of the men walking three or four miles to their work in the new quarries.

It was important that the Eisdalsa Company should fulfil its contract with Dunedin in full, as Malcolm Logie had made it very clear that there were other slate companies waiting eagerly on the sidelines for any sign of failure. Not the least of these was the one at Ballachulish.

Elizabeth's observation of McPhee, in contact with the rival firm, worried William. There was no doubt that, unpopular as he had been as a Manager, he was quite capable of enlisting the support of certain employees who, for whatever reason, thought that they had a grievance against the Eisdalsa Company.

What if some ill-considered word from McGillivray had alerted the ex-Manager to the proposed dealings with Dunedin? Whatever the method used, the other company was clearly alive to the possibility of taking over Eisdalsa's market, should they fail to keep up with the contract. He must be wary of any scheme to delay production in the quarries.

Although Malcolm Logie's function as negotiator was now accomplished, William sent word for him to stay in New Zealand for a further three months, until the first of the shipments had arrived at its destination, and until Logie himself felt satisfied that the contract was fulfilled to the letter.

Late in November, on a particularly unpleasant day when the wind swept mountainous waves across the rocks and covered the trees and bushes of Tigh na Broch with a fine spray of salty water, David was disturbed in his study by the sound of frenzied pounding on the outer door of the surgery. He rose reluctantly from his desk, which was strewn with microscope slides. The Koch staining system had proved invaluable in the location and identification of microbes, in samples both of drinking water, and from the drains in the village.

He had been trying for some weeks to complete a treatise on the subject, for publication in the *University Medical Journal*. This afternoon had afforded a rare opportunity for study.

He rose from the desk, drew on his working jacket, smoothed down his rumpled hair – he had a habit of pushing his hands through it when he was thinking – and walked through to the outside door. The pounding stopped at his approach. When he opened up, the doctor was surprised to find that it was McCulloch the minister who was making the disturbance.

'Thank heaven you are here, Beaton,' the man gasped, as David ushered him inside and helped him to remove a saturated topcoat. 'I feared that you might have been called away, to the Island perhaps!'

'On such a day, even the hardiest of the men would be unlikely to venture far into the quarries. I think I shall be untroubled in that quarter.' He invited his caller to be seated, and offered him a dram to keep out the cold.

McCulloch swallowed the stiff whisky gratefully, and set the glass down with a sigh of satisfaction.

'Just what the doctor ordered,' he declared, then realising the pun, laughed in a high-pitched, near-hysterical fashion.

'Tell me,' urged David, 'what brings you out on such a foul afternoon?'

'It is my wife's niece, Beaton. She has come to stay following a bout of fever . . . to recover, you understand. She arrived two days ago, and seemed tired and pale but otherwise in good spirits. Today however, she awoke complaining of headache. My wife persuaded her to remain in her bed. Now she is vomiting and has diarrhoea, and seems to be burning up with fever. My wife has done her best to reduce the temperature, but nothing she can do seems to help.'

'You say she has already suffered a bout of fever. Where was that pray?'

'She is a nursing sister. She works in Glasgow's Western Infirmary.'

'There has been a serious outbreak of cholera in Glasgow in recent weeks . . . are you saying that it is cholera from which she is recovering?'

'Yes, that is so.'

'Then we have a job on our hands. At all costs, the disease must be prevented from spreading here. In the villages, with their poor sanitation and overcrowded houses, cholera would rampage like wildfire.'

As he spoke, David was gathering together the medicines and equipment he needed. Soon he was ready to accompany McCulloch. He thrust his head round the kitchen door to tell Morag where he would be, if needed, and then the two men went out into the storm.

Annabel Douglas lay tossing on her narrow bed. Her long brown hair, dark with perspiration, straggled across the pillows. Her skin was blotched with red marks, the only colour on her otherwise grey face. Her eyes stared, unseeing, at the sloping ceiling, only a few feet above her head, in the dimly lit, attic room.

The smell was intolerable. It was clear that the patient had no bowel control and that Mrs McCulloch, try as she might, was unable to cope with the constant demand for clean linen.

David had seen many cases of cholera in the slums of Edinburgh in his student days. It was no less distressing to find a case here, in the relative cleanliness and comfort of the manse.

Pausing only for a short word with Mrs McCulloch, he approached the bed. His patient was in a state of collapse, her pulse fluttered feebly, and although her brow was burning hot and she shivered and perspired profusely, her hands and feet were clammy and cold.

'First thing, Mrs McCulloch, is to make her as warm as possible. Hot bricks, water bottles, whatever you have . . . plenty of blankets . . . and bank up the fire. This room is like an ice house!'

Mrs McCulloch hurried away to summon her servants and to carry out his instructions.

David took from his bag a solution of permanganate of potash which he had prepared before leaving the surgery. Lifting his patient's head he forced her to swallow the bitter mixture in small painful gulps.

Satisfied at last that she had taken sufficient of the draught, he laid her back on the pillows, rubbing her hands all the while to increase the circulation.

Soon the minister's wife was back, bearing a pile of blankets. Her husband followed with coals and wood for the fire, while the servant approached the bed carrying some large bricks, wrapped in flannel.

'Ah,' cried David, approvingly, 'these will do very well, thank you.' He smiled reassuringly at the timid maidservant and lifted back the covers so that she might insert a brick alongside each of the patient's thighs and another at her feet.

'Right, Mrs McCulloch, it will be some time before we know if the treatment I have given will work. Meantime we must look to prevent the spread of infection to the rest of the household.'

Until this moment, Myra McCulloch had considered only the welfare of her niece. No thought of danger to herself or her family had crossed her mind. She cried out in dismay as the import of David's words struck her.

Quick to allay her fears, he issued his instructions, knowing that she would now obey them to the letter.

'Everything your niece has used must be scalded, boiled or burned. Make absolutely sure, for instance, that any cup or plate is used only by her, and washed separately from the family's utensils. Her bodily fluids must be disposed of in a pit, dug especially for the purpose, well away from your own privy and from the water supply. I suggest that you add some granules of this to each chamber-pot, before you empty it.' He handed her a bottle of carbolic acid crystals.

'As for the patient herself, get her to drink as much liquid as she will swallow . . . force her, if necessary. The greatest danger is one of dehydration. Boil all the fluids which you give her.

'On no account should you allow the children into this room, for whatever reason, and you and your servant must take every precaution to avoid direct contact with Miss Douglas's body fluids. Wash your hands thoroughly after handling the patient or items she has used. Soiled linen must be soaked in carbolic acid solution, and boiled for at least thirty minutes before you attempt to rinse the articles by hand. Now, do you think you can remember all that?'

David's question was addressed to the young servant as much as to the mistress. The girl's face was white with terror, but, at the doctor's question, she managed a shy smile, nodded and curtsied.

David was aware of the commonly held belief that all fevers were borne on foul air and could be eliminated by good ventilation. His own researches, following those of Lister and Pasteur, had indicated without doubt that diseases such as cholera were water-borne and usually resulted from a contaminated water or food supply. Once one accepted that it was the combination of overcrowding, poor drainage or none, and inadequate water supplies, which was responsible for the spread of the disease, it was possible to understand why such epidemics occurred mainly in towns, or in closely packed accommodation such as prisons and workhouses.

David did not doubt that Miss Douglas had carried the infection with her from Glasgow. Her weakness, coupled with the long, tiring journey by sea, had resulted in a recurrence of the disease which must have lain dormant in her blood. If he could isolate the patient immediately, and here in the manse there were the facilities for that to be possible, he could yet prevent an outbreak among the quarriers.

The extra warmth had revived Annabel. Her eyes no longer appeared glazed. She directed a questioning glance at David.

'I am Dr Beaton, Miss Douglas,' he reassured her. 'You have suffered a relapse, I fear. We shall soon have you back to rights.' He patted her gently on the shoulder and smiled. She was too weak to respond, but her eyes told him of her gratitude.

It had been foolish to set out on such long journey, she knew that now, but the situation in the nurses' hostel had been unbearable. Two of her friends had died; others were so overworked that they could not fail to fall ill. Her own attack had been relatively mild and when she had recovered sufficiently to travel, she had begged to be allowed to go to her relatives to recuperate. Only now did she appreciate what harm she might have done, by bringing the disease here. From the mists of her delirium she had heard David's voice. The instructions he gave to her aunt were the very ones she had been trying to give herself, but her attempts had been interpreted as fevered ramblings.

Satisfied at last that the matter was in capable hands, she relaxed, and almost immediately fell into a natural, untroubled sleep.

In the days that followed, David called often to assess the progress of his patient who, once past the crisis point, began to make a good recovery. The doctor was pleased to see the care that the minister's household was taking to prevent any spread of the infection. So far there had been no further instances of the disease. He was satisfied that the case was an isolated one and that, with continued vigilance, the outbreak would be contained.

*　　　*　　　*

As the days grew shorter and the festive season approached, Elizabeth began to make plans for the anticipated visit of her future mother-in-law. Gordon had at last persuaded Mrs McIntyre that, unless she agreed to join himself and Elizabeth on Eisdalsa for New Year, she would be celebrating Hogmanay alone.

With his new command already on the stocks at Clydebank, he felt it was time to approach William on the subject of suitable accommodation for himself and his bride-to-be. Elizabeth was determined to remain on the Island. As a married woman she would be forced to resign her position in the school, and as a consequence would be obliged to give up her present house.

William agreed to seek approval from the Factor for Gordon to build a house on Eisdalsa.

'I am sure that the Marquis will consent to your friend purchasing the lease of a parcel of land,' Lugas agreed. 'He must appreciate, however, that any building which he may have constructed legally becomes the property of the Marquis when the term expires.'

William, unaccustomed to the Scottish system of land-law, found this rather surprising.

'Is there no compensation in such a case?' he enquired.

'The matter would be one for mutual agreement between the landlord and lessee,' replied the Factor. 'I have no doubt that His Lordship would look favourably upon some modest form of compensation.'

Somewhat disconcerted, William had conveyed the substance of this conversation to Gordon. His friend was not in the least perturbed.

'Provided the lease is a long one, what have I to lose?' he said. 'We must have a permanent home, and Elizabeth has set her heart on remaining here on the island. She will inevitably be alone a great deal of the time. I would certainly be happier for her to be amongst friends.'

The matter was settled. A lease for seventy-five years was drawn up, and the planning of Elizabeth's new home was begun.

Whatever dreams William may have nurtured, concerning his own relationship with Elizabeth, had finally been dispelled by Gordon's tentative enquiries about housing.

After his experience in Cornwall, William had believed that he could never love any other woman. His initial encounter with Elizabeth, however, had quite dispelled that notion, but being a realist, he had known for some time that his cause was hopeless. One had only to witness Gordon and Elizabeth in each other's company to recognise the strength of the bond between them.

He had long since resigned himself to the role of friend and counsellor, and, should need arise during Gordon's frequent absences, protector. For the moment he was flattered that they placed such confidence in him that he was to be included in the planning of their new home.

Late into the night, the three friends pored over plans for the new house. It was to have the most modern arrangements for supplying water to the kitchen, and a range with a back boiler to provide hot water. Most exciting of all, there was to be a bathroom and the very first water closet in Eisdalsa. William had been studying the arrangements which had recently been installed in the Queen's residence, Osborne House, on the Isle of Wight. What was good enough for Her Majesty should be good enough for Elizabeth! With its own ash pit for processing the household effluents, this was to be the most sanitary dwelling in the district.

Once the design was agreed, William engaged a small body of masons to begin building. There was much speculation as to what the purpose of the structure might be. For many weeks the site was the focus of several interesting, and often highly imaginative, suggestions.

Mrs McIntyre arrived two days before the end of December and Elizabeth endeavoured to make her comfortable in the schoolteacher's house. The old bothy was now distinguished by the title of 'house', since it possessed a bedroom and a scullery, separate from the living room. Elizabeth had retained the cot which had been there when she took over the accommodation, so that she was able to provide her guest with the luxury of a private bedroom while she herself slept in the living room. But despite all her efforts, Elizabeth failed to find favour with Mrs McIntyre. The days before the Hogmanay Ball were fraught with problems, which were relieved only when William called upon them. Mrs McIntyre was of that school of females who believe that the world was made by men, for men, and that the only duty of women was to see to their comfort.

Elizabeth failed to live up to expectations because she presumed, in the first instance, to work for her living. Secondly, she was intelligent, and never slow to air her opinions upon matters which the older woman considered unsuitable topics for a female to discuss. Most damning of all, it was clear that Gordon was besotted with the girl. Mrs McIntyre could not forgive his disloyalty to his mother, and blamed the girl for alienating his affections, instead of accepting that her son was in love and determined to marry.

Elizabeth felt that she must tell David herself about her forthcoming engagement. It would be unfortunate if word were to reach his ears before she had an opportunity to speak with him.

She sent a note to Morag asking her if it would be convenient to call at Tigh na Broch one afternoon in the hope of seeing David. She was disconcerted to receive a note by return explaining that since he was attending a case of cholera in the district, he thought it inadvisable for them to meet. He was concerned to ensure that the disease did not spread via the schoolchildren.

Unwilling to take the easy way out by writing a letter, Elizabeth decided to wait until David was free to see her.

She knew there had been rumours of fever in the village; someone had suggested that there was a case of cholera, although it was hard to believe that the scourge of the cities could have reached out to this backwater of Argyll. At any event, David had been kept busy on Seileach, while the population of Eisdalsa Island enjoyed the robust health which renewed prosperity and well-filled larders had brought to the quarrying families.

Annie and Elizabeth had planned to wear new gowns for the Hogmanay Ball. Together they had drawn patterns, and cut out the fabrics which Gordon had been commissioned to purchase in Glasgow. Sewing and fitting the dresses had taken up all their spare time in the past few weeks. Now Elizabeth's gown, a jewel-rich red, hung in the closet.

As she stroked the silky fabric, she remembered the previous Hogmanay Ball, and recalled what had taken place between herself and the doctor on that occasion. She experienced a moment's unease as she considered David's possible reaction to her forthcoming marriage.

He had never once, since that evening, mentioned either his love for her or the plans he had made for their future together. Not for the first time, she assured herself that his proposal had been a momentary whim brought on by the moonlight and the romance of the situation. He must surely have observed how close she had become to Gordon in the last few months. When all four friends were together, he could not fail to be aware of the habitual pairing: Elizabeth with Gordon, William with David.

Well, it was too late to say anything now. She did not even know if he would be coming to the ball. It was possible that his duties would keep him on Seileach. There had been some suggestion that he was discouraging too much interchange of people between the Village and the Island because of the risk of infection, although she had not observed any undue restraint in the numbers of people using the ferry.

When the day of the ball arrived at last, Elizabeth was up early, making sure that the fire was banked up to provide sufficient hot water for her guest and herself to bathe in the old galvanised iron tub which was brought into the house when required.

Elizabeth dragged the heavy bath through to the bedroom, trying not to disturb Mrs McIntyre until the water was hot.

Unfortunately, that lady was already awake.

'Lord 'a mercy!' cried Mrs McIntyre. 'Have I overslept? Whatever is the time that you disturb me so?'

'It is still quite early,' Elizabeth explained, 'but there is a great deal to be done, helping to prepare for tonight's festivities. I do hope you will not mind my preparing your bath a little early?'

'Bath . . . what should I want with a bath? I am quite clean, and will wait until I return to my own home before I take another bath!' The elderly woman sat up in the bed, her woollen shawl clasped tightly across her chest. Straggling wisps of grey hair escaped from her lace bed-cap and for the first time Elizabeth understood why it was that Mrs McIntyre always seemed to stare right through her when she addressed her directly. On the night stand, beside the bed, resting upon a crumpled handkerchief, lay a single glass eye.

Noticing Elizabeth's startled expression, Gordon's mother immediately reached out and with a deft movement fixed the eye into its hollow socket. Embarrassed only because she had uncovered the poor woman's secret, Elizabeth turned her back to make an unnecessary rearrangement of the bath, and to allow her guest to regain some composure.

As she straightened her back, Elizabeth explained, 'It has always been the custom in my own family to take a bath on the eve of the New Year . . . a form of ritual cleansing, I suppose. I do apologise for presuming to expect you to follow the same habit. Now that I have brought the bath in, perhaps I may leave it here so that I may take one myself later on?'

'Do as you please, girl,' was the harsh retort. 'You are the mistress of the house.'

Elizabeth smiled to herself as she quietly closed the door behind her. The poor woman was so embarrassed by her defective eye; it was a pity Gordon had not mentioned it. In future she resolved to knock and give her guest time to arrange herself properly before bursting in upon her.

Throughout the day, Elizabeth joined in with the general toing and froing of the islanders between the Drill Hall and their own cottages.

By midday, the decorations were complete and the food began to be delivered, to be arranged at convenient places around the sides of the Hall.

At three o'clock the *Lord of Lorn* docked at the pier on Seileach, and Elizabeth waited impatiently to greet her lover as he was rowed across from the steamer.

He came ashore, laden with parcels. As she approached, he looked as if he longed to throw them down and clasp her in his arms. She, however, was conscious of many surreptitious glances, particularly from some of her pupils who were gathered on the shore to welcome their own visitors for the festivities. She held out her hand in formal greeting.

'Good afternoon, Mr McIntyre,' she said decorously.

Gordon laughed aloud. 'I do not believe there would be too many here who would be surprised if I were to kiss you here and now,' he murmured in her ear, eyes sparkling with suppressed laughter.

Elizabeth glanced in the direction of the children and smiled. 'It has been very difficult for me to keep our secret,' she agreed. 'Children are often more observant than their parents!'

Gordon greeted the boys and girls as they passed, and the young lovers walked on together to the schoolteacher's house.

'How has my mama been behaving herself?' Gordon enquired as they neared the door.

'She is still rather frosty, I am afraid,' replied Elisabeth. 'I wish that you had told me about her eye. It has not helped that I discovered her disability by chance!'

Gordon roared with laughter. 'Oh dear,' he chortled, 'I am sorry not to have warned you. Mama is particularly sensitive in that quarter. She cannot abide imperfection in anything or anyone. That she should herself be so afflicted is more than she can bear to admit!'

'It is very unfortunate for her.' Elizabeth felt that Gordon was unjustifiably flippant about his mother's misfortune. 'How did she come to lose her eye?'

'It happened when she was a child. She was playing with my grandfather's shotgun, threatening one of her brothers, I believe, when the gun went off accidentally. It is a wonder she was not killed.'

Elizabeth had paled at his explanation. He put his arm around her to reassure her, and added, 'It was all a long time ago, and best forgotten. Come, let us go and face the foe.'

Laughing, he pushed open the door and walked in.

'Why, Mama, how well you look,' he exclaimed. 'The Eisdalsa air must be good for you.'

'How you can contemplate living in such a place, I will never understand,' was her reply, but she held up her cheek to be kissed nevertheless.

'How have my two favourite girls been getting along then?' Gordon's rather arch question was asked with a twinkle of the eye.

'Well enough,' conceded his mother. 'Aye, well enough.' She looked towards Elizabeth, but could read nothing in the girl's face that would betray any alternative response to Gordon's question. The older woman again felt that her son was taking up sides against her. 'Needs must when the Devil pleases,' she added with a sigh.

Having distributed his largess, perfume and a corsage of white orchids for Elizabeth, a colourful silk scarf for his mother, Gordon hoisted his carpet-bag over his shoulder, saying, 'I will go and find William. It will take a deal of scrubbing and titivating to make us both fit to escort such lovely ladies to the ball this evening!'

He was gone, the whole building shuddering with the force of his departure.

'When will that boy learn to close a door quietly?' Mrs McIntyre enquired of nobody in particular. She had been asking the same rhetorical question for the past thirty years, to little effect.

David felt the strong, steady beat of Annabel's pulse. Warming his stethoscope between his fingers, he placed it on her snowy bosom, and listened to the satisfyingly rhythmic heartbeat.

'You have made a remarkably quick recovery, Miss Douglas. Your nurse is to be heartily congratulated.' He paused to beam a smile of approval in the direction of Myra McCulloch.

The minister's wife, flustered by such unaccustomed praise, seemed tongue-tied. It was Annabel who put the question which had been exercising both ladies for days past.

'Am I well enough to attend the celebrations this evening?' she enquired. 'My aunt would be so disappointed to miss the ball, but she quite refuses to go without me. The children, too, have been looking forward to the festivities, and Myra will not hear of their going without us.'

David looked doubtful for a few minutes, but seeing the eager expressions on both faces, felt it would be churlish to refuse them.

'You are certainly clear of the disease,' he agreed, 'but I fear the possibility of a relapse if you tire yourself. How will it be if you attend the function, but promise not to tire your strength? It will be frustrating, I know, for such a lively young lady to resist the temptation to accept the many invitations which you will undoubtedly receive. Will you be able to resist the pleas of your suitors?' His eyes twinkled and she knew that he was joking with her.

'I promise, doctor, that I shall not dance without your express permission.'

'Then you shall go to the ball!'

With something of a flourish, David bowed himself out of the room, and laughed to hear the squeals of delight as the children were made aware that their prayers had been answered.

On the doorstep, he encountered the minister returning from his duties.

'Your household is in turmoil, sir,' he said to the bewildered cleric. 'Whether you wish it or not, your family is bound for the Island this evening. I do hope you will not hold it against me!'

'Is Annabel so much recovered?' McCulloch looked doubtful.

'She will do very well, provided she obeys my orders,' David assured him. 'More importantly, your wife deserves a little diversion. Her ministrations have left her tired and wan. Take her to the dance, man, let her enjoy herself for a while. There is a long winter ahead of us!'

As he picked up his medical bag and turned to go, he added, 'My mother and I will be passing the manse at about seven-thirty. If your ladies are ready, I will give them a ride to the pier. There is no need to tire our patient unduly.'

3

William and Gordon arrived at the schoolhouse in good time on the evening of the ball.

William, preceding his friend into the cosy living room, addressed himself immediately to Mrs McIntyre.

'You will do me a great honour, madam, if you will allow me to escort you to the ball this evening.' He bowed low and presented an astonished Mrs McIntyre with a corsage of hothouse flowers.

That formidable lady's cheeks flushed with pleasure, while she actually managed a most uncharacteristic smile.

'Why, Mr Whylie, thank you. I shall be pleased to accept your kind invitation.'

Elizabeth dared not look at Gordon. She was having the greatest difficulty restraining the giggle which threatened to escape her. Could this really be the woman who had complained endlessly about the need to dress up for a party in a village hall?

'Ball, indeed!' she had uttered at one point. 'These peasants cannot know the meaning of the word!'

'Unfortunately,' William now turned his attention to Elizabeth, 'I am obliged to arrive early at the Hall. Will you excuse us if we leave immediately? There is no reason for you and Gordon to accompany us, if you are not quite ready.'

The two men exchanged a conspiratorial glance and, without waiting for a response from Elizabeth, William offered his arm to Gordon's mother and politely guided her out of the door.

Gordon watched them depart before turning to Elizabeth. He thought she looked breathtaking. Whoever had said that a person with red hair should not wear red had certainly not seen this particular vision of loveliness. Her gown of scarlet silk, shot with orange, glimmered a kaleidoscope of hues in the firelight. Lit from behind, by her mother's old oil lamp, Elizabeth's hair formed a shining halo around her delicate features. Her green eyes sparkled with happiness.

Temporarily tongue-tied, Gordon withdrew his hand from behind his back and held out a pretty posy of everlasting flowers, trimmed with lace and ribbons.

'Oh, how beautiful!' Elizabeth exclaimed in delight.

Then, eagerly, he took from his waistcoat pocket a small box, and fumbled in his anxiety to get it open.

'Why, whatever have you there?' Elizabeth demanded. Could she be teasing him?

'How can you pretend that you do not know?' challenged Gordon, his face clouding with frustration as he wrestled with the unyielding fastening.

'It is clearly an engagement ring.'

Ignoring all those hours of planning for their future home, she assumed an air of surprise. 'And for whom is this ring intended?'

'Why, you, of course, you ninny,' he exploded. The lid of the box flew open.

'Why, Mr McIntyre, you have made no formal proposal of marriage as I recall,' she chided. 'Although I am not unwilling to listen to such a proposition, should you make one!' she added hastily.

In an instant he was down on one knee, and grasping both her smooth white hands in his own brown and roughened ones.

'Elizabeth, you are the dearest person in the world to me. Unless I have you by my side always, my life will be a miserable, meaningless journey. I beg you to become my wife.'

'Oh, my darling,' she murmured, tears glistening in her eyes, all archness gone. 'Of course I will marry you. Could you ever doubt it?'

For a moment they clung together, then taking her left hand, Gordon slipped the diamond ring on her finger.

Elizabeth could not take her eyes off the rose-cut solitaire. She turned her hand this way and that as the stone flashed rainbow colours in the light from the lamp. Then she turned up her face to him and kissed him full on the lips. He returned her kisses and for a little while neither spoke.

It was Elizabeth who finally broke the spell.

'We must be going,' she said. 'William will wonder what has been keeping us.'

'I do not think so,' Gordon assured her. 'He is all prepared to announce our betrothal at the party. In fact, he has been rehearsing that portion of his speech all afternoon!'

'What a good thing I decided to accept you,' she laughed. 'He might have had to change it at the last minute!'

Arm-in-arm, they set off for the Hall, where the music and sounds of merriment were sure signs that the party was well under way.

David had prepared for the ball that evening with extreme care.

The battle to prevent the spread of cholera had caused him to be more than usually cautious these last weeks. Indeed, intent upon confining the disease to the manse, he had purposely refrained from making contact with either of his friends on the Island. Considering Elizabeth's aversion to the smell of disinfectant, perhaps it was just as well that he had avoided her so assiduously!

David rubbed a second application of pomade into his scalp, and combed his hair back into a sleek, shining skullcap. He was sure that the scent of carbolic still lingered, but knew of no other way to disguise it.

It was a year since he had last approached Elizabeth on the subject of marriage. During that time, they had seen a great deal of each other, always in company with others of course. He felt that she had had time enough to exploit her talents in the schoolroom.

She had certainly convinced Mr Ford that she was a force to be reckoned with, he mused. She had only to lift her little finger in that direction, and she was receiving all manner of benefits for her beloved school. There were times when he had wondered if Mr Ford's interest went further than a concern for Elizabeth's work. These disturbing ideas had been quickly dispelled when he considered the age of the Inspector, coupled with his pedantic manner. The latter characteristic certainly tried David's patience and, he assumed, must weary the ebullient Elizabeth to distraction.

No, whatever was in her mind, with regard to her future, David was convinced that Mr Ford had no place in her plans.

There would be no more schoolteaching once they were married, he assured himself. Elizabeth would soon have babies of her own to care for and worry over.

She would still be expected to take an interest in the village children, of course, and there would be all the Parish functions normally expected of the doctor's wife to keep her sufficiently happy and occupied.

Taking a final appraisal of his appearance in the heavily framed mirror, he was well pleased with the full effect of his laborious preparations. One last tug at the carefully knotted cravat, a brush with the back of his hand at an invisible thread upon his sleeve, and he was satisfied.

From a drawer situated beneath the mirror stand, the doctor withdrew a small leather box. He examined its contents intently for a few seconds before tucking it into his waistcoat pocket. He turned down the lamp and slammed the door behind him.

As he took the stairs two at a time, he called out to Morag.

'Hurry up, Mama. I promised to give Myra McCulloch and Miss Douglas a lift to the ferry. They will be waiting for us!'

Morag emerged from her own bedroom and descended the staircase, more sedately than her son but equally anxious for the evening's festivities to begin.

David had confided in his mother his intention to propose to Elizabeth for a second time. Surely the silly girl would not turn him down again, Morag thought to herself as she followed him out into the night air.

Only the two McCulloch ladies remained at the manse when they arrived. The minister and the children had already started walking towards the ferry.

Annabel was waiting in the hall, and quickly stepped forward to open the front door when she heard the doctor's carriage pulling up. When David entered, she stood back. The light fell advantageously upon her, and he perceived the intended effect. Her rich chestnut hair had been washed and curled, and was pinned back to allow the ringlets to cascade down her back, reaching nearly to her waist. Her pallid skin had been enlivened with a little carefully applied rouge. She looked very different from the sick and fevered patient he had first set eyes on only a few weeks ago.

Her dress was of cream silk, in an elegant style currently the height of Glasgow fashion. The bodice was cut low, and lavishly trimmed with the finest coffee-coloured lace which tumbled over her white bosom and emphasised the deep brown of her eyes. The same lace edged the frills around the skirt, its colour repeated in the brown ribbon sash which hung down behind, almost to the floor. Having formerly seen her only when she was drained by illness, David was at first startled at the transformation. He admired her charms, even if they were a little over-elaborate for his taste, and congratulated himself on having been instrumental in procuring such a successful recovery.

Seeing Annabel in all her finery led his mind back to Elizabeth, remembering how lovely she had looked last year in her green evening gown.

With Annabel and Myra safely aboard, he whipped up the mare and the tidy little chaise rattled off over the stony road in pursuit of the rest of the minister's family.

They passed the group of walkers as they were approaching the ferry landing. Laughing and shouting, the children ran alongside the carriage until it reached the water's edge.

The Hall was so crowded when the doctor's party arrived that they had difficulty in finding a place where the ladies could sit down. Mary and her brother quickly disappeared in search of their comrades, and David and the minister were left to scramble at the bar for fruit punch for the ladies, and something just a little stronger for themselves.

There was a strong temperance influence in the Village and on the Island, and at most times of the year one would be hard pressed to discover any alcoholic beverage other than inside certain well-recognised houses.

At the festive season, however, the bottles of whisky normally kept for medicinal purposes came to the fore. Men, and ladies too, normally noted for their sobriety, were not averse to taking a dram or two at the New Year.

Most households brewed their own ale from whatever grain was available. On social occasions, each participant would contribute his or her special potion. Long-standing rivalries existed regarding the quality of the various products, and those in the know chose to sample only the best!

Whisky, too, produced its share of competitiveness. The village boasted its own official distillery, but there were, in addition, a number of illicit stills, usually in the outlying crofts, where a barn or byre provided suitable camouflage from the eagle eyes of the Revenue Men.

David had need of a little Dutch courage this evening if he was to fulfil his purpose. Before carrying away the glasses of punch to the ladies, he swallowed a good measure of whisky, and replaced his glass on the table. Instantly it was refilled.

With some difficulty, the doctor forced his way through the crush of bodies, carrying high above his shoulder a tray of brimming glasses. He arrived eventually, with the glasses more or less intact, at the table chosen by Morag and the McCulloch ladies.

Surrounding quarriers and their partners applauded his prowess with a tray, one even going so far as to place a white napkin over David's uplifted arm to lend authenticity to the act.

The fiddlers and their accompanying accordionist struck up a waltz.

David tried to catch sight of Elizabeth in the throng. He was looking for the emerald green dress which he remembered. He was startled therefore to see a vision of scarlet and auburn whirling towards him on the arm of Gordon McIntyre. So surprised was he to find the steamship officer at the party that he failed to notice the radiant look on Elizabeth's face as they danced past him.

William, in more sedate fashion, waltzed by with an older lady in his arms, one whom David did not recognise.

So many strangers, he thought to himself, as he noticed a number of new faces in the group surrounding Jamie McGillivray. I must ask William to give me the names of the men brought in to dig the new quarries. They should be signed up for medical insurance.

The music came to an end. David moved forward in the hope of demanding the next dance of Elizabeth. Across the room, he saw her respond to an invitation from young Michael Brown, on leave from his medical studies in Glasgow.

What a fine strapping fellow he had grown into, David reflected. At sixteen, he was as tall as his father, and fast developing the broad shoulders which would have stood him in good stead had he chosen to follow Brown into the quarries. He would make a fine surgeon, David told himself with satisfaction. After all, was it not on his own recommendation that the boy had been given a bursary by His Lordship?

David was aware that Annabel was regarding him with an anxious, almost pleading gaze. Oh, well, he thought, if Elizabeth was otherwise engaged, perhaps he should have a gentle turn around the floor with the visitor from Glasgow.

'Miss Douglas, will you do me the honour?' he enquired.

Annabel smiled with pleasure, her wide mouth slightly open to display a set of gleaming white teeth. As though to ensure that David did not change his mind before the music finished, she stood up and came towards him, her arms wide and inviting.

He was surprised at how well they danced together. The nurse had a well-proportioned figure, if a trifle heavier than David would have chosen. She was light on her feet, as larger people often are. Her rather plain features were alight with animation . . . so many weeks had passed without entertainment of any kind, she was determined to enjoy every minute of these festivities.

The music stopped again and it was clear that the band was going to take a rest. David and Annabel had come to a standstill beside the bar.

He ordered drinks for them both. Annabel was looking a trifle flushed and he did not wish his erstwhile patient to become faint, and have to be carried out! He watched her sipping at her fruit cup while he downed yet another generous dram of whisky.

He was beginning to enjoy the evening, finding himself engaging in flippant exchanges with those about him, and laughing rather more than was his habit.

He found Annabel a seat nearby. It was hopeless to try to force a way to where his mother and the other ladies were seated. Looking around in search of Elizabeth, he spotted her near the platform, deep in conversation with McIntyre and Whylie . . . cooking up some nonsense or other, no doubt!

William chose this moment to make his Chairman's speech.

'Ladies and gentlemen . . . friends . . . last year, on this very occasion, I told you something of my own hopes for improvement in the future.

'Through the good offices of our colleague Malcolm Logie, who is even now on his way home from New Zealand,' William smiled down at Katherine Logie, standing amongst a group of friends below the platform, 'we are assured of a ready market for all the slate we can produce for the next twelve months!' There was a general murmur of approval.

He continued, 'The New Zealand contract has not only brought the improved sales that we hoped for, it has also brought into our midst a number of new faces whose presence amongst us we acknowledge with satisfaction and gratitude. Welcome to them and their families.'

There were shouts of appreciation, and not a little ribaldry. William raised his hand to quell the noise.

'I have one final and most agreeable task to perform before the clock strikes. I am asked to announce tonight the betrothal of our much admired schoolmistress, Miss Elizabeth Duncan, to First Officer Gordon McIntyre of the *Lord of Lorn*. I am sure that you will all join with me in wishing them happiness.'

There was a sudden hush in which the only sound was the shattering of the glass which had slipped through David's paralysed fingers. Then the whole Hall erupted in a wave of cheering, clapping, and shouted congratulations. Elizabeth and Gordon stood encircled by glowing, smiling faces. Hands were shaken, backs were slapped, kisses liberally applied to the cheeks of the blushing schoolmistress.

Elizabeth was ecstatic, her happiness plain for all to see.

'Oh, how radiant she looks!' gasped Annabel, enviously, admiring at the same time the smartly uniformed figure of Elizabeth's fiance. 'Is Miss Duncan a friend of yours by any chance?'

'I thought so,' David muttered. 'Until tonight.'

He caught sight of his mother's ashen face on the far side of the room. Her eyes brimmed with the pity that she felt for her poor boy. He had set out so happily tonight, assured of claiming Elizabeth for himself.

'Oh God,' David seemed unaware that he was speaking aloud, 'I must get out of here.' He grabbed another glass, brimful of whisky, and threw it back. Then, catching Annabel by the hand, he all but dragged her from the Hall.

At the door she drew back, studying him intently for a moment. Realising that this was no time for explanations, but understanding his need for her companionship, she allowed him to steer her out into the night.

There was a sharp wind blowing from the north-east. The odd icy flurry of rain set them walking a little faster.

Annabel was not sure where they were going, or why, but clung to David's arm with one hand while they the other she pulled her flimsy stole tight about her head.

They strode blindly into the wind for some minutes until David, realising that his partner was shivering and stumbling miserably along beside him, pulled her closer to protect her from the gale.

'I should not have brought you out here,' he shouted above the wind. 'You will catch a chill.'

A dark building loomed in front of them. David fumbled along the rough stone wall, searching for the door. Finding it at last, he thrust it open and pulled Annabel inside.

For a short while they stood, gasping for breath. Then, his eyes becoming accustomed to the darkness, he searched around for some form of lighting. His hand contacted the cover of an old storm lantern. In moments he had the wick alight, and the shield in position.

Annabel looked around her, wondering about this place to which he had brought her. An array of fishing nets hung from the rafters. More nets were piled neatly in one corner. Fishing creels were stacked against one wall, together with an assortment of anchors, oars, marlin-spikes, rowlocks – anything and everything associated with boats and fishing. The air held the salt tang of the sea, mingled with a mustiness of damp netting and the all-pervading odour of long departed fish.

David led her over to the heap of folded netting and invited her to sit down.

'Forgive me for that hasty departure, Miss Douglas. What must you think of me?' He looked at his companion with some concern.

'I cannot imagine what I was thinking of, to drag you out into the cold night air . . . and without a cloak too.' He took hold of her fingers, which were quite blue, and began to rub and blow on them, to restore her circulation. He took off his own coat and draped it about her shoulders, and then sat down beside her on an up-ended barrel.

Even with the additional covering, she still shivered, so he placed his arm around her shoulders and held her, willing his own excessive heat to pass to her.

Soon Annabel had sufficiently recovered to sit up straight, and begin to pat at her dishevelled hair.

'Are you going to tell me what that was all about?' she asked him. It was clear that the announcement of Elizabeth's betrothal had been the source of his discomfiture . . . but why, she wondered, was his reaction so violent?

'Mr McIntyre and Miss Duncan were good friends of mine.' David knew it sounded a lame explanation even as he gave it. 'I suppose that I was offended that they did not confide their intentions to me, before making so public a declaration.'

Ignoring the past tense which he had used, involuntarily perhaps, Annabel probed further.

'Do you not approve of their engagement . . . is it that you consider them unsuitable for each other?' she enquired.

David recalled his dreams of life with Elizabeth, always at his side, within his house, tending his garden, playing with his children. Tigh na Broch had seemed to ring with her laughter and pulsate with her presence. It had been but a delusion. How blind he had been. While he had dreamed and made his plans in secret, McIntyre had stolen her from under his nose!

What of William, his friend? He must have known of her treachery, yet had said nothing; given no indication of what was happening.

Annabel watched dark shadows flitting across his face as he replied, 'I am sure that if Elizabeth finds Mr McIntyre to her liking, then they are admirably suited to each other.' His attempt at indifference gave only an impression of petulance. Annabel was reminded of her young cousin, who behaved in just this way when he lost to her in a game of chess.

'Is Miss Duncan a good schoolmistress?' she queried, wanting to keep his attention. She felt that he needed to talk about what was bothering him. She could only guess at the reason for his strange behaviour. She had become increasingly warm towards him in the past weeks, and it alarmed her to see him so distraught.

He started at her question, remembering those cosy discussions around his mother's table, recalling his fierce defence of her interests at meetings of the School Board. How could she have betrayed him thus?

'I believe so,' he answered darkly.

It was Annabel now who took hold of David's hand, stroking it gently as she continued in a calm, soothing tone.

'Whatever your friends have decided, I am sure that they know what they are doing. If you care about them both, you should be very happy for them.'

David bowed his head, not wanting her to see how utterly miserable he felt.

'For everyone on this earth there is a partner,' she told him consolingly. 'Perhaps you have not found yours yet.'

David looked at her and was startled by the intensity of her gaze. A smile played about her lips, which were slightly apart, displaying a row of perfect teeth. As he watched her, the pink tip of her tongue flicked for an instant between the lips invitingly.

He pulled her to him and kissed her hard upon the mouth. So tight was his grasp that she had to push him away at last, gasping for breath. He smelt of whisky and his face was hot beneath her hands as she gently traced the contours of his brows, his cheek-bones, his mouth.

Again his mouth was hard on hers. He forced her back amongst the soft, yielding nets until they lay clasped in one another's arms.

David began to grope for the fastening of her bodice. Fearing for the delicate fabric, she released herself from his grasp, slipped off the bed of ropes, and quickly removed both gown and frothy petticoats.

Before he realised what was happening, David found the girl naked beside him and entwining her limbs about his.

Slowly she removed his cravat. Delicate, nimble fingers released the diamond studs which fastened the stiffened linen across his chest.

She ran her fingers lightly at first, and then more urgently, over his bared breast, grasping painfully at the bright red bush of hair.

There was more of the delicate fingering, and more buttons were released.

Despite the whisky, David found himself aroused and ready to meet her advances. In a moment they were together, tearing, scrabbling, clinging, moving as one in violent lustful motion.

All passion spent, the two white bodies lay in each other's arms, the girl panting faintly, her recent illness having weakened her.

David, now sober and full of remorse, was confused in his emotions. As his body had responded to the lure of the flesh, his mind had been elsewhere. It was Elizabeth's face he had seen, not Annabel's. As he grasped and pounded wildly in his passion, it was against Elizabeth that he was venting his anger. He had used Annabel to assuage his despair for the love that he had lost. Now he felt ashamed and full of regret.

Whether or not she was aware of the strange nature of their encounter, he was never to know.

Recovering somewhat, she began to gather her clothing, and stepping modestly into the shadows, pulled on her dress.

With his back to her, David too began to put himself to rights.

Perhaps it was the incongruous surroundings, or maybe the total unsuitability of their attire, requiring as it did that each should assist the other with the final touches, which made Annabel's naturally buoyant spirits come to the fore.

Dropping David's impossibly screwed-up necktie back on to the nets, she sat down, giggling like a schoolgirl.

David looked startled, then catching her mood, he too began to laugh.

Annabel got to her feet, straightened his hair, and tried again, more successfully this time, with the cravat. She stood back so that he could examine her for any defects in her attire. Satisfied that they would pass muster, as merely having taken a stroll in the breezy night air, they made their way back to the Hall.

Before they went in, David took Annabel gently in his arms one last time, and kissed her on the forehead.

'Thank you,' he said.

She made no reply. Smiling knowingly up at him, she took his hand and led him inside.

The wild music for dancing had given place to the usual solo singing which preceded the departure of the families and less energetic guests.

As the party began to break up, and before the serious drinkers became too heavily engaged in the real business of their night, David made his way to where Elizabeth and Gordon stood, receiving the congratulations of the departing guests.

As he approached, he could feel his composure deserting him.

McCulloch was chattering away to Gordon about where and when the wedding would be held.

Touting for business! thought David uncharitably.

Mrs McCulloch was twittering in her usual foolish fashion about dresses and bridesmaids to the sour-faced lady who had been William's partner.

Seeing David hovering in the background, Elizabeth dragged him forward.

'Why, David, where have you been all evening? We were so sorry not to have been able to share with you our little secret, but you have been so elusive of late!' She turned to the stiff lady in black at her side.

'Mrs McIntyre, you must meet our local physician, Dr Beaton. David, this is Gordon's mama.'

David took the fish-like hand in his and greeted the woman politely. Turning to Gordon, he said, 'My congratulations, McIntyre . . . it is amazing the power that a uniform holds over the ladies!'

It was meant to be a joke, but David was unable to disguise his sarcasm and even William looked startled at the sharpness of the doctor's tone.

The good-natured sailor, ignoring, or in his elation unaware of, the slight, shook David warmly by the hand and expressed the hope that he would join William in supporting him at the wedding.

He replied, unenthusiastically, that he would be pleased to assist in any way he could.

Gathering his party together, like an anxious sheepdog, the minister approached David.

'Are we ready for the ferry, doctor?'

'It seems we are all here,' he agreed.

In a perfectly natural gesture of concern for his patient, he offered his arm to Annabel Douglas, and led the way out of the Hall.

4

T he early spring days passed quickly for Elizabeth. The new house was fast nearing completion, and she and Annie pored endlessly over catalogues of furniture, draperies, crockery, and other household equipment.

Like most young women of her day, Elizabeth had chosen a design for her wedding dress which, once it had fulfilled its primary purpose, would serve her as a suitable gown for special occasions.

Gordon had taken her to Glasgow one cold wintry day in late January to choose the materials for her trousseau. In addition they had ordered many of the household items which she had already decided upon, with Annie's advice.

Leaving Elizabeth at the house of an old schoolfriend, Gordon continued his journey to Edinburgh, to make one of his increasingly infrequent calls upon his mother.

It was five years or more since Elizabeth had set eyes upon Helena McDuff. In their last year at school, Elizabeth's proposed visit to the McDuff family home on the Island of Mull had been forestalled by the death of the Reverend Duncan. While Elizabeth had continued at the school on the Solway Firth, first as a pupil, and then as a registered teacher, Helena had gone home to help her mother in raising numerous additional small McDuffs. Then, one summer, she had met a young businessman called Mackintosh, on Mull for a fishing holiday. Their easy friendship turned quickly to a true courtship and by the spring of 1876 the couple were married, and living in a small semi-detached villa in Bearsden, on the outskirts of Glasgow.

The girls had kept in contact by letter during the intervening years, but had met only once, on the occasion of Helena's wedding. When she had heard of Elizabeth's forthcoming marriage, Helena had insisted that her friend spend a few days in the Mackintosh household, to enable her to do her shopping.

Helena was almost as excited as Elizabeth about the approaching event and, like a mother hen, hurried her friend round from shop to shop, in a frenzy of viewing, trying on, measuring, choosing, and above all, spending.

Elizabeth had saved what she considered to be an adequate sum of money for this expedition. In addition, Gordon had pressed upon her twenty pounds, for the purchase of some of the smaller household items they required. It was soon gone.

Laden with packages, the two young women fought their way into a rather grand coffee shop, which Helena declared was the place where she treated herself when she was feeling particularly festive.

The building was indeed ornate, although rather vulgar for Elizabeth's taste. Crystal chandeliers were suspended from a ceiling which was encrusted with elaborate plaster mouldings. The walls were hung with huge mirrors in heavy gilt frames. Thick crimson velvet curtains draped every window, alcove and archway, and the floor covering was a crimson carpet so thick that Elizabeth could feel herself sinking into its cushion-like pile at every step.

Waitresses in frilled and starched snow-white aprons bustled to and fro with huge, heavily laden trays. A tall, excruciatingly thin waiter in morning dress moved sedately from table to table with a large, three-tiered trolley, piled high with confections of all kinds. Chocolate, mocha, glazed or crystallised fruits of every description, mounted upon sponge or shortcrust bases, and everywhere thick, yellow cream.

Elizabeth shuddered when she contemplated the spread, thinking of the wedding gown for which she had been measured only that morning.

'I know this is a mistake,' she confessed to Helena, as she chose a fruit tart, lavishly decorated with thick creamy whirls. 'It is just as well that I am to return to the quiet life of Eisdalsa tomorrow.'

'The time has gone by so fast,' complained Helena. 'Now that we have managed one meeting, we must certainly make sure that we do not allow another two years to pass before we see each other again.'

'You must come to visit Gordon and myself on Eisdalsa, once we are settled in our new home,' Elizabeth suggested.

'Henry and I will spend some weeks on Mull during July and August. He still loves to fish, and I like to spend time with my parents. Now that most of the family are gone away, Mama does miss us all so!'

Elizabeth, following her train of thought, replied, 'When Gordon has a few days' leave, he likes nothing better than to go sailing.' She realised how odd this must sound when he was constantly at sea anyway. 'He borrows a yacht owned by a friend on the Island,' she added hastily.

She dabbed delicately at a stray blob of cream which had escaped to the corner of her mouth. 'Maybe we can arrange a visit to Mull . . . your house is near Bunessan, is it not?'

'Why, yes, of course,' Helena reflected eagerly. 'It stands on a promontory, facing out towards the mainland. One can see Eisdalsa on a clear day. It would be a short distance only by sea. Oh, what a splendid notion!'

On the last evening before their departure for Eisdalsa, Elizabeth and Gordon had been invited to accompany the young Mackintoshes to the theatre. They were to dine at an exclusive restaurant and occupy a box at the Playhouse.

As the two young women prepared themselves for the evening's entertainment, Helena startled Elizabeth by asking her, 'Are you troubled at all by the prospect of being married?'

Elizabeth, who could think of no reason for anything to cloud her vision of the future, looked at her friend's reflection in the mirror and was surprised to see that Helena blushed with embarrassment.

'The wedding night may come . . . as a shock.' She had put down the brush with which she had been dressing Elizabeth's hair and sat beside her friend on the long dressing stool, finding it easier to talk into the mirror.

'Without your mother to advise you, I wondered . . . are you prepared?'

Elizabeth had listened to the conversations between Annie and the Marchioness, only half understanding some of the references they made. She had only a vague notion of what was described as 'a wife's duty' to her husband.

'I went to my bridal bed,' Helena was saying, 'believing that men are animals whose carnal appetites must be assuaged by a dutiful partner. My mother instilled in me the belief that the relationship between married people is intended as a means of procreation only, and that it is sinful to gain any enjoyment from the physical union.' Relaxing now that she had set herself upon this course, and determined to advise and encourage her friend, Helena smiled triumphantly as she concluded, 'I can assure you, dearest Elizabeth, that far from being a torment to be endured, the sexual act is a most enjoyable experience, sinful or not!'

Both girls collapsed in a paroxysm of noisy laughter, sufficient to bring Henry Mackintosh knocking on their door, demanding why they were not yet ready to leave.

At last the visit came to an end. In the early dawn of a cold February day, the *Lord of Lorn* set sail from Glasgow, with First Officer Gordon McIntyre in charge of the bridge, and the future Mrs McIntyre comfortably ensconced in the Captain's cabin. The Skipper, as Gordon always described him, was taking a short leave himself while Gordon took over the run around the Mull of Kintyre and northwards to Fort William.

Normally, the steamer plied daily between the Fort and Crinan, disembarking her passengers for the short journey along the canal to Ardrishaig. On this trip however, the *Lord of Lorn* having been brought right into Port Glasgow for repairs, it was necessary for her to undergo the somewhat stormy passage beyond Ailsa Craig and out into the Irish Sea.

Elizabeth had experienced some fairly heavy seas, even on the normal route to Crinan. Never had she been so overcome by the motion of the vessel, however, as she was today. She was thankful for the seclusion of the Captain's cabin for she was constantly seasick and shuddered to think of the condition of the main passenger lounge, if there were many people in the same state as herself.

While the steamer navigated the worst of the seas, Gordon was obliged to remain on the bridge. He sent the steward down to Elizabeth from time to time with offers of refreshment, all of which were refused.

At last the ship slipped into the narrow channel between Jura and the mainland, and the heavy swell reduced sufficiently for Gordon to go below to see his fiancee.

Elizabeth, pale and listless, was lying upon the narrow bunk. The scene reminded Gordon of their first encounter; the sight of her red-gold hair and freckled brow bringing those other moments flooding back.

He recalled how the three of them, David, William and himself, had competed for her attention and vied with each other to bring her solace. It never ceased to amaze him that it was he whom she had chosen. She could have had any one of them!

He thought he understood why she would not have accepted Whylie, even if he had summoned the courage to ask her. William was a good man; a man of substance, position and integrity; but he lacked that sparkle, that touch of excitement which was required as a foil for Elizabeth's ready wit, and sense of adventure. He felt that William was a man to be relied upon to be a good friend in adversity. There were no certainties in a sailor's life. It was a comfort to know that Elizabeth would always have one true friend upon whom she could depend.

David was a different kettle of fish altogether. There had been times, at the very beginning, when Gordon had felt sure that it would be Beaton who would win the fair lady. He was a good-looking chap with that particular charisma so often exuded by doctors, guaranteed to win all female hearts. Gordon had often wondered if David had declared his feelings for Elizabeth. It was plain to see that she held a special place in his affections.

On the one occasion when Gordon had put this question to Elizabeth, she had murmured something coyly about a romantic moment when David had clearly had too much to drink, but had quickly dismissed the idea with a laugh.

'Can you really see me as the wife of the village doctor?' she had scoffed at the suggestion. 'Carrying soup to the needy, chairing the village sewing party and even, in the absence of the Marchioness or the minister's wife, opening a sale of work?'

Gordon could envisage her in all those capacities, and knew that she would perform the functions exceedingly well. No, there was more to it than the kind of life which she would be expected to lead.

The note of the engines changed suddenly; they must be approaching Blackmill Bay and he should be on deck. He rose to leave.

The sleeping Elizabeth stirred. Then, sensing his presence, she opened her eyes and stretched out her hand to him.

'Oh, my dearest, what a bad time you have had,' he said. 'Do you feel any better for your sleep?'

'A little, I think,' she replied. 'What is happening, why are we slowing down?'

'Just approaching the southern tip of Luing,' he explained. 'We are unlikely to meet any more rough seas now. Would you like to come up on deck? The fresh air would do you more good than lying here in this stuffy cabin.'

She sat up and began to rearrange her hair and button her jacket.

'How glad I am that you do not command a transatlantic steamer,' she declared. 'I fear that I would not survive even one such voyage!'

'You would become accustomed to the motion, I am sure,' he replied, smiling. 'It was a very heavy swell this morning,' he went on. 'There was not a passenger aboard who did not succumb.'

His assurance made her feel less foolish. She smiled up at him, loving him for his careful consideration of her feelings.

'I will wash and tidy myself a little, and then I will come up and join you.'

It was Wednesday morning, the height of the February influenza period, and the waiting room was full. Old men with raucous coughs, which came up from their boots and continued, long and loud, for minutes at a time, competed with the wailing of snotty-nosed children, whose steaming bodies owed more to their red-flannel underwear than the influenza germs.

David listened to the rhythmic beat of his third worn-out quarryman's heart of the morning, heard the dull sounds of a fluid-filled lung, and wondered why any human being should have to live under the conditions experienced by so many of his patients.

'Well, Angus, you know as well as I do what ails you. A warmer, drier climate is what you need. If you go on working at all times in a foot of water, soaked to the skin more often than not, I cannot clear your lungs for you. It's an early grave that you will go to, if you do not stop working in the quarries.'

'Just give me the usual bottle, Master David, and let me get back to ma work,' the man insisted. 'Ye know as well as I do that I canna leave here. Where would we go?'

David thought of the dark, dirty, city streets and the closely packed tenement blocks of his student days, and had to agree with his patient. He nodded his head, submitting to the pure logic of the man's argument, and lifted down yet another bottle of the sweet brown mixture he had been dispensing all morning.

What would we do without ipecacuanha and camphor? he wondered as he made a neat parcel of the two mixtures, one to loosen the congestion and the other an expectorant. He wrote the instructions on the packets in a clear hand . . . hearing as he did so, his father's words.

'Never use an indecipherable hand when it comes to prescribing and labelling. You could cause more problems than you seek to avert!'

Angus Fraser shuffled out of the consulting room, clutching his bottles, a satisfied grin on his face.

The next patient was a Mrs McAlister, the general help at the manse. Before she began to describe her own symptoms, a tale of woe to which David had been subjected on many previous occasions, she handed him a note.

'It is from my mistress, doctor,' she explained. 'Miss Douglas is bad again, vomiting and headaches, the poor lass . . . just like before!'

David looked up in alarm. Could it possibly be that Annabel had a recurrence of the cholera? He read the letter, the contents of which were much as Mrs McAlister had suggested, although Mrs McCulloch made no mention of cholera. This led him to suspect that whatever was the cause of the girl's trouble, it was not the dread disease.

He folded the note and proceeded to listen carefully to the well-rehearsed list of symptoms expanded upon by his portly patient, whose only real problem was her own insatiable appetite.

The morning wore on until, putting his head round the waiting-room door, David found that the one remaining patient had melted away. His courage must have failed him at the last moment or, more probably, he had departed to try out one of the multitude of remedies offered by his fellow patients.

Morag had David's meal ready and waiting. This he ate in silence, his mind upon Annabel.

When he arrived at the manse at three o'clock he found Myra McCulloch anxiously awaiting him. He was immediately shown into the now familiar bedroom, with its sloping ceiling and small dormer windows.

Annabel, wearing a bed-gown, and with a multi-coloured quilt thrown over her shoulders, was seated before a small grate in which a fire of coals glowed cheerfully, brightening the gloomy afternoon.

She looked up as David entered and smiled wanly.

'I fear this is a great to-do about nothing, Dr Beaton,' she exclaimed, looking accusingly at her aunt. 'I was a little unwell this morning, but as you can see, the patient is now quite recovered.'

'Nevertheless,' he responded good-naturedly, 'perhaps I may be allowed to make my own diagnosis, nurse!'

Many times during her long illness they had addressed each other thus. David had come to appreciate Annabel's knowledge of medicine and to respect her as a professional colleague.

Inviting her to lie on the bed, he proceeded with his examination.

He took her pulse, which was racing. He listened to her heart, which beat strongly if a little erratically. He felt her breasts, palpated her abdomen, tested her reflexes, all the while quietly enquiring as to the nature of her symptoms. After a while, he discreetly turned his back whilst she covered herself.

'I think, Mrs McCulloch, that your patient and her physician would be much better for a cup of tea,' he suggested.

The minister's wife looked from doctor to patient, suddenly understood that her presence was no longer required, and made a somewhat flustered departure.

'Miss Annabel is well enough to take her refreshment in the parlour,' David called after her from the doorway. 'We will be down directly.'

He turned to Annabel, seated once more before the fire.

'You know, of course, that you are pregnant?' He fired the words at her, all pretence of professional etiquette now gone.

'I had hoped to be away from here before you could find out,' Annabel replied, in a matter-of-fact manner. 'Unfortunately, my aunt caught me unawares during a bout of morning sickness, and became alarmed that I was again falling ill of a fever.'

'What had you intended doing, if you expected to leave without my knowing?'

'There are ways of dealing with these things, as you must be only too well aware. I shall go to a woman whom my friends have told me about, when I return to Glasgow.'

'An abortion?' David was outraged. 'How dare you suggest such a thing! What kind of a man do you think I am?'

'I know you to be a good, kind, honourable person. One who does not deserve to have his life shattered by a momentary indiscretion at a time of great distress.' Annabel smiled up at the tall rigid figure.

David stared at her in disbelief. However he may have regarded her in the past, and whatever his reasons for bringing her to this sorry state, he could not but admire the woman's determination that no recriminations should be allowed to obscure her judgement.

She had risen from her chair and come to stand before him, her gaze steady.

'Please, David – I suppose I may call you David, under the circumstances – do not distress yourself. I was as much to blame as you. I am not a simple village girl, ignorant of the consequences of such an encounter. You needed me, I gave myself willingly, fully aware of what might happen.'

'You make it all sound so clinical.' he complained, knowing that what she said was right, and yet unable to accept her bald assessment of the situation.

'We must find a way of discussing this further,' he declared. 'Promise me that you will wait for a day or so, until I can find a reason for us to be alone? Long enough to talk it out properly.'

'Very well,' she agreed. 'My aunt will wonder what is keeping us. You go on down, while I dress.'

Before leaving her, he took both her hands in his and looked at her, long and hard.

It was as though he were seeing her for the first time.

He was filled with admiration for her confident air. He found her figure attractive, was taken anew by her luxuriant chestnut brown hair and clear, honest eyes. Surprised by the strength of his feelings for the woman at this moment, he wondered if perhaps he had been wrong all along. Could he perhaps love Annabel?

Without a word, he kissed her gently on the cheek, then held her at arm's length.

'Please do not worry,' he beseeched her, 'we will work it out.' At the door he paused. 'Please tell your aunt that I could not wait for tea,' he begged her. 'I will be in touch in a day or two . . . never fear.'

He was gone.

Annabel passed one hand gently across her belly, and smiled at the thought of his outrage at her suggestion of an abortion. She had judged him correctly. He would do the right thing by her, she knew. Anyway, what could be a more appropriate apprenticeship for the wife of a country doctor than a nurse's training? She would be a professional assistant, always on hand when needed.

Morag had been careful to make no reference to Elizabeth's betrothal. She knew that David would bring the matter up, in his own good time.

She found it hard to accept that her hopes for the future of her son and her dear friend had been dashed so abruptly. Unreasonably she blamed Annabel Douglas, and her illness, for what had occurred. All this must have happened during those weeks when David had insisted that Elizabeth should remain on the Island and not risk visiting Morag, in case of cross-infection.

Morag was only too conscious of the dangers of the schoolmistress contracting such an infectious disease as cholera . . . it would have spread to the children and hence throughout the village. Nevertheless, David's absence from Elizabeth's life had, she considered, left the girl vulnerable to the advances of First Officer McIntyre. He was so handsome in his smart uniform, any young woman would find it hard to resist his charms.

David returned from his visit to the manse and went straight to his study. Mechanically, he sorted through his records of the morning's surgery. There were a number of outstanding bills to be sent out. He tried to concentrate on the dates and figures but they became a blur before his eyes.

Throwing down his pen, he went to the window and gazed out at the stormy sea. White horses crested the waves and great billowing creamy breakers swept along the shore of the island.

He imagined Elizabeth, closing up the school for the day and making her way back to her little house. How he envied McIntyre those intimate glances, those tender, loving words.

Would he ever cease to feel that stab of injured pride whenever her name was mentioned? He had been so certain she felt as he did. Had he assumed too much to begin with? Had she found him arrogant in his approach?

What then of Annabel? He must be careful not to make the same mistake a second time.

At last he faced up to the problem he had been avoiding all afternoon. There really was no question. He must marry the girl.

Matters could have been worse, he supposed. After all, Annabel Douglas was a very intelligent woman. On matters of medicine, they had much in common. She was capable of making a useful contribution to the practice.

Annabel was handsome – not beautiful as Elizabeth was beautiful, but certainly attractive. There would be no difficulty with childbearing either. He remembered the petite figure of the poor dead Marchioness, and was thankful that Annabel would not have to suffer so.

Most of all, she was kind. It was her kindness which had led her to this pass. She deserved his protection . . . and affection. He could never feel for her as he did for Elizabeth, but he was determined to try to make her happy.

David gave up all further pretence of working. Taking from his desk drawer the small jewellery box which he had gloated over with such anticipation on New Year's Eve, he opened it and examined the ring. A twisted band of gold was the setting for five diamonds, the largest at the centre, the others diminishing in size to the outer edge.

He turned the ring so that the inscription on the inner surface could be seen. The initials, DAB and ED were separated by a tiny heart.

A clever engraver could change the E to an A with little difficulty, he thought to himself. I will ride into Oban in the morning and have it altered.

There was no point in prevaricating; the deed must be done, and the sooner the better. With determination, he snapped the box shut and pushed it securely into his inner pocket. Then he strode out into the kitchen in search of his mother and a cup of tea.

'Annabel Douglas will be leaving for Glasgow in a few days,' he told Morag. 'Will you not wish to invite Mrs McCulloch and her niece for a farewell tea-party?'

Morag was surprised. David did not usually take so much interest in her plans for entertaining.

'Of course I will invite them,' she agreed, 'but I understood that Miss Douglas was feeling poorly again.'

David always found it disconcerting that his mother seemed to know as much, if not more, about his patients' ailments than he did himself. He assumed that her long association with the practice, and her intimate knowledge of the villagers' lives, gave her a head start when it came to diagnosis. Also, she was connected to that invisible chain of information which keeps all small communities aware of events.

'Miss Douglas is well enough to return to Glasgow, although I doubt if she will take up her nursing again for a while,' he assured her.

'Then I shall send Sheilagh up to the manse immediately and invite them for Wednesday afternoon, if you think Miss Douglas will be leaving so soon.'

Morag never needed an excuse to entertain. Sheilagh was dispatched upon her errand and Morag shooed her son out of the kitchen so that she might prepare her baking.

David, having successfully negotiated this first step in his plan, now retired to his study to write a few letters.

Argyll Times   31 March 1878

The wedding took place this week, in Glasgow, of Miss Annabel Douglas, daughter of the late Mr Angus Douglas and Mrs Douglas of Bishopbriggs, and Dr David Beaton of Eisdalsa. The ceremony was conducted by the bride's uncle, the Rev. James McCulloch, Minister of the Parish of Seileach and Eisdalsa in Argyll. The couple will honeymoon in London before returning to live on Seileach Island where Dr Beaton has his medical practice.

Elizabeth put down the newspaper and stared out of her window.

She knew that David had been bitterly hurt by her failure to give him even a hint of her intention to marry Gordon before the betrothal was announced in public. Explanations involving her isolation during the cholera scare had fallen upon deaf ears. Since the Hogmanay Ball, David and she had exchanged only a few, impersonal words on his infrequent visits to the schoolhouse.

She wondered if William had been aware of David's intention to marry Miss Douglas. Surely, had he known, he would have passed on the information?

Morag too had been quite evasive of late. Elizabeth valued her friendship with the kindly woman, and hoped that her disappointment over Elizabeth's engagement to Gordon would soon pass.

Annabel Douglas was really an excellent choice for David, Elizabeth mused. She was an elegant person, with all the right attributes for a doctor's wife. She was intelligent, knowledgeable in medical matters, and would be able to hold her own in the social strata in which David and his mother moved. Yes, thought Elizabeth charitably, Annabel will make David a very suitable wife.

Morag was still stunned by the events of the past few weeks.

Following the tea-party with Mrs McCulloch and Annabel, when David had appeared unexpectedly and whisked the young lady away to his study to look at his collection of slides of bacteria, her life had become one long round of surprise and confusion.

The young people had rejoined the ladies in the parlour, and announced their engagement. Annabel appeared overwhelmed with delight at the ring which David had given her.

With almost indecent haste, they had arranged for the wedding to take place at Annabel's home in Glasgow. They would have foregone the presence of any members of either family at the ceremony, had not both Morag and Myra McCulloch insisted upon being there. Annabel's uncle must officiate at the wedding and such of Morag's family as could make the journey had to be invited.

Annabel's parents were both dead, but she retained the family house in Bishopbriggs, a village to the north of the city of Glasgow, and lived there when she was not required at the hospital. It was a convenient venue for the wedding and ensured that the Eisdalsa people would be left in ignorance of the marriage until it was all over. Anxious to avoid too many wagging tongues, and too much mental arithmetic giving rise to speculation later in the year, David was determined that no actual date should be fixed in any of the local minds.

The ceremony was conducted in the little church where Annabel had been baptised. Her aunt wept happily throughout the ceremony while Morag, still stunned by the speed with which the whole affair had been managed, stood stony-faced between her two other sons, John, on leave from his regiment, and Angus, who had travelled from Mull.

There had been little time for Annabel to become properly acquainted with her brothers-in-law, although Angus had seemed very amenable. John, who spent much of his time in remote corners of the world, in a totally male-orientated society, found conversation with females difficult. She had exchanged only a few words with him during the proceedings and found him to be shy, tongue-tied even, in her presence.

The wedding breakfast over, the newly-weds were driven to Central Station to catch the train for London.

The days spent in the capital were full of delight for Annabel who had never before ventured across the border.

They shopped in Oxford Street and Regent Street and wandered aimlessly around the cobbled alleyways of Bloomsbury. They sat and watched the passers-by in the tree-lined squares around Lincoln's Inn, and strolled past Buckingham Palace, and on to view the fashionable great houses of Eaton Square and Belgravia.

They paid a visit to the hospital where David's friend, Joseph Lister, was now enjoying a growing reputation for his revolutionary work in aseptic surgery, and spent the afternoon walking the wards with the great man. Annabel had heard of Mr Lister during her nursing days in Glasgow. He was now regarded as the leading figure, in the fight against infectious disease.

Joseph was pleased to receive the young couple in his home, where Annabel set up an immediate rapport with the recently married Mrs Lister. While the two ladies made plans for an expedition on the following day, David and Joseph arranged a session in which to discuss their respective researches.

Two weeks passed all too quickly. In the excitement of the wedding and the subsequent travelling, Annabel quite forgot the discomfort of her pregnancy and was able to announce to David at the end of their stay in London that she had felt neither sick nor faint during the entire fortnight.

As the days lengthened into summer, it became more and more obvious to Morag that her daughter-in-law was pregnant. Neither David nor his wife had said anything about Annabel's condition, which made her all the more suspicious that the child had been conceived prior to the wedding.

If Morag could make such a deduction, there were plenty of females in the village who would soon be coming to the same conclusion. She resolved to have it out with Annabel at the earliest opportunity.

Her chance came on the following morning when the two women were companionably collecting eggs in the hen-house.

Annabel, forced to stretch over the wooden nesting box to reach a clutch of well-hidden eggs, drew back suddenly as though in pain.

Morag thrust her gently to one side.

'You should take more care, in your condition,' she said quietly.

Annabel, who was leaning against the grain trough, panting heavily from her exertions, looked up, startled.

'I have not been a doctor's wife all these years for nothing,' Morag told her. 'When is the baby due?'

'September.' Annabel's reply was almost defiant, challenging her mother-in-law to make the obvious conclusion.

'So that is it!' The answer to all her questions. The puzzling events of these past months now fitted neatly into place. Annabel had been available at the time of David's extreme disappointment over Elizabeth. It was obvious to Morag that Myra McCulloch's niece had taken advantage of him in his weakest moment, and secured her own future as only an artful woman can.

'Do not think too badly of us, Mama,' Annabel pleaded. 'We made a mistake, but both David and I are happy with the outcome now.'

'If you believe that my son would have married you, had you not made it impossible for him to do otherwise, then you are much mistaken!' Morag knew she had gone too far, but pride prevented her from mollifying her words.

Annabel was crushed. The light of happiness, which had scarcely left her eyes since the day of her engagement, was quite extinguished.

She had always accepted that David did not love her at the time her child was conceived. She hoped, however, that he had come to regard her with more than mere affection during the short period since their wedding. He gave her every consideration and appeared to be looking forward to the birth of their baby.

Morag must know how he felt about his marriage, she thought, he would surely have confided in his mother, for they were very close. Annabel's unhappiness was so intense that only momentary oblivion could relieve the built-up tension. She fell in a dead faint on to the hen-house floor.

Morag was terrified at what she had done. David would never forgive her interference. What if her stupid remarks had harmed the baby?

She ran to the house to call him out of the surgery.

Annabel regained consciousness almost at once. By the time that David arrived, she had pulled herself up into a sitting position, resting against the wooden shelving where the hens roosted.

Anxiously, he counted her pulse, examined her for fever, and then, much relieved, turned to his mother who hovered in the doorway.

'No harm done,' he declared, helping his wife to her feet. 'Quite normal, in fact, under the circumstances. What were you two discussing to cause such agitation?'

His cheerful acceptance of her faint, and apparent lack of concern, made Annabel unreasonably angry.

'You had best ask your mother for the answer to that question!' she cried. She could feel tears of despair and frustration welling in her eyes. On no account would she give Morag the satisfaction of seeing her weep. She threw off David's restraining hand and fled to her bedroom.

'I take it that Annabel has told you that she is expecting?' he asked his mother.

Morag considered his attitude to be far too casual.

'I worked it out for myself,' she replied, rather frostily. 'I am also able to perform simple exercises in mental arithmetic . . . the immoral hussy!'

'Oh, come now, Mama, she is no more to blame than I. It was a moment of madness only. I have no regrets. Annabel makes an admirable wife. I am very fond of her.'

'And what of me?' demanded his mother. 'How am I to hold up my head amongst my neighbours? What of my reputation in the village? Have you no sense? Do you not understand what this means? Why, were Annabel a crofter's daughter, she would be castigated in the kirk, made to stand in her shift on the cutty stool, shamed in front of the whole congregation!'

'She is a married woman, Mama. With the wedding such a quiet affair, no one will even remember the date,' David laughed, still not appreciating his mother's concern.

'She will have to be sent away until after the child is born.' Morag was quite adamant. Her mind now working to full effect, she outlined a plan that even David found acceptable.

At that moment Sheilagh came to the kitchen door to ask should she take Mrs David a cup of tea.

'You make it, Sheilagh,' said David, all jocularity, 'and I will carry it to her myself.'

Annabel lay on the bed, her eyes red with weeping. David came to her and folded her in his arms.

'Come, my dear, what is all the fuss about? You must not heed Mama. She does not understand.'

'She believes that I have entrapped you by becoming pregnant. Is that what you think of me also?' He found her very attractive when she was angry like this, but knew it really was not good for her to become so emotional.

'Calm yourself, Annabel,' he ordered, quite severely. 'You are making far too much of this silly incident. Now I will tell you what I have decided.

'Mama, quite rightly so it seems to me, believes that the village women will denounce you as a loose woman if you remain here during your pregnancy . . . she even threatens you with the cutty stool in the kirk!' He was laughing when he said it, but Annabel could detect Morag's influence in his words and did not appreciate that there was any humour in the situation.

'You shall go to stay with my brother Angus on Mull, before your condition becomes too obvious. It is only a half hour's sail away. I shall come to visit you often. We shall tell the villagers that you are pregnant, and that I have sent you away, fearing any infection you might incur from my patients. Angus is good at babies . . . he will be delighted to take care of you.'

'Does your brother not have infectious patients also?' Annabel enquired coldly. She could not forgive his casual attitude to her difficulties.

'His practice is widespread, mainly in a farming community. His patients seldom bother him. In fact, he spends most of his time writing. His published works augment his income to such an extent that he hardly needs to work as a doctor at all!'

Annabel remembered the pleasant encounter which she had enjoyed with him at her wedding breakfast. She was, however, determined not to appear too willing to concede to her husband's wishes, knowing that Morag was behind the idea.

'You and your mother just want me out of the way because I am an embarrassment to you both,' she declared, pouting like a spoilt child.

'The last thing I want is to be away from you when our baby is born,' David protested. 'I promise you that I will be there. But Mama is correct in her assessment of the village women. They could make your life very miserable, believe me. Some unmarried girls have been driven out of the Parish entirely for giving birth to an illegitimate child!'

'What does your brother say to this arrangement? Presumably you have consulted with him previously, even if you have not bothered to ask my opinion before finalising your plans?'

She can be very cutting, thought David. There is a hardness here that I have not recognised before. Poor girl, it must be the shock of all this. He resolved to ignore his wife's uncooperative attitude, putting it down to her condition.

This, of course, merely served to infuriate Annabel further, but she was too tired to argue any more.

'Angus knows nothing of the plan, I assure you. I have only just thought of it myself.

'I shall sail over to Bunessan on the first fine day, and explain our problem to him.'

He tightened his hold on her persuasively.

'Why do you not come along with me? The trip will do you good. You shall see where you are to stay, and become better acquainted with your physician.'

She relaxed in his comforting embrace and, at last, found herself smiling into his anxious eyes.

When, after some time, they eventually rejoined Morag, Annabel's composure was fully restored.

Morag, satisfied that she had not, after all, been the cause of a major disaster, assumed a wounded air, and treated them both to a stony silence.

5

The man that the ex-manager of the Eisdalsa Quarries needed to contact was Alan McClintock. McPhee had dismissed the idea of visiting the island again. He had no wish to arouse the suspicions of William Whylie. Knowing that Alan frequented the old coaching inn in Oban, he decided to chance a meeting with him there.

Three steps up from the street and a sharp turn to the right brought him into the dimly lit taproom. The place was sufficiently crowded to allow a stranger to pass amongst the customers unnoticed.

Although it was the end of July, and the light remained for most of the twenty-four hours of every day, the evening was dreich, a dismal sea mist having closed down over the coast.

McPhee pushed his way to the bar, and ordered a glass of ale. He observed his quarry, a solitary figure seated where he had been told to find him, on a bench in the inglenook. A low fire of peats glowed red in the grate, a welcome sight on such a raw day.

After weeks spent in an almost perpetual drunken stupor, Alan McClintock was an unprepossessing figure. His face was unwashed and covered in several days' growth of ginger stubble. His clothes, little more than rags from rough living, hung about his emaciated frame as though made for a man three times his size.

He viewed the foaming tankard with satisfaction, tipped the contents down his parched throat and sighed contentedly.

'The first today!' he declared to no one in particular. He wiped one sleeve across his mouth and set the emptied tankard down, noisily, on the table before him. He would have yelled loudly for the landlord to refill it, had not a familiar figure addressed him.

'Allow me, friend,' purred McPhee temptingly. He lifted the empty vessel with his free hand, and called for its replenishment.

Setting the overflowing tankard on the table before McClintock, McPhee slid on to the bench beside him.

He immediately regretted the move. The smell arising from the unwashed body of his companion was almost more than he could stomach. McPhee realised now why it was that in that crowded bar there were empty seats beside the fire.

'Well, Alan, this is a happy coincidence.' The insincerity of McPhee's greeting was not lost on the quarryman.

'What of it?' he snarled. Without a word of thanks, he lifted the tankard and drained half its contents. 'Who are you to interrupt a man's drinking, eh?'

'Just an old friend who seeks a service from you . . . for which I am willing to pay.' McPhee placed a golden sovereign on the table, allowing McClintock to see the coin clearly, before covering it with the flat of his hand.

'Oh, aye?' Alan could not hide the fact that his interest was aroused.

'There is a service that you can render me which could benefit us both,' McPhee continued.

'What might that . . . service . . . be?'

'I am told that you are dissatisfied with the Fiscal's verdict of Accidental Death on your boy. No doubt you seek redress for the episode – someone should be held responsible?'

McClintock rejoiced to find someone who agreed with him, that his son's death could have been avoided.

'Aye,' he muttered, 'a few pieces of rusting machinery were considered more important than a young boy with all his life ahead of him.'

'It was McGillivray who gave the order to cut the cable, was it?'

The question was intended to inflame McClintock, and it succeeded.

'I am just biding ma time, sir, waiting for the right opportunity, you might say. Ah'm goin' to get the twa buggers . . . ha' nae fear!' He slapped his fist down so heavily on the rickety table that McPhee's half empty glass rolled onto the floor and shattered.

The noise attracted the curious glances of other customers. McPhee hastily silenced his companion, not wishing his own presence to be noticed by anyone who might recognise him in company with the man from Eisdalsa.

'There is a way in which you can help me, and at the same time take your revenge upon both McGillivray and Whylie,' he said, in low tones.

Alan McClintock had never thought very highly of the former Manager of the Eisdalsa Quarries. The workers had been suspicious that their master was not strictly honest in his dealings, either with themselves or with their employers. These suspicions had been confirmed by the marked improvement in their working conditions since the appointment of William Whylie. Nevertheless, McClintock blamed Whylie and that arrogant swine McGillivray for his boy's death. He was willing to listen to any plan which would see the downfall of the two of them.

McClintock cleared his throat noisily and expelled a globule of thick yellow phlegm which sizzled loudly as it hit the red-hot iron fire basket.

McPhee recoiled.

'What had you in mind?' McClintock resolved to consider the proposition. If he did not like it, he could always refuse.

McPhee drew closer so that they might not be overheard, and spoke earnestly for some minutes.

McClintock would have called for another drink but McPhee deterred him. This operation required a clear head, not one befuddled by strong liquor. As McPhee continued to outline his plan, the quarryman listened intently, nodding from time to time. When McPhee had finished, there was a long pause before McClintock said, 'Very well, Mr McPhee,' and stretched out a grubby hand, 'it is a bargain. The night of the schoolmistress's wedding, a week from today. The people will be enjoying themselves too much to concern themselves with activities on the other side of the Island.'

McPhee slid the sovereign across the table and McClintock swiftly pocketed it.

'And there will be four more just like it when the job is done!'

McClintock looked wistfully at his now empty tankard.

Ignoring the unspoken request, McPhee rose to his feet and sauntered to the far end of the bar where he ordered himself another drink. He drained his glass quickly and set it down.

The transaction had taken a few minutes only. He was satisfied that no one had taken any particular interest in his exchange with the quarryman. Had their encounter been noted at all, it would surely have been interpreted as the benevolent action of a traveller, seeking local information from one of the town's characters.

Donald McPherson stepped back into the shadows when he observed McPhee, deep in conversation with his brother-in-law. McPherson had good reason to mistrust the sacked Quarry Manager. What business could he have with Alan? He moved a little closer in order to overhear what they were saying, but apart from the mention of Saturday night and Miss Duncan's wedding, heard nothing of value. He did, however, observe the transfer of the golden sovereign to McClintock's pocket and the promise of further payment to come.

He held back until McPhee had moved away to the far end of the bar.

When he did at last approach his brother-in-law, Donald said nothing of what he had seen and overheard. He was very disturbed, however, and for several days considered the possibility of mentioning the encounter to the quarry clerk, McGillivray. Jamie would know what to do. To every Eisdalsa man, the presence of McPhee in their midst meant trouble.

McClintock tied up his boat and made his way reluctantly towards his cottage on the far side of the green.

He saw his wife standing at their door looking out for the children coming home from school. She did this every day, as though hoping that her own wee Colin would come running, knees skinned, trousers at half mast, dirty and happy at the end of a long day in the classroom. Alan could not bear to see her so. His own solution to their bereavement, found at the bottom of a whisky glass, seemed more natural.

'So you've come home at last, ye awful wee man you!' shouted old Fanny Fraser, their neighbour. 'It's takin' care of that poor wee wife of yours that ye should be, not sticking yer heed forever in a tankard!'

Alan incensed by her interference, yelled back.

'Aw, shut yer noise, ye stupid owd *baobh*, you!' He thrust his wife, none too gently, inside the house.

'You have no cause to call Mrs Fraser a hag, Alan, she has been kindness itself to me all these weeks.'

Mairie McClintock began to busy herself at the fire. Nowadays she had no idea when her man might appear. Since Colin's death, he sometimes went missing for days, and rarely appeared before midnight.

He would go off, crossing the channel in his little rowing boat, to the distillery in the Village, or even further afield for all she knew. She often wondered how he navigated himself back across the water, drunk as he was, and in the dark.

One day, she said to herself, he will lose an oar, or pass out on the crossing, and come to, to find himself floating towards America. She wondered if she would care.

'Where have you been? My brother Donald came looking for you when you did not turn out for work again last week.'

'He found me, in Oban.'

'Oh, Alan, what are we going to do if you do not work? And Donald . . . he can ill afford to waste his time coming looking for you. Colin is dead. He cannot be brought back. We have to go on living.'

'Is that why you stand at the door every afternoon, hoping he will come out of school with the other children?' he retorted bitterly.

'My memories are all I have,' she replied, choking back threatening tears. 'At least I try to run the house properly. But I can't go on doing that if you do not work. Mr McKay at the store drew a line under our tally today. He will give no more credit until you do an honest day's toil.'

McClintock fumbled in his filthy waistcoat pocket and drew out a few coins, all that remained of the sovereign he had been given by McPhee.

'Here, take this, it will have to do you for the time being.'

She dared not ask where he had got the money. She knew it was not by working. Taking down an ornately decorated tea caddy from the mantelshelf, she counted into it eight shillings and fivepence halfpenny. It would not go far, but was better than nothing.

'Will you go back to work tomorrow, Alan?' she asked.

'Aye. Aye, I will,' he said reluctantly.

In order to carry out McPhee's wishes, he had to go back to working normally; the other men must get used to seeing him about the place again.

Elizabeth's coming wedding was the talk of the island.

For weeks the older children had been rehearsing in secret, under the guidance of Miss Logie. Nothing short of a full-blown choir was good enough for Miss Elizabeth's ceremony.

The little ones, whose skills at making paper flowers had already been demonstrated at the many ceilidhs held during the year, now turned out mountains of white blooms which were to decorate the hall for the wedding party.

Elizabeth and Annie had worked together on the dresses for the bridesmaids, Kirsty McGillivray and Mary McCulloch.

Their dresses were to be of white muslin, embroidered with tiny sprigs of heather. Elizabeth's gown, which she had ordered earlier in the year, had already arrived, and even now reposed, sheathed in layers of paper and scented with shoots of lavender, in her living-room press.

The dress was of lilac silk. The bodice was neatly tucked, with a high neckline, while the skirt was pulled back into a fashionable bustle. The simple decoration consisted of a single frill which fringed the front panel of the skirt to form a false apron. This was edged in lace of a lighter shade than the silk. The same lace decorated the collar and the cuffs on the sleeves, which billowed out at the top but were drawn in tightly below the elbow.

Defying all convention, Elizabeth had refrained from selecting fashionable black, which was still often chosen to commemorate the death of Prince Albert nearly twenty years before. Instead she had decided upon a colour which would complement her own complexion, and would be a useful addition to her wardrobe. Annie suspected that the village matrons would find this choice difficult to accept, but then, they had long ago ceased to wonder at the strange notions of their 'modern' schoolmistress.

If Elizabeth's choice of gown had been made with usefulness in mind, her hat could certainly not be placed in that category. It was a confection of feathers and flowers in all shades of mauve, from pale lilac to deep purple. As a concession to the summer breezes, it could be tied prettily about her head with a scarf of finest lilac chiffon.

On her feet, she was to wear dainty leather Russian boots of white kid, buttoned from ankle to just below the knee.

Since David was already married, Gordon had chosen the bachelor, William, to be his best man. David, now reconciled to his own situation, and looking forward to fatherhood, was content to join Jamie McGillivray as an usher.

Elizabeth was disappointed that Annabel, David's wife, would not be attending the wedding. It seemed that she was already pregnant and, fearing complications arising from her recent illness, David had sent her away to rest in a more agreeable climate.

Annabel's destination had not been revealed, but somewhere overseas seemed likely. Whenever Elizabeth had mentioned the matter to Morag, her friend had been evasive, quickly changing the subject. Elizabeth began to wonder if there might be something wrong with the marriage but, since Morag was clearly disinclined to discuss the matter, she asked no further questions.

The wedding day dawned bright and clear. There was a soft breeze from the south-west which suggested rain later, but for the moment, all was perfect.

The bride was to be rowed to the landing below the church. Her barge was the finest, newest fishing boat on the island. Propelled by four stout oarsmen in their Sunday clothes, white ribbons streaming from the masthead, the bridal party was carried across the Sound of Lorn. All about them other vessels, loaded with the islanders, quarrymen and their families, skidded over the waves, racing for the landing where they would line up to greet the bride.

Once ashore, the merry party made its way up the hill to the little church. Ladies picked up their skirts to avoid the muddy patches left by last night's rain, while toddlers were hoisted on to their fathers' shoulders as they began to flag on the steep hillside.

Elizabeth, with her two bridesmaids tripping merrily at her side, picked her way cautiously along the stony path, trying to preserve the whiteness of her boots. By the end of the day, which would be followed by an evening of dancing, she could cast them aside, heedlessly, but now she was determined to arrive immaculate for her groom.

The men had arrived from Tigh na Broch, where all three had spent the night together with some of Gordon's seafaring comrades. It had been a wild party and all three were showing signs of wear and tear. After a long night of eating and drinking they had finished, in the early hours, by taking a walk over the hill to Ballahuan, arriving back at the doctor's house in time for breakfast.

Now they stood, like three naughty schoolboys, thought Morag, awaiting the arrival of the bridal party. Oh, they were clean and tidy enough, she had seen to that, but there were shadows beneath the eyes and a tell-tale whiteness about the gills.

Why did men always have to abuse their bodies in order to enjoy themselves? Morag pondered. What a stupid ritual the stag-night was. Thank goodness David's wedding had been a far more decorous affair. There had been none of this nonsense when it had been just him and his elder brothers.

When at last she caught sight of the bride, her mouth went dry and there was a lump in her throat. Oh why, she cried inwardly, why couldn't this be my daughter-in-law coming to meet me?

Elizabeth's mother-in-law to be was already ensconced in her seat, in front and to the right of the aisle. She had no intention of exposing her careful coiffure to the coastal breezes.

The bride and her maids, the groom and his supporters, filed into the vestry at the rear, while the remainder of the congregation began to fill the church. Soon every pew was squashed full. People stood crowded into the side aisles, and even sat on the steps which led up to the pulpit.

During the civil ceremony, which took place behind closed doors, the children's choir sang sweetly the sacred songs that Katherine Logie had taught them.

The formalities completed, the *Wedding March* by Mendelssohn was struck up on the harmonium, and the bride and groom walked down the aisle to receive the blessing of their Lord.

For Annie McGillivray, it was the culmination of weeks of planning and sewing. She could not help but feel pride in her own daughter, for Kirsty looked so self-possessed, standing behind the bridal pair, holding the posy of white roses, carnations and Parma violets. What a fuss there had been obtaining those, at this time of the year!

She caught herself thinking again of the little boy who would now have been two years old. How proud she would have been to have him seated here beside her. Quickly she brushed away a tear. Jamie looked at her, concerned. She smiled up at him and squeezed his arm.

For David there was a strange feeling of remoteness. Present in body only, his mind floated back to that trip on the water when he had come home for a short time . . . just to set things to rights before he went off to London.

He remembered his first encounter with his three friends . . . the heart-stopping moments when he had caught Elizabeth in his arms and carried her to safety.

He saw her again as she was on the day of the sail to the Holy Isle, her fiery hair floating on the breeze . . . the look of sheer happiness as she stood in the stern on the homeward journey. With a sudden jolt of recognition, he knew that this must have been the day when all his hopes of making her his own had been thwarted.

The minister was droning on in his usual boring fashion. It was a pity, thought David, that McCulloch could not be more forceful in his attitude to his Parishioners. He allowed the elders too much say in the affairs of the Parish.

Their bigotry and their hypocrisy sickened David. The quarrymen were doing quite well at the moment, but on many occasions in the past year he had gone to the Parish Council and begged for support for

crofters bowed down by the excessive rents which Lugas was obliged
to levy on behalf of the new tenant of Ballahuan House.

Their attitude had been entirely negative. The crofters were idle
wasters. They must work harder, take on extra crofters on the Estate
to augment their income. The children should be put to work. It never
did the previous generation any harm. Education for farm labourers
was a waste of time.

David seethed with indignation as he recalled the plethora of excuses
which accompanied every denial of support.

The sick and the old could be hidden away in the workhouse, out of
sight and out of mind. David recalled the piper, Iain Leakie, who only
last week had died at the age of eighty. The bothy in which he had
lived latterly with his widowed daughter had half its roof collapsed. The
windows were unglazed, and the wooden shutters and door so ill-fitting
that the wind howled through the house, putting out the meagre peat
fire which was all the old man could afford. Iain had marched at the
head of Stirling's Company at Sebastopol. He had piped his comrades
to victory at Balaclava. His reward, for a life of dedication to his Laird,
had been a roofless hovel, and slow death by starvation.

David did not blame the Marquis for this neglect. He had delegated
responsibility for such matters to his Factor and to the members of the
Parish Council. Despite their representation on that body, William and
he were two lone voices shouting in the wilderness.

'. . . joined together, let no man put asunder.'

There was an audible sigh from the body of the church as Elizabeth
turned to her husband for the chaste kiss which was considered appropriate at the end of the ceremony.

Donald McPherson watched his brother-in-law all evening, never letting
him out of his sight.

The wedding party was at its height, the wedding breakfast had been
consumed, speeches had been made, and now the dancing was in full
swing. The festivities would probably continue throughout the night.
Only the necessity of appearing in kirk the following morning would
eventually send the islanders to their beds.

Alan McClintock had worked solidly all week. He had appeared at
the quarry every morning, ready to take his place alongside the other
members of the crew. His companions, relieved that he seemed at last
to have put the tragedy of his son's death behind him, welcomed him
back into the fold.

Only Donald suspected that his brother-in-law's apparent change of
heart had more sinister connotations. The encounter with McPhee
bothered him and he wished now that he had confided his apprehensions
to McGillivray.

The company clerk was chatting animatedly with his companions when Donald interrupted.

'Jamie, I need your help for a minute. Can we talk, privately?' Donald tried to make the request sound like a light-hearted conspiracy, associated perhaps with the imminent departure of the bridal pair.

Jamie was instantly on his feet, ready for the fun.

'At your service, my man!' he cried merrily, and hobbled to the end of the hall where they would not be overheard.

'It is not what you think, I'm afraid,' confessed Donald, when they were out of earshot. 'I have reason to believe there may be mischief afoot in one of the quarries.'

Jamie's jocular demeanour changed instantly to one of serious concern. He had often discussed with William the possibility of sabotage. There had been a great deal of antagonism generated amongst their rivals in Lochaber as a result of the success of Eisdalsa in the Antipodes. They were jealous of the New Zealand contract, and might go to any lengths to interfere with it to their own advantage.

In the recent weeks of outstandingly good weather, output from the island workings had improved above all expectations. It would, however, require only a single set-back, an exposure of poor slate, or a failure of the pumps, to prevent the Company from fulfilling the terms of its contract.

'What is it you suspect?' Jamie drew his companion aside as a pair of dancers brushed past them.

'I saw McPhee a few days ago, in the Oban Inn, speaking with one of the men.'

'Who was it?'

'I don't know his name . . . one of the incomers.'

Donald was reluctant to expose his own brother-in-law. If the fool was to be caught performing some act against the interests of his employers, McPherson would prefer that it was one of the Company's officials who made the discovery.

'What caused you to be suspicious about the encounter?' Jamie asked anxiously.

'I heard only the last few words of their conversation: Saturday night was mentioned. Money changed hands.'

'You mean to say that McPhee paid money to one of our men?' The matter was indeed serious.

McPhee was famous for his lack of charity to his fellow men. It must have been a very good cause for him to part with even a single bawbee!

During his conversation with McGillivray, Donald had withdrawn his attention from McClintock for the first time that evening. Now his eyes searched the throng for that familiar stocky figure, and the head with its monkish tonsure. Alan was nowhere to be seen.

'What will you do?' he demanded of Jamie, anxious to be rid of the terrible responsibility which he felt.

'I shall go out directly, and take a look round. You must find Mr Whylie and tell him what you suspect.'

'Can you not talk to Whylie yourself? He is more likely to take notice of what you say.'

'There is no time to waste. Every minute might be important, if we are dealing with sabotage. Mr Whylie is well aware of such a danger. We have spoken often about the possibility of trouble of this kind. Just tell him what you have told me, and say that I have gone first to Number Two.'

The mischief intended could involve any one of a number of actions. Instinctively Jamie felt that a breaching of the sea wall to the largest of all the workings, the quarry from which the best slate was being drawn, would do the most damage. Were he himself hell-bent on ruining the Company, this was the target he would choose.

He was reluctant to alert any of his mates, all of whom were enjoying themselves at the far end of the hall. If the whole matter were a figment of Donald's imagination, he would be made to look a fool. Better to confirm the quarryman's fears first, and then take whatever action seemed necessary.

Jamie pointed out to Donald where William Whylie stood, in a group which consisted of the bridal pair, Morag and Katherine Logie, and the tall severe figure of the groom's mother.

'Get along with you, man,' he ordered sharply. 'I'm away to the mine.'

Donald stared helplessly after the vanishing figure of McGillivray. Then, forcing himself to appear at ease and even to acknowledge the pleasantries of his comrades as he made a passage for himself across the crowded space, he approached the Quarry Manager.

'Mr Whylie, sir, may I interrupt you for a moment? An urgent message from Mr McGillivray.'

William, startled by the serious expression on Donald's face, excused himself politely and led the quarryman away.

'Mr McGillivray has reason to suspect an act of sabotage, planned for tonight. He has gone to Number Two quarry in the first instance.'

'Alone?'

'Yes, sir. He was anxious not to interrupt the proceedings unnecessarily. He has just gone to have a look round and report back.'

'What gave him cause for his suspicions, McPherson?'

Donald hesitated before making his reply.

'I overheard part of a conversation in the Oban Inn, sir . . . between McPhee and one of your men.'

William looked at him sharply.

'One of *my* men, do you say? Which one of the men was it?'

'I would rather not say, sir.'

William felt that he knew the answer to his own question. He would not press Donald to betray his own kinsman, but had little doubt that the man in question was McClintock. It was common knowledge that Alan had made threats against both William and McGillivray, blaming them for his son's accident.

This thought led him to the realisation that Jamie, crippled as he was, might be in great danger.

'McGillivray's crewmen are over there,' William indicated a merry group in the corner near the musician's podium. 'Without making too much disturbance, have them muster outside with whatever weapons they can lay hand to . . . just in case.'

While Donald gathered the men together, William sought out David. 'There is some trouble in the quarries, Beaton. I would be obliged if you will stay on for a while longer. Your services may be required.'

'What kind of trouble?'

'It may be something planned to prevent us from fulfilling the New Zealand contract. Will you remain here and try to keep the ladies calm? I will get a message back to you as soon as I know anything definite.'

For two days after returning to his place in the gang, Alan McClintock made every effort to persuade his brother-in-law that he had put the past behind him.

Eager to convince himself that he had been wrong to be suspicious about Alan's encounter with McPhee, Donald watched with relief as Alan regained his confidence, and re-established his authority with the crew.

For some years past, Alan had been powder man. He it was who laid the charges to blast out the huge chunks of rock into the neat square blocks which could be split into roofing slates, with the minimum of wastage. It was the most skilled and dangerous of the work carried out by the team. McPhee had known exactly what he was doing when he had chosen the disgruntled McClintock as his inside man.

Alan had been aware all evening of Donald's eyes constantly upon him. Each time he had thought to slide, surreptitiously, out of the hall, he had been unable to shake off his kinsman's concentrated surveillance. It was almost as if he were aware of what was about to happen.

Not for the first time in the past few days, Alan thought about the encounter in the inn. Was it possible that Donald had overheard his conversation with McPhee?

He watched McPherson approach McGillivray. They talked for a moment, laughed conspiratorially and wandered off, presumably bent on some practical joke.

Now was the moment, while his brother-in-law's attention was elsewhere. He slipped behind a screen decorated with evergreens and the children's paper flowers. It was only a few steps to the outer door.

He glanced over again to where the conspirators stood talking, Donald not looking in his direction. Without further hesitation, he pushed open the door and went outside.

The square was deserted and all the houses in darkness. Alan hurried around the harbour, aware that he was already late for his appointment.

The door to the company office was locked, but McClintock was aware that the ancient mechanism could be forced with a piece of wire. In McPhee's day he had been called upon to perform the trick on many a chilly morning when, the manager being late for work, the men were impatient to get started on the job.

In a few minutes his efforts were rewarded. He heard the tumblers click into place and when he turned the handle, the door swung open. The small room was almost dark. A little evening light penetrated the single grubby window, allowing McClintock to locate the row of keys hanging behind the clerk's desk. He pocketed the one he needed and, relocking the door behind him, hurried to the rendezvous.

During the afternoon the clouds had thickened and the warm sunshine had given way to a chilly mist which rolled in from the sea in patches. One moment all was clear; the next, houses, boats, the hillside, were enveloped in an impenetrable mantle of clammy vapour.

The noise from the hall receded as he made his way, via the railway track, to the western shore.

When there was a swell on the ocean, it was almost impossible to land a boat on this side of the island, but tonight the sea was glassy in its stillness. Under cover of the fog, McPhee's men had drawn their craft up on to the rocky beach. It was now turned, bows to the surf, ready for a quick escape.

As Alan made his cautious approach, McPhee came forward out of the mist to greet him.

'My God, man, you took your time. I was beginning to think you had changed your mind!'

A band of five or six men sheltered beside the squat building which housed the explosives. Alan pulled his cap down firmly and turned up his coat collar in a futile attempt to disguise his features. The additional help was essential, but he had no wish to be identified by one of these strangers, should things go wrong.

'Position your men along the wall yonder.' He indicated the solid wall, ten feet in height, which had been made at the seaward end of the quarry. Built of huge slabs of slate, set vertically and packed dry without the use of mortar, this structure was an effective barrier against the sea in normal tides. When the tide was exceptionally high, or the waves unusually rough, some water could pass between the stones, thereby reducing the strength of the forces against them. The pumps could cope with the amounts of water thus seeping into the quarry.

Were the wall to be breached, however, the sea would come flooding in at high tide and completely overwhelm the pumps.

McPhee had timed his enterprise with expert precision. Tonight, the difference between high and low tide would be the maximum, fourteen feet. Charges could be laid on both sides of the wall and would remain dry until well after the tide had turned, and he and his men were out of sight of the island.

'Where is the powder?' he demanded. It had been part of the bargain that McClintock should provide the means of blowing up the wall.

'I have the key to the magazine,' McClintock told him. 'It would have aroused their suspicions if I had taken any explosives before the stock was checked at the end of the week.'

'Well then, hurry, man, and get it. Someone could discover our presence at any time!'

'Not tonight they won't.' Alan dug the iron key out of his pocket and put it into the lock. 'They're all too busy celebrating in the Drill Hall.'

While McClintock selected the fuses and explosive that would be necessary for the task, McPhee signalled to two of his men to carry the materials to others, stationed beside the wall.

Among them were a number of experienced men from the Ballachulish Quarries. They would know how to fix the charges, but McClintock had helped to build the wall, and could tell them where best to place the explosive in order to do the greatest amount of damage.

Although it was long after midnight, there was still a vestige of light in the night sky. Jamie McGillivray had climbed the narrow ridge, which sloped up from the end of the village. From the top of the hill he could look right down into Number Two quarry, but with the black shadow of the hill lying over the landscape, it was difficult to see anything happening.

He heard, from somewhere below him, the rasp of wooden cases being dragged across the stones. There was a clink of metal and a low cursing as someone dropped a tool.

The sound seemed to come from the far side of the quarry . . . the seaward end! It was as he had feared, they were going to attack the sea wall.

Jamie's eyes were now accustomed to the gloom, but mist lay over the quarry itself. Figures drifted in and out of sight as the light breeze shifted it capriciously. He had already counted half a dozen men, maybe more. Too many for him to handle alone.

He turned back and half-climbed, half-slid down the hillside, away from the western shore.

Hampered by his game leg, Jamie could make ground only slowly. Great was his relief, therefore, to find a group of his own friends making their way towards him, along the track.

Try as he might to be discreet about what was happening, William had found himself obliged to explain the situation to Gordon. Never one to shirk a good scrap, even though it was his wedding day, he had summoned those of his own crew who were present, and they too had joined the party.

Jamie had made a shrewd assessment of the situation as he had sat, concealed, on top of the ridge.

It was clear that the invaders depended upon McClintock for something . . . explosives probably. Yes, that had to be it. Also, McClintock would know how and where the explosives should be laid for maximum effect. The charges must be set off just before high tide, which would occur at three o'clock. Any earlier and the islanders, alerted by the explosion, might be in time to prevent major flooding.

Jamie sought out William Whylie.

'There are at least six men, sir, maybe more, I could not see all that clearly, from the top of the hill.'

'Any suggestions as to how we should tackle this, Jamie?' William asked, deferring to his clerk's experience.

'If half our number take the north side of the hill, and the rest the south side, we can approach them from both ends of the wall. That will stop at least some of them from reaching their boat. I could not see it, but I expect it to be lying somewhere on the shore, near the quarries.'

'What of the charges . . . will we have time to reach them?'

'It seems clear that they have nearly finished laying them,' said Jamie, 'but they will not light the fuses for half an hour or so. Just before high tide would be my guess.'

'Right then.' William turned to his little army of defenders. 'McIntyre, if you will take your men, with McGregor to guide you, via the north end, I will lead my company round by the southern path. I do not need to remind you, gentlemen, that a silent approach is essential if we are to surprise them!' Turning to Jamie he continued, 'You have already done your part tonight, McGillivray. Go back to the Hall and report to Dr Beaton. There is no need for you to expose yourself to injury.'

McGillivray did not appreciate the Manager's concern for his safety. He had come to terms with being crippled in his leg, but the notion that he should be excluded from the fray annoyed him.

'If you have no objection, sir,' he replied, 'I think that I should make my way to the magazine. It will be useful to know how much powder has been taken.'

'Oh, very well, McGillivray.' William was disinclined to waste time arguing. 'But stay out of the fighting. A blow on that metal plate of yours and it will be all up with you!'

6

Jamie climbed back up the path by which he had just descended, and made his way over the crest of the hill. Down below he could see William's men moving between the shadows cast by the rocks. To the north, the seamen with McPherson at their head were making slower progress, across what was to them unknown territory.

He regained his vantage point and stared down to where the saboteurs were laying their charges on either side of the great sea wall.

McPhee was becoming agitated. Although his boat had been hauled far up the beach, it was now only a few feet from the water's edge. If they did not board her in the next few minutes, she would float off without them.

'McClintock,' his harsh whisper carried along the face of the wall, 'how much longer?'

Alan McClintock stepped back to view his work. From holes forced between the hard-packed stones, the fuses protruded and came running towards him from both directions. He bunched them together and led them up and over the wall. Here he fanned them out again, so that each could be lit separately. Should any one of them go out, the others would still carry a flame, unimpeded, to the charges.

He hauled himself up on to the top of the wall, and slipped down the other side to wait for the appointed time.

McGillivray, from his perch on the cliff, spotted the lone figure and guessed his intention.

With great relief, McPhee responded to Alan's low whistle, the signal that his own part in the business was complete.

'Everyone to the boat. No noise! We do not want to alert anyone, even at this late stage.'

William's men had spotted the boat drawn up on the beach. The fast-approaching surf had reached the bows, and water lapped along the sides of the vessel as each wave surged forward.

They lay in wait behind the rocks, sticks, pipes, whatever weapons they had been able to lay hands on, at the ready. Soon, three shadowy figures were seen, approaching stealthily. William allowed the first two men to pass him before giving the order to attack.

The intruders were totally surprised. Overwhelmed by the incensed islanders, they quickly gave up the struggle and, but for a few bruises and the occasional gash, were unharmed. William commanded them to lie down, out of sight amongst the rocks. Their guard, Tam McTavish, a wild-looking giant of a man from the outer isles, made doubly sure that they made no sound to alert their comrades, by a most effective demonstration of the use to which his heavy, gnarled walking-stick might be put!

Before making for the boat himself, McPhee went back to check on McClintock. The role of the Eisdalsa man was essential, and he wanted to be certain that Alan understood the consequences of any failure on his part.

McClintock was in place, and ready to light the fuses when the time came. McPhee spoke quietly to him.

'Now then, Alan, give us fifteen minutes to get clear of the rocks. Remember our meeting . . . the same time as before. If you should fail, you may be sure that your own part in this affair will reach the ears of William Whylie and you will never work again in Scotland!'

McPhee spat out the words with so much venom that McClintock cringed in fear.

McPhee, believing his own night's work was now complete, cast all caution aside, and climbed up on to the wall.

Clearly silhouetted against the sky, he ran along the top, covering the distance to the boat in half the time his men had taken to pick their way tentatively among the rocks.

McPhee's movements alerted the group of seamen led by Gordon who came howling out of the darkness in pursuit.

More of McPhee's men, disturbed by the onrush of attackers from the north, fled directly into the path of William's defenders. Batons whirled, and fists flew, as the parties engaged in hand-to-hand fighting. In the mêlée, two of the captives in the charge of Tam McTavish managed to escape. As the third tried to follow them, he received a mighty blow from Tam's stick, which left him lying unconscious on the beach.

The two escapees joined McPhee in a desperate attempt to push the boat out into the surf. Ever anxious for his own safety, McPhee leapt aboard, leaving his two companions to continue heaving at the heavy vessel. At last they could feel the water under the keel. The vessel swung away from the beach on the next receding wave.

The first man managed to haul himself aboard, falling head-first into the boat. The second was just too late. McTavish, angry at having lost his charges, had followed them into the surf. As the fugitive tried to clamber aboard, Tam grabbed his legs. The gunwale was out of reach. The man made a second lunge and fell, flat on his face in the surf. He would have drowned had not Tam hauled him up out of the water and slung him across his shoulders, clambering to safety across the rocks with his load.

McPhee managed to grab an oar. His partner, too, was quickly in place upon the thwart, struggling to get his oar into the rowlock. Once, twice . . . three times, they managed to pull the heavy oars through the surf. As the oars dug in for the fourth time a great wave arose out of nowhere, and smashed the stricken vessel back towards the shore. McPhee and his companion were tipped into the sea, as the timbers were dashed to pieces against the sharp rocks. William's men could only stand and watch as the two intruders disappeared in the hungry surf.

From his perch on the hillside, Jamie McGillivray watched the activity below, and was grateful to William for having excluded him from the fight. He was not a man to admit readily to incapacity, but knew that he would have been less help than hindrance to his friends, in the circumstances.

He could hear shouted instructions from below, and watched as a number of dejected figures were bundled together and frog-marched along the path, back towards the village. Several men on both sides held makeshift bandages to heads and limbs . . . it had been a hard fought battle and no mistake!

William and Gordon stood with two of the Eisdalsa men, and watched the weary party retreating.

'They had obviously finished laying their charges,' said William. 'We surprised them on their way back to the boat. Malcolm and Franklin,' he ordered his two powder men, 'you take the outer side of the wall. Mr McIntyre and I will search along the inner side. If you find anything, just rip out the fuses but leave the charges in position. We must have evidence to show the Sheriff's men.'

To Gordon, he observed confidentially, 'I am thankful McClintock was not among the captives. I would not like to think that he was involved.'

The four men began the treacherous climb across the rocks to the seaward end of the quarry. Believing that all the conspirators were either dead or captive, they made no attempt to disguise their presence.

McClintock, crouched down below the wall, waiting for high tide, heard all the activity, but was unable to see the outcome. At one point in the battle, he had cautiously climbed up the inner face of the wall in time to see McPhee and his partner launch the boat. Realising that he himself was doomed if they found him here, he quickly regained the shelter of the wall. He saw nothing of the final outcome of McPhee's attempt at escape. Believing him to be safely away, McClintock knew he must carry out his part of the operation or McPhee would ruin him, as he had threatened.

He could not wait for the highest point of the tide, that was clear.

Now that the plot had been discovered, he must light the charges and retreat, before he himself was arrested. That the men seeking him out might be caught in the explosion, and that a charge of murder might be added to the list of his offences, did not occur to him. At that moment, all he could think of was McPhee's threat to expose him.

He turned to the bundle of fuses, hanging by the wall. The damp air made it difficult to strike a lucifer. The first one sparked, burned momentarily, and died, leaving behind an acrid smell of sulphur. He tried again. This time the stick caught light, and gave him enough flame to set the first of the fuses glowing. The flame began to travel along each of the separate pathways, up to the top of the wall . . . and over.

Jamie had watched the activity from the hillside, and had seen McPhee's men making for the boat. He realised that if, indeed, sabotage was intended, then someone must have been left behind to fire the charges.

He scrambled down the hillside, pausing behind the solid stone building where the explosives were housed. The magazine stood in an isolated position well above the quarries and away from the engine house and pumping equipment.

Jamie felt his way along the wall in the deep shadow cast by the hillside. At the corner, he stopped and took a cautious peep to ensure that none of the men had been left behind. The building appeared to be deserted.

He found the door open. The key was still in the lock. This confirmed their suspicion that an Eisdalsa man was indeed involved. He pushed the door open wider and went inside.

The stocks of explosive had certainly been disturbed. He himself had carried out the weekly stocktaking, and it was clear that a large quantity of material was missing. On the floor, obviously kicked and scuffed by a number of pairs of muddy boots, lay a distinctive tartan scarf. McGillivray recognised it at once. There was only one family of McClintocks on the island, and Alan made a great play of displaying his clan tartan. Stuffing the scarf in his pocket, Jamie went out on to the hillside.

The noise of the battle below had died down a little. He observed what he took to be Whylie's men, marching off towards the village. A small group remained over near the beach, but McGillivray's attention now centred on the great wall, at the end of Number Two quarry.

He saw a movement in the shadows at the base of the wall. The mist had cleared somewhat, and it was possible to detect the figure of a man, bending over. A lighted match spluttered and went out, but it was sufficient to assure McGillivray that the man was, indeed, intent upon blowing up the wall.

Ignoring William's order to stay out of the fight, Jamie hobbled down the path and along the edge of the quarry. The turf here was quite thick, and his approach went unnoticed by the saboteur who was preoccupied with his task.

Jamie covered the last few yards with more caution. Obliged to tread on loose rocks and boulders spread along the base of the wall, he was in danger of alerting his quarry. He bent down and seized a sharp piece of rock. As he did so, others beneath it moved and one was dislodged, falling down the steep side of the quarry. McClintock turned his head at the sound and Jamie struck.

It was not a heavy blow, but McGillivray hoped it was sufficient to stun his adversary and buy him the time he needed to prevent the explosion.

McClintock had toppled backwards, away from the wall, and sprawled helplessly on the slippery rocks at the edge of the quarry. Jamie was intent upon safeguarding the wall. He could spare only a second to ensure that McClintock was in no position to retaliate before he set about extinguishing the spluttering fuses.

Those nearest to hand, he put out immediately with his feet. The ones which had been led up and over the wall to the charges on the outer face, he had to scramble for.

Soon, all but one had been put out. The last fuse led to the nearest charge, on the far side of the wall. Instinct warned Jamie that this one was going to reach its destination at any moment.

Leaving the final charge to do whatever damage it might, he dropped down from the wall, and pulling the still dazed McClintock behind a large boulder, forced him to crouch down in its shelter.

The explosion, only a fraction of what it might have been, was sufficient to deafen both men. Rocks flew in every direction and it was some moments before the air was clear enough to see what damage had been done.

It was fortunate that the charge had been laid near the top of the wall. Although a section, some twelve feet long and eight feet deep, had been dislodged, the bulk of the surrounding stonework remained intact.

Satisfied that the damage was minimal, Jamie turned to his captive. 'You fool, McClintock! What possessed you, man? Whatever the cause, you had no right to endanger the livelihood of your fellows!'

Shocked by the events of the night, and perhaps by the explosion itself, McClintock could only stare at Jamie, speechless, his mouth hanging open like that of an imbecile. His eyes were red-rimmed from the dust, but there was no mistaking their expression. It was one of hatred so intense that McGillivray took a step back, as though to avoid the power of the curse that McClintock put upon him.

'By God, McGillivray,' he cried, 'I swear I will make you pay for my boy's death, one way or another. No matter how long it takes, I will get my revenge!'

At the departure of so many of William's men, the wedding party had broken up in confusion.

The village women decided to occupy themselves in clearing the remains of the feast and tidying up the hall for bible class in the morning.

Although the Island could not boast a church of its own, the smaller children attended Sabbath School which was conducted by Miss Logie and some of the older pupils in the day school.

David had sent Sheilagh away with Ian, the ferryman, to collect his medical bag. Annie and some of her neighbours had gone off to gather blankets and clean linen, which might be needed for binding wounds.

Elizabeth, who had anticipated spending her wedding night in the wonderful new house that had been built for her, went back to the schoolhouse with Mrs McIntyre and persuaded her new mother-in-law to go to bed and rest.

She herself changed out of her wedding gown into a more practical day dress, realising that the night would be a long one, and that the departure planned for tomorrow . . . today . . . might have to be postponed.

Back at the hall, the first of the quarrymen were arriving.

There were quite a few black eyes, several severe gashes and not a few strained muscles, but nothing serious as yet.

Annie greeted each returning party, eagerly searching for Jamie. She knew that Mr Whylie would not allow him to enter the fray but why had he not returned with the others?

There was a considerable lull in proceedings. David had bound up every wound and administered witch-hazel to the bruises. The women were dispensing huge mugs of sweet tea to everyone and there was a general air of excitement, not to say gaiety.

Only one group remained sullen and uncommunicative. These were the captives who had been herded into a space set aside for them at the far end of the hall. They had received the same ministrations as the islanders but, naturally, there was no elation among them, only apprehension.

The Sheriff's men had been summoned. The saboteurs knew that the court would frown upon their activities. The lightest punishment they might look forward to would be a long prison sentence.

William, looking tired and dishevelled, arrived at last. He was followed into the hall by two men, bearing between them a stretcher. This they placed discreetly in a corner, behind one of the decorated screens. Slowly a stream of water began to flow from beneath the screen, out into the Hall. Annie would have gone to mop it up, but William held her back.

'Best not to look,' he urged her. He had witnessed more than one body, fished from the sea, and had no wish to expose Annie to such a sight.

William's men had searched along the shore for some time before, finally, they had found the body of McPhee, caught between rocks which were exposed as the tide fell. Of his companion, there had been no trace.

While the recently appointed quarrymen and their wives stared, uncomprehending, at the body of the ex-Quarry Master, the old hands looked on, unmoved by the plight of this man who had exploited them for so long, and had intended to deprive them of their living, possibly for ever.

Jamie entered at last, gripping Alan McClintock firmly by one arm. The saboteur was held on his other side by Tam McTavish, who was determined that there would be no more escapes that night! In truth the prisoner looked in no fit state to make any such attempt.

Blood flowed freely from a gash on the back of his head. His eyebrows and whiskers were singed and blackened, his face and hands blistered as though he had been in a fire.

Jamie McGillivray looked little better than his captive. The boulder had taken the worst of the blast from the explosion but their close proximity had caused both men to receive minor burns on their exposed skin.

David took McClintock away, to attend to his wounds. He was helped by Tam, who was reluctant to hand over his charge to anyone.

Annie led the weary Jamie to one side and gave him a cup of tea before bathing his scorched face with a solution of boracic, and applying ointment to the blistered areas.

William, mighty pleased with the result of the night's work, came up to Jamie and Annie where they sat silently, grateful to be together and unharmed.

'Well, McGillivray, you disobeyed orders . . . but I'm mighty glad you did! It is thanks to you that we shall still have the New Zealand contract, despite McPhee and his marauders.'

'Had McPherson not alerted us, sir, the mischief would have been done, and us none the wiser until the dust had settled!'

'That is true.' William lowered his voice. 'But I think he would not thank you for saying so. He considers that he has betrayed his kinsman, and believes that his wife and her sister will never forgive him.'

It was Annie who spoke up in Donald's defence. 'All the families on this island owe a debt of gratitude to Donald McPherson. I cannot believe that either his wife or his sister-in-law would hold it against him.'

'Let us hope you are right, Annie.' William smiled at this quiet, practical woman whom he had come to admire for her compassion and commonsense. 'But perhaps we should keep the knowledge to ourselves? McClintock need never know who it was who betrayed him.'

Gordon had joined the group, having assured himself that his bride was still happy to be his bride, and his mother was safely tucked up in her bed!

'Well,' he declared, laughing, 'I expected my wedding day to be memorable . . . but this was not exactly what I had in mind!'

'My dear fellow,' exclaimed William, thumping his friend on the back, 'I cannot thank you and your men enough for what you did. We would have been hard put to it to overcome the devils, had you not been there to help us.'

'Oh, I don't know,' laughed Gordon. 'It seems to me that McGillivray could have taken the whole lot of them on his own, game leg and all!'

Jamie looked embarrassed while Annie frowned, not having realised to what extent he had placed himself in jeopardy.

It was William who reminded them of the real purpose of the day.

'What will you do about your trip to Mull, Gordon? With no sleep for two nights, you must be feeling the need for bed, rather than sailing.'

Elizabeth, who was unaware that her husband had had no sleep at all the night before, spoke for them both.

'I think we should be on our way as soon as the tide is right. When will that be? About three o'clock?'

'I may be delayed, dealing with the Sheriff's men,' said William, 'but if you are willing to set out then, I shall try to be ready.'

He had offered Gordon the use of *The Saucy Nancy* for the two weeks of their honeymoon but both Gordon and Elizabeth had agreed that they could not deprive their friend of his vessel during the best of the sailing season. They had however been grateful to accept his offer to ferry them across to the Ross of Mull, where they were to spend their holiday in a cottage on the estate belonging to the father of Elizabeth's friend, Helena Mackintosh.

Fearing practical jokers, neither Gordon nor Elizabeth had revealed their destination to anyone other than William. It was widely believed that the happy couple would be leaving the island for Glasgow on the morning steamer, and any plans for a wild send-off were geared to that end.

Even David had no idea where they were going.

Whatever Elizabeth's expectations of marriage, nothing she had dreamed of matched the sheer ecstasy of those two weeks spent on Mull in August 1878.

There were golden days, and there were days when the skies opened and the rain fell in sheets. Nothing bothered them.

They strode across the countryside, following sheep tracks into the wilderness. They climbed to the top of every hill in the vicinity and paddled in the mountain streams.

Borrowing a couple of horses on one occasion, they made their way to the foot of Ben Mor and climbed partway up that extinct volcano.

On another day, Mr McDuff lent them his small sailing dinghy and they covered the short sea trip to the island of Iona. There they explored the ruined Abbey Church and the old Nunnery, before wandering across to the southern shore of the island, to bury their bare toes in the sparkling white sand, and paddle in the blue waters of Camas Cuil.

The McDuffs were kindness itself. Apart from a cordial greeting on their arrival on Sunday evening, when they had been escorted by Helena's father to the door of the cottage, Gordon and Elizabeth had been left to their own devices for much of the first week.

William had helped Gordon to unload their small stock of provisions, and carry them to the house. Then, despite their entreaties that he spend the night with them before returning to Eisdalsa, he had set sail. With a following westerly breeze, *The Saucy Nancy* was soon lost to sight against the backdrop of the hills of Argyll, crouching on the horizon.

When the weather was bad, they stayed indoors and watched pictures form and disintegrate in the peat fire. They confided their hopes and their dreams, delighted in the books they read together, and revelled in shared memories.

At night, in the downy refuge of their huge feather bed, they made love. Elizabeth rejoiced that she had confided in Annie her qualms and uncertainties about the marriage bed. The frank discussions which they had had gave Elizabeth some idea what to expect.

Despite this, and the revelations of her friend Helena, Elizabeth's initial encounter with the naked male form had been a shock.

Gordon, the gentle knight, understood her confusion and apprehension. He folded her in his arms and stroked her until she relaxed. Then, when she was ready for him, and only then, he took possession of her.

The hypocritical modesty of Victorian society, which sent young women into marriage in a state of ignorance, marred many an otherwise perfect match. Elizabeth was spared that, and for her their passionate and tender love-making was sheer joy. For Gordon, not without previous experience in such matters, the union was perfection. All that remained for them to pray for was that their marriage should be fruitful. Elizabeth wanted babies, as many and as soon as possible!

Just when they had begun to feel that this idyll would never end, the last Saturday of their holiday was upon them.

A message was sent down, early in the morning, from the McDuffs at the Tower House. Mrs McDuff requested the honour of their presence that evening at a small dinner party she was giving for a few of her neighbours.

Reluctant as the honeymooners were to spend their last evening in anyone's company but their own, they felt it would be churlish and ungrateful to refuse the invitation.

They arrived at the appointed hour, looking as spruce as they could manage with the limited wardrobe that each had brought along on the holiday.

Elizabeth wore the green gown which David had so much admired the year before. Gordon had put on his only suit, of a tweed rather too heavy for the season. As the evening wore on he began to show such signs of distress that McDuff, with disarming politeness, discarded his own dinner-jacket and encouraged Gordon to follow suit.

On arrival, Gordon and Elizabeth were shown into the drawing room where they were greeted by their host and hostess and then introduced to a number of farmers and their wives.

Elizabeth noticed a tall, red-headed figure standing at the far end of the room, in front of a chair whose back and wings completely obscured the occupant. So engrossed was he in his conversation that he had been unaware of their arrival. Elizabeth was sure that she had not met him before, and yet there was something familiar about him.

'And finally we come to our physician, Dr Beaton,' Mrs McDuff introduced the remainder of her guests. 'Dr Angus Beaton, Mr and Mrs Gordon McIntyre.'

Elizabeth started on hearing the name. Then, realising why she had felt that she knew him, she advanced towards David's brother, Angus.

'Dr Beaton,' she shook his hand politely, 'This is an unexpected pleasure. David is one of our dearest friends. Perhaps he has mentioned us?'

Angus, two years older than his brother and seemingly several years wiser, smiled knowingly as he replied, 'My brother has certainly mentioned you, Mrs McIntyre.' Then, almost as an afterthought, 'And your husband, of course!'

To Gordon he bowed as he took his hand and greeted him.

'Congratulations, McIntyre. You are a very lucky fellow!'

Gordon accepted the compliment, beaming at his bride who blushed prettily by his side.

'Well, thank you, Beaton. No one is more conscious of my good fortune than I am myself.'

Mrs McDuff interrupted, flushed with embarrassment. 'What can I be thinking of?' she exclaimed. 'You will of course know Dr Beaton's sister-in-law, Mrs David Beaton?'

Unable to hide in the chair any longer, Annabel rose rather clumsily to her feet and turned towards them.

She looked the very picture of good health, her skin fairly blooming with her condition. Because of her broad frame, she held the child inconspicuously, her loosely fitted gown disguising the bulge most effectively. Nevertheless, it was clear to Elizabeth that the pregnancy was well advanced.

'Why, Annabel!' she exclaimed. 'How well you look. David assured us that you were too poorly to attend the wedding. I am so pleased that he has underestimated your powers of recovery.'

Desperately, she sought for words which would sound natural. She recalled how evasive both David and Morag had been about the coming baby, how they had been at pains to avoid mention of where Annabel had been sent, how the implication had been that the pregnancy was likely to be a difficult one. Yet here was Annabel, apparently in blooming health and in the care of her brother-in-law.

She was clearly as uncomfortable about the encounter as was Elizabeth. The men, on the other hand, were quite oblivious to the strained atmosphere. They were soon engaged in conversation about the merits of the new steamers, currently in construction on the Clyde, which would soon be replacing the *Lord of Lorn* and her sister vessels.

The evening passed quickly; the company was well mixed, and Elizabeth and Gordon were after all surprised at how much they enjoyed talking to so many new people.

As they picked their way across the park towards their own little cottage, they laughed together about the anecdotes they had heard from both McDuff and from Angus and chewed over the characters of some of the farmers. Gordon reflected aloud that Annabel's looks were so much improved by her pregnancy, he wondered what that state would achieve in Elizabeth's already perfect body.

For this remark, he received a severe slap, where it would hurt him the least, and they ran off, hand in hand, to their cottage by the shore.

PART V

PART V

1

August continued to bring a mixture of bright days and stormy ones. The sea would be still as a mill pond for a few hours, then a wind would get up and soon the channel was a seething cauldron in which the slate-boats were tossed unmercifully, and those fishermen caught out of the shelter of the island feared for their lives. Old seamen who had travelled the oceans of the world likened the storms to the Indian monsoons.

September arrived at last, and with it a period of calm weather. Each day was filled with changing colour, from the moment that the red skies dawning in the east turned to vivid, cloudless blue, until the sun set behind Mull in one glorious burst of scarlet and orange.

The hills bloomed with purple heather and yellow whins. Bracken died to a splendid chestnut brown while the rowans bent to the weight of their profusion of bright red berries.

Swallows which for weeks past had soared and swooped after the midges swarming in the long grasses by the roadside, and the myriad insects which darted across the still waters of the lochs, gave way to flocks of noisy starlings; while on every post and vantage point buzzards perched, awaiting their own particular harvest of unwary young rabbits and voles. On the high crags, golden eagle fledglings tried their wings. Abandoned to their own devices by parents weary of the summer's hunting, they hovered over upland lochs and pastures, ready to swoop on anything which moved.

It was the time for harvesting. Every croft in the parish now needed extra help to get in the meagre crop of oats and barley. Potatoes, too, must be lifted and stored before the wet weather set in again. Along the valley bottoms, the flax was cut, and the women, up to their ankles in the cold mountain water, took up the sheaves, banged them on the rocks to loosen the fibres, and laid them back to rot further.

The countless and varied tasks called for every man, woman and child to work from dawn until dusk. On many a croft, there were insufficient bodies to carry out all that was required. It was the time for the 'travellers' to arrive.

From the Lowlands they came, where the harvest started earlier. They followed the West Coast northwards, only turning south again when the severe winter weather threatened to strand them in desolate mountain country. They moved around with their homes on their backs, or in the flat, horse-drawn carts which they called yokes.

These were true travellers, the real tinkers of the Highlands. They had no fixed abode, they drank and they smoked tobacco, but they lived by a code as strict as that of any church elder. They took no pride in possessions . . . what they had they used or they gave away. When a friend or a kinsman was in trouble, the problem became everyone's to solve. No widow was left to fend for herself; no orphan went for long without a foster family.

Because they were outside the law, the tinkers often fell foul of the Sheriff's men. Some landlords had them moved on, not allowing them to pitch tents on their land, even for a night.

Others were more benevolent. Stirling had never discouraged the travellers, appreciating the value of such an industrious, itinerant workforce.

This summer, however, as the tinkers drove their yolks in to the familiar camping ground, above Ballahuan farmhouse, they met the Factor's men, armed with staves and pitchforks, barring their way into the glen.

Most of the travellers turned back and found their way to friendly crofts or else moved further north to other estates.

When Mary Black and her family came trudging along the path which wound its tortuous route around the headland, she was dismayed to find that the glen was empty of tents, and there were no familiar faces waiting to greet her.

She had been so sure that they would arrive ahead of her . . . after all, they had yokes and were not forced to walk, weighed down by their heavy packs.

Mary had owned a yoke when her man was alive. She had been forced to sell both cart and pony to get food for the weans during the last winter. Hampered as she was by her slow method of travel, she was unlikely to accumulate enough provisions to see them through the next.

Her last hope had been to catch up with the clan and throw herself upon their mercy.

Despairing, she sat down on a stone at the head of the glen. Her children, releasing the burden which each of them carried, its size appropriate to the age of the child, collapsed beside her.

Wee Rab clung to her skirts. She looked down at the boy, noting his flushed face and watery eyes.

'Are ye tired, ma wee Rabbie?' she queried in her soft lilting voice.

'Aye, Mither, and so hot!' As he spoke the little lad, perhaps five or six years old, tore off his frayed and patched jersey, exposing his frail limbs to the cool September breeze.

Mary noticed the rash at once. She touched his brow, and frowned when she felt the heat. The child had a fever, no doubt about it, and she with no roof to put over their heads.

An elderly man, supporting his rheumatic legs by means of a stout walking stick, approached them slowly from the village of Ballahuan down the glen.

When he came abreast of the weary group of travellers, he halted and peered intently at Mary for a few minutes.

'Why, I do believe it is Mrs Black back again!' he declared. 'You and your husband were working at Ballahuan Farm last autumn, were you not?'

'Oh, yes, sir,' she exclaimed, delighted to be recognised by a friendly face. 'You will be the good doctor who took care of my Johnny when his chest was bad.'

Major Lovat took off his hat politely and enquired, 'How is Mr Black keeping now?'

'He died in the spring, sir, as the snows were melting. We were on Arran, sheltering in a cave. It was gey cold, and there was little enough for the bairns to eat. I didna know he was giving his share to the weans until it was too late. Coughed up a tuil of blood, he did, and died in ma arms.'

'I am sorry to hear that, ma'am,' said the Major, showing a genuine compassion for her plight. 'Were you hoping to find work here again?'

'Word went round that Johnny's family were meeting up here. I thought they might take one or two of the wee ones off ma hons.'

It was not callousness which prompted the woman to seek to farm out her children. Mary knew that some childless couple in the clan would be pleased to raise one of her boys as their own. Male children were at a premium, for they soon developed strength enough to perform the kind of work which would earn good money. The girls were less easy to place, but she knew of one cousin who was anxious to complete her family of three sons, and unable to have another child of her own.

She took a quick glance across the path to where her eldest girl, Emily, was playing with ten-month-old Christopher. No, she could not spare Emily, but Patty was another matter altogether. Patty was seven years old, with golden hair and the face of an angel. No one could fail to love her. Farmers' wives fell over themselves to give her sweet-meats and clothes. She was an asset to any travelling band. Yes, it would have to be Patty.

Her thoughts were interrupted by Major Lovat. What was that he was telling her?

'Yes, things have changed greatly around here in the past year,' he was saying. 'The new tenant no longer farms the estate. I fear there is no harvest to gather this year, other than the few brace of pheasant that his new gamekeeper has managed to rear.'

Mary stared at him in disbelief.

'But His Lordship's estates have always been well farmed,' she cried in dismay. 'How has he allowed such a thing to happen?'

'It seems that since the tragic death of his young wife, the Marquis has stayed away from his Argyle lands. He leaves his interests in the hands of Mr Lugas, his Factor.'

'Surely some of the farmers have crops to harvest?' Mary pleaded. She could not believe that the Marquis could desert his lands and leave those who depended upon him for work, who had worked for his forefathers as far back as anyone could remember, without a place to stay and food for their bellies.

'I believe that most of the farmers have sufficient help already with their crops,' the Major said gently, hating to see the anguished expression on her face. 'There is just one possibility,' he added hastily. 'The crofter McDougal who has the small farm on Eisdalsa Island needs help. One of his children has left home, and his younger daughter is in school. A very bright girl they do say. He is trying to gather in his crops with just his son Jack and his wife. You might try there.'

As Mary began to thank him, he added, 'Of course, McDougal is a poor man himself. You may have to work for food, and shelter in the barn.'

'Anything will do, just so long as we can get in out of the cold tonight. Thank you kindly, sir.'

'Tell McDougal I sent you,' called Lovat as they went on their way.

He watched the little party gather up their belongings and turn to follow the path, back the way they had come. The curly-headed boy, clinging closely to his mother, looked flushed. As he gathered his pack and heaved it on to his narrow shoulders, he coughed, a dry rasping sound which shuddered through the wasted little frame. The old physician wondered how soon it would be before the child followed his poor father to the grave.

McDougal was pleased to see Mary arrive. Most of the energetic travelling men, having discovered the change in circumstances at the Ballahuan Estate, had already taken work on the larger, more productive crofts on Seileach.

Mary required no introduction from Major Lovat. Both she and her husband were known to the local farmers as a hard-working pair who could be trusted to do an honest day's toil for a fair wage.

McDougal was sorry to hear of Johnny Black's sad demise, of course, but the widow and her children could do the work he required, and would not demand hard cash in payment.

'I wilna pay wages, Mary, you must understand. But you and the weans may have all the food you can eat, and shelter in the barn while the work lasts.'

'I canna ask for mair. Thank you kindly, sir.'

In a very short time, Mary's little family had made itself at home in the loft of the old stone barn. The roofing slates were loosened, missing even in one corner, but there was plenty of clean sweet-smelling straw.

Rab, worn out by the walking and the added burden of his fever, lay down in the straw and instantly fell asleep.

As Mary settled her little ones for the night, determined that they should sleep well and be ready for arduous work the next day, a young girlish voice called out to her from below: 'My mother has sent you out this dish of broth, Mrs Black, and a few bannocks. May I climb up with the food?'

'We shall be pleased to see you, my dear,' called Mary, 'but you must let my lad come and help you with the pot.'

Unbidden, her eldest son Calum climbed halfway down the ladder and reached for the steaming stew-pot which Ellen McDougal handed up to him.

Calum pulled up the pot and placed it in the straw at his mother's feet. The children gathered round, their bright eyes wide with wonder at such largesse, nostrils quivering with anticipation at the delicious scent issuing from the round iron vessel.

Ellen's head now appeared above the floor level. In an instant she was standing upright before them, a basket of bannocks and apples dangling from her right hand.

'The bannocks are special,' she declared as she laid the basket beside the pot of broth, 'I made them myself. They have fish in some, and those at the bottom have the first of the brambles!'

'It is a wonderful feast, little lady, you must thank your mother kindly for her generosity.'

'May I stay awhile and talk?' the girl asked eagerly. 'My mother tells me that you have been in these parts before.'

'Every year since I was a girl no older than yourself.'

Ellen watched the children devour the food she had brought as though they had not eaten for a week.

When they had all had their fill, Mary herself finished what was left of the broth. Then, taking the remaining bannocks, she wrapped them carefully in a clean cloth and placed them in her own, well-scrubbed basin.

'These will do fine for their breakfast.' She smiled at Ellen as she handed her the empty basket. 'My, but you are a fine wee baker, miss.'

Ellen hesitated before standing up to leave. She looked wistfully at the tinker woman. Mary thought she knew what was coming next.

'Mrs Black,' Ellen began, choosing her words carefully, because she did not wish to cause any offence, 'do you have the second sight? Would you tell my fortune for a piece of silver?'

Mary smiled at the crofter's daughter.

'Why, bless my soul, but you are a trifle young to be thinking of a lover, are ye no'?'

'I am thirteen years old next month.' Ellen drew herself up as tall as she could. 'Other girls have had their palms read, and they are much younger than me!'

'Show me your sill'er then, missy, and I will see what I can do.'

Eagerly, the child searched out the silver threepenny which was carefully tied into the corner of her apron. She placed it in the woman's outstretched hand, and watched as it disappeared into a copious canvas sack which hung from the tinker's belt.

Squatting down beside Mary, the girl stretched out her hand for the woman to see.

She examined the grubby little palm in silence, pausing in her scanning from time to time; going back occasionally over an area she had just passed; rubbing at a particularly dirty spot so that she could see more clearly. She let out an involuntary cry of dismay at one moment, then noticing the anxious look on her client's face, she laughed.

'Such a dirty little hand. How can anyone make a proper reading, and in this light?'

'Oh, please, Mrs Black, what do you see? Shall I marry young? Will he be a handsome husband? Shall I have many children . . . boys? Oh, how I hope they will be boys!'

Mary closed the little hand with her own large roughened brown one.

'Your future will be a rosy one, with all the good things that you wish for yourself, my dear. Have no fear, the Lord will take care to see that you are happy.'

Emily Black looked sharply at her mother. What could her words mean? The tinker girl had studied palm reading alongside Mary ever since she had been able to understand its purpose, but she had never heard her mother give such a strange reading.

'I am studying the reading, miss,' she declared. 'May I see your hand too?'

As Ellen willingly offered her hand to Emily, the tinker's daughter caught sight of her mother's warning look and noted the almost imperceptible shake of her head.

She studied the girl's hand and understood. Without the slightest sign that there was anything amiss, she smiled at Ellen and released her, saying brightly, 'My mother is always right, you know. The Lord will take good care of you.'

Ellen seemed satisfied. Mother and daughter avoided each other's gaze until their visitor had climbed down the ladder with her pot, and had caught the basket which Emily handed to her.

When they heard the barn door close, Emily came and sat close behind her mother. Her eyes filled with tears.

'There, there, little Emily,' crooned Mary Black, 'you must not take it so hard. Some of us are born to suffer. It cannot always be good news that we see.'

Wee Rabbie slept fitfully that night and by morning the rash had reached the extremities of his wasted little body.

Leaving the other children in Emily's care, Mary climbed down the ladder with the boy in her arms and carried him to the door of the croft house.

Like many such houses, the family lived at one end of the building, while the cattle were housed at the other. When the cold winds of winter swept across the island and engulfed the house, it was the steaming bodies of the milch cows which helped to keep the family warm.

She found the door to the byre open, and the cheerful sound of milk squirting into a pail was music to her ears.

'Good day to you, ma'am,' she called out to Mrs McDougal who, crouched over her task, had not noticed the presence of her visitor. She jumped up, startled. The cow protested with a low moan and rattled the bucket with her back foot.

'Oh, I am sorry to disturb you, ma'am,' Mary apologised, 'but I wonder, could you spare a wee drop of milk for the wean? He is no' well at all.'

Mrs McDougal wiped her hands on her sacking apron and came to look at the child.

'Oh, the poor wee thing,' she cried. 'Sit you here, Mrs Black, while I fill your cup.'

The good woman took Mary's tin cup and dipped in into the bucket.

Rab needed no coaxing. Eagerly he drained the cup and held it out for more. The good woman refilled it but said warningly to Mary, 'Do not give it to him all at once. It will make him sick.'

'Thank you, ma'am.' She took the milk and had turned to leave when the farmer's wife called her back.

'You will not be taking the child to the field all day?' she demanded.

'I have nowhere else to leave him,' replied Mary. 'All the children, save only the baby, must work beside me. I canna spare ony of ma girls, to watch over him.'

'Leave him here with me,' was the kindly suggestion. 'You can make him a bed in the sweet straw yonder and I shall keep my eye on him while I make the cheese.'

'Thank you, lady,' replied Mary, grateful to her hostess for her thoughtful offer. 'I thought I would brew up a small potion of pennyroyal to give him. Would you be so kind as to dose him when he wakes?'

'Anything you wish,' replied Mrs McDougal.

Mary Black had learned her skills from her own mother. Calling across the yard for Emily to accompany her, she strode down to the water meadow beside the burn, searching for water-mint. Soon she spotted a clump of the blue flowers and pointed it out to Emily.

'Yonder is the pennyroyal,' she exclaimed. 'Pick me a good bunch of the stems . . . flowers and leaves.' Emily would carry on the work of healing when her mother was dead and buried. So it had always been, mother to daughter, the healing art passed down the centuries.

'Go you back to the house and ask if you may boil water over the fire. When it is boiling, pour the water over the mint and leave it to stand. Tell Mrs McDougal to give it to wee Rabbie when he wakes.'

The little band of workers toiled throughout the long, hot day.

McDougal congratulated himself on his foresight in accepting the traveller woman and her brood. The lad, Calum, worked as hard as any man, and the eldest girl too proved able and willing to do more than her share. As for the pretty little one . . . Patty did they call her? . . . well, what she lacked in application, she made up for in charm.

It was the last Wednesday in the month, the day set aside for Martha, the eldest McDougal daughter, to visit her parents, bringing with her young Iain, her son, now nearly three years old. The bairn was a bright wee fellow, lively as a cricket and forever in mischief.

At the Castle where he spent most of his time, he ran riot through the kitchen and up the back stairs. In his shadow pranced little Lord Edward, just a week or two his junior but a great deal less precocious than his companion.

There was a native wit about Iain which was to stand him in good stead all his life. He was strong, for such a small child, and had never ailed for a day since he was born.

Edward was of more delicate material. His frame was narrow like that of his mother, the late Marchioness. His skin was fair, hair so blond as to be almost white. His eyelashes and brows too were so light that they were almost invisible. The penetrating gaze from his deep blue eyes was quite startling in its intensity.

While Iain seemed immune from all ills, Edward succumbed to every childhood disease that appeared in the district. Even had David not given his word to the Marquis to keep an eye on the child, he would have been a constant visitor to his young Lordship.

It was because of yet another sniffle that Edward had not accompanied Iain and his mother to the McDougal household today. Usually on fine Wednesdays Mrs Lugas was happy to allow her charge to take the ferry to the Island with his nursemaid. Little Edward loved the animals, and relished the welcome he received at the hands of the kindly crofter and his wife.

Martha found her mother hard at work in the cold little cellar where she made her cream and butter and stored the fruits of her labours.

The women hugged one another and settled to exchange gossip accumulated over the past month. Neither paid heed to little Iain who, having received his customary hugs and kisses from his grandmother, had wandered off into the byre to talk to the cows.

He stumbled over a small pair of legs, poking out of the straw. When he picked himself up he found that he was looking into the watery eyes of a rather scruffy boy, several years his senior.

The boy seemed startled and looked around him in a dazed fashion.

Rab had slept soundly all morning and felt much better. His rash was itching but his head did not ache so much, and the bright rays of the sun, piercing the gaps in the roof of the byre, no longer troubled him.

'Who're you?' enquired the infant, in his engaging little lisp.

'Rab,' replied the stranger. 'What's your name then?'

'Iain James McDougal,' said the mite proudly. 'This is my grandfather's croft,' he added, making sure that the stranger appreciated his importance.

It was as though the little lad needed to establish his role in this household in order to counteract the fact that, up at the Castle, he was always relegated by the staff to a position subordinate to that of the 'young Master'.

'What are ye doing here?' Iain demanded.

'I'm sick,' Rab replied, rather proudly. 'Ma mither and sisters are working in the fields alongside ma brother Calum . . . getting the harvest.'

'What's "harvest"?' enquired the tot. The previous year he had been barely walking, and the idea was new to him.

'It's when the corn is cut and the tatties lifted,' explained the bigger boy. 'We travel all about, wherever a farmer needs help with his crops.'

'Would you go as far as the quarries?' asked Iain, his eyes wide with admiration. 'The quarries' was a place at the edge of his experience. His world ended there. Factor Lugas had promised to take him there one day, and Edward, when they were *big* boys. It was a dream world which lay just over the horizon.

'Which ones?' asked Rab, who in his few short years had passed by many quarries, both by the shore, and away inland, where great boulders of granite were gouged from the mountainside and crushed to make road stone, or dressed and carted to the city for building.

Iain's eyes opened wide as the traveller boy told him of the things he had seen and the people he had met. He spoke also of his father, telling the infant the same little stories upon which he had himself been reared.

After a time the wee boy grew silent and his eyes filled with tears. Rab asked him, 'What ails you? Do ye no feel well?'

Iain sobbed, a great big tear rolling down his cheek. 'I dinna have a faither,' he wept. 'It must be grand to have a faither.'

Rab nodded sombrely. 'Aye,' he agreed, 'it was so.'

'Was?' The younger child did not understand. 'Do you no have a faither the noo?'

'He is deid.' Rab tried to sound matter-of-fact but the word still hurt.

'What's deid?' asked Iain.

'He is gone to live with Jesus.' Rab gave the answer he had been given himself. He did not understand it either.

Iain would have sought further clarification had not his mother come to find him at that moment.

She started when she saw the other boy, sitting up now in the straw, with little Iain close beside him, hanging upon his words.

'Why, who is this ye have found, wee Iain?' she demanded.

'His name is Rab and he is my friend,' announced her son.

Martha sought out her mother.

'Is that no a wee tinker's boy in the byre, Mother?' she asked. While Martha knew that Mrs Lugas had few reservations about a visit to her parents, she was quite sure that consorting with travellers would not be so readily accepted and was thankful that the young master had not come with her today.

'Och, he is just a sick wee child,' said Mrs McDougal. 'His mother left him with me while she works in the field.'

The kindly woman went over to Rab, felt his forehead and examined his rash.

'How do you feel now, ma wee man?' she enquired. 'Your fever has gone, thanks be.'

Martha stood dumbstruck, 'Fever, Mother!' she cried. 'Do you tell me the lad has a fever and young Iain here has been with him all this time!'

'Oh, it is the measles just,' the good woman waved away her daughter's fears. 'All the weans must get it sometimes, better sooner nor later.'

A thought struck her then. 'Mrs Black, the boy's mother, has made up a potion for him. It certainly has done the trick. Come, my wee laddie, it is time for another dose.'

She reached down the bottle which Mary had given her that morning, shook it and poured a generous measure into the spoon.

'I will ask Mrs Black to make up a bottle for you to take back with you, Martha, in case the wean should need it!'

By the time that Mary and her family returned from the fields, Martha McDougal and little Iain were well upon their way. Martha was terrified lest Iain should contract the disease and pass it on to Master Edward. She had no fears for her own healthy boy, but the Laird's son was another matter.

Annabel's child was due in two or three days.

David had crowded his work into the past week, making a number of routine calls upon his patients and ensuring that those on regular medication had sufficient to keep them going for a while.

William had promised to sail *The Saucy Nancy* across to Mull on the following day. High tide was near noon and David felt that one more morning surgery would be sufficient to keep all his patients happy.

He had sent a note to Major Lovat requesting him to see to any unforeseen accidents while he was away. The sooner he reached his brother's house now, the better he would be pleased. Annabel expected him to be by her side for the birth of their child, and he wanted it so.

He passed through the waiting room and heard not one but two . . . no, three rasping dry coughs.

He took a quick look at the young patients, each seated upon a parent's knee. He felt a forehead here, counted a pulse there, looked behind ears and pulled up a shirt to find the tell-tale rash.

His heart sank. 'Measles,' he muttered under his breath, and cursed himself for not having left for Mull the day before.

To the mothers who patiently awaited his verdict, he gave instructions to take their little ones home at once, and put them to bed.

'Keep the patient warm but not too warm. Plenty of boiled water to drink, and whey, not milk. Otherwise, starve them until they are well enough to ask for food. Keep your child out of the direct sunlight,' he urged them, 'and if there is sickness or diarrhoea, give a dose of castor oil.'

The Village women were used to children's ailments; he felt sure that they would cope in his absence.

Having cleared the waiting room of measles cases, he was left with a few elderly quarrymen with lung troubles, and a pregnant woman. The latter he dismissed without ceremony.

'You have another two months to go, Mrs McFee, and as far as I can see there will be no complications. I would advise you to steer clear of the measles, if you can, but have no fear. Newborn infants are unlikely to contract the disease, at least while they are feeding on their mother's milk. Should you have any worries while I am away, go to Mrs McGillivray. She will help you I am sure. I shall be back before the week is out!'

He nearly got away.

He was aboard the ferry in which old Ian had agreed to carry him out to *The Saucy Nancy*, anchored in the Sound, when he saw Lugas's stable boy, signalling wildly from the shore. He asked Ian to row closer to the steamer pier so that he might hear what the lad was saying.

'Thank you for stopping, doctor,' called the boy. 'I have an urgent message from my mistress.'

David sighed, Mrs Lugas was over-anxious about her charge, she had probably heard about the measles epidemic.

By the time that Ian had pulled them up to the pier steps, the doctor had all but given up the idea of sailing for Mull that day.

The stable lad took the steps two at a time.

'My mistress says to come quick, sir,' he cried. 'Miss Martha's boy is sick with fever, and the mistress is afeared that the young master will catch it.'

This was indeed worrying news. Little Edward had had several chest infections in the last few months. He would not fare well if he caught the measles now.

Turning to the ferryman, David requested him to row out to *The Saucy Nancy* and tell Mr Whylie that their trip would have to be cancelled.

'Ask him to wait until tomorrow, will you, Ian? Say that I have been called to the Castle. He will understand.'

Yes, he will understand, thought David as he mounted the mare offered to him by the Factor's man. But will Annabel?

Little Iain McDougal lay in a darkened room on the top floor. Sun tried to penetrate around the edges of the thick curtain which had been drawn across the dormer window.

David strode across and pulled the curtains apart, throwing open the casement.

Mrs Meecham pursed her lips but remained silent. She knew about measles. Children should be kept in the dark lest they go blind!

Martha sat beside her boy, sponging his hot little body with cool water.

David felt his pulse, noticed the rash behind the ears and searched inside the child's mouth for tell-tale white spots.

This caused Iain to cough, the familiar rasping, choking sound which David seemed to have been hearing all day.

'Well, as I am sure you know, Mrs Meecham, we have a perfect case of measles here. It is the fourth that I have seen today.'

'The child has been nowhere near the Village,' said Mrs Meecham. 'Why should wee Iain have caught it?'

'Has he not been with any children outside the Castle?' asked David, mystified. 'He must have had contact with someone who had the disease already.'

Martha, in fear of losing her employment if Mrs Lugas should hear of the traveller's child, shook her head and remained silent.

'Well,' said David, 'you are doing all that can be done for the poor little mite. Here is a mixture which should help the cough and settle his stomach. Give him a spoonful every four hours.' He handed Martha a bottle containing ipecacuanha, bicarbonate of soda and camphor. He had made up a batch after morning surgery, expecting a heavy demand for the medicine.

'If he suffers from colic, or his bowels are affected, a dose of castor oil should do the trick.'

As Mrs Meecham pointedly walked to the window to draw the curtains closed, he intervened.

'Leave the window, Mrs Meecham, the light will do no harm if he is not looking directly into it, and the room is too small to be adequately ventilated with the curtains drawn.'

The housekeeper did not hold with his new-fangled ideas, but held her tongue. Mrs Lugas would not have a word said against the young doctor, and Mrs Meecham knew her place.

David took his leave of Martha, and allowed the housekeeper to see him down the stairs.

'Will you take a look at the little master, now you are here, doctor?' Mrs Lugas has emerged from the nursery as David was led along the corridor to the main staircase.

'The boys have been together all the time until today. Surely if Iain has measles then Master Edward has it too?'

She was right, of course. David had hoped that the children had been kept apart when the McDougal boy started to ail. If they were together until the rash appeared, then Edward had already been exposed.

'Oh, very well, Mrs Lugas,' he agreed, 'perhaps I should look at him, but I will wash my hands before going in.'

When they entered the nursery, the little boy looked up from his haphazard pile of coloured bricks. They had held his attention for fully fifteen minutes and he was ready for some new diversion. Instantly recognising his friend, Edward came running to David, arms wide, ready for a welcoming hug.

'Hello, my little man!' David beamed at him as he gathered the child in his arms. 'What are you building, eh?'

'Bridge,' announced the little boy.

'A bridge, do you say? What a fine one it is too.' David admired the structure and at the same time checked behind his patient's ears. No sign of rash there.

He felt the child's forehead. It was cool.

'Now, young Edward,' David sat down on the low nursing chair and pulled the boy towards him, 'I want to see what you have inside your mouth . . . open wide.'

To persuade the boy to do as he wished, David opened his own mouth as wide as he could.

Lord Edward Aberfeldy, heir to the Stirling fortune, gazed with interest into the yawning chasm.

'Dark in there!' he lisped, pointing right inside at the black circle where David's throat began.

'Now you,' he encouraged. The boy opened wide. The doctor studied the walls of the cheeks but could find nothing to give any indication of the disease.

'What else did you see? What did you see?' demanded the imperious little voice.

'I saw . . . right down . . . inside your BIG . . . TOE!' cried the doctor, and the small boy squealed with delight.

'My toe, my toe, he saw my toe!' he ran laughing and calling out into the gallery.

Once more, David washed his hands solemnly while Mrs Lugas and the majestic housekeeper, her face softened now by the presence of her precious charge, waited anxiously for his verdict.

'He has no symptoms as yet,' he said, 'but the infection can take up to three weeks to show itself. If the boys have been together until now, there is little hope that Edward can escape infection. Let us pray that it is a mild attack.'

By the time that David reached home, he had decided that to go to Mull now might be unwise. The epidemic seemed to be widespread. He could only think that it must have been carried into school for so many cases to appear on one day. He had probably seen only a small sample of the children affected. The majority of women were only too familiar with the course of the disease, and would think it money ill spent to call in the doctor. Only the quarrymen, with their health insurance scheme, could afford such luxury.

Measles was not itself a life-threatening disease, but in a poor community where damp houses and meagre diet sapped the natural resistance of young bodies, the complications arising, particularly in the lungs, could be dangerous.

He called out to Morag as he strode into the dispensary and began mixing further supplies of the potions he felt sure he would be needing.

She came and stood in the doorway, watching him work.

'It is quite a serious epidemic, is it not.' It was a statement, not a question.

'So it seems, Mama.'

'You cannot go to Annabel now.'

'No. I am needed here.'

'What can I do to help? Let me do the dispensing, I do know how.'

She thought wistfully of the many times that she and Hugh had worked together during just such a crisis as this. She wanted so much to be needed.

'You could help me most, Mama, by going across to Annabel, and being with her when the child is born.'

David understood Morag's resentment of the way they had deceived her about their need to marry. He had hoped that time would heal the rift, but try as she might, Annabel had been unable to thaw the icy atmosphere between herself and her mother-in-law.

For a long time, Morag worked silently at his side; handing him the ingredients he needed; fetching out the little glass bottles; filling and labelling them as the potions were completed.

Their task was nearly done when a loud knocking at the surgery door broke the silence.

David went himself to open up.

An urchin of about ten or eleven years, dressed in an assortment of rags and clearly a tinker's child, stood before him, panting from having run a fair distance.

'Are you the doctor?'

The child struggled to get his breath.

'Yes,' David replied, holding the boy's arm, lest he collapse from his exertions.

'I am come from McDougal's croft, across the water there.'

'I know it,' said David. 'What is amiss?'

'It is the young lady . . . Miss Ellen. She has a sore fever and the mistress is beside hersel. Ma mither has done all she can, but Miss Ellen just lies there as if she were deid!'

'I will come at once,' David promised. 'Run to the stable and tell my man to saddle the mare. I will fetch my bag.'

He packed the medical bag hurriedly, while Morag completed the dispensing.

As he was about to leave, she at last broke her silence.

'I shall not be here when you return,' she told him. 'I shall send Sheilagh to the pier to engage a fisherman to take me across to Bunessan.'

Overwhelmed with gratitude, David pulled her into his arms and kissed her lovingly. He knew what it had taken for her to make such a decision.

'Oh, Mama, thank you,' he exclaimed. 'I promised Annabel that nothing would keep me away . . . only you will convince her that for me to leave now is out of the question. Apart from my duty to my patients, I would not wish to carry the infection further afield.'

'How will you manage here while I am gone?' She gazed at the evidence of their afternoon's work.

'Sheilagh will take care of me, and I can always enlist Annie McGillivray's help if things get worse.'

The mare was waiting in the stable yard when he emerged from the house. There was no sign of the boy. David supposed that he had already set off, back along the road to the croft.

As the doctor's horse carried him towards the village, a little knot of figures watched from the hill above the house.

Satisfied that the doctor had heeded the urgency of her message, Mary Black waited for Calum to catch up, before following her little family round the bend and out of sight.

She had done her best for the crofter's child, but from the night that she had read the girl's palm, she had expected disaster. If the villagers got to know that it was her wee Rabbie who had brought the disease, they would hound her from the district.

She would not give them that satisfaction.

2

T he tinker's boy had given a very graphic description of the coma which Ellen McDougal presented. David examined her for vital signs, finding little response even to tests for the most basic involuntary nervous activity.

He stood up slowly, shaking his head.

'You are doing everything that can be done for her, Mrs McDougal,' he assured the girl's mother. 'The measles germ usually confines itself to the respiratory and digestive systems, but in a few cases, and this is one of them, the lining of the brain is affected.

'Ellen is still able to breathe, and her heart beat and pulses are regular, though weakened. She may stay like this for days, or she may revive within hours.' He paused, feeling it would be unkind to give them false hopes. 'She may never emerge from the coma, in which case her heart and lungs will eventually fail altogether.'

The mother's hand flew to her lips to stifle the cry of anguish which rose from the depths of her being. When at last she removed it, her livid finger marks remained.

McDougal stared, unbelieving, at the doctor.

'You canna mean that, doctor?' he murmured. 'Not ma' wee angel. No . . . not ma wee clever little bird.'

David cleared his throat which was constricted with emotion. Practical advice was what was needed here, activity to occupy these poor distraught people.

'Continue to bathe her with tepid water,' he instructed. 'A little calamine will ease the irritation.' Although unconscious, the child continuously made scratching motions, tearing at her inflamed skin.

'If she regains consciousness and can swallow, get her to take plenty of fluid . . . boiled water or a little thin broth. Give her a dose of this medicine every four hours.'

He placed the standard mixture on the kitchen table, knowing in his heart that it would not be effective.

'I will call in again in the morning.'

At the door of the croft, he paused.

'What of your other children? Do they have any symptoms of the disease?'

'There is only the boy now, he had measles as a tot,' Mrs McDougal replied mechanically. 'Martha is away up at the Castle. Her wean has it, as well you know, doctor. Otherwise there was just the wee tinker laddie, but he was fine by the time they left us the day!'

'Tinkers?' David was startled. 'Was that the boy who came to the house to fetch me?'

'Oh, no,' protested McDougal, 'that would have been young Jack. He wasna sick. No, it was his young brother . . . Rabbie, she called him. Aye, he was right as rain when they went away. None of the others was sick.'

'Have they been staying here for long?' David demanded.

'Three weeks tomorrow,' replied Mrs McDougal. 'Wee Rabbie had the fever when they arrived.'

'Ellen was with them, was she?' David was making rapid calculations in his head.

'Oh, aye, we couldna keep her out of their road. Every afternoon, straight out o' school, she was up in the fields alongside the bigger girl . . . Emily was her name. They were quite inseparable!'

There was his answer. Ellen had carried the disease to school with her. Twenty odd days for incubation, and then the outbreak he had witnessed today.

It was some time later when he realised that, while this accounted for most of the reported cases, it did not explain how Master Iain McDougal came to have the disease. He suspected the truth but, realising the effect such knowledge could have upon the prospects of the McDougal's elder daughter, decided to keep it to himself. The damage was done now. Whatever his investigations should reveal, these poor people had paid too heavy a price for their carelessness.

As David prepared to leave, Mrs McDougal begged him to wait. In a few minutes, she emerged from the dairy carrying a basket, the contents of which were concealed beneath a white cloth.

'We canna pay you, doctor.' The woman spoke quickly in her embarrassment. 'Will you take these few things to your good lady?'

David would have waved her away in protest, but McDougal himself had followed his wife.

'Do not deny Katrina her pride, doctor,' he pleaded. 'She has little else to sustain her.'

Unable to argue further in the race of such stoicism, David took the basket and thanked her. He touched his hat in salute, and strode off down the track which led to the ferry.

Ellen McDougal regained consciousness after three days. At first her parents attributed the changes in her personality to weakness following her illness. They were not unduly concerned, assuming that when she regained her health, her mind would also clear.

David, only too aware of the extreme poverty of the crofting family, restrained himself from making professional calls upon Ellen during the period of her recovery. He did, however, deliberately make a detour past the McDougal croft whenever he was called to attend patients in the vicinity.

Many of the quarriers' children had succumbed to the disease, so that hardly a day went by when he did not have an excuse to pass the McDougal home. If he managed to catch sight of Mrs McDougal, he would enquire about his patient's progress, but without an invitation to enter the cottage, had no opportunity of seeing Ellen. Mrs McDougal answered his enquiries cheerfully enough.

'She is doing well now, doctor. The fever is quite gone.' Or, 'No so bad, thank ye, doctor, the little lassie will be back at school soon enough.'

Today when he called there was no sign of the farmer's wife. The door to the cottage stood open and a thin wisp of smoke suggested the fire had been left burning in the grate.

He looked in through the low doorway, his eyes requiring a few moments to accustom themselves to the gloom.

At first it seemed that the kitchen was deserted. He noticed a slight flutter of something white near the fireplace and stepped into the room, clearing his throat so as to warn whoever was there of his presence.

The sound seemed to have had an effect. The white shape became still.

David advanced further into the gloom and discovered that the person he had disturbed was little Ellen McDougal herself.

The child squatted on a 'creepy' stool, close to the meagre fire of peats. She clasped her arms around her chest, as though to protect herself from a blow. Her head was bent and she gazed, unseeing, at the dusty rag rug under her feet. She did not look up when he spoke.

'Good morning, Ellen,' David said, very quietly, so as not to frighten her. 'Where is your mother?'

The girl did not respond other than to commence a backwards and forwards rocking motion.

The doctor knelt on the floor before her. Very gently, he put his hand under her chin and lifted her head.

The child's white face was without expression. Her eyes stared vacantly into the fire. When David spoke directly to her, there was the smallest flicker of a response, but it was clear that the old Ellen, the clever vivacious child who had been destined, despite her sorry beginnings, for an academic career, had become a hopeless mental cripple.

A slight movement from the doorway alerted David to the presence of the girl's mother. He stood up and advanced towards her.

'Mrs McDougal, why did you not tell me? Has she been like this ever since she regained consciousness?'

The mother wrung her hands, and broke into a terrible, heaving sobbing.

David put his arm comfortingly around her shoulders and led her out into the crisp autumnal air.

'I feared that this might happen,' he said, as he sat her down on the rough-hewn seat beside the door. 'When you said nothing, I assumed that Ellen had recovered completely.'

'At first we thought it was something that would pass. Then, as the time went on, I grew impatient and tried to insist that she got up and about. She tries to do my bidding, but it seems that after a few minutes, she forgets what she has started to do and I find her back on the stool as you saw. Is it always to be like this now, doctor?'

David could see that the woman anticipated, despairingly, a future filled with nothing but heartbreaking memories.

'No one can say how such a case may turn out, Mrs McDougal. What you must do is to keep on trying to stimulate her mind. Talk to her, keep her on her feet doing something, no matter how simple or routine it seems. Even if it means constantly supervising her every activity, persevere.

'There is a spark of intelligence there, I am sure of it. Maybe, if you work really hard at it, she will improve.'

Katrina McDougal was not a woman to be defeated for long. The doctor's words put new vitality into her. There was some hope . . . something to work towards . . . something to look forward to after all.

She straightened her shoulders, drew the back of her hand across her tear-stained face, and rose to her feet.

'Och!' she cried, tugging at her apron and smoothing her bushy brown hair. 'Here am I wailing and moaning, and you with not even a dish o' tea to wet your whistle. Will you no come ben and take something?'

David politely declined her invitation, fearing he had already imposed himself upon the poor wretched woman for too long, but as he strode through the gate which she held open for him he said, 'Mrs McDougal, Ellen's case is of particular interest to me. I would like to follow her progress for my own researches. If you have no objection, I will call upon you from time to time to make my observations of her condition. At no cost to yourselves, of course!'

How could Katrina McDougal refuse the good doctor? It was the least she could do after all his kindness.

'Any time you wish, Dr Beaton,' she replied. 'We shall always be pleased to welcome you.'

It had been a difficult decision for Morag to take. She still could not bring herself to forgive Annabel for the wanton behaviour which had led to a marriage of convenience quite contrary to anything she had imagined for her youngest son.

She had convinced herself that the whole affair had been contrived by the hussy who was now her daughter-in-law. At times, she wished that David had never agreed to stay here, but had gone to London with his friend Joseph Lister. Had he done so, all this would never have happened.

Annabel would not thank her for making the journey to Mull. Had it not been for the prospect of spending some time in the company of her son Angus, of whom she saw so very little, she might never have agreed to David's request.

She went ashore at the sheltered inlet of Port Uisken, on the southern shore of the island of Mull.

The village boasted a small number of cottages, a schoolhouse and a tiny church. It was unlikely that she would find any means of transportation in the middle of the afternoon. Everywhere seemed to be lifeless and quite deserted.

Suddenly, from the direction of the forge which stood back from the track on the edge of the village, she heard a rhythmic clanging of steel upon steel. A horse whinnied and there was a sharp, deep-throated rebuff . . . how much more expressive was a swear word in the Gaelic, she reflected, smiling to herself.

She approached the door of the forge and placed her bags on the hard-trodden earth floor.

'Good day to you, Dougie McKerral,' she called.

The hammering ceased. From the dark interior the smith emerged. He was a mountain of a man. His bare, muscular arms, with hands like huge black dinner plates, were spread wide in welcome.

'Why, it is Morag MacAdam hersel,' he cried in delight. 'It iss too long you have been away, so it iss.'

'Nothing seems to have changed here, Dougie.' She smiled up into the heavily bearded face which she had known since her childhood.

'Och, we keep going just the same, Miss Morag.' He had never used her married name. In the way of the Highlanders, a woman retained her rights to property and, if she chose, her maiden name, even after her marriage.

'You will be away to see your Angus, I am thinking.' The smith sat down on a handily up-turned barrel to light his pipe.

'Yes, indeed,' Morag replied. 'Will it inconvenience you if I leave my bags here until he can fetch them?' she enquired, indicating the two carpet-bags with which she had struggled from the pier.

'Aye, leave them down by,' he replied. 'I will get McDuff's man to drop them off when he comes for the mare here.' He indicated a glossy grey hunter who gazed round at him mournfully, no doubt anticipating the hot iron shoe, glowing redly amongst the coals.

'Thank you, Dougie.' She tied her bonnet more firmly and hitched up her skirts, for the track was rough.

'You will be here for the birthing.' It was a statement, not a question.

'Master David's wife is a bonny lass. It will be a braw wee lamb she'll be having, and nae mistake.'

'Let us hope so,' Morag replied. 'As long as the child is strong and healthy, I am sure that Annabel will be satisfied.' If her answer was a trifle stiff, Dougie did not appear to notice.

'We shall be along to wet the babbie's heid, never you fear!'

'You will be more than welcome,' she responded, and set off along the road to Bunessan village.

The rough track wound upwards, away from the shore. Despite the lateness of the season it was a warm afternoon, and Morag soon shed both cape and bonnet. With her arms bare, and her hair blowing in the stiff breeze, which strengthened as she ascended the highest crest upon the two-mile route, she felt as though she were a young girl again and her mind went back to the day when she had first met Hugh Beaton.

So wrapt was she in her memories that Morag failed to notice a tall figure approaching her along the track.

When at last she raised her eyes and peered into the distance, she started, obliged to pause for a moment to catch her breath.

With Hugh so recently in her thoughts, it was natural enough for her to have mistaken her eldest son for his father. Here was the same tall, willowy frame, the flashing red hair, and bold easy movement which had, long ago, won her heart so inexorably.

'Why, Mama,' he called to her, as they approached one another, 'this is a surprise. I had thought to meet David coming up from the pier. I did not know that you intended to accompany him.'

'David will not be here today,' Morag replied bluntly. 'I am come to explain his absence to Annabel.'

'Not coming, eh? Annabel will not take kindly to your news. She has been hanging upon every footstep for the last two days, expecting to hear him come bursting through the door!'

'There is an epidemic of measles,' Morag explained. 'David feared that he might carry the disease across with him, and did not wish to endanger Annabel or the baby.'

She said nothing of the case of Ellen McDougal, and David's concern at the virulence of this particular epidemic. Ellen might have died. Perhaps other children would be less fortunate than she.

Whether intentionally or not, her words seemed to convey something more than this simple explanation. Angus looked at his mother thoughtfully, but refrained from making any further observation. He knew as well as David that there was no chance of his brother transmitting the disease. It was conveyed from patient to patient. He also knew that there was no danger to a newborn babe. Why then had his brother declined to be here for his child's birth? Was the epidemic of measles just an excuse?

*   *   *

Unaware of the strain under which her husband had been working, Annabel too was only too ready to be unconvinced by her mother-in-law's explanation.

Hearing Angus returning to the house, she had hurried to the large bay window of the drawing room, anxious to catch her first sight of her husband for nearly three weeks.

When Morag explained David's absence, Annabel viewed the message at first with disbelief, and then anger.

'But he promised he would be here,' she cried, and burst into floods of most uncharacteristic tears. So distraught was she that Angus feared she would do herself a mischief, and ordered her to rest.

Lying on the couch in her bedroom, languid from the mild sedative which her brother-in-law had administered, she went over in her mind this sudden alteration in their plans.

Angus, naturally, understood the circumstances of Annabel's pregnancy. Early in her stay in Bunessan, they had talked of the problems to be faced after the child was born, when it was taken back to the village. His own suggestion, that she should remain on Mull until the baby was a few weeks old, to confuse the gossips, she had accepted most gratefully. At the back of each decision they had made, however, lay the clear certainty that David wanted the child as much as she did. Why then was he holding back now?

Was he ashamed to admit his parenthood after all? Was he doubting his ability to love their baby?

Tormented by these doubts, which loomed in and out of her thoughts like dark shadows, she fell into a drugged sleep only to be aroused, suddenly, at some time in the early hours of the morning, by unmistakable labour pains.

She rang the little brass bell beside her bed and, in seconds, Angus was beside her.

He had suspected that her time was very near. Having passed the evening comfortably in the company of his mother, when at last she retired to bed he had settled down to a nightlong vigil. His patience was rewarded by a relatively short, perfectly straightforward labour which gave neither his sister-in-law nor her physician the slightest trouble. It was only the lusty yelling of her first grandchild, penetrating her deep slumbers, which brought Morag on the scene.

Still fastening her robe over her night-gown, she advanced into the room. One glance at Annabel told her that everything was well in that quarter.

Angus was bending over the crib which had been moved from an obscure corner to stand now beside the bed.

When he saw his mother, the doctor stooped and gathered up a tiny bundle. He came towards her, smiling at the child in his arms.

'Here you are, young Beaton, meet your grandmother!'

Morag took the baby from her son and gazed down at the tiny wrinkled form. In his turn, the child stared back at the elderly woman, his deep blue eyes unfocussed but acutely aware.

In that moment, overwhelmed by maternal feelings long forgotten, Morag put aside all her disappointments, all her frustrations of the past months. There came over her a marvellous awareness of her love for this tiny creature, such as she had never experienced even with her own babies.

The infant features, as yet unformed, gave promise of a new generation of bold young men, golden-haired, blue-eyed, straight and tall and fearless.

Morag hugged the child to her for some time, the tears streaming down her face, then turned to the woman in the bed.

'Annabel, forgive me, my dear. Please forgive me.'

Annabel smiled sleepily at her mother-in-law, and stretched out her arms to receive her son.

'Thank you . . . oh, thank you,' whispered Morag. She kissed Annabel gently on the forehead. It was the first such physical contact that the two women had ever had. As Morag drew back, Annabel caught her hand and held it tightly.

'Thank you for coming, Mama,' she sighed. 'If only . . .' Her voice drifted off. The laudanum had taken over.

Angus lifted the baby and laid him gently in his crib.

'She will sleep now, Mama. Perhaps we should have a few minutes' shut-eye ourselves. It may be the only chance we get for some time!'

While measles raged in Seileach, and the crofters fought to complete the harvest before the autumnal gales ruined the year's work, at Inverary another drama was drawing to a close.

The court-house was full. So many were the defendants that an enlarged dock had had to be constructed to accommodate them.

Each man had heard his name called and each had received a guilty verdict. All that remained was for the Sheriff to decide upon the punishment.

'It is clear from the evidence in this case that the major perpetrator of this crime was Charles McPhee. He has been pronounced guilty posthumously. For his part in this sorry affair, a fine of three hundred pounds is placed upon his estate, to be paid into the court by his beneficiaries.'

From somewhere at the back of the courtroom there came a stifled cry of dismay.

'In the case of the deceased, Martin Leven, a fine of fifty pounds is imposed.' The courtroom was silent now. Leven, who had drowned with McPhee when the boat capsized, had had no wife dependent upon him, but his aged parents would be made destitute by the fine.

'As for the defendants before us in the dock . . .' The Sheriff continued, in his monotonous voice, to award sentences of imprisonment with hard labour, ranging from six months to two years.

'Finally, I come to perhaps the most heinous crime of all. Alan McClintock, you have been found guilty of conspiring with Charles McPhee to destroy the quarry workings of your own employers, the Eisdalsa Slate Quarrying Company. It has been shown that you did, on the eighteenth of August 1879, lay explosive charges with the intention of destroying a quarry wall, to let in the sea and drown the said quarry. This callous disregard for the property of your employers, and the livelihood of your fellow workers, deserves the harshest sentence which I am empowered to give. You will serve a period of fifteen years' hard labour, in an appropriate penal institution.'

There was a gasp of dismay from a contingent of men from Eisdalsa. They had sympathised with McClintock when his son died, although few would agree with him that there was blame to be laid at any door in connection with Colin's accidental death. But Alan had been their friend and colleague. It was true that he had threatened to deprive the quarries of the valuable New Zealand contract, and there were some who could not bring themselves to forgive him for that, but their hearts went out to Mrs McClintock, who had lost her son, and now her husband. The chances of Alan's surviving the rigours of such a sentence were few. His wife was unlikely ever to see him again; she might as well regard herself as a widow already.

William Whylie folded his documents away in his portfolio and turned to the Company's lawyer. There was no look of triumph on his face, only sorrow. The atmosphere of excitement and anticipation which had been generated in the quarries by the winning of the new contract seemed now to have been soured.

He shook hands solemnly with the advocate and turned to smile wanly at McGillivray, seated on the bench behind him.

The two of them rose, intending to leave the courtroom together. At that moment, the prisoners were being shepherded out of the dock, no more than twenty feet away.

McClintock, last in the file, leaned over the barrier and spat his venomous words in McGillivray's direction.

'D'na think ye have heard the last of Alan McClintock, James McGillivray. I shall be back for ye!'

Startled by the vehemence of the outcry, every eye in the room was turned upon the man to whom these taunting words were addressed.

McGillivray's white-knuckled grip on the bench rail was the only indication that he had even heard the threat. Slowly, he turned his back on the raging figure in the dock and addressed his companion.

'Shall we be going, sir?'

William cast one final glance in the direction of McClintock, shook his head as though to dismiss the whole sorry episode, and followed the broad back of Jamie McGillivray from the courtroom.

Little Iain McDougal recovered rapidly from his bout of measles. Tough child that he was, the rash had been a mere inconvenience to him, and after two days confined to his bed, he was prancing about his mother's quarters as though nothing had been wrong with him.

From the day of her visit to her father's croft, Martha had been fearful that the infection might pass to young Edward. After her encounter with the sick tinker's child, she tried to separate her charges as much as possible, without drawing attention to the fact and provoking speculation.

She organised their routine to avoid close contact between the two boys, taking every opportunity to send her own child out of the nursery. In this ploy she found Iain to be a willing participant, since he liked nothing better than to make an expedition to the servants' quarters where he would be made more than welcome. With Iain out of the way, Martha would bundle up his young Lordship in layers of warm clothing and hustle him out into the garden to play.

It had been a great relief when, at last, Iain developed the symptoms which necessitated Mrs Lugas calling in the doctor. Now Martha could legitimately separate the boys. Indeed, for the week when Iain was feverish, Mrs Lugas insisted on keeping Edward with her, releasing the nursemaid to attend to her invalid son.

The two women were actually congratulating themselves on the success of their strategy when, three weeks to the day after Iain had first become ill, Edward woke with a headache, became very fractious as the day wore on, and cried because his eyes hurt him.

Within a few hours he was in the throes of the most severe attack of the disease which David had seen, barring only that of Ellen McDougal. It was this comparison between patients which first set alarm bells ringing. Although he knew that His Lordship would be annoyed if he were asked to travel so far on a false errand, David advised Lugas to write instantly, requesting his presence at the little boy's sickbed.

Edward's lungs, afflicted throughout the previous winter by one infection after another, now became the centre of attention for the measles germ.

Day and night the child coughed and vomited until not only phlegm but also blood appeared on the endless supply of fine linen kerchiefs.

By the time the child's father arrived, David was almost constantly in attendance at the Castle. He accompanied George Stirling to the nursery, and together they looked down at the wasted little body, lying so still and pale beneath the snowy covers.

Sensing their presence, Edward opened his eyes. He looked puzzled at seeing them there. Then, suddenly recognising the big bear of a man who stood beside the familiar figure of Dr David, he smiled.

'Papa!'

It was to be the first and last word that George, Marquis of Stirling, heard from the lips of his only child.

In a paroxysm of coughing, during the late afternoon of a cold October day, the infant heir to the Stirling fortunes suffered a massive haemorrhage and died without regaining consciousness.

Following the death of his son, the Marquis suffered a complete breakdown. David visited the Castle every day, but nothing that he could say or do seemed to relieve the terrible depression which had settled upon Stirling. Torn between his duty to his patients and the desire to see his own newborn son, the doctor allowed his head to rule his heart and stayed at home. After all, he told himself, Annabel had both Angus and Morag to care for her. She would come to no harm with them on Mull.

Because of the Marquis's own condition, the child's funeral was held in the local kirk, McCulloch performing a very simple committal service in the presence of the castle staff. Throughout his short life, this had been Edward's home. It was fitting that he be laid to rest amongst the only friends he ever knew.

When William returned from Inverary, he felt the need of an understanding ear. He thought of calling upon Elizabeth, whom he knew was alone, Gordon having been stranded in Glasgow by yet another breakdown of the old *Lord of Lorn*. It seemed that the steamship company had run into difficulties concerning the commissioning of its new fleet of steamers. Gordon had begun to think he would never receive his own command.

Elizabeth was not at home, so William decided to seek out David Beaton.

He hailed the ferry, and persuaded Ian to set him ashore on the beach below Tigh na Broch, saving himself the walk from the village.

As he strode up the drive he could see lights in the study window, and knew he was in luck.

He found David to be a shadow of his normal self. His sleep had been disturbed, on two nights out of three, for weeks past. The doctor had been deeply affected by the death of the Marquis's little boy, whom he had come to love as though he were his own son.

William greeted David warily, not sure what kind of reception he would get, arriving without invitation. He need not have worried.

David leapt from his chair, delighted to see his friend.

'I hope that I am not intruding on a rare moment of rest?' William hesitated in the doorway.

'Not at all . . . not at all.' David made a space for William on a sofa which was piled high with papers and unopened letters.

'Everything is in a bit of a mess as you can see. The women usually look after things in here. Can't get the hang of filing and such myself. It's a job they do so much better!'

'You look tired, man.' William was concerned at his friend's uncharacteristically dishevelled appearance. It was so unlike David to let himself go. A half-empty bottle of whisky stood on the side table beside an assorted collection of unwashed glasses.

David now lifted a couple of these, wiped each with a less than clean cloth, and filled them with the spirit.

Handing a glass to William, he downed the other in one swallow and refilled it.

'I heard about young Edward, Beaton. I'm sorry. I know you were fond of the little fellow.' It was a gruff attempt at consolation. He did not anticipate its effect.

David's eyes filled with tears. He hurriedly pulled out a crumpled handkerchief and blew his nose loudly. 'Bloody weather,' he protested, as if to explain away the moment of weakness.

William's heart went out to his friend. He sought for some distraction, and found it in relating to David the events leading up to the sentencing of the wreckers from Lochaber.

'What of McClintock?' David asked, grateful for the diversion. 'What is his punishment to be?'

'Fifteen years' hard labour.'

'Poor devil.'

David visualised the prison at Barlinnie where he had attended during his student days. While the harsh conditions of the road gangs held little threat for an Eisdalsa man, the foul, overcrowded and disease-ridden cells would almost certainly bring about his demise.

'Well, we are unlikely to see him again,' he reflected, and made a note to visit Mrs McClintock. There might be something he could find for her to do in the village; she would need employment, without her man to support her.

'Tell me about your own boy? How is he doing? And Annabel, is she quite well now?' William had heard from one of the seamen that Annabel had been delivered of a son. It seemed that the villagers of Bunessan and the surrounding district had spent more than one night wetting the Beaton baby's head. By all accounts, the celebration had been a wild affair, into which those Eisdalsa fishermen who called regularly at Port Uisken had become drawn.

So much for secrecy, thought David, smiling at Morag's naive belief that they could confuse the villagers about the baby's birth date.

'I believe that both mother and child are doing splendidly, but I have not seen the baby yet. Thought it best to stay away until this measles thing was out of the way.'

In truth, it was at first a fear for the safety of his wife and child which had kept him away. He knew these fears to be irrational, but the memory of what had happened to Ellen, and now little Edward, served to increase his concern to keep his own child as far away from the danger as possible.

Annabel had had to make do with a few hurriedly scrawled notes, conveyed by any fisherman conveniently sailing in the vicinity of Bunessan.

The death of Edward, and subsequent collapse of His Lordship, had been the cause of yet another delay in David's departure for Mull.

'The fact is, Whylie,' he confided to his friend, 'I fear the man may take his own life. No one could remain unaffected by the tragedies the poor fellow has undergone in these past two years. What he really needs is some robust company, a few weeks of rough riding, shooting, fishing . . . even a few days' sailing might be sufficient to snap him out of his present melancholia.'

'If I can do anything to help, you can count on me,' William assured him. 'I will have a word with Lugas and see what can be arranged. If the weather remains as mild as it is today, a short sailing trip might be possible.

'On the subject of sailing,' he continued, 'it is time for you to visit your own family. Your patients will have to look out for themselves for a spell.'

'Oh, I hardly think I can leave things here at the moment . . .' David began to protest, but William was insistent.

'I will send someone to old Lovat and ask him to take over for you for a few days. You pack a few necessities, and I will get *The Saucy Nancy* ready for sea. High tide is at six this evening. We will set sail on the ebb.'

Too tired to argue, David allowed his friend to take over. Sheilagh, who had for days past been desperately worried about her master's condition, expressed her relief to William as she saw him out by the front door.

'I am so thankful you have come, Mr Whylie,' she confessed. 'The doctor has not been himself these past weeks, and without Mistress Morag to advise me, I have not known which way to turn.'

'We are sailing across tonight, Sheilagh, and with luck shall return in a day or so with both Mrs Beatons and the latest member of the family.'

At this news, Sheilagh pursed her lips. She had been, to say the least, surprised at the manner of Mistress Annabel's departure to Mull. Now the baby was born, and two months earlier than it should have been by her reckoning. What annoyed her the most was that she, who had been present at the birth of all the Beaton sons, had not been there to see the first grandchild brought into the world.

'I shall be pleased to have the mistress back where she belongs,' was all that the old servant would say. She was aware that there was little love lost between the two Beaton women, and knew where her loyalties lay.

With a good following wind, *The Saucy Nancy* made record time to Port Uisken. By nine o'clock that evening, William and David were approaching the Old Manse where Morag had been born.

On the death of Minister MacAdam, the house had become vacant, the new minister choosing to live nearer to Iona on the far side of the Parish. Angus, looking for a medical practice which would allow him time for his more academic pursuits, found his grandfather's residence to be admirably situated for the purpose, and settled comfortably into the community in which his mother had spent her childhood.

William and David crested the last hill and stopped to look down on the stone house, standing amongst sombre yews and pine trees, beside an ancient church.

David felt a pang of remorse. He should have been here for Annabel's confinement. He had given her a promise, and had failed her abysmally.

He shuddered as at a chill premonition of disaster, and tried to push such an idea out of his mind.

William, who had throughout the voyage and the long walk from the Port kept up a jovial conversation, now fell silent.

Both men were weary, and looked forward to a warm fire and a good meal. They took the downward path almost at a run, anxious to cover the remaining few yards between them and the lighted windows in the valley.

3

E lizabeth's marriage was as perfect as the circumstances of her husband's occupation would allow. It seemed to consist of one long honeymoon which was, inevitably, interrupted by weeks of separation. As the months became years, the partings were no less painful, nor the reunions less enjoyable.

No longer able to occupy herself with her work at the school, Elizabeth at first found time hanging heavy on her hands. Katherine Logie had taken over as the island's schoolmistress, continuing with the same style of education which had been laid down by her predecessor. In an atmosphere of cheerful industry, the children were encouraged to develop their own individual talents.

Each year's intake of pupils contained both high-fliers, and those with little ability to learn. None, however, seemed to match for intelligence and initiative that group which had so impressed Elizabeth when she had first come to the school.

There had been Annie's children, Kirsty and Dougie, Peter McFarlane, Mary Campbell and Mary McCulloch, the minister's daughter. Poor Ellen McDougal was now sadly excluded by the effects of her illness.

Peter Lugas should also have been included in the list. As the son of the Factor, a bursary for his continued education was a foregone conclusion but, unfortunately for Peter, the Academy insisted upon a high standard of attainment in all of their entrants, no matter how wealthy they might be!

If these aspiring academics were to pass their entrance tests, they would require extra tuition. So it was that, a year after her marriage to Gordon McIntyre, Elizabeth set up her Evening Institute.

Enlisting William's assistance with mathematics, and related topics of mechanics, astronomy and navigation, she began to take pupils into her advanced classes.

The charges made for this special tuition were minimal. Elizabeth would have given her services free of charge, but both Annie and William insisted that the work should be undertaken in a professional manner. Nevertheless, William made sure that no deserving case was allowed to suffer neglect for want of money. If a pupil was unable to pay, mysteriously the money appeared from another source. Since it was William who kept the books, Elizabeth knew that she did not have to look any further to find the benefactor.

Not only the older children, still in school, attended her classes. A number of the young apprentices in the quarries, and in particular the children of quarrymen newly arrived in the district, availed themselves of the opportunity to better their chances in life.

William and Elizabeth determined to pursue the Marquis's promise to provide the means for talented pupils to extend their education at school or university. Regularly, during the past year, names of suitable applicants had been put forward for approval by the School Board but, unfortunately, for some time there had been no response from the Marquis to any of the Board's requests.

The two great tragedies in George Stirling's life had left him drained of any consideration for his workers. He appeared to have lost all interest in life itself.

Following the death of little Edward, it had been many weeks before David could pronounce His Lordship sufficiently recovered to make the journey to his residence in Perthshire. For a further year, there was no word of reply to the many requests for action of one kind or another which came to his Estate Office from his tenants across the country.

At last, in the spring of 1881, more than two years after the death of his heir, George Stirling found himself compelled to revisit his estates in Lorn.

In a cloud of dust, His Lordship's carriage rolled through the Castle gateway and clattered to a halt before the great door. The horses were sweating in the heat of the day, and the carriage was so covered in filth from the deeply rutted roads, that the Stirling crest on either door was quite obscured.

Stiff and ill-tempered from the long and uncomfortable journey, His Lordship had scant words of greeting for his Factor who waited at the foot of the stairs to welcome him.

Stirling mounted the steps, two at a time, while Lugas struggled to keep up. With a curt greeting he thrust his hat and gloves at Mrs Meecham, nodded a brusque acknowledgement of Alicia Lugas's deep curtsey, and burst into the library.

'Bring me a whisky, someone, and be quick about it!'

Mrs Meecham hurried away and soon a servant appeared with the life-giving liquor.

'As we drove through the glen,' the Marquis turned upon his Factor, 'I noted that the Leakies' croft is lying fallow. What's amiss with old Iain? It is unlike him to allow things to get out of hand.'

'The Leakie croft reverted to the Ballahuan Estate at Michaelmas two years ago,' Lugas explained. 'It was a matter of inability to pay the rent. I had to send in the bailie's men.'

'The bailie, you say?' snapped the Marquis angrily. 'Surely you could have come to some accommodation with the tenant, without resorting to such drastic means?'

'Alas, no, My Lord.' Lugas's reply smacked of condescension. 'The tenant had received several warnings, all of which were ignored.'

He laughed unpleasantly.

'Leakie had the effrontery to tell me that he had written to Your Lordship complaining of the amount in dispute, and refused to make any further payment until he received your reply. Since there was no word from your office, I assumed that the man was simply trying to delay the inevitable by inventing this letter of appeal.'

'Hurrrumph!' The Marquis cleared his throat in an embarrassed manner. He had ignored his responsibilities for two years; he could hardly take his Factor to task now for taking decisions in matters about which he, himself, had been negligent.

'What happened to the family? I roamed these hills with the Leakie boys when we were young. Old Iain taught me to fish.' The Marquis indulged in reminiscences for a few minutes whilst Lugas, despising him for such sentimentality, listened poker-faced.

'I believe that the sons took their families away to Glasgow to find work,' the Factor offered, hoping to close the conversation there.

George had seen the mean, overcrowded tenements in which factory workers were obliged to live in the city. He thought of the two sprightly youths who had spent their childhood tickling trout in the mountain streams, and stalking deer in the woodlands, and his heart bled for them.

'Old Iain?' he asked eagerly. 'What has become of him?' At least he could make amends to the elderly crofter.

'Leakie went to live in a cottage with his daughter. They were supported by the Parish until the old man died. I believe that the girl has now gone to join her brothers.'

So even that reparation was to be denied him. His Lordship poured another large whisky for himself, and gave Lugas a cursory wave of dismissal.

The Factor hurried to his own small office at the rear of the building. He sorted rapidly through the contents of a folder marked 'Ballahuan Croft Tenancies', discovered the letter he was seeking and carried it to the fire. Better His Lordship's clerks at Aberfeldy or the postal system be blamed than that Leakie's letter should come to light, still waiting to be forwarded to The Marquis.

Anxious to hear what other difficulties had arisen as a result of his neglect, George Stirling summoned the local dignitaries to the Castle.

William and David wasted no time in addressing His Lordship on the subject of student bursaries.

'It is important,' William was insisting, 'that there is a steady supply of well-schooled engineers to open up the new quarries and to take over from the older men who are less well acquainted with modern methods of working.'

'Don't let the men hear you talking like that,' Alexander Lugas interrupted with a somewhat cynical expression. 'You could have a strike on your hands!'

'Our men are too well aware of their own good fortune to jeopardise their employment,' William laughed. 'Those industries experiencing such troubles have only themselves to blame. Low wages and poor working conditions are what breed discontent.'

'Nevertheless,' insisted Lugas, 'seditious literature has been infiltrating the quarry villages. You cannot deny it.'

Irritated by the interruption, William ignored Lugas's comment.

'I had not intended that the older men should be put out of work,' he insisted. 'Not while they are able to undertake a full day's labour. There is, however, a requirement for a younger, more energetic team to get things moving along. Naturally one will be obliged to introduce changes gradually. Negotiations will need to be very delicate.'

'If the men get wind of your ideas, no matter how delicately they are put,' commented Lugas darkly, 'there will be hell to pay, make no mistake.'

David, anxious to get back to the discussion in hand, addressed the Marquis.

'You may not be aware, My Lord, that Mrs McIntyre is conducting advanced classes for young aspirants to higher education. There are now more than a dozen students, all told, who are claiming support for their further training.'

'You will recall, My Lord,' William pressed the point home, 'that you did agree in principle, some time back, to consider worthy applications for financial support?'

For a moment, George's mind went back to a happier time. He recalled his discussion with Jane upon the subject. It was as though she were standing before him now, nodding her agreement, even as she had then.

'The Marchioness once mentioned how impressed she had been with the Eisdalsa school, and how much she admired the teacher. Would that be your Mrs McIntyre?'

William nodded.

'She would have wanted to help.' The Marquis lapsed into a thoughtful silence, so prolonged that both William and David began to fidget uncomfortably.

Ogilvie, the schoolmaster, overhearing the subject under discussion and not wishing to have his own opinions discounted, felt it was time for him to add his weight to the conversation.

'Your Lordship will appreciate that such an investment can bring nothing but benefit to Your Lordship's estates. You will be guaranteed a loyal body of professional people who will remain because they are under an obligation to you.'

David felt that the dominie might have put it better. However, the comment seemed to strike a chord for the Marquis straightened his shoulders and cleared his throat before speaking. He wanted his position heard and understood by everyone present.

'Perhaps you will compile a list of the candidates, Whylie, to be presented at your next Council meeting . . . with justification for your selection, of course. Lugas shall convey the agreed list to me without delay.'

This last remark was intended to convey his Lordship's displeasure at the way other of his instructions to the Factor had been ignored. The implication was not lost upon Lugas.

With a surprising lack of grace, he replied, 'As Your Lordship pleases.'

The Marquis turned now to David.

'Tell me, Beaton, how are you progressing with your plans to clean up the villages?' He placed his hand beneath the doctor's elbow and deliberately steered him away from the gathering. The truth was, he was tired of talking and sought solace in the company of this young man with whom he had shared some of the most painful and dramatic moments of his life.

David knew that His Lordship had no wish to discuss drains and water supplies. Once inside the library, with the door shut on the world, each man sank into a well-upholstered chair.

A servant responded immediately to His Lordship's summons, and soon they were sipping generous measures of whisky.

It took Stirling a moment or two to summon the energy to enquire, 'Well now, doctor, how do you find married life? A father too, I hear? Congratulations! You must bring your wife to meet me sometime. Mrs Lugas shall arrange a garden party when the weather is warmer . . . in the summer.'

'I am very happy, sir,' David responded readily.

'And the . . . the boy. He is well?'

'There are two boys now, sir. Both fine healthy children. Hugh has his mother's good looks and his father's uncertain temperament, but the baby, Stuart, is bright as a button. A splendid little fellow!'

Conscious of the empty silence which had followed his reply, David proceeded to discuss the Marquis's own health.

'The Eisdalsa air has certainly worked its usual miracle on you, My Lord,' he commented. 'I trust that you are keeping to the strict regime which we managed to impose upon you when you were here before?'

With Stirling's manservant, David had drawn up a programme of exercise and healthy activity which the Marquis was persuaded to follow in order to improve his general well-being and also to impose some pattern upon his disrupted life.

'Thank'ee, Beaton,' he grinned in reply, 'your scheme lasted exactly one month. Then, much to old Burton's dismay, I flung out the dumb-bells, threw away m' soft shoes and m' flannel running drawers, and started to live a normal life!'

'I'm glad to hear that the stratagem achieved its objective,' David laughed.

'Mind you, doctor,' the Marquis confided, 'that was a heavy blow to fall upon any man. I do not believe it is possible to forget.'

'Nor should you try,' David reassured him. 'Lady Jane will be remembered by all who knew her, for her grace and kindliness. Little Edward will always have a special place in my heart. He was like a son to me.'

His Lordship blew his nose loudly before rising from his chair.

'I am pleased to have had this opportunity to speak with you, Beaton. Wanted to thank you, don't y'know? I reckon you somehow understand a fellow's feelin's as no one else can.'

David, his own heart too full to be able to make a reply, pushed open the heavy door and stood back to allow the Marquis to return to his guests.

In truth, little Hugh had been an exceptionally good baby. He basked in the affection of his mother and the unashamed adoration of his grand-mother. On those infrequent occasions when David had time to spend with his son, however, the child was more likely to howl than to smile.

His father's gruff voice and boisterous approach frightened the baby, who was more comfortable with the muted, gentle tones of the female members of the household.

The absence of David in the weeks following his birth seemed to have created a division between parent and child, which had, in the beginning, been exaggerated by the coldness of Annabel towards her husband.

The parents eventually healed their rift.

Annabel was sufficiently aware of the peculiarities of the female psyche following childbirth to realise that her reaction to David's absence at the birth had been a little unreasonable. Children in greater need of his attentions than she had priority. It was a harsh fact of life for a physician's wife.

Once returned to their own home, their relationship flowered, nurtured in no small part by the change in attitude of Morag and, consequently, Sheilagh.

Morag, resigned now to her role of dowager, finally relinquished the reins of household management to her daughter-in-law, while Sheilagh found herself able to refer to Annabel as 'the mistress', without too much pain to herself!

The infant, however, having sensed his parents' differences from a very early age, appeared to set himself against his father to such an extent that David left him alone, assuming that when he reached a more discerning stage, Hugh would come around to accepting him. Unfortunately, by the time that this occurred, David had become accustomed to ignoring the child, leaving him to the willing hands of his wife and his mother.

Stuart had arrived a month after Hugh's first birthday.

In accordance with medical etiquette, Angus had been summoned to attend Annabel's accouchement. Sheilagh resumed her role of midwife, one which had been denied her at Hugh's birth, and when the child had been cleaned and wrapped, the first person to hold him was his father.

From that moment, Stuart was David's son, just as Hugh would always defer to his mother.

At first, Alan McClintock had found his life in prison unbearable. In the overcrowded cell, the air was foul with the stench of rotting humanity. The prison walls seemed to bulge with ever-increasing numbers of Glasgow's felons.

Some of them were desperate men who, unable to find work, evicted from their homes and deprived of the means to make provision for their wives and families, had been forced to choose between the workhouse and a life of crime. Their offences were often as minimal as the stealing of a stale loaf or the poaching of a single salmon.

Others were the scum of the city's underworld, wicked men who preyed upon their fellows and would stop at nothing to gain their ends.

Thieves, murderers, swindlers and bankrupts rubbed shoulders in conditions which levelled all men to the lowest common denominator.

Deprived of the solace of alcohol, Alan McClintock had taken several weeks to pass through the painful process of withdrawal from his addiction. At last, freed from the craving, he began to indulge in a far more deeply rooted obsession: hatred and the desire for revenge. This passion had absorbed his every waking moment of the past two years.

In the close confines of the prison, a man must seek privacy within himself. For hour upon hour, while McClintock sat silent, ignoring all those about him, he was scheming. Volunteering nothing of his own thoughts, he would listen to the idle chatter of his cell-mates, absorbing any information which might help him in his endeavour.

He knew that escape would mean certain recapture, but, with careful planning, not before he had achieved his objective. After that, he could anticipate, and would indeed welcome, the death penalty.

When first he had been transferred from the gaol at Inverary, it was December and thick snow lay on the mountains, drifting along the valleys and making any kind of outside work impossible. The men had been forced to languish in prison without occupation, deprived of all physical activity except for a short period in the exercise yard each day. In their thin prison uniforms, the inmates were frozen to the marrow by the biting east wind. Within minutes, those who had demanded most vociferously to be let out, were begging to be allowed to return to their cells.

Alan took every advantage of these short periods in the open. He breathed deeply, despite the freezing air, filling his lungs until his head spun with the rush of oxygen to his brain. He flung his arms up and down, took short, energetic running steps, using every second of the time to condition his body. His companions stared at him, uncomprehending. Some even dared to pass ribald remarks, but the menacing glare which was McClintock's response to any gibe was sufficient to silence them.

At last the cold spell ended and the snows began to melt in the valleys and on the lower slopes of the hills. The ground was still frozen, but there was no further reason to keep the men incarcerated. It was time to get them back to work.

Throughout the Highlands, the age of industrial development was making its mark upon the landscape. Roads and railways were, year by year, inching their way across the map, opening up vast areas of countryside which, formerly, were closed to all but a few hardy travellers.

Road building required a small number of experienced engineers and a great deal of manual labour, supplied for the most part by itinerant workers and convicts.

To Alan McClintock, the effort of breaking hard granite into pieces small enough for road metal was not punishing. As spring advanced, and the days lengthened, his insistence upon maintaining his muscle tone paid off. Hands softened by weeks of idleness quickly hardened, and his daily output of crushed stone reached record-breaking proportions. He was soon brought to the notice of the guards who marked him down as a diligent and trustworthy worker.

His fellow convicts were not impressed by Alan's application to the tasks he was given. What one man could achieve today, the rest would be expected to perform tomorrow! While his cell-mates muttered oaths against him, between themselves, and were openly hostile towards him at mealtimes and in the bathhouse, no one dared confront him. He was clearly a hard man, and one who would be unlikely to emerge from any physical battle on the losing side.

In this manner, for two years McClintock laboured in the quarries or along the roadways. It suited his design that the road they were building in the spring of 1881 was that which would carry traffic westwards from Stirling, towards Oban to the south and Fort William to the north.

Alan's continued application to his work and his exemplary behaviour had brought him a number of privileges. His expertise in blasting was exploited to the full. This distinction brought two benefits. He was no longer expected to perform so many of the hardest physical tasks, and he had access, always carefully supervised of course, to explosives.

At Tyndrum, both road and railway divided. Alan was assigned to the route going south-westwards towards Dalmally, along Glen Lochy, following the old military road built a hundred years ago.

It was familiar territory for the man from Eisdalsa. He was now ready to complete his plan to escape and to wreak his revenge against an enemy whose perfidy had not diminished, in his mind, during the long years of confinement.

The road wound through Glen Lochy, skirting sharp hillocks of glacial moraine. In order to reduce the number of curves that it must take, it was necessary to blast away considerable quantities of rock. As day followed day, Alan was given more and more responsibility for handling the explosives. The three engineers had parted at Tyndrum, two being assigned to the Fort William route and an Englishman, Bland, being delegated to oversee the work on the Oban road. The guards were competent enough in controlling the activities of the ordinary prisoners, but had little knowledge of the work being carried out by Alan, who was under direct instruction from Mr Bland. Bland's interest was in the road itself. He took no responsibility for the security of the workforce.

The engineer and his powder man surveyed the next obstacle.

'I have taken some boreholes on the southern slope, McClintock. It's mainly granite boulders with an infill of sandstone and clay. A moderate charge should suffice.'

Alan shook his head and paused dramatically before murmuring a reluctant agreement.

'Come, man, what bothers you, eh?'

'Nothing, sir . . . only . . .'

'Well then, out with it. Do I have it wrong . . . again?'

Bland had learned, the hard way, to respect McClintock's superior knowledge when it came to blasting. He had no wish to act contrary to the quarryman's advice.

Alan had built up this measure of respect for a purpose. It was about to pay off.

'Well, sir, it is my belief that three small charges, correctly placed, will take the side of the hillock right away at one go.'

'What do you mean by small charges?' Bland enquired, trying to visualise the three positions in his mind's eye.

'Say three or three and a half pounds of powder of each site.' Alan indicated the positions he proposed on a sketch map which he traced in the dust.

Reluctant to waste further precious time in discussion, the engineer decided to go along with the more experienced man.

'Oh, very well, carry on as you see fit McClintock. Masters!' The guard assigned to keep an eye on the stocks of gunpowder came running.

'McClintock will require eight . . . no, nine pounds of powder and three sets of fuses.'

'Sir!' The guard stood back, rifle at the ready, to allow the convict quarryman to gain access to the powder wagon.

Nine pounds of powder were carefully weighed into three equal portions and placed in suitable-sized leather pouches. Alan selected a handful of fuses and set off up the slope of the hillock, his own personal guard at his heels.

Weighed down by the quantity of material and equipment he was carrying, McClintock soon stumbled. The guard, who had some regard for the quiet quarryman, stooped and lifted the heavy auger which had been perched across McClintock's shoulders. Alan retrieved the bundle of fuses he had dropped and the two men continued on their way.

At a point still in view of the main body of the workforce, Alan stopped and laid down his equipment. The guard also put down the auger and his rifle. He squatted on a boulder while Alan proceeded to work the auger into the hillside.

After some minutes the drill was removed, leaving a clean, circular opening into the rock to a depth of about three feet.

Chatting disarmingly to his guard, Alan began the process of packing explosive into the hole.

'I used to travel the old track from Eisdalsa to Aberfeldy with my father when I was a lad,' he commented.

'That's a sizeable journey,' said the guard, thinking of his own little dark-haired laddie waving goodbye to his father. Was it really six months since he has last seen him? He would be quite unrecognisable by now! 'A long step for a small boy.'

Alan rammed home the charge, leaving a trailing end of fuse which snaked out of the hole and followed the downward slope.

They moved on to the next site. The guard insisted on carrying the auger once more and even offered to take the empty powder sack, but Alan would not hear of it.

'Yes,' said Alan, as he turned the auger first one way and then the other, to make the second hole. 'On a fine day, much like today, I have seen golden eagles cavorting up there amongst the crags.' He indicated the crest of Beinn Chuirn to the south, and the guard could not resist the temptation to scan the rocky summit for signs of the elusive bird.

Alan thrust powder into the second hole, rammed home the plug and ran out the fuse.

'One more to go,' he announced, and the guard scrambled to his feet, following the quarrier round the side of the hill and out of sight of the rest of the workers.

Bland, Alan had noticed, was deep in conversation with a messenger, probably from the main site on the Fort William road. The timing was perfect.

He made a hole with the auger, as before. Withdrawing the long iron rod, he fumbled with uncharacteristic clumsiness and it slipped out of his hands. It rolled to the edge of a steep bank of scree and slid some thirty feet to the bottom.

The guard, completely disarmed by the pleasant atmosphere and congenial company, did not hesitate to scramble down the slope to retrieve it.

By the time he had climbed back up the scree, McClintock had managed to thrust into the hole not only the three pounds of powder allocated, but in addition, two-thirds of the explosive destined for the other two holes. The charge would be enough to dislodge a huge quantity of rock, sufficient to start an avalanche down the scree slope. Alan calculated that the amount of rock which would pile up at the bottom would block the way for several hours.

'Ready now to light the fuses?' the guard asked. McClintock raised a hand in agreement.

'I will report to Mr Bland. Come on now, look sharp.'

Prisoner and escort scrambled over the rough ground to join the engineer.

'Ready for firing,' reported the guard. Alan smiled to himself. Anyone would think that the man had laid the charges himself.

'Very well,' replied Bland, then turning to the remainder of the squad, shouted: 'Five minutes to firing. Prepare to take cover.'

He signalled to Alan to accompany him and strode up to the position of the first charge.

'I have laid suitable fuses so that all three charges will go off together, for maximum effect,' explained Alan. 'It will be possible for one person to fire the first two charges, but the last one will need someone else. It is quite a climb to the third site. Whoever fires it will need to sprint very quickly for cover,' he added, slyly.

The engineer was a man who enjoyed his food and paid little attention to fitness. Alan knew that he would certainly not volunteer to do any of the running.

Bland, unaccustomed to the wiles of prisoners, saw no harm in allowing Alan to make the dash.

'Very well then, McClintock. I shall shout the order to take cover. Give the men time to respond, then light your fuse. At the same time,

I will light the others. Off you go now. Wait for my command.'

With a warning to the guard that, for his own safety, he had best stay where he was and take cover, Alan scrambled over the rocks. Ignoring the engineer's instructions, he set light to his exceptionally long fuse immediately, and waiting only to assure himself that it was properly ignited, disappeared behind a jutting piece of rock. He was already more than a hundred yards from the site when Bland's call came.

'Fire in the hole!' The order rang through the valley and every man took cover.

Almost instantly, the first of the charges exploded. It was an unimpressive thud, which was quickly followed by a second, equally unremarkable eruption. Alan stumbled and slithered to the floor of the valley, and ran off down the track towards the west. At the last minute, he flung himself down behind a jutting boulder. Holding his breath, he waited for the last explosion.

Like a huge clap of thunder, the sound rolled down the glen, echoing from the hard rock surfaces and reverberating into the distance. A cloud of dust and rock fragments soared into the air and, with a staccato stutter, fell all about him. There followed a sound of rock clattering as it tumbled down the scree slope, accompanied by a further cloud of blinding dust. In the confusion, he was able to escape, unseen.

He had witnessed enough to know that his plan had succeeded. The track was blocked, and it would probably be some time before anyone realised that he was missing. When his escape had been discovered, there would still be a delay while a path was made through the rubble, by which time he would be well on his way. In home territory, he would make faster progress than his pursuers.

Kirsty McGillivray ran across the square, clutching a large white paper which she waved like a banner. Her hair, carefully plaited when she had set out for school that morning, now straggled in the cold February wind. Her pinafore ribbon was undone and trailed behind her as she ran. One dark stocking had slipped down, to sag untidily over her boot, but she did not care.

She threw open the cottage door, startling Annie who dropped the bannock she was moulding and lifted both flour-covered hands to her face.

'Mercy on us, Kirsty, what is all the fuss about!'

'I've passed the scholarship, Ma, I've passed! I am going to be a teacher like Miss Elizabeth!'

She danced around in the confined space, gathering Annie into her arms and waltzing with her until both were covered in flour. Laughing, they collapsed, Annie into the single rocking chair, and Kirsty on to her brother's bed.

'Wait 'til your father hears!' cried Annie, tears of happiness pouring down her face. 'He will be so proud.'

'Shall I run up to the office and tell him?' suggested her daughter, and would have set off immediately had not Annie restrained her.

'Your pa will not thank you for interrupting him at this end of the day. He has all his reckoning to do. You can help me to make a special celebration supper.' Annie wiped her hands and finished preparing the bannocks.

'If I may not disturb Pa, can I go and ask Mrs McIntyre to join us for supper? She is all alone.'

Annie had placed the first of the bannocks on the iron griddle above the stove.

'Go along to Mr McKay and fetch me a pound of ham and a dozen eggs. Then you may go to Mrs McIntyre and invite her to join us.'

As she handed her the shopping basket, Annie could not resist giving her clever daughter a further hug . . . to think that she would go to college and become a teacher!

Jamie McGillivray surveyed his family with a satisfied smile.

Elizabeth, at his right hand, observed the love in the look which he exchanged with his wife. After all the years, these two still lived only for each other and their children, of whom they were justly proud. She hoped that she would be able to say the same about her own family in years to come.

Jamie lifted his glass. 'I give you a toast,' he announced. 'To my clever daughter, congratulations on her success and good fortune in all her endeavours!' They all toasted the girl, who blushed prettily, embarrassed by the attention lavished upon her. The clear spring water might have been French Champagne, so elated was the party seated around that simple board.

Elizabeth turned to Dougie on her other side.

'Now that Kirsty has shown the way, you are next, Dougie.' She raised her glass. 'To Dougal McGillivray, Mining Engineer.'

'I'll drink to that,' cried Jamie. He downed another draught of pure water and reached behind Elizabeth's back to give his son a friendly thump across the shoulders.

It seemed to her that the boy did not look too pleased to be so addressed.

The evening wore to a close. At last Elizabeth excused herself and prepared to leave. It was Dougie who insisted on accompanying her to her own house.

She turned in the doorway to say good night, and took in the cosy scene once more. Firelight played in her friend's hair making it appear golden although Elizabeth knew it to be fading and greying at the temples. The light that sparkled in Annie's eye was one of devotion for the man who stretched his aching, mutilated leg before the blaze. Kirsty, darker than her mother, but with that confident look which marked her down as having emerged from the same mould, was quietly clearing the dishes.

Elizabeth caught her breath. She felt a cold shiver across her back, and wondered if the moment had some particular significance.

'Good night, Annie, and thank you. Good night, everyone,' she called.

Jamie lifted his hand in farewell and smiled. Kirsty curtsied, as much out of habit as respect for her mother's friend. Annie blew her a kiss.

'Well done, Kirsty,' Elizabeth added. She stepped out into the chill March evening to find Dougie offering her his arm like a gallant twice his age. She took it straight-faced, and thanked him.

'I hear that you have begun working in the quarries, Dougal?'

'Yes, I am apprenticed to my father's old crew,' the boy replied proudly. 'But only on condition that I attend evening classes. Pa says that I am to try for the College of Mines in London.'

'And is that not what you want also?' Elizabeth asked.

'I think so,' replied the boy, as though unconvinced, 'but I believe that I shall find the mathematics very hard.'

She laughed gently, and squeezed his arm.

'Mr Whylie will see to it that you do not fail. He believes that you will be a very good pupil.'

'Oh, does he really, miss . . . Mrs McIntyre? Does he really think that I can do it?'

'We have both had you marked down for an engineer, for a long time.' Elizabeth let go of his arm as they approached her door. She stood back while he opened it for her and thanked him for his company.

'I shall invite you all to dine with me the very next time that Mr McIntyre has a few days' leave. Thank you so much for this evening, Dougie. Good night.'

'Good night miss . . . Mrs Elizabeth!'

He disappeared into the gloom and she shut the door on the chill evening air. Removing her cloak, Elizabeth wandered into the kitchen where a fire burned low in the grate. She took the bellows and blew some life into the dying embers, then piled on a few more peats. Soon there was a cheerful blaze. For a long time she sat drawing imaginary pictures in the flames, remembering the enchanted days of her honeymoon and wishing, oh, how she wished, that she could sit with her children about her, as the McGillivrays had done tonight. More than two years had passed and still there seemed no hope of their having a child. How much longer would they have to wait?

When Dougie returned home he seemed happier than he had appeared all day. Annie thought about it and decided that Kirsty's success had somehow put pressure upon the boy.

She tucked her son in his bed, and called up the stairs to Kirsty who now had the loft room to herself. She closed the kitchen door and joined her husband in their tiny bedroom.

She shivered as she removed her gown and slipped in beside him.

'Are you cold, love?' he asked her gently. 'Here, let me warm you.'

'It was good tonight,' she whispered. 'If only the baby had lived,' she voiced the thought which was never far from her lips, 'he would have been old enough to join in the fun!'

'Do you know what I think?' Jamie stroked her shoulder then allowed his hand to slide down and over her breasts. 'I think it is time that we laid that poor wee bairn to rest, and I know how.'

Annie knew that Jamie had been as saddened as herself about the stillborn child. It was not heartlessness but concern for her that had made him speak so.

'What do you propose to do about it?' she enquired provocatively.

'We could try and make another,' he murmured in her ear.

Elizabeth heard the ship's siren as she was gathering a bunch of early daffodils from her garden. Most islanders used any available land for cultivating vegetables. No one else was prepared to waste time growing flowers. Elizabeth, however, had insisted that there should be one spot, beside the house, where she might have a small lawn and a flower garden.

Old Angus, who tended the garden in Gordon's absence, thought she was crazed to have such a notion. 'Why grow something you cannot eat?' he had grumbled, but he did as she requested and would not have a word said against her by anyone else. When his friends laughed at him for scything the grass and planting bulbs and seeds, he ignored them. It was sufficient for Angus that Mistress Elizabeth was pleased.

The siren hooted again, by which time she had run into the house and thrust her daffodils into a waiting vase. She grabbed her cloak from a hook by the door and flew across the green, towards the shore.

Usually she must make do with a cheery wave from her husband as he supervised the unloading of passengers and cargo before sailing off again. Today, however, was the start of a three-day leave. In a few minutes he would be pushing off from the pier and would come ashore with the other passengers for the island.

Yes, there he was, standing in the prow of the sturdy ferry-boat, shading his eyes in an effort to catch his first glimpse of her.

In minutes they were in each other's arms. Hand in hand, they hurried around the harbour to their house and were soon inside, out of the glare and away from prying eyes.

He kissed her long and hard before pushing her from him and holding her at arm's length. He inspected her thoroughly, noting with a tut here and a gasp of feigned astonishment there, the mud-caked shoes and blackened fingernails of his bride.

'Not a very prepossessing figure!' he declared, 'For the wife of a sea . . . Captain!'

'Oh, Gordon,' she cried, flinging her arms about him yet again, 'it has come. You have your new orders! When will the ship be ready?'

So excited was she that he had to cover her mouth with his hand in order to silence her.

'Wait! Let me tell it!'

'Forgive me, my darling, but you have waited so long for this news. You cannot blame me for being excited.'

'The work will be completed next month,' he told her. 'There is to be a great commissioning ceremony, which you will be expected to attend.'

'Oh, dear,' she cried in dismay. 'Whatever shall I wear?'

He roared with laughter.

'My wife hears that her husband is to be Master of his own ship, and all she can think of it what she is going to wear?'

Elizabeth collapsed in giggles, realising how silly she must have sounded.

'It is only that I wish to look my best for you,' she excused herself. 'I shall be so proud.'

'It will mean that I shall not see you on such fleeting visits in future,' he warned. 'The new vessel is destined to make the longer trips, around the outer islands. It means that we shall be away for several weeks at a time. But . . .' he paused before making his crowning revelation, '. . . a Master is allowed, nay, encouraged, to take his wife along as often as she wishes!'

Elizabeth experienced a quick stab of dismay. She remembered the time they had sailed around the Mull of Kintyre, and how sick she had been. Nothing must mar this moment, however. She put her reservations out of mind, and rejoiced with her husband.

4

Tigh na Broch now rang with the sounds of a family whose individual members pursued their own particular interests with little concern for what the rest were doing.

Hugh's childish prattle could be heard throughout the house, either talking to Sheilagh, whose shadow he was, or to his grandmother. In the absence of an adult audience, he would regale his baby brother with his stories, and when Stuart was tucked up in his cradle, told them to the cat.

Annabel fulfilled her role of doctor's wife admirably. She knew most of the patients by name, their family histories and the complexity of relationships which, in a small community, were enough to confound even the most assiduous student of anthropology.

By her careful recording of David's work, and her meticulous book-keeping, she had managed to place the finances of the practice on an even keel at last, and was able to show a small profit, which she was careful to salt away against the time when her boys would need education.

While the village school would suffice in their earlier years, David was determined that when they reached the appropriate age, Hugh and Stuart would go away to school in Edinburgh, and then to University. Annabel sometimes wondered if he was right to assume that both children would wish to follow in his own footsteps, but for the time being held her tongue, and determined to make the most of the years in which she was able to keep them by her side.

Morag was content to settle into a more relaxed way of life, allowing Annabel to take control of the household while she concentrated on amusing her grandchildren, pottering in the garden and helping Sheilagh with the cooking.

Sheilagh was happy to have the bustle of family life to contend with again. She could remember when it was Master John and little Angus who had been skipping about the place, while the baby, wee Davy, sucked his fists and squawked from his cradle.

David found many distractions outside his daily round of wheezy chests and creaking joints. He went sailing with William whenever he had the opportunity, and when the season was right exercised his privilege of being allowed to fish and shoot on His Lordship's land.

The winter months were filled with the business of the Parish

Council. With Annabel to act as his secretary, he was able to carry on an endless correspondence about the inadequacies of the school, the disposal of refuse, and, most important of all in David's eyes, the provision of an isolation hospital.

These were good years for David and Annabel. Their earlier differences, born of the stresses imposed upon them by a rigid notion of what society expected, and by the unrelenting demands of David's profession, had been put behind them.

Determined to play a full part in the work of the practice, Annabel would help David in the surgery when there were limbs to set or small children to hold still, and when minor operations were performed. She would also accompany her husband on those occasions when he required her assistance at some more major surgery in the patient's home. She dressed wounds, comforted grieving relatives, and gave advice when, in the doctor's absence, patients came knocking at her door.

The demands of his practice kept David away from his children during the day. By the time that he did have a few moments to spare for them, they were fretful with tiredness and ready for their beds.

Only once, in those early years, did Hugh wander down the dark passage which led from the house to his father's consulting room. Undaunted by the forbidding oak door, he gripped the shiny brass knob in his pudgy hands, and tried to turn it. The hinges were kept well oiled. As the little body was forced to lean against the door in order to get a purchase on the handle, his weight caused it to swing open, bearing the intruder with it.

Mrs MacNab had at last, with much argument, and only after insisting upon the presence of Annabel as chaperone, been persuaded to shed her bombazine jacket and snowy white camisole in order that David might examine what she described as an uncomfortable something in her breast.

The patient now stood with huge pink bosoms enjoying a moment of unaccustomed freedom. She stared straight ahead, teeth gritted, trying hard to pretend that this was not happening to her.

David, concentrating on his examination, was unaware of the tiny figure who stood, transfixed, in the doorway.

Hugh was enchanted. Aunt Elizabeth always took him to McDougal's croft when he visited her on the island. Animal anatomy was no mystery to him. He had watched Katrina milking on many occasions, and had even been allowed to try himself. At the sight of Mrs MacNab, the little boy let out a whoop of delight and shouted in his lisp: 'Juth like Bet-thy, juth like Bet-thy. Thall we get thum milk?'

Mrs MacNab screamed, grabbed at her undergarments and fled behind the screen. David stared, open-mouthed, at the diminutive figure of his son, while Annabel, stifling a sound which was somewhere between a cry and a giggle, ran to gather the child in her arms and remove him from the scene.

Over his mother's shoulder, Hugh watched his father's figure receding down the length of the passage. First, David's face turned every shade of purple, and then his voice came tearing through the gloom.

'Get that child of yours out of my sight, Mrs Beaton! I do not wish to see him in here, ever again!'

Hugh had gained considerable satisfaction from the effect of his innocent remark, but his father's response terrified him. It was to be many years before the boy ever ventured along that passage again, and even when, eventually, Stuart too discovered the way into his father's domain, Hugh did not follow him.

Mrs MacNab, recovered from the initial shock of exposure, gained an entirely different perspective on the event. The doctor's words to his wife confirmed what she had always believed. The child had been conceived out of wedlock, and the good doctor had married the girl to save her from disgrace.

There had been much speculation in the village about the child having been born less than nine months after the wedding. Although Annabel had stayed with Angus until Hugh was six weeks old, there was no doubt in the minds of the village matrons that this was no premature baby. He was far too bonny and bright-eyed. The encounter in the surgery added fuel to the story, and for many years there were those who insisted that Hugh was not the doctor's son at all. Even when the child developed the tall stature, the red-gold colouring and determined chin that were all Beaton characteristics, Mrs MacNab could still be heard, insisting: 'And did not the doctor himself declare the truth, in a moment of anger?'

While the incident was to leave its own particular mark upon Hugh, it was, for the present, merely a source of great amusement amongst the adults.

Annabel related the event to Morag as she prepared a cup of tea, and Sheilagh scraped carrots in readiness for their luncheon.

'Och, that Dolly MacNab,' observed Sheilagh, 'so full of her hoity-toity ideas. It will do her good to be brought down to earth for once.'

Morag had laughed at little Hugh's exploit, but was also concerned for the patient.

'Hush, Sheilagh,' she reprimanded the servant. 'The poor woman may be desperately ill for all you know.'

'Not that one,' retorted Sheilagh with conviction. 'She is just fat from over indulgence. The only thing she is likely to suffer from is a sore nose through sticking it into other people's business!'

David, his morning surgery finished, joined them in time to hear the last remark.

He too had seen the funny side of his son's exploit, but was determined not to allow the child to gain any kudos from the event.

'You really must see to it that the children do not stray into the surgery again,' he warned Annabel. 'I would not want them to be exposed unnecessarily to anything contagious.'

'Had I not been there myself, at Mrs MacNab's insistence, Hugh would have been here with me,' she replied. 'I do not think he will venture there again, not after the way you behaved.'

'Well, what was I to do? Mrs MacNab standing there in all her nakedness, and the boy . . .' He tailed off into silence as the three women gazed at him, then all of them burst out laughing.

Morag placed a steaming cup before Annabel who stirred her tea absent-mindedly for a moment, before raising the cup to her lips. Suddenly she put it down again on the saucer and stared at the brown liquid. A feeling of extreme nausea overwhelmed her, and she thought she was going faint.

David, alerted to her distress, came quickly to her side and thrust her head between her knees.

'Take a few deep breaths,' he commanded. As he held his wife's shoulders, he exchanged glances with his mother.

Morag, alarmed for an instant, was now calmly smiling at her son. Without a word, she signalled to Sheilagh and the two elderly women melted from the scene.

'Better now?' enquired the doctor in David. He held his wife's wrist, counting her pulse. With his spare hand, he slid the teacup to the far side of the table.

Annabel straightened her back, gratefully acknowledging the removal of the offending beverage.

'How long have you been feeling like this?' he enquired, taking in every detail of his wife's appearance, and noting the tell-tale signs of early pregnancy.

'This is the first real indication,' she replied. 'I found tea distasteful when I was carrying Stuart, but never such a strong reaction as this.'

'Well,' declared David, 'it looks as though there will be another tiny mouth to feed in the Beaton household.'

For an instant her eyes searched his, looking for a sign.

'Do you mind?' she asked tentatively.

'Do you?' he countered. 'After all, you are the one to be most affected.'

'You know how I love the children,' she protested. 'A third will make a perfect little family.'

'Just make sure that this one is a daughter, to care for me in my old age,' he teased, smiling at her.

He kissed her tenderly, then helped her to her feet.

'Anything you do, my dear, will be sure to make me happy. Now, are you fit to carry on, or would you like me to tuck you up and make an invalid of you?'

'I am quite well again, thank you,' she assured him. 'Now that I know, I can conduct my life accordingly!'

David knew that she spoke the truth. Annabel was one of the most organised and practical women he had ever met. She would carry this child without fuss, and in due course she would give birth to a healthy baby. He really did hope that it would be a girl. Perhaps he would have an easier time showing his affection for a daughter?

When David had departed on his rounds that afternoon, Annabel confirmed what Morag had already suspected about her condition. The two women spent some time indulging themselves in the kind of speculation and planning which only mothers can understand. So concentrated were they on the subject of the new baby, that they were taken completely by surprise when their guest for afternoon tea was ushered in.

'Mrs McGillivray is here, ma'am,' Sheilagh announced, as she showed Annie into the drawing room.

After the formal greetings were over, Annie sat back in her chair and regarded her two friends with a solemn expression.

'Well,' she asked, 'is someone going to tell me what you two are being so conspiratorial about?'

'It seems,' Annabel responded, with an air of self-congratulation, 'that I am to have another child.'

Annie looked almost disappointed.

'When?' she enquired.

'Toward the end of November, I think. David is not quite sure yet.'

'How extraordinary,' Annie exclaimed. 'You have quite stolen my thunder. You see, I came here today full of the news that I, too, am pregnant, and my baby also is due at the end of November!'

'Oh, but that is wonderful!' cried Annabel. 'We shall be able to enjoy our "interesting conditions" together!'

At that juncture, Sheilagh appeared bearing a heavily laden tea-tray.

As Morag began to pour, and Sheilagh to hand round the delicate china cups, Annabel laughed.

'There is just one problem,' she declared. 'Afternoon tea is banned . . . from now on.'

'For you maybe,' said Morag defiantly, 'but not for Annie, and most assuredly not for me!'

Gordon's new command was commissioned that summer, and on her maiden voyage, with the Captain's lady aboard, she paid a courtesy visit to each of the ports along the West Coast route. The winds were unseasonably kind, so that the passage was calm and Elizabeth could extract the maximum enjoyment from the experience.

Believing that the invigorating atmosphere on the upper deck would prevent her from having any seasickness, she walked slowly up and down, taking in the changing view as the ship slid past the islands of the Inner Hebrides. From time to time, she would pause to look up to where Gordon, the gold braid of his new cap as yet untarnished, commanded the vessel from the bridge.

Her heart swelled with pride. She caught his eye and they exchanged a wave. Not wanting to attract attention to herself, Elizabeth turned back to the rail and leant upon it, watching the water churning and frothing as it fell away from the great paddle-wheel.

'It is an awe-inspiring sight, is it not?'

Elizabeth turned to face the stranger who had addressed her.

'A veritable miniature of the Victoria Falls, on the Zambezi River,' he concluded.

'I fear that I am not in a position to make such a comparison,' she asserted, somewhat put out by the effrontery of this stranger who addressed her without formal introduction.

He was a young man in his mid-twenties whose loose-fitting, lightweight clothing disguised a lean, muscular frame, hardened by Spartan living, and burned brown by tropical sunshine.

'Forgive the absence of formal niceties in a wild colonial, ma'am.' The stranger raised his hat. 'I fear that five years in the African bush have eroded the few good manners I once had.' He was laughing at her haughty attitude. She knew it, and it made her blush.

'In five years, you do not seem to have lost your West Coast accent,' she remarked. 'Are you returning home?'

'Indeed I am, ma'am, to the Island of Eisdalsa.'

'That is where I live!' she declared, then added, perhaps a trifle ironically, 'Should I have heard of you?'

'If you are acquainted with a Miss Katherine Logie, then I sincerely hope so,' he replied.

'You must be Murdo Campbell!' she recalled Katherine's excitement when she had received notification some months back that Murdo was on his way home. He had promised to inform her when he landed in England.

'Then you do know her!' he cried. 'How is she? Is she well? Does she speak of me at all?'

'I have worked alongside her for the past five years, and I would say that not a day has passed without your name being mentioned at least once.' Elizabeth regarded this bronzed young man, with the smiling brown eyes and overfamiliar manner, with some constraint. No doubt Katherine would be delighted at his return, and she ought to be very happy for her friend.

'You must be the schoolmistress, Miss Duncan, whom Katherine mentioned in her letters?'

'No longer Miss Duncan, I am happy to say, I am now Mrs McIntyre.'

'My congratulations, madam.' He took her hand with exaggerated courtesy. 'And where might Mr McIntyre be?'

'Up there on the bridge behind you,' she replied. She had been conscious for some minutes of Gordon's gaze upon them. He would no doubt be wondering who was this stranger conversing with his wife.

She waved to him reassuringly. He gave her a smart salute, and acknowledged the fact that Campbell had raised his hat in greeting.

'I am impressed,' murmured Murdo, and Elizabeth again sensed that he was laughing at her. 'I fear that I have intruded upon rather exalted company.'

'Does Katherine know you are coming?' Elizabeth hastily changed the subject.

'No. My ship docked in Liverpool two days ago. I thought a letter would reach her no sooner than I myself, so decided that my arrival should be a surprise.'

A steward, smartly turned out in the new livery of the Clyde River Company, approached them and saluted Elizabeth.

'The Captain's compliments, ma'am,' he said, 'would you and your companion care to visit the bridge?'

'What a splendid idea.' She was pleased at the interruption, not too certain that she was capable of continued sparring with this very astute and worldly-wise young man. She turned to Murdo with an enquiring glance.

'I shall be delighted to accept the invitation,' he said, and offered her his arm.

'I see that not all the polite formalities have been lost in the African jungle,' she laughed.

Murdo Campbell was not the only Eisdalsa-bound passenger making his way homewards after service abroad. Malcolm Logie, once foreman of the Eisdalsa Quarries, and now a private agent, negotiating contracts for the supply of building materials between Scottish producers and the developing countries of the Empire, was taking his ease in the smoking lounge, on a lower deck.

Logie had been indebted to William Whylie for placing his feet upon the first rung of this particular ladder. The deal negotiated with the city fathers of Dunedin had led to similar contracts for the supply of slate. He had then branched out into other materials and now travelled the world arranging for the transportation of stone, lime, aggregates, and even timber, from source to the point where they were required. His major consideration, however, remained the export of Eisdalsa slate. It was Logie who had been responsible for the considerable increase in export orders over the past years.

William felt that the confidence he had placed in his ex-foreman had been fully justified, and had even discussed, with the Board of Directors, the possibility that Logie might be reinstated. The Chairman, Sir Alexander Campbell, had shown his willingness to comply with this request, but Logie himself, when he was approached, declared that he had moved on from being a quarry foreman, and preferred his present situation.

On the rare occasions when Malcolm had returned to visit his daughter he had maintained his friendship with Douglas Brown and Jamie McGillivray. At the same time, there had been a subtle change in his relationship with William Whylie. The two men now met on equal terms, discussing trading prospects and developing schemes for improving the position of the Eisdalsa Quarries in the world markets.

Malcolm had been proud to find his daughter, Katherine, promoted to schoolmistress on the island, but worried that her marriage prospects were so limited. When Murdo Campbell had left for the African gold fields in '76, it had been on the understanding that he would be back to marry her once he had amassed his fortune. That fortune had been a long time coming, and whilst, in every letter, he had declared his undying love for her and implored her to wait for his return, Katherine's father saw every year that passed as diminishing the chance for his daughter to settle down with a man to protect her. The fact that she was earning a salary which kept her in reasonable comfort, and that she was completely self-sufficient, did not enter into his reckoning. He would not rest until some suitable male person had taken responsibility for his girl. Then he could go off on his travels with a clear conscience.

As the sparkling new steamer slid alongside the pier at Eisdalsa, passengers for the Island gathered at the companion ladder where the ferry-boat was, even now, preparing to tie up.

Logie returned when he recognised Elizabeth McIntyre's voice and, intending to help the lady with her baggage, held back, allowing others to pass down the ladder before him. As she approached, he realised he need not have waited. She already had an escort who was totally engrossed in assisting her.

Malcolm started. The man was familiar to him. Could it be . . . He let out a wild cry.

'Murdo . . . Murdo Campbell! By all that's wonderful! Does Katherine know? Why, man, it's good to see you. Welcome home!'

The two men, oblivious to everyone around them, shook hands vigorously, and clasped each other in a rough bear-hug.

Neither noticed that the Captain himself had come up behind them, grasped Elizabeth's baggage in one hand so that she could cling on to his free arm, and assisted her into the ferry.

He had kissed her farewell and remounted the ladder before either of the two men were aware that she was gone.

'I am sorry to hurry you, gentlemen,' Gordon addressed them in a courteous manner, 'but unless you wish to walk the sixteen miles back from Oban, I suggest you disembark right away!'

Campbell shook him by the hand.

'Thank you for your invitation to the bridge, Captain. Shall we be seeing you on the Island in the near future?'

'This is a longer trip than usual, we shall be visiting a number of the outer islands, but I should be back for a short leave in ten days.'

'Then I hope you will take a dram with my father and myself, and bring your charming wife. I believe she and my fiancée are good friends.' Campbell shook him by the hand, exuding bonhomie.

'I shall look forward to it.' Gordon acknowledged the invitation with an uncharacteristic lack of warmth. He wondered why he should have been affronted by the stranger's casual approach to Elizabeth. He was, after all, a true native of Eisdalsa, and probably felt he had every right to address her, with or without a conventional introduction.

He turned to Logie. 'Good day to you, Mr Logie. I am sure that Katherine will be delighted to have both of you home at last.'

They climbed down the ladder to where Ian was becoming agitated at the extended wait. He could have made two trips in the time it had taken to load this group of passengers.

When David had first approached Elizabeth on the subject of finding employment for Alan McClintock's wife, she had been rather hesitant. As she pointed out to him, there were plenty of other women in dire straits who were perhaps more deserving of her consideration.

'Don't you see,' he urged, 'if a well-respected figure like yourself were to befriend the woman and indicate that she has your trust, then others would follow suit.'

'If I could only be sure that Mrs McClintock does not harbour feelings similar to those of her husband,' protested Elizabeth, 'I might consider taking her on myself. You must be aware that Alan McClintock has sworn revenge against my dearest friends. What will Annie and James McGillivray think, if I employ the wife of their enemy?'

'I do not believe that McGillivray regards McClintock as anything other than a poor deranged fellow. A few years' incarceration will surely set his thoughts straight. Anyway, the chances of his surviving fifteen years in prison are very slight, whereas his unfortunate spouse is left to fend for herself in hostile surroundings. I would engage her myself, but both Annabel and Morag insist that three women are quite adequate to run our household.'

'Oh, very well.' Elizabeth found it difficult to deny any request from David when he was in missionary mood. 'I shall certainly have need of a servant when we start our family.'

He looked up sharply.

'Are you with child?' he enquired bluntly. He had been somewhat concerned that, after three years of marriage, the McIntyres had not yet produced offspring. He had even conveyed his disquiet to Annabel who had suggested that there might be some problem with the relationship, perhaps connected with Gordon's long absences from home. Having observed the closeness of the couple, he had dismissed this notion. He felt that he knew Elizabeth well enough to sense in her any such unhappiness.

She blushed at his directness, and thanked Providence that this discussion was taking place in the privacy of her own home.

'I am not yet pregnant,' she told him, 'but I fancy that it will not be long . . . now.'

'You mean that until recently you have actively avoided pregnancy?'

'Gordon has taken certain . . . precautions. It was important, you see, that we should not have children until his future was assured. Now he has gained his promotion we are actively attempting to have a child.'

'I am delighted to hear it!' declared David, to whom any interference with the natural order of things was anathema. 'You should be aware, however, that in avoiding the natural sequel to marriage, you may have encouraged your body to resist fertilisation in the future. Do not be surprised if it is some time before you can bear a child.'

Elizabeth was alarmed by his frank appraisal of her situation. She had trusted to Gordon's judgement in these matters. Her husband had assured her that she need not be involved, that he would do what was necessary to avoid conception until such time as they could afford a baby. Now here was David suggesting that what they had done was wrong, and that they might now find it difficult to have any children!

Relenting a little when he saw that he had alarmed her, he tried to redress the balance.

'Come,' he said, 'do not look so distressed, I am sure that everything will soon be back to normal, and that you will have a quiverful of beautiful babies.'

Elizabeth thought longingly about Gordon's next leave, and smiled her relief.

'I hope that you will come and see me as soon as you suspect anything,' he continued. 'I like to keep a careful watch on the progress of my young mothers.'

Elizabeth, struck by the pomposity of this last remark, wanted to laugh. Instead she resolved to store it up, with the rest of this encounter, to relate to Gordon when the time was right.

Mairie McClintock sang as she worked. Her voice, a soft resonant contralto, had been sorely missed at the ceilidhs these months past. Today she felt as though a great cloud had lifted. She had been invited to take part in the Social on Saturday night, by none other than the minister's wife herself.

She acknowledged her debt to Mistress McIntyre, knowing that it was only Elizabeth's example which had persuaded the village women that they, too, should accept her presence without rancour. Mairie felt included once more.

She lifted down a delicate figurine of Chelsea porcelain and rubbed it carefully with her soft cloth. Admiring its exquisite detail, she replaced the dainty lady in the cabinet alongside the rest of Elizabeth's precious collection, and lifted out her partner.

There was a furtive tapping on a window somewhere at the rear of the building. Mairie, alone in the house, was apprehensive. The mistress had not mentioned that there were any visitors likely to call. She replaced the porcelain shepherd and closed the door of the cabinet. As she did so, the tapping came again, louder and more urgent.

In the scullery, Mairie paused for a moment, listening for any sound which would indicate the identity of her visitor. There was a slight scratching noise followed by a sharp click as the lock on the kitchen door flew apart. Cautiously the intruder pushed open the door,

'Mairie . . . Mairie, are you there?'

She caught her breath, fearing that she was confronting a ghost. There in the doorway stood her husband Alan. He was unshaven and dirty. His sodden garments clung to him, revealing a body wasted by starvation. It was clear that he had spent many days and nights in the open. So great was his fatigue, he could hardly stand.

'Alan!'

Her strangled cry ceased abruptly. The shock of seeing him was too much for her. Mairie sank to the floor in a dead faint.

When she regained consciousness, she found herself in her husband's arms. She would have cried out a second time, had he not covered her mouth with his huge roughened hand,

'Are you alone in the house?'

She nodded, eyes wide in alarm.

'If I release my hold, will you promise to make no sound?'

She nodded her assent and Alan let her go.

'How did you know where to find me?' she asked, curiosity overcoming her apprehension.

'I swam the channel before dawn. Since daybreak I have lain in the heather, up on the hill, watching the comings and goings in the village. I saw you enter this house, and then I watched the schoolmistress leave and cross on the ferry. I guessed the house was empty but for you. What are you doing here?'

'I work here . . . as a servant.'

'What!' Alan was outraged. 'You allow yourself to take orders from a woman who openly befriends that monster McGillivray and his whore! How dare you betray me in such a fashion?' He lashed out at her, clipping the side of her face where a red weal quickly appeared.

She reeled away from him.

'You don't understand, Alan,' she cried. 'Mrs McIntyre was the only person who would help me. She has given me work so that I may hold up my head amongst my neighbours, and try to lead a normal existence again.'

'Oh, I see, you are ashamed of me, is that it? There's wifely loyalty for you.'

'What was I to do, with you locked away for fifteen years? How was I supposed to live? The Sheriff's men left nothing. They stripped our house of everything of any value to pay your fines. I have stayed alive solely through the charity of the Parish Council, and now the benevolence of Mrs McIntyre. Believe me, Alan, there have been times in these last years when I have thanked God that Colin is not here to see me come to this pass.'

'Why, you stupid woman! Were Colin here, none of this would have happened. Had McGillivray not killed him, we would all be together and there would be nothing amiss.'

'Have years of imprisonment taught you nothing?' she asked, despairing.

'They have sharpened my mind and focussed my thoughts,' he replied, in a tone which sent shivers of alarm through her body.

She looked about her in despair. What if Elizabeth were to come back now? She would feel betrayed, her kindness thrown back in her face. Mairie knew she must get rid of him quickly before her mistress returned.

'What do you want of me?' she asked him.

'Food, fresh clothing, money. I have to hide out for a while until the Sheriff's men give up the chase.'

She started. She had not considered how he came to be here. He had escaped, and no doubt half the countryside was on his trail. Were he to be found on the Island, she herself would be accused of harbouring an escaped criminal and arrested. She must give him what he wanted and send him on his way.

'Wait here,' she commanded. 'If Mistress McIntyre returns, you must slip out of the back door and hide until the coast is clear.'

She busied herself with preparing a meal of bannocks and cheese. There was a little broth left in the larder. This she poured into a pan which she stood on the iron range to heat.

'I will go to our house and gather up what you will need to camp out. While I am gone you may wash in the sink there.' She handed him a rough towel. 'Have you any idea where you will go?'

He gave her a penetrating stare. 'How can I be sure that I can trust you not to tell the Sheriff's men where I am? All you need to know is that I am here, that I will be watching out for you, and that soon I shall take my revenge upon the McGillivrays. After that, nothing else matters. I shall probably do away with myself!'

She knew there was no time to waste arguing. There was no changing his mind. If she tried to dissuade him from his purpose he might well attack her.

First she must get him away from here. Later she would talk to Mistress Elizabeth. She would know what to do.

Mairie made her way to her own cottage on the green. She tried not to hurry unduly, unwilling to attract the attention of the other villagers. Soon she was returning by the same path, carrying a bundle containing what he needed.

'Go quickly,' she urged him, 'The men will be leaving the quarries shortly. You do not want to be recognised by any of them.'

He would have stayed to try and persuade her of the rightness of his actions, but could see the wisdom of her advice.

'Don't think you have heard the last of me,' he warned menacingly. 'If you give me away, it will not be Jamie McGillivray's head alone which will roll!'

He snatched up the sack of provisions and opened the door. 'I shall take cover on the Island until dark. Remember, I will be able to watch all your movements, so be careful.'

He was gone.

Mairie slammed the door behind him and locked it. She shot home the bolts in case he should try to gain entry a second time.

Overwhelmed by a mixture of emotions – relief that her husband was alive, despair at his determination to take revenge on James McGillivray, and terror that his visit might be discovered – she sank into a chair and wept.

Alan hid on the hillside behind a group of boulders until it was quite dark. Fortunately for him, it was a moonless, cloudy night.

Midsummer was long past and the evenings were beginning to draw in. The air was chill. It was unlikely that there would be many village folk about after eleven o'clock.

He stretched his cramped limbs, muscles painful after a day in damp clothing. He grasped the precious sack which Mairie had brought for him and made his way cautiously down towards the shore.

Most of the boats were secured inside the harbour. To take one of those would be to risk drawing attention to himself. Ian, the ferryman, might well be called out before Alan could get away. He dared not risk an encounter with the old man.

He made his way along the shore of the Eisdalsa Sound. Here he found what he was looking for. A fishing smack had been drawn up on the rocks, ready for launching at high water which would be about one o'clock. She would be afloat a good hour before the vessels inside the harbour.

His time with the road gangs now stood him in good stead. He had developed a superior strength in his arms and particularly his shoulders.

Recovered after his day's rest, and refreshed by the food which Mairie had provided, McClintock found himself able to lift and heave the heavy boat by turns across the rocks.

The wooden hull scraped noisily on the sharp stones. He stopped, his heart in his mouth. Nothing stirred.

One more mighty effort, and the cumbersome vessel slid silently into the surf.

With the tide on the flood, the water flowed southwards, carrying his craft between the Island of Eisdalsa and the Village on Seileach. With a deft movement of the oars he avoided the stout pillars of timber which supported the steamer pier. Then, suddenly, without warning, his craft shot out of the shadows cast by the pier, and into the bay.

It required little more than a light pull on one oar or the other from time to time to guide the boat towards the landing below the church. Alan pulled ashore at last, threw the sack up on to the grassy shelf of an ancient raised beach, and leapt out after it. He gave one final shove with his foot on the gunwale, and the wooden vessel glided out into the waves once more, where the current carried it onwards.

Satisfied that the boat would continue, propelled by the fast-flowing tidal race between the islands, Alan turned his back on the sea and began to climb up the cliff.

5

Mairie waited anxiously throughout the afternoon.

She knew that Elizabeth had an appointment to see Dr Beaton. No doubt she would remain to take tea with Mrs Beaton and her mother-in-law.

The hands of the clock moved so slowly. Should she wait? Should she warn Annie McGillivray? Alan had said that he intended to go into hiding . . . McGillivray was not in any danger yet. Not until the Sheriff's men called off their search.

At last Mairie heard the sound of Elizabeth's voice, calling merrily to one of her neighbours as she hurried along the pathway to her house.

Poor Mairie's heart sank. Mrs McIntyre sounded so happy. How could she bother her mistress with her own problems?

Elizabeth threw open the door and called: 'Mairie, the steamer will be docking in half an hour. I hope you have the fire going well? You know the Captain likes to take a bath as soon as he gets in!'

She burst into the parlour, arms full of autumnal blooms from the Beatons' garden.

'Are they not beautiful?' she cried as she laid the bouquet on the polished table, and began to loosen the strings of her bonnet.

Mairie prepared to speak, but Elizabeth interrupted her.

'I want everything especially perfect for the Captain tonight,' she declared. 'I have some very . . . very important news for him.' Her eyes were sparkling with excitement.

'Shall I bring a vase, ma'am?' Mairie asked. 'Will you arrange the blooms yourself?'

'Yes, please, Mairie. Then put on the water for the bath, and make some tea.'

She went to do as she was ordered, fighting back tears of frustration. What was she to do now? Perhaps she should go to Mr Whylie? He had been most considerate and understanding, despite the terrible troubles which Alan had brought upon him.

Yes, she determined, I shall go to Mr Whylie just as soon as I am dismissed.

'You are looking uncommonly beautiful this evening, my love,' Gordon remarked as they lingered over the supper table.

Elizabeth's skin, smooth as peach-bloom, glowed rosily in the mellow light of the oil lamp. Aware of his admiring gaze, she blushed a little and glanced away. She concentrated on the simple wedding band on her left hand, turning it on her finger, summoning the words she had to say. She reached out tentatively, taking his hand between her own.

'My darling,' her voice was hardly more than a whisper, 'I went to consult David Beaton today.'

He looked at her, more sharply now, anxiety clouding his brow.

'What is it, my love? Are you unwell? I notice that your cheeks are unusually flushed.'

'Oh no, I am quite well . . . very well indeed.' She continued to hold his hand, her eyes laughing into his. Suddenly, he knew what she had to tell him.

'You are going to have a child!'

'Yes.'

'But that is wonderful news!' He pushed back his chair, pulled her up and into his arms, crushing her to him with such fervour that he made her cry out.

'Gordon, I cannot breathe!'

Full of contrition, he held her away from him, gazing searchingly into her face.

'Did I hurt you, my darling? That is the last thing I would wish to do.'

All solicitude, he helped her into the armchair beside the fire, lifted her feet on to the footstool and searched about for a suitable shawl to cover her legs.

Elizabeth burst out laughing.

'You must not make an invalid of me,' she remonstrated. 'I am perfectly well, and it will be a long time before you need to cosset me so.'

'I cannot tell you how happy you have made me,' he murmured, kneeling beside her and stroking the long delicate fingers which now lay relaxed in her lap. 'You must know that nothing in this world is as dear to me as my wife . . . and my son.'

'Or daughter,' she corrected him hastily, and looked anxiously for a sign that it would not matter if the child were a girl.

'It's strange,' he mused, 'but from the moment that you told me we were to have a child, I have thought only of a son. Though a daughter will do very well,' he added hurriedly, 'especially if she is as beautiful as her mother.'

'Whatever it is,' observed Elizabeth, 'it will be only the first of many, of both kinds!'

'Of course.' He put her fingers to his lips and then took her in his arms and kissed her fondly on the mouth.

She lay back upon the cushions and challenged him, 'You have not asked me when.'

'Oh, some time in April, I would think.' He was laughing now, at her perplexity.

'How could you know?' she demanded, irritated that he could be so smug, as well as accurate.

'There was one particular reunion, when I came back after that long summer cruise last July . . . I willed that it should happen.'

'And I too.' She smiled at him and blushed as she remembered the abandonment of their love-making on that occasion. Oh, yes, this was to be a child born of joy, no mistake about that.

Ian tipped his cap as the officer and his two escorts climbed out of the ferry-boat. It was not often that the Sheriff's men were required to visit the island. The quarrymen were a law-abiding bunch for the most part. Tam assumed that this was something to do with that McClintock fellow. He had heard tell that the foolish man had escaped from a road gang. When they caught him, they would hang him. And good riddance!

Mr Haydon helped himself to tobacco from the jar which William held out to him. He stuffed the pungent mixture into the bowl of a white clay pipe, reached for a lighted spill, and puffed thoughtfully for a few minutes.

'You say that McClintock threatened vengeance upon one of your men?'

He leaned back in the chair and placed one highly polished boot upon the fender.

'Has this person himself had any indication that the absconder is in the vicinity?'

'No, McGillivray would most assuredly have told me had he seen or heard anything. I am certain that McClintock has not been seen hereabouts since he was committed to prison two years ago.' William was adamant.

'No unusual occurrences in the last two or three days?' Haydon's men had traced McClintock as far as Taynuilt, and had found evidence that he had been holed up for some considerable time in a disused sheiling in Glen Lonan.

William considered the question for a few minutes. He seated himself opposite the law officer and said thoughtfully: 'There was a boat went missing from the foreshore last night. The discovery was made in the early hours when Fraser, the owner, went down to launch it just before high tide. At first he thought that it was his own carelessness which had caused the vessel to be cast adrift, but on closer observation it became clear that the painter had been cut.

'It was also confirmed that, from the position in which the boat had been left, the water could not have reached it before the time the owner arrived. Someone must have pushed it over the rocks, well before high tide.'

'Did no one go in search of this vessel?' asked Haydon.

'Fraser persuaded a friend to take him across the bay, in the hope of seeing it, but the current is strong when the tide is as high as it was last night. Even if it is drifting, unmanned, the boat will almost certainly be miles south of here, probably dashed to pieces on the rocks.'

Haydon nodded in appreciation of William's local knowledge.

The Quarry Manager hesitated before remarking, 'It hardly makes sense to suppose that McClintock is responsible for the loss of this boat, though. If he was here on the Island, why should he leave before accomplishing his purpose?'

'As you say, sir,' the officer agreed. 'Unless, of course, he came to his family for help. He is likely to be in a bad state after all this time on the run. Is it possible that he would obtain assistance here?'

'Even his wife has denounced him,' William protested. 'By involving himself with the attack upon the quarries, he alienated himself from all his former friends and colleagues.'

Accepting the logic of William's reasoning, Haydon rose to leave.

'No doubt if the boat is found you will hear about it?' he enquired.

'Once the message gets about, every vessel in the district will be on the look-out,' agreed William, 'but it may be days before it is found. The loss of a boat is a serious matter to these men, Mr Haydon. You can rest assured that the search will be thorough.'

'This may have no bearing upon our search of course, Mr Whylie, but if there is any possibility that it was McClintock who took the boat, then its discovery may provide a clue to his present whereabouts. He is a patient fellow . . . every move he has made so far has been carefully thought out. Have no doubt that he will be back for his man.'

'There is nobody on the Island who will give succour to McClintock,' William assured him. 'Once it is known that he is on the run, every man here will be on the watch for him.'

'Well, Mr Whylie, I see that I do not have to convince you of the importance of tracking down the offender. I have to make a report to my superiors at Inverary, but I will leave two of my men here on the Island. Perhaps you will arrange for them to accompany the search vessels in the morning?

'Should there be any sign of our quarry, I would be obliged if you would see to it that a message gets through to me, as soon as possible.

'One last warning,' he added. 'McClintock knows that recapture will certainly mean a death sentence. He has nothing to lose. Your man . . . McGillivray, is it? . . . should take every precaution to avoid an encounter with him. On no account should any of your people attempt to capture him by themselves.'

'Rest assured, Mr Haydon, I will make sure that McGillivray stays well out of the way until this matter is cleared up.'

William rose to usher his visitor to the door.

Outside, the two constables were stamping their feet to keep out the cold. It had been raining most of the day and now, although a light breeze had at last moved away the grey clouds, the wind was cold. There was a nip of autumn in the air.

'I will find your men suitable accommodation, Mr Haydon,' William assured the officer.

Haydon gave the constables a few murmured instructions, saluted William, and bade them all good night.

As he stood in the open doorway of his house, William followed the progress of the dark-suited figure, with its distinctive military bearing, until Haydon was out of sight. He shuddered. Who would want to be on the run from the law in weather like this? Turning to the two constables, shivering in the gloom, he said, 'Gentlemen, come in. It is late to be seeking accommodation for the night. Tomorrow, I shall find suitable families with whom you may lodge for a few days. Tonight, my fireside will have to suffice.'

Gratefully the two men accepted his invitation. They entered, closing the door firmly behind them.

Mairie had approached William's house somewhat cautiously. She had no wish to be observed visiting the Quarry Master at this late hour. The neighbours had quite sufficient gossip to keep their tongues wagging as it was.

When she observed the two policemen at the door, she slid back into the shadows. She recognised one of them as having been with the party who had arrested her husband on that terrible night.

If these men were on the Island, it could mean only one thing: they already knew that Alan had been here. There was no need for her to get herself involved. If Mr Whylie already knew that Alan was at large, he would take whatever precaution was necessary.

She crept back towards her cottage, on the far side of the harbour.

The wedding of Katherine Logie and Murdo Campbell was set for the first Saturday in December. Mr Ogilvie vowed that his next assistant would be male. He was tired of losing his female staff, every year or so, to the dictates of the heart.

As Elizabeth observed during one of their infrequent conversations over the use of the schoolroom for the Mechanical Institute classes, the rule demanding the resignation of women teachers immediately upon marriage was a stupid one. She herself could easily have continued with her teaching duties these past two years. Pregnancy was an obvious drawback to full-time employment, but many married women did not achieve that happy state for some time after the wedding. Also, women with children of their own might bring an extra dimension to the classroom, a greater understanding perhaps of child psychology.

Ogilvie could not agree.

'A married woman, particularly one with her own family, could not be expected to give her full attention to her professional duties,' he declared.

'But men who are husbands and fathers manage to sustain an occupation also,' she protested.

'Ah, yes, but men are men, and women are women,' observed the dominie, his expression suggesting that no more need be said!

Elizabeth would not be silenced.

'A professional woman who has gained her status by learning and experience is in every way the equal of her male counterpart,' she maintained. 'I note that a farmer's wife does not lose her capacity to work alongside her husband, no matter how many children she bears. Married women work in the mills and factories. Indeed, such organisations could not function without female labour.'

'But these are lower-class women, my dear Mrs McIntyre. You can hardly equate the function of a crofter's wife with that of a schoolteacher.'

Speechless with indignation, she had stalked out of that conversation, only to vent her annoyance upon her poor unsuspecting husband.

Gordon loved to see her in high dudgeon. It was her capacity for argument which had first attracted him to her. He remembered that day aboard *The Saucy Nancy* when she had been so cross with David about conserving wild animals.

'When will the *Marquis* be sailing again?' Elizabeth changed the subject, knowing that Gordon had no intention of taking sides in her argument.

'November the fifteenth,' he replied.

'Will you be back for Katherine's wedding on the fifth of December?'

'I most sincerely hope so,' he replied. 'You know that I am the last person to forego any opportunity for a good party.'

Elizabeth jumped up from her chair and went into the bedroom. She took from the press first one dress, then another, trying them against her swollen figure.

On David's insistence, she had discarded all aids to a slim waistline. Gone were the corsets with which she had been able to squeeze herself into the red ball gown. The dress she wore now hung loosely from the shoulder, with only the hint of a constriction at the waist. Ample folds of softly flowing muslin disguised her fuller figure.

Gordon had crept up behind her. He flung his arms around her ample bosom and gazed at her reflection in the long mirror.

'I presume that this demonstration of your entire wardrobe is in order to point out that you have nothing suitable to wear to the wedding party?'

She smiled radiantly at his mischievous face in the glass.

'How well you understand women. Perhaps too well . . . for an old married man,' she chided.

'An old married sailor,' he corrected her, laughing. 'That is very different.'

He went to his valise which lay on the chaise longue where he had thrown it when he arrived home that afternoon.

'I somehow thought this matter would arise shortly,' he declared, with a self-satisfied grin. 'Which is why I felt compelled to purchase this length of fabric when I just happened to be strolling down Sauchiehall Street last week!'

Elizabeth squealed with delight at the sight of the cloth. It was a fine wool in the McIntyre tartan.

She caught up the length of material in her hand, and looping one end over her shoulder, draped it about herself. She danced around the room, making the stuff swirl with her movements.

'It will be wonderful for the reels,' she gasped. 'What remarkably good taste you have!'

The material sank to the floor as she put her arms around her husband and gave him a bear-hug.

'No other woman can possibly be so well taken care of,' she declared.

'A school-marm who uses such appalling grammar does not deserve so much consideration,' he replied. 'I think I will take it back!'

He gathered the fabric up and laid it on the bed.

'Indeed you will not,' she cried, in mock anguish, and they tussled playfully until, quite exhausted, she lay back in his arms.

He kissed her gently on the lips, then harder and more passionately.

Alan McClintock made his way stealthily through the rough pasture towards the cave which had been his home these many weeks. In the sack which hung from his shoulder was a pheasant and two hares. Not a bad haul for a night's trapping.

What he craved was sweet fresh milk and cheese. He would give anything for a wedge of hard cheese.

His supply of meal had run out long ago. For the last two weeks he had eaten only stew, made from the game he had been able to snare.

There had been no sign of the Sheriff's search party for a very long time. He assumed that the boat had been found as he had hoped, and that he was presumed drowned. They would soon appreciate their mistake!

It was time for him to make his next move. Tomorrow he would take the shore road to the Village and steal a boat. It would then be a matter of hiding out on the Island until he saw an opportunity of getting McGillivray on his own.

The weeks of inactivity in the cave, only venturing out at night in order to find food, had merely served to increase Alan's determination to take his revenge upon his sworn enemy.

When he lay down to sleep that night, it was in the certain knowledge that it was the last he would spend in the cave.

A too-bright November sun rose only a short distance above the hills. Since the cave was north-facing, it was noon before light penetrated and finally wakened him.

Alan was instantly alert, sensing a distinct change in the weather conditions.

The temperature had fallen considerably. The wind was freshening and moving into the north-west.

Below him, on the shore, the waves were dashing wildly against the rocks, sending up huge plumes of spray.

The gale blew fitfully, gusts coming suddenly and with great force. Last season's bracken, chocolate brown, lay flattened against the hill-side. Rowan and willow, their leaves finally blown away, bent before the salty wind, presenting the least resistance to its force.

Alan gathered his most necessary belongings, pocketing what he could and tying what remained into a ragged cloth, which he slung over his shoulder on a stout pole. His unshaven face and ragged clothing would provide ample disguise. On such a day, the villagers would pay little attention to a traveller trying to find shelter from the storm.

He cast an approving glance about the cave. No sign remained of his presence. He had worked late into the night, destroying all evidence of his occupation. Now, he stamped out the fire and scattered the ashes with his foot.

Taking a branch torn from one of the whins near the cave mouth, he swept the floor carefully from side to side, backing out of the cave. Satisfied at last that all traces of footprints had gone, he tramped off along the sheep track, taking a circuitous route towards the Village. Should there be a hue and cry after his attack, he would stay clear of the cave until a search had been made, then make his way back there. It had served him well as a hide-out and might well do so again.

McDougal's croft occupied that area to the north-east of the Island where the ground was littered with glacial mounds. These hillocks were a heather-covered mixture of granite, basalt and dark red sandstone; boulders torn from their bedrock millions of years before, and carried hundreds of miles across country by the relentless ice floe. Natural weathering had provided a variety of soils which accumulated between the hummocks, providing a medium for growing a limited number of food crops. The task of protecting the young plants from the salt-laden

She slid from under the covers, shivering as her foot touched bare floorboards.

Drawing on her gown, she went to the window. The sea was wild this morning. Mountainous, billowing black clouds were gathering in the north west.

She shuddered and was thankful that Angus had already arrived the previous evening.

Her brother-in-law, summoned to attend yet another confinement, had assumed that she would perform in her usual efficient manner. He had left his journey until the last moment, reluctant to set aside his books before it was absolutely necessary.

Looking out at the threatening sky, Annabel felt another twinge of discomfort and knew that he had not left Mull a moment too soon. She prayed that David would not be called out into the storm. If he once went over to the Island today, he was unlikely to get back.

Long ago, Annabel had come to terms with her husband's dedication to his work. She was fortunate to have her own personal physician for the confinement; it would be sheer greed to deny others her husband's services.

She wondered if Annie, too, was feeling the change in the atmosphere. It must be the storm which made her head ache so.

Annie's baby was due any day now. David had warned his wife that he might be called out to attend her when Annabel herself was in labour. They had laughed together at the strange coincidence of the two friends having conceived at the same time.

'It is as though you had both conspired in the matter, just to make my life complicated!' he had teased.

Annabel was pleased for Annie. The quarrier's wife had confided to her their sadness at the loss of her stillborn child. She had related in detail the events of that awful night when Jamie lay in a coma and David and Elizabeth had fought to save both mother and baby.

Annabel's thoughts turned to Elizabeth. Gordon was away at sea. Elizabeth should not be alone with a storm of this magnitude brewing. She would suggest to David that he call in and persuade her friend to return with him to Tigh na Broch. She wondered why she was so certain that he would be called to the Island before the day was over.

The pain came again.

She knew that her time had come. No need to disturb anyone just yet. Let them sleep on, as long as they could. It was going to be a busy day for them all.

The rain began to fall towards the middle of the afternoon. The hours of daylight were short enough in November anyway, but today it seemed there was to be perpetual twilight.

The sunlight which had awakened Alan McClintock had long since become obscured by the gathering clouds. The walk from the cave to the outskirts of the Village had taken him less than an hour. Rather than risk being seen by people who might recognise him, despite his disguise, he planned to seek out a suitable craft to get him to the Island, and then lie in wait until it was dark enough for his crossing to go unnoticed.

He could not believe his luck when he came upon just such a vessel, well outside the Village, in a spot where there was ample shelter and even a source of food.

Alan had spotted the little rowing boat on the beach, below the doctor's house. He contemplated taking the larger sailing craft, which was drawn up alongside it, but decided that the rowing boat would be more easily handled and less conspicuous.

He hid, during the remaining daylight hours, in the hen-house behind the Beatons' residence. Chickens' eggs, although raw, were a rare treat for one who had lived for so long on what the hedgerows could provide.

At last it was dark enough to launch the boat without being observed. He made his way cautiously to the beach, and thrust David's sturdy little craft out into the surf.

McClintock had not reckoned with the ferocity of the waves. The wind had become very strong during the afternoon and was veering to the north-west. The tide was nearing full height and the current flowing through the Sound was unexpectedly powerful.

Determined not to be defeated by the elements, he rowed against the mounting forces of wind and waves, pulling with the strength of a maniac.

Where he had chosen to cross, the channel was fairly narrow, but because the current was so strong he was obliged to steer diagonally across it, north-westwards, in order to make a landing by Camas Quarry at the most southerly tip of the Island. He could feel the bows veering away to the west and struggled to right their direction.

Another dozen or so pulls on the oars and he would be safe . . . one . . . two . . . one . . . two . . . he timed himself, willing his arms to keep up the steady rhythm which would get him across.

Suddenly, he was in slack water. The boat ground hard against the gravelly beach. In seconds he had leapt ashore, dragging the painter with him to secure the craft. He tied up to an iron stake. His escape route was clear.

Gordon's contribution to Island living had been the introduction of a signalling system, to summon aid from Seileach and to convey weather warnings and other information.

On the southernmost point of the Island, a ship's mast had been erected from which signal flags could be flown. With so many exmariners in the community, it was certain that someone would read the messages so displayed and relay them to the appropriate body. It was not long before most of the children could read the signs also.

The doctor had his own signal. Three red globular floats, hoisted to the top of the mast in daylight hours, and three lamps, in the same position, after dark.

Annie McGillivray had begun her labour soon after midday, but waited until Jamie came in from the office before sending for the doctor. Anxious not to trouble David unnecessarily, she had left it over-long.

Leaving Kirsty to take care of his wife, Jamie set off for the signal mast. Blown by the force of the wind at his back, he had difficulty keeping on his feet. More than once he was thrown forward by the blast and had to struggle to remain upright.

At last, with the gloom of the wintery afternoon settling around him, he arrived at the place.

From a box at the foot of the mast, Jamie drew out the three signal lamps and, after a number of abortive attempts, managed to light them all.

He attached one of the lamps to the halyard and began to draw it aloft. It swayed violently in the wind, striking the mast with such force that Jamie was afraid that the glass would shatter. At last, however, the first lamp was hoisted safely into position.

He continued with the operation until all three lamps swung from the topmost yard-arm. As he stepped back and gazed aloft, assuring himself that the signals were going to stay in place, their combined light fell full upon his face.

Alan McClintock had discovered a tarpaulin thrown carelessly over winding gear erected on the lip of the Camas Quarry. Under this makeshift tent, he had spent the past hour, waiting for the men to leave the quarry for the night, for no one was likely to linger in such a gale. He had been about to leave the cover of his hideout when a man had appeared, apparently intent upon lighting signal lamps. The mast was an innovation since he had left the Island. Its message meant nothing to the escaped prisoner.

As the man stepped back to hoist the third lantern, the light revealed his features and McClintock recognised him. He could hardly believe his good fortune.

Unaware that he was under observation, McGillivray began to make his way back towards the harbour. His boat would have to be lashed down.

Cursing himself for having missed a perfect opportunity, McClintock followed.

Even from the far side of the green, Jamie could see that the water level in the harbour was exceptionally high. Waves were beating on the walls, sending up showers of spray twenty or more feet into the air.

He moved closer to the edge and noticed that McDougal's boat had come adrift at the stern and was causing damage to other vessels.

He jumped down into one of the smaller slate-boats, moored against the harbour wall. From here he could reach the boat which was being beaten unmercifully by McDougal's vessel.

He was aware of another man behind him, on the wall, and was grateful for the company. It would take two of them to secure the fishing boat.

Jamie leant forward and grasped the loose painter which dangled in the water. Swiftly withdrawing his hand, he was just in time to avoid having his arm crushed between the two boats. As McDougal's vessel, held by the rope at its bows, smashed its stern once again against its neighbour, McGillivray turned to hand the painter to his companion – and looked up into the wildly staring eyes of Alan McClintock.

At the instant of recognition, Jamie saw the marlin-spike descending. Too late, he put up his arm to ward off the blow. The weapon landed on the back of his head, dislodging the silver plate which had protected him for so long, and smashing into his exposed brain.

McClintock, opportunist that he was, realised that the death could well be attributed to an accident, in these circumstances. The dead man already had the painter firmly in his grasp. Giving the rope a further two or three turns about McGillivray's wrist, he rolled the body out of the boat and into the water.

As McDougal's boat drifted out into the centre of the harbour, the body of Jamie McGillivray, was towed with it. When found, it would be clear to all concerned that he had lost his footing, attempting to secure the vessel, had hit his head upon some sharp iron, and had been dragged into the water to drown.

McClintock shivered. Shock and cold combined had slowed his circulation. He must get into the warm, if only for a short while.

He climbed back on to the harbour wall, and dodging from one shadow to the next, made his way around the square, using the cottages as a shield.

There was a light in the window of his own home.

He looked in. Mairie was crouched over the fire, cooking her evening meal. There did not seem to be anyone with her.

Quickly, he made up his mind. He thrust open the door and stepped inside, pulling it to behind him.

6

The *Marquis of Stirling* dropped anchor in Tobermory Bay in mid-afternoon.

Anxiety had been mounting amongst the crew for some hours. The new ship had never been tested in seas of this magnitude and had a surprising tendency to roll.

Not for the first time, Gordon found himself wondering if those who built paddle-steamers to sail on the Clyde had any real notion of the forces to which a ship could be exposed in Hebridean waters.

With the small number of passengers travelling at this time of the year, he had no hesitation in sending them ashore until the storm was over, knowing that the town would be able to accommodate them in comfort. Such members of the crew as could be spared were sent with them.

Gordon was also able to persuade the local auctioneer to open his cattle pens to the animals on board, which were bound for the market in Oban.

Having dispensed with these two major responsibilities, he was free to concentrate on keeping the *Marquis* afloat, in what was threatening to be the worst storm he had ever experienced.

He steered the steamer out into the channel, laid additional anchors, and prepared to ride out the gale.

Annabel's daughter was born soon after two o'clock. Angus was in attendance, but it was David who delivered the child.

Although he had officiated at countless births, and each time had marvelled at the miracle taking place before him, this was a unique experience.

He held the slippery, writhing little being in his firm hands, and was overcome by exactly the same feelings of awe and inadequacy as those of every father before him.

Annabel was aware of his emotion and loved him all the more for being so vulnerable.

Angus, busy with his patient, left it to the proud father to clean the tiny babe, wrap her in a shawl, and lay her in her mother's arms.

David sat beside his wife, his arm resting easily on the pillow behind her head, and regarded his daughter. The tiny fists tightened, the wrinkled brow reddened, and she let out a defiant cry.

The two parents looked at each other and laughed.

'She is a very determined little creature,' mused her father.

'She will need to be,' commented Angus as he approached the bed, drying his hands. He discarded the towel and pulled back the shawl to expose his little niece's head.

'It's a harsh world out there, little one,' he whispered, 'but we will do our best to shield you from it.'

'Don't be too sure she will thank you for that,' Annabel remarked. 'The next generation of women is unlikely to be as dependent upon male protection as the previous one.'

The two men were startled by the vehemence of her tone. They exchanged a knowing look, putting her outburst down to the strain of childbirth.

'Time for you to take a little rest, my dear,' Angus decided, handing her a small medicine glass of brown fluid.

She took the glass but before swallowing the sedative, begged David to fetch Morag and the children.

Angus watched his brother's family gather, with fondness and not a little envy. His mother, seated on the nursery chair, held her tiny grand-daughter in her arms, and the toddler, Stuart, clung tightly to her skirts. Hugh stood straight and tall beside his father, trying hard to appear nonchalant in this unusual situation. Having given a cursory glance at the squawking bundle in his grandmother's arms, he concentrated upon his mother. Why should she be so uncharacteristic in her bed in the middle of the afternoon?

They had assured him that she was not really unwell, and would soon be up and about again, but he was not convinced. Her incapacity was related in some way to the presence of this strange infant. He was not too sure that he welcomed her.

Quickly tiring of the novelty of the situation, he wandered away to stare out of the window. It was nearly dark. Black clouds towered in the western sky over Mull. He lowered his sights until his gaze came to rest on the mast which Captain McIntyre had erected on the island. Three lanterns hung from the highest spar.

'Papa!' he cried. 'Papa, your signal is hanging from the masthead!'

David was beside the boy in an instant. He turned towards the bed. Annabel smiled up at him, sleepily.

'It will be Annie,' she murmured, and as he hesitated for an instant, urged him, 'You must make haste, dearest. Soon the sea will be too rough for you to cross.'

'There is nothing for you to do here, old chap,' Angus persuaded him. 'Mother and I can take care of Annabel and the children.'

David kissed his drowsy wife, rubbed his hand through little Stuart's tousled curls and took one last peep at his new daughter.

'I think,' he said, willing Morag to understand, 'that we should call her Margaret, after Annabel's mother.'

'It was your grandmother's name also,' she nodded approvingly. Annabel's mother had not lived to see her daughter married. Morag was happy for her name to live on in her grandchild.

Annabel added sleepily, 'Margaret Elizabeth. I shall ask her to be godmother.'

Ian had seen the signal and had rowed the ferry across in anticipation of the doctor's rapid response.

When David arrived at the harbour, the innkeeper's son was already on hand to take charge of Bess. He led the horse away to shelter in the barn, while David descended to the landing stage, taking the steps two at a time.

Even in the sheltered Sound, the waves were reaching incredible heights. Ian had his work cut out to row the boat and steer at the same time.

Seeing his difficulty, David took hold of the spare oars and, slotting them into a second set of rowlocks, pulled for all he was worth.

The boat moved slowly out into the deepest part of the Sound. Here it was caught by the current, and had it not been for David's additional strength, would certainly have been carried past the Island and out into the bay.

Together, the two men eased the frail craft out of the current and into slack water at the mouth of the harbour. With relief, David stowed his oars. Ian tied up the ferry-boat at the landing, and turned to help his passenger with his bag.

'There will be no more crossings the night, Dr David. Now that you are here, you will be staying, I am thinking.'

'I am not likely to be finished until the early hours anyway, Ian. Should there be any emergency on Seileach my brother is there to take care of it. By the look of this weather, my services could be needed for more than a birthing tonight!'

As he took the path up from the harbour, David was aware of the large number of men gathered there, working at securing a multitude of sailing craft. Small boats were lifted bodily from the water and upended on the grass in the square. Larger vessels were stripped of their sails and nets, and these were carried away by the older children to be stored in the drill hall. Everything which could be moved, was moved. What could not, was lashed securely. The larger vessels were roped to both sides of the harbour, so that they were prevented from swinging and crashing into each other as the tide changed.

With so much activity going on all around him, David was not unduly surprised to find that no escort awaited him at the pier. Assuming that the call was indeed to Annie McGillivray, he made his way directly to her door.

His knock was answered by Kirsty who looked smart and extremely efficient in a clean white apron.

'Good afternoon, doctor,' she greeted him politely. 'Will you step inside?' Before closing the door she peered out into the gloomy afternoon, hoping to catch sight of her father. There was no sign of him.

David, amused at the child's serious expression and very proper greeting, took off his hat and coat, handing them to her as he stooped to enter the tiny lobby.

'How is the patient, nurse?' he enquired.

'She is in there.' Try as she might Kirsty could not restrain her giggles. She indicated the kitchen. 'I tell't her she should be in her bed, but she will tak no heed of me.'

Annie was on her knees, scrubbing the hearthstone as though her life depended upon it. When she saw David she struggled to her feet, clutching her back with one soapy hand while, with the other, she swept her straggling hair out of her eyes.

'Thank goodness you have come, doctor,' she declared, 'the pains are so regular and so strong, I cannot think it will be long before the child is born!'

'What on earth are you doing, woman?' he demanded, steering her to the arm-chair and forcing her to sit down. 'Remembering the last occasion, I would have thought you might take more care of yourself.'

Annie laughed at him.

'There will be nothing amiss with this child, David. It has been clamouring to be let out for weeks past!'

'Well, I cannot examine you properly here,' he observed, 'so perhaps you will be so good at to make yourself ready for the event?'

Kirsty had been well instructed by her mother. As David prepared his patient for the delivery, the girl was always to hand; water, towels, bowls appeared as if by magic. His every request was answered immediately. A trained nurse could have done no better.

As Annie had predicted, the baby, while certainly causing her mother considerable agony in her passage into the world, made the journey swiftly, and arrived yelling.

David tied off the umbilical cord and severed the connection with the placenta. He lifted the baby to find Kirsty standing beside him, ready with a towel in which to wrap the infant.

'Wipe her over gently with a soft cloth,' he said.

'I know what to do,' she replied. 'Just you look after my mother.'

Confident that the baby was in safe hands, he turned to his patient. Annie was smiling up at him.

'She is a good girl, and so quick to learn,' she told him. 'I suggested she should train to be a nurse. Do you know what she replied?'

David shook his head, only half listening as he attended to his work.

'She said she had no intention of becoming a nurse. She has decided that she is going to be a doctor.'

David did take note of that.

'Medicine is no occupation for a woman, Annie. Indeed, I know of no Medical School which admits females. I hope you managed to put that notion out of her head?'

'Oh, you know what young people are, doctor, always changing their minds, following whatever whim is popular at the moment. I have no doubt she will be a teacher . . . she has talked of nothing else all these years, until just recently. In fact, it was Mrs Beaton who put the idea of medicine into her head in the first place.'

'I cannot believe that my mother would recommend such a thing!' David protested.

'Not Mrs Beaton Senior,' Annie explained. 'No, it was Annabel who suggested it. She believes, that in the next twenty years, we shall see women taking on many of the roles presently filled exclusively by men. Have you not heard her on the subject of women's suffrage?'

Indeed he had not. But then, he scarcely listened when Annabel and his mother got into one of their arguments about the functions assigned to the sexes. He must listen more carefully in future.

At that moment Kirsty returned, with her little sister cosily swaddled in a soft shawl, and handed the infant to her mother.

Annie gazed down into the bright boot-button eyes which stared back at her, unblinking. Then, quickly remembering the efforts of her elder daughter, she smiled up at her.

'Having been so important during her birthing, Kirsty, you shall be the one to name your sister.'

She swelled with pride to be given such a responsibility and looked hard at the tiny mite, noting the shock of dark hair and the inquisitive frown which creased the wrinkled forehead.

'Why,' she cried, 'that frown is so exactly like your own, Ma. I think we should call her Annie too. Wee Annie McGillivray!'

Annie smiled sleepily. Jamie will like that, she thought. He had always said that he wanted another daughter, one who was just like herself.

In the fading light, it was hardly surprising that one boat should have been overlooked.

The McDougals were busy out on the hill, trying to round up their small herd of beef cattle. The cows were safe in the byre, but the remainder of the stock would have to weather the storm. All that McDougal could do was to see that they were confined in a securely walled paddock where they would get some shelter from the over-hanging cliff.

It was late in the day when Jack McDougal made his way to the harbour to attend to the boat. So densely were the vessels packed together, that he could not locate her from the harbour wall.

He asked among his friends, but during their efforts to tie everything down, no one seemed to have noticed the McDougal craft.

Jack returned home concerned, but not so perturbed that he felt he should worry his father. There was nothing that anyone could do about it now. In the dark, and in the face of the ever-increasing force of the gale, he knew that it would be foolhardy to go back out again.

In fact, McDougal's fishing boat, some fourteen feet in length and sturdily built for ocean sailing, had been cast adrift before the general activity to secure the harbour had begun. In the gathering gloom, at the very time when Ian had taken the ferry-boat across to collect the doctor, it had followed the receding tide out of the harbour, and drifted beyond the point. Wallowing in its wake, and acting as a sea-anchor, was the body of Jamie McGillivray.

Mairie started up when she heard the outer door burst open, carrying with it a blast of cold air. The wind must have blown it open again.

Before she could reach the kitchen door that, too, was thrown open and Alan McClintock, wild-eyed and soaking wet, thrust her aside so that he could reach the fire.

It had been three months since Mairie had last seen her husband. The discovery of Fraser's boat, wrecked on Scarba, had convinced her that he was drowned.

'What are you gawping at, woman?' he snapped, irritated by her dumbfounded expression. 'What! Did you think I was dead? Put me out of mind, had you? Well, so much the worse for you!'

His unreasonable anger frightened her. It was not just his appearance . . . ragged, filthy, weeks of unkempt growth on his face . . . no, there was something else. He seemed to have lost all control. Had he also lost his reason?

'Well, don't stand there staring. There is no time to lose. Food . . . dry clothing . . . something to drink.'

'What is it, Alan?' she asked fearfully, praying that it was not as she suspected. 'What has happened? What have you done?'

'Done! What do you suppose I have done? I have finished what he began, that's what I have done!'

'Oh, Alan!' She sank into a chair, covered her face with her hands and began to wail, a high keening sound which only increased her husband's fury.

Angrily, he piled what food he could find on to the tablecloth and tied it into a bundle. He tore open the clothes press, unearthing flannel drawers, an old pair of moleskin trousers and a flannel shirt. He stripped to the skin, and pulled on the dry garments. For the moment he had run out of steam. He glanced around distractedly.

'Oilskins . . . where are my oilskins?' He shook her roughly. Unable to find the words, she looked up at the ceiling.

'In the loft?' He set the ladder up and scrambled into the roof-space. She could hear him swearing as he stubbed his toes on the boxes and discarded furniture stored there. Soon he was back, carrying the heavy canvas quarryman's coat which had been soaked in oil to keep out the wet.

At the door, he paused.

His wife had uttered no word during all his activity. Could she be trusted to keep her mouth shut once he was out of the way? Why take the risk?

Slowly, he put down his sack of provisions and moved towards the grate. As Mairie watched him, wondering what was coming next, he took the poker and hit her again and again until her head was an unrecognisable mass of blood and bone.

McClintock found his stolen rowing boat where he had left it. In a matter of moments, he had launched the vessel into the surf and leapt aboard.

Using the oars merely as a rudder, he allowed the boat to be carried south towards the sparsely inhabited coast of South Lorn.

Having done all that he could for Annie and her baby, David left his patient in the care of Kirsty, and battled against the wind towards the Quarry Manager's house.

At the head of the harbour, he encountered Dougie McGillivray on his way homeward.

'Good evening to you, doctor,' the boy shouted, in order to be heard above the noise of the gale. 'How is my mother?'

'You have a beautiful little sister,' he bellowed. 'Mother and child are both very well!'

'Thank heavens for that,' the boy declared, remembering the last time when he was nearly deprived of both his parents in one night. 'Is my father with her?'

Dougie had searched for his father in order to gain his permission to haul their own vessel ashore. Failing to find him, he had taken the initiative and collected a few friends to help him carry the boat to safety.

'No,' David replied, 'Jamie was not there when I left. Annie assumed he was busy in the quarries.'

'No doubt that is where he will be sure enough.' But Dougie was unable to disguise his concern for his father's safety. Since the day that Jamie had returned from Inverary and related the events of the trial, making a joke of McClintock's threats, Dougie had kept a close watch on his father. There had been a scare when Fraser's boat went missing, and the constables had searched all along the coast. Even when the shattered hull of the vessel was found on Scarba, the boy had not accepted his father's assurances that there was no longer any threat.

With a wave to the doctor, Dougie hurried on, praying that Jamie was now in the safety of his own home.

At every step, the force of the wind appeared to increase. It blew from the north-west and David, doubled up against the blast, was headed straight into it. When at last he reached William's door, it was all that he could do to pull himself upright in order to raise the knocker.

William had only just returned from the quarries, where he had been overseeing the securing of valuable equipment against the storm.

He had sent some of the men to help with the boats, and trusted that they would include *The Saucy Nancy* in their ministrations.

David shrugged off his sodden greatcoat and gratefully accepted a generous measure of whisky from his friend.

'Annie McGillivray has given birth to a daughter,' he announced.

'Mother and baby doing well, I hope?' William enquired. He had a great fondness for the McGillivrays. They had endured more than their share of misfortune, it was time that they had something to celebrate.

'Both doing splendidly.' David sighed with satisfaction as he stretched his legs and pointed his toes to the fire.

'My second birthing today,' he observed, triumphantly, recalling events earlier in the afternoon. 'Annabel gave birth to a daughter also.'

'My dear fellow, congratulations!' William slapped his friend on the back and refilled his glass. David tried to affect a casual air, but his pride in the new baby was clear to see.

'Incidentally, I shall need to beg shelter for the night,' he told William. 'Had I not taken up the oars myself on the way across, the ferry would never have made it. There is no persuading Ian to take me back again, not while this storm lasts.'

As if to confirm his assessment, the wind increased in strength and changed its pitch as it howled around the buildings.

'I have seen some strong gales in Cornwall,' William confided, 'but nothing quite as wild as this. Why, it might even be classed a hurricane!'

A loud knocking at the door brought him to his feet. A small group of men stood outside, supporting one of their number who was clearly in considerable pain.

'We heard that the doctor was with you, sir,' said one of the men. 'Wullie Mackay has damaged his arm, may we bring him inside?'

William held the door wide to allow the injured man to enter. David helped his patient into a chair, near to the light.

As the night wore on, David had plenty of such cases to deal with. Any suggestion of the doctor taking to his bed was quickly dismissed.

'What chance have we of sleeping with all this noise?' he demanded.

'Might as well stay alert and ready for whatever action is necessary. It's my belief the worst is yet to come.'

Towards three o'clock, the wind dropped a fraction, the clouds drew back and a full moon lit the Island as thought it were the middle of the day.

William cautiously opened the door, ready to close it immediately should a gust threaten to tear it off. Although the wind still seemed to be blowing with some force, it was possible to move about outside now, without fear of being blown away.

He turned to David who, despite his protests to the contrary, had fallen into a deep sleep. Not wishing to disturb him, William decided to go out on to the hill by himself, and assess the storm damage.

He climbed up the cliff behind the house, and made his way along the upper railway track towards the northern end of the Island. The white moonlight gave a strange cast to the landmarks so familiar during the day.

The sea was boiling around the rocks on the foreshore. It was nearly high tide. Waves thundered against the seaward end of the largest quarry, sending up clouds of spray which showered the iron girders of the lifting gear and, jumping the wall, fell a hundred feet or more to the quarry floor.

The pumps will be working full pelt for days, to clear that lot he told himself.

He lifted his eyes now towards Mull, which lay dimly on the horizon. There was something strange about the profile . . . quite unlike any view of that island that he had noticed before.

He stared into the distance, trying to make out a thick white band which seemed to stretch across the Sound, drawing a horizontal line from Mull to the Island of Kerrera. He swung round and saw a similar effect between Kerrera and the mainland.

'Oh, my God!' he cried, and scrambled down the hillside as fast as the rough terrain would allow.

He must warn the people, but how?

Tearing past his own house, he raced to the harbour where the coalree stood, convenient for the unloading of the coal which was stored there.

Some time before, William had had a bell erected, to be used for warning of accidents in the quarry or to call the islanders together for whatever reason.

This was his only hope.

Without the key to the padlock, he must smash open the door to the building, an action which took a few seconds only. Clambering up the ladder to the loft, he found the bell-rope and pulled for all he was worth.

The urgent clanging was sufficient to alert those men who, like the

Manager, had been fearful of the damage which might be wrought by the gale, and had stayed awake.

Soon, doors were opening all around the village and William could stop the ringing.

He ran to the nearest houses, calling to the dazed occupants: 'Make for the higher ground . . . a monstrous wave . . . go to your lofts . . . it is nearly upon us!'

The cry was taken up and soon the whole population seemed to be on the move. Some took to the hill, scrambling up the steep slope, their children clinging to them in the wild rush. Others chose to gather their families in the lofts of the houses. A few, despite the rain which had begun again, broke through the slates and climbed out on to their roofs.

Satisfied that everyone would be made aware of the danger, William ran back to his home to find David still slumbering beside the fire.

'Hurry, Beaton!' William shook him roughly, 'Wake up, man, for God's sake!'

Bleary-eyed, David followed the engineer up the stairs and into the loft room. Instinct had made him grab his medical bag as he woke . . . he had it with him now.

As they stood at the dormer window, which faced up towards Kerrera, the clouds parted again and the scene was once more bathed in moonlight.

For the crew aboard the *Marquis of Stirling*, it seemed that the night would never end.

Anchored in moderately sheltered waters, between the peninsular of Ardnamurchan to the north and the shores of Mull, she was somewhat protected from the full force of the gale but the squat profile was not suited to the Atlantic rollers, and the motion had laid low all but the most hardened seamen.

Soon after midnight, the vessel began to drag her anchors and Gordon, fearful that she might end up on the rocks, chose to ride out the gale at sea.

The engines were started, the anchors drawn up and the *Marquis* headed south-eastwards towards Oban bay, where there was a greater degree of shelter.

The experts were to spend many weeks compiling their reports of what happened that night. A combination of factors, they claimed, produced the disaster.

It was full moon, and the tide was at its highest spring of the year, with the sun and moon acting in unison to draw the liquid surfaces of the globe upwards against the forces of gravity. At the same time, a low pressure belt was moving across the British Isles and into Scandinavia, drawing after it winds of a magnitude seldom experienced, even in the hostile waters around the Hebrides.

An exceptional volume of water was travelling from north to south along both coasts of Scotland. To the west, that water was forced to travel between numerous islands, the outer surfaces of the flow meeting resistance against the shoreline, while the centre moved forward at a faster rate. The build up was so great that by the time it hit the Sound of Mull, the water had formed into a tidal wave of enormous proportions.

Gordon, wedged in a corner of the wheel-house, concentrated on chart and compass, using all his skills to keep the helmsman on a course which would avoid the treacherous rocky islands to be found to the west of the Sound. He could not understand the shouts of his lookouts, and waited for his Mate to appear, drenched and full of alarm.

'Change course, Skipper, for God's sake. Have you not seen what is coming on the port side?'

Gordon ran to the port window and stared out.

The wave seemed as high as a Glasgow tenement. In the moonlight the waters appeared black and the white foam at its crest glowed with phosphorescence.

'Hard a'port,' he yelled, and sprang to the wheel to lend his weight to that of the helmsman.

The flat-bottomed vessel shuddered under the strain as the rudder moved. Slowly the ship began to turn into the wave. She was now deep in the trough before the watery cliff. For an instant the force of the wind dropped and the vessel moved more swiftly to face the onslaught.

The wave hit as her bows were still turning. The force of the water caught the cumbersome housing of the paddle-wheel on the vessel's starboard side, lifting her up and turning her over as though she were a child's toy.

There was no time for orders. Those members of the crew who were on deck were thrown into the sea. Below, in the engine-room, men were tossed like rag dolls against the machinery. Those who did not die instantly were scalded to death as the steam-pipes shattered, or were drowned by the water which smashed its way through hatches and doors, contributing its weight to the vessel's list.

The helmsman had been thrown across the wheel-house and lay unconscious on the sloping floor. Gordon, too, had been tossed aside, but his fall had been broken by the body of his First Mate, whose head having been nearly severed from his neck by a jagged piece of glass, had died as the wave struck.

The Skipper disentangled himself from the corpse and struggled towards the other man.

The helmsman was alive, but unconscious. Grabbing the man beneath his arms, Gordon dragged his limp body across the steeply sloping deck and managed, with superhuman effort, to force open the wheel-house door.

The tidal wave had passed on down the Sound, leaving the *Marquis* wallowing in its wake. The list on the ship was increasing by the second. All that he could do was to drag his companion to the deck rail, now almost awash. Miraculously, at that instant, a loose lifebelt floated by. Gordon made a grab for it and, forcing it down over the helmsman's shoulders, tipped the unconscious seaman over the rail.

He looked about him in despair. The deck was almost vertical and he had to hold on to the rail to stop himself being swept overboard. He could see no one. In another minute the ship would turn over. He jumped.

Down, down into the dark waters he sank, in his ears the screaming of the men still trapped in the hull.

He felt his lungs would burst.

Now he was rising once more, rising towards the light. How could there be light, he wondered, as a dark shadow fell on the water?

With deck lights ablaze, the ship turned over, trapping her Master in the rigging. Together they sank to the ocean bed.

Awakened by the insistent ringing of the bell, Elizabeth dressed hastily and hurried outside. She caught hold of Malcolm Logie as he ran past, making for a pair of cottages on the point where the occupants appeared to have slept on, despite the warning.

'What is it, Mr Logie?' she shouted to make herself heard.

'The sea . . . a huge wave . . . like to engulf the island!' He rushed on.

There were women and children hovering uncertainly, looking anxiously for guidance. Some of the men were hurriedly adjusting ropes on the already secured boats, or attempting to erect barricades before their doors.

Racing for the schoolhouse, Elizabeth called to each group as she passed: 'The schoolhouse . . . make for the schoolhouse . . . it will be safer there!'

She thrust open the heavy door and went to find oil lamps. As the islanders piled into the building, more and more willing helpers came to her aid.

'We must find a way of blocking up the door,' she cried. 'The windows are high enough to keep out the water, but it could come in through the doorway.'

Canvas screens were ripped from their frames, and the material stuffed into cracks in the door frame. Heavy tables were piled up against it and wedged into place by window poles, blackboard pointers, whatever came to hand.

Elizabeth, in the forefront of this activity, gave no heed to her condition. She heaved and pushed the heavy furniture, strained and stretched to secure it, and soon found herself gasping for breath, but with the schoolhouse as secure as she could make it.

The wave broke first at the north-west point of the Island. The great gaping hollows of the two main quarries absorbed some of the volume, and slowed the water in its approach to the village.

Swirling and churning, around the base of the hill it came, breaching the walls of McDougal's fields and engulfing them in its progress.

Cattle, chickens and the McDougals' two pigs were all swept away by the torrent.

The water hit the first of the sturdily built stone cottages. These resisted the impact, although doors and windows were smashed, and the sea passed through at a height of several feet.

The harbour filled, and the vessels lashed to its walls rode so high it seemed they might sail off across the square.

More cottages were flooded. Their occupants, most of whom had taken to the lofts, now broke through the roofs and sprawled across the slates, clinging to the ridges of the buildings.

Having been restricted in its passage between the houses, the deluge of water hit the door of the schoolhouse with renewed strength. It held, but glass was smashed as some of the lower panes of the tall windows gave way.

On the far side of the green, another row of cottages stood between the surging water and its escape into Camas Bay. Built hurriedly to accommodate the additional workers, these were of less robust construction than those cottages set further from the harbour. Here walls collapsed and furniture was swept away. Thankfully, by this time all the occupants were sheltering in the schoolhouse or had taken refuge on the hill.

It was fortunate that the terrace of houses which contained the McGillivray home was one of the older buildings on the island, situated at the southern end of the ridge and elevated some fifteen feet above the other dwellings.

Thus it was that the exhausted Annie and her new baby slept undisturbed by the deluge. Kirsty and Dougie, waiting anxiously for James McGillivray's return, stoked up the fire, and stood by the tiny window, watching the progress of the storm with mounting apprehension. Their father must have gone to help secure the boats and then decided to take shelter in another house. Oh, how they wished that he would come home!

Two doors down, another island inhabitant was quite unaware of the turmoil going on about her. A wide pool of blood was already drying beneath the lifeless body of Mairie McClintock. The weapon of her destruction lay beside the cold ashes in the untended grate.

Now the deluge made its final thrust against the islanders. Water poured over the rim of the two-hundred-foot deep Camas Quarry and filled it, carrying away cranes and pulleys, and tearing up the railway track. Tools and equipment lay abandoned on the quarry floor, buried under piles of loose rubble and fathoms of sea water.

Across the Sound, the Village of Seileach was also awash. The deepest quarry, that which lay behind the steamer pier, closest to the sea, was also filled. Here the impact against the man-made sea wall was so great that it collapsed completely and the quarry filled rapidly. This saved the village itself from the full force of the water and it was a flood of only two or three feet in depth which flowed along the streets and quickly dispersed.

After the wave had passed, an eerie silence fell over the Island. The wind seemed to abate and the rain ceased. It was as though the elements themselves were exhausted by their efforts.

The silence was broken first by the wailing of a child. The chorus was quickly taken up. Shouts could be heard as families, separated in the turmoil, gathered their number together. One or two cries for help came from those trapped and injured by debris.

Elizabeth's assorted collection of refugees began to take down their barricade. Soon they had the door open, the lights from within giving a welcome signal to others to come and take shelter.

Little could be done until the dawn light revealed the full extent of the damage.

Elizabeth organised the women and children to collect water, and coals for the stove. She sent people to forage for dry clothing and what food they could lay hands on. They returned very soon, carrying armfuls of blankets and baskets and bowls of provisions.

The school was soon milling with people, all striving to make each other comfortable. Children were laid to rest in makeshift beds. Kettles were boiled on the stove, and soon everyone was drinking hot tea or steaming broth and munching on bannocks.

The people may have had their homes swamped, and their treasured possessions destroyed, their boats may have been carried away, and their animals drowned, but they themselves were alive, and for that they were thankful.

William and David had watched the approach of the wave in horrified silence.

They saw it engulf the walled vegetable gardens and tear away the enclosure protecting McDougal's cattle. The poor beasts could be heard above the tumult, lowing pitifully as they struggled to swim against the torrent.

William thought of the crofter's flock of sheep on Eilean nam Uam, and hoped that they had found shelter. That poor family could ill afford a further blow of this kind.

Although the water had swept through the lower part of William's house to a height of some three feet, it had receded almost as quickly as it had come. The solid slate floors were unaffected, although furniture and rugs had been soaked.

Ignoring the chaos around them, the two men wrapped themselves in their heavy overcoats and set out for the main part of the village, to see what could be done to help the people.

Lights from the schoolhouse suggested that many of the islanders were gathered there, so David and William made their way in that direction.

It was nearly dawn as they crossed the green. William thought he recognised the outline of *The Saucy Nancy*, riding in the harbour, tightly lashed against the side of one of the larger slate-boats. He could not help letting out a sigh of relief, while commiserating with those fishermen who had not been so lucky.

Inside the schoolhouse, David found plenty to occupy him. Most casualties were bruised or cut by flying debris; a number were suffering from shock; others from submersion and exposure.

Elizabeth moved about the hall, ensuring that the children were warm and comfortable. She would have turned her attention to the women also, but they could see that she herself was close to collapse and insisted that she should take a seat and a warming drink. When David approached, he found her sitting close to the stove, a mug of rapidly cooling tea in her hands, shivering violently.

'You should be in your bed, Elizabeth,' he told her, with concern. 'Was your house swamped?'

She managed to shake her head, but could not stop shivering. Suddenly a stabbing pain in her lower back made her cry out. Several women nearby came running to her side.

Calling to William to accompany him, David gathered Elizabeth in his arms and carried her out into the early dawn and across the square to her house.

While William busied himself with the lamps, David laid her on the bed, already stripped by the islanders.

'See if you can find some clean linen and a blanket or two, if any are left,' he instructed William.

The engineer, following Elizabeth's gasped instructions, located clean sheets. Blankets were another matter.

'They have all been taken to the hall for the children,' she murmured faintly. 'There is my travelling cloak in the press by the front door.'

While William sought out the cloak, David made his examination.

Soon he put down his stethoscope and held her hand, finding it difficult to tell her what he must.

'It is the baby,' she murmured. 'Will I lose it?'

'I fear so.' He could find no way to soften the blow. 'It will not be long now.'

As if to confirm his prediction, the tearing pain came again, and Elizabeth could not contain her anguish. Her scream brought William to her bedside.

Together the two friends witnessed the agony of the woman whom both had continued to love for so long. At nearly five months, the foetus was fully formed. It was a boy.

While David attended to Elizabeth, William went away, returning some time later with a small, highly polished wooden box. It was made of walnut, the grain carefully matched to create an exquisite pattern. William recalled the hours of loving care which had gone into its construction, and the Cornish sweetheart for whom it had been intended as a wedding gift.

Elizabeth, heavily sedated, slept.

During his frantic search for bedding, William had discovered the hoard of baby garments which she had been preparing for her child. A lacy shawl, gossamer fine, was used to wrap the infant.

With extreme gentleness, David laid the boy in the box, and closed the lid.

To William's unasked question, he replied, 'Place him in the parlour. We will ask her what she wants done when she awakens.'

William carried the casket into the living room and laid it on the table. Elizabeth had gathered the last of the roses from her garden, before the storm destroyed them. In the heat of the room, the buds had opened. He lifted the lid of the casket and contemplated the tiny form for a few moments, before laying a single white rose alongside the boy's body.

'Sleep well,' he murmured.

EPILOGUE

To W. Sproat Esq.   Tigh na Broch
Procurator Fiscal   Seileach
Tobermory   Argyll

On Tuesday, 24 November 1881 I examined the body of Mrs Mairie McClintock.

The woman was thirty-five years of age and apparently in good health at the time of her death.

Extensive damage had been caused to her head and upper torso, the wounds being commensurate with a frenzied attack with a heavy metallic object.

An iron poker, covered with blood, and with a quantity of flesh and hair attached, lay close to the body. The nature of the wounds suggest that this could have been the murder weapon.

Time of death is estimated to have been between seven and eight o'clock on the evening of Sunday, 22 November.

I hereby certify on soul and conscience that Mairie McClintock died as a result of head injuries probably administered by the use of an iron poker.

David Alexander Beaton MB, CM   24 November 1881

To W. Sproat Esq.   Tigh na Broch
Procurator Fiscal   Seileach
Tobermory   Argyll

On Thursday, 26 November 1881 I was called to examine the body of James McGillivray of Eisdalsa Island. The deceased was found drifting in the Firth of Lorn, off Garbh Eileach.

The body was attached by a rope to a small fishing boat, later identified as belonging to Mr John McDougal of Eisdalsa.

From its condition, I would estimate that the body had been in the water for approximately three days, which would lead me to suspect that the unfortunate victim met his death during the great storm of 23 November.

Mr McGillivray, a quarry worker, was forty-three years of age, and appears to have been in good health at the time of his death.

A post mortem revealed that death occurred before McGillivray entered the water. Despite the deterioration which had taken place during immersion, I was able to identify the body by means of a metal plate inserted in the skull, this operation having been carried out by me following an accident in the quarries, five years ago. Major Lovat of Ballahuan, who was present during that operation, can confirm my identification.

The plate had been dislodged. This fact, together with extensive damage to the cranium, would suggest a blow from a heavy object as being the cause of death.

It is impossible to say how this blow was struck. In the circumstances prevailing at the time, it is possible that McGillivray may have been hit by flying debris whilst attempting to secure the boat against the storm.

I hereby certify on soul and conscience that James McGillivray died as a result of a blow to the head and was subsequently immersed in seawater.

David Alexander Beaton, MB, CM   27 November 1881

Extracts from the
Argyll Chronicle
25 November 1881

Islanders in the Firth of Lorn are today assessing the damage caused by a tidal wave of extraordinary proportions which devastated western shores in the early hours of Monday morning.

Among those lost in the storm are the Master and five members of crew of the steamer *Marquis of Stirling*, the most recent addition to the fleet of the Clyde River and Western Isles Steamship Company.

Only the foresight of her Master, Captain Gordon McIntyre of Eisdalsa, prevented a much greater tragedy. Captain McIntyre had sent all his passengers and several of his crew ashore at Tobermory, before the storm reached its height. Six crewmen managed to swim to safety, and are being cared for by the villagers of Craignure. Among them is Mr William Stuart, helmsman of the *Marquis*, who is believed to have been the last person to have seen the Captain alive . . .

. . . Many crofts have been devastated and farmers are fearful that their families will not be able to survive without assistance . . .

. . . Some slate quarries on the Island of Seileach, and all of those on the Island of Eisdalsa, have been flooded. Valuable equipment has either been destroyed or washed out to sea.

Mr William Whylie, Manager of Eisdalsa Quarries, told our reporter:

'The great thing is that the people are safe. With hard work and perseverance we shall get the quarries working again. I have already assessed the damage and estimate that at least two of the larger quarries will be operating again by Christmas.' . . .

. . . Mystery surrounds the discovery of the unidentified body of a man, washed ashore on the north coast of Scarba. It appears that he was at sea during the great storm of Sunday night, Monday morning. A boat, the wreckage of which was scattered along the shore nearby, has been identified as belonging to Dr David Beaton of Tigh na Broch, Isle of Seileach. No member of Dr Beaton's family or staff is missing. Prior to this discovery, it had been assumed that the boat had been washed away during the storm.

They brought Elizabeth the news on the day after the storm.

William had thought to keep it from her until she regained her strength, but David insisted that the sooner she knew the truth, the sooner she would be able to come to terms with it.

Elizabeth was numbed by the sheer magnitude of the devastation which had befallen her world.

Unable to weep, she carried on her normal daily routine like an automaton.

The loss of her child and her husband on the same dreadful night appeared to her to be a punishment. She did not know why she deserved such harsh treatment, but supposed that it was because she had been too carefree, too extravagant with her happiness.

When they had shown her the casket in which her son was to be buried, she had examined it carefully before she enquired its origin.

'William provided it,' David had told her gently. 'I believe that he made it a long time ago, for quite another purpose.'

'It is very beautiful,' she had replied. 'I must remember to thank him.'

It was the custom to bury stillborn children in any grave conveniently open to receive an adult. Annie had come to her on the day that Jamie's body had been found adrift in the ocean.

'Will you allow them to bury your baby with my Jamie?' she had asked her. 'He will be glad of the company.'

Elizabeth, agonising over the fact that her beloved Gordon was fathoms deep on the ocean bed and could never lie in the kirkyard, nodded her agreement. The two women clung miserably together, their unspoken grief lightened by the sharing.

So it was that James McGillivray was buried, together with Elizabeth's son, in the cemetery at the crossroads below the kirk.

Annie and her family could not afford the luxury of an extended period of mourning. The day after Jamie's funeral, Annie presented herself at William's door with a proposition for him.

'It is absolutely essential that Dougie goes to college, Mr Whylie,' she asserted. 'If I am to persuade him to continue to work at his books and, when the time comes, to leave us and go off to London, then I must be able to prove to him that Kirsty and I can look after ourselves.'

William was taken aback by the directness of her approach. He found himself, not for the first time, full of admiration for her spirited nature.

'What would you have me do, Mrs McGillivray?' he enquired, expecting a request perhaps for financial assistance or other practical help.

'Let me take on Jamie's work.'

He was quite unprepared for this. For the moment her proposal left him speechless.

The question of who would take responsibility for the financial records of the company, particularly the intricate compilation of work done and pay owing, had been tormenting him since McGillivray's death. While the quarries were underwater, there was no problem. The men were receiving day wages while they operated the pumps, worked at repairing the sea-walls or restored the machinery.

Once the quarries were operational again, the more complicated method of payment by results would mean a return to the sophisticated book-keeping which Jamie McGillivray had initiated. William had trawled his list of workers for a suitable replacement, but so far had found no one.

Annie waited patiently while he thought about her proposal.

'Your husband held a position of respect amongst the workforce,' he tried to explain gently. 'The men recognised his exceptional knowledge of both local geological formations and the engineering systems which we employ in the quarries. If he decided that a section was good or bad, and paid accordingly, there was no man who would argue with him.

'How could you, a woman, convince the men that you were sufficiently knowledgeable to make those decisions?'

'For the past five years I have helped Jamie to build up his files of information on the various sections,' she protested. 'Night after night we have sat together over the lists of figures. I would check his addition and be mine. There is no area of the work in which I have not had a hand.'

William had often admired the accuracy of his clerk's records. He had not appreciated that it had been Annie's hand which had guided him.

'When new faces are opened,' she persisted, 'you will be able to tell me which are good workings and which poor. I shall keep up Jamie's records and expand them as necessary.'

Despite his misgivings, William had to agree that the woman's arguments made sense.

'Let me think about it, Mrs McGillivray,' he said. 'I will let you know my answer when I have discussed this with my foremen.'

Two days later, Annie took up her new post as clerk to the Eisdalsa Slate Quarrying Company.

Argyll Chronicle
1 December 1881

A memorial service for the crew of the steamer the *Marquis of Stirling*, which foundered in the early hours of Monday 23 November, is to be held at 11 am on Sunday 6 December in St John's Cathedral, Oban.

Elizabeth had no difficulty waking early on the day of the memorial service. She slept only fitfully these days. It puzzled her that in all those weeks that Gordon had been away at sea she had never once considered the possibility that he would not return to her. Despite his absences she had never lost a night's sleep.

Now that she knew he would not come again, she lay awake, listening, hoping, starting up at the least suggestion of a footfall on the path outside.

The hooting of a steamer's whistle would bring her instantly to her feet. Once she had been away down to the harbour before she remembered that her journey would be fruitless.

She began to dress in her widow's weeds. Gordon would have hated to see her in black. Nor would she have worn mourning dress, were it not for his mother. Mrs McIntyre would expect her to observe the custom of the day. She could not heap further distress upon the poor woman by defying etiquette. With her son's death, all purpose had gone from Mrs McIntyre's life. Even the prospect of a grandchild had been denied her.

How kind it had been of Annabel and David to accommodate Gordon's mother. She did so hate the sea crossing on the little ferry-boat.

From the back of the press Elizabeth withdrew a large hat-box and took out the black hat which she had worn to church in those first weeks after her arrival on the Island.

She stroked down the long black feathers and smiled as she recalled the day they had all sailed to the Holy Isle. She had remonstrated with David about shooting the birds, and he had condemned her as a hypocrite because she owned this hat. She had never worn it since.

She opened a drawer in the bedside table, and reached for her prayer-book. Beneath it she discovered Gordon's own small bible, which he normally took with him when he went to sea. She wondered idly why he had not had it on the night he died. She picked it up, deciding upon impulse to take it to church with her.

The clock struck eight. She must hurry if she was to catch the ferry in time to meet David in the Village. She snatched up her reticule, and in her haste, dropped Gordon's bible. The book fell open at a page in which her husband had inserted a thin sheet of paper.

She reached for it, thinking to stuff it in the drawer to be read later.

It was one of his poems which she had not seen before. Regardless now of the urgency of her departure, she sat on the edge of the mattress and read his words.

The sighing of the wind shall be my breath;
The salt air, and the sweet whins my scent.
See me in the red sunset glow, and in the purple heather on the braes.
Let your laughter echo from the cliffs, and hear my voice.
In the dark moments, feel my presence all around you.
When your days grow short, and the long night beckons,
I will be waiting for you by the shore.

She was hardly aware that she was weeping. Weeping for the first time since they had brought her the terrible news.

Great tears flowed down her cheeks and, falling on the writing, threatened to wash away the words.

Faster now, the tears flowed. Then, from the depths of her being, came the sobbing. Her shoulders shook with the force of her emotion. So loudly did she continue to wail that she did not hear the knocking.

Suddenly William was there.

His arms were about her. She clung to him as she wept, and he consoled her as one would a child.

The crying stopped at last. She lifted herself away from his shoulder and smiled a watery smile.

'How is it,' she asked him, 'that you are always here when I need you.'

He kissed away the last salty tear as it trickled down her cheek.

'It's what friends are for,' he replied.

For some time they sat together, neither speaking. At last, he stood up.

'We must go now,' he told her quietly. 'David's carriage is waiting on the other side. He will think we are never coming.'

Elizabeth straightened her back, and gave him a faint courageous smile. She rose to her feet.

'I'm ready now,' she said.